FIREFLY

BRET JOORSEN

Published by The Oracle
Paperback ISBN: 978-1-7394873-0-0

FIREFLY

"Nothing vast enters the life of mortals without a curse." – Sophocles

For my long-suffering wife Lisa,
without whose endless patience this book
would never have been possible.

INTRODUCTION

Have you ever gone outside on a clear, moonless night, gazed up into the sky and marvelled at the sheer incomprehensible vastness of the star-studded firmament, only to be drawn to wondering at our place in it all?

Presupposed as early as the 1930s and confirmed in more recent times, through calculation and supercomputer modelling, that as much as ninety-five percent of our universe comprises of something we simply do not understand. Now, consider for a moment what this signifies; that humankind's ability to conceptualise its raison d'être is essentially restricted by our current technological and intellectual capacity. There is much about the cosmos to which humanity remains blithely ignorant, an empty chasm of understanding yet to be gained, before we truly comprehend.

The storyline of this book is a work of fiction, touching on the polarising yet alluring debate over whether we are indeed alone in the universe. Advocates believe we are being "visited", or monitored by other-worldly beings, pointing to innumerable reported sightings of unexplained phenomena, stretching from early man's pictorial recordings, right up to modern times. Considered apocryphal by mainstream theologians, The Book of Enoch asserts that our earliest ancestors were placed here by a deity, under the stewardship of supernatural entities, the Watchers. Paradoxically, the indiscretions of humanity's supposed guardians have echoed throughout ensuing ages, recurrently manifesting in the inherently darker facets of our nature. Sullied, mankind repetitiously orchestrates mass self-destruction, putting to the torch, or sword, anything that is good and pure in pursuit of individual, tribal or national enrichment.

Not everything in this story is however fictitious, since real characters, places, events and purported occurrences serve as a backbone, all referenced with utmost deference and portrayed in a historically accurate context. Similarly, most underpinning scientific principles described are either established fact, possible or technologically plausible. You, the reader, are invited to differentiate.

Carl Sagan once said: "*We live on a hunk of rock and metal that circles a humdrum star that is one of 400 billion other stars that make up the Milky Way Galaxy which is one of billions of other galaxies, which make up a universe which may be one of a very large number, perhaps an infinite number, of other universes. That is a perspective on human life and our culture that is well worth pondering.*"

He also held that: "*It is far better to grasp the universe as it really is than to persist in delusion, however satisfying and reassuring.*"

CHAPTER 1

"And once the storm is over, you won't remember how you made it through, how you managed to survive. You won't even be sure whether the storm is really over. When you come out of the storm, you won't be the same person who walked in." – Haruki Murakami

Blazing relentlessly from a coppery, pale blue African sky, the sun had by mid-afternoon heated the air to a brutal level of intolerability, rendering every drawn breath acutely unpleasant. Stripped down to an old pair of rugby shorts, Craig opted for shelter, whiling away what remained of the day under the rear porch's wide overhang. Finding a modicum of relief in the shade, he lounged in a wicker chair and nursed a half tumbler of iced water, long since warmed tepid. Getting up to refill the glass felt like way too much effort, besides, knowing he'd neglected to put another pack of bottles in the fridge to chill. Planting a small vegetable patch with assorted seedlings during relatively cooler morning hours, he'd called time when the soaring mercury drove him from the land. Personal discomfort aside, the heat's intensity fostered a niggling insight, suggesting it left far too late in the season for cultivating such delicate crops.

Representing a clear affirmation of climate change, the day it all began started out like most that summer, nothing remarkable but undeniably different to previous years. Approaching the season's hottest period, recent weeks had seen the familiar golden disc of sunrise replaced by a dirty orange, amorphous blob. Presenting a virtual insight to an inescapable eventuality, occurring aeons in the future, when our host star burns up all hydrogen and becomes a distended red giant, engulfing and incinerating the Earth. In truth, recent daybreak's pre-apocalyptic countenance fortunately less portentous; an optical distortion, created by an atmosphere choked in a blend of airborne dust and smoke from countless bushfires. An all-pervasive, sickly-sweet charcoal scent filled the air, every static surface bedecked in a fine coating of powdery ash and gritty dust.

After abandoning his morning's pursuit, Craig had warmed last night's leftover lasagna and garlic bread, washing both down with a chilled beer. Thinking to finish the day's objectives, he'd returned to the plot's ordered beds, except the meal had left him feeling lethargic and drowsy, too darn hot anyway. Indifferent, he had stood staring downslope across the river to where scatterings of clustered, thatched wattle-and-daub houses marked the homes of subsistence farmers. Even from over a kilometre distant, not a single soul could be seen tending the maize, madumbe [taro] or sweet potato fields, all choosing to shelter from the sun.

Apathy won over and Craig had returned to the shaded porch, resignedly gazing through half-closed eyes at rows of newly planted tender seedlings succumbing to the sun's scorching rays. Their potential saviour, a roll of shade netting, still leant against the garage wall where he'd left it yesterday, on returning from a garden centre. An unfulfilled goal, unrolling and draping the close-woven mesh over a series of wooden goalposts straddling the beds. Tomorrow was another day…

Seasonal afternoon rainstorms hadn't materialised that summer, approaching weather fronts simultaneously deflected back into the Indian Ocean by an intense high-pressure cell. Tenaciously dominating South Africa's interior and stifling normal weather patterns, this weather system had effectively turned the country into a tinder-dry dust bowl.

Some weeks back, Craig had stopped at a local Spaza Shop (an informal micro convenience store) to pick up a few supplies. Busy mending a puncture on his bicycle at the roadside, the local sangoma (a traditional spiritual healer and fortune teller) had greeted Craig, and they chatted awhile. Typical of any impromptu meeting of virtual strangers, the drought and its effects had served as the principal topic of conversation. Striking a chord with the medicine man, who passionately proclaimed these dire conditions attributable to his people having displeased their ancestors' spirits. Witnessing the Zulu nation increasingly abandoning traditional customs in favour of the trappings of Western culture, the Amadlozi [ancestors] had entreated the rain gods to punish their people with famine.

At the opposite end of this spectrum, so-called climate experts conversely placed the blame squarely on El Niño and human-accelerated global warming. Whatever the reality, circumstances were unquestionably bleak, the country's outlook becoming worse by the day. Rapidly emptying dams drying up, livestock starving or dying of thirst and fresh produce in short supply were all factors driving skyrocketing food prices.

Despite widespread doom and gloom, little could diminish Craig's appreciation of the far-reaching panorama afforded by his hilltop vantage point. Beginning to doze when, from over a fluidly dancing heat haze, movement in the valley caught his attention. On the far bank of a barely trickling Little Tugela, a racing pickup truck negotiated the winding dirt road leading to a rustic, hutted campsite set deeper within the foothills. Evidently in a hurry and taking the wide bends at speed, weirdly giving an impression of the vehicle being hotly pursued by the billowing dust cloud churned up in its passing.

Holding Craig's interest for only a short while until, as if vying for his attention, a gentle breeze lazily stirred a patch of dry leaves and flowers collected on the porch's slasto paving. Fallen from a bougainvillea growing on a trellis enclosing the far end, these cast-off flora remnants reluctantly tumbled about whisperingly, then settled again. Moments later, a more insistent gust spurred them into an excitedly rustling airborne cluster, also ultimately collapsing in a dry and dusty heap.

It wasn't so much these observable distractions, rather a subtle change in the air that roused Craig from uncomfortably sweaty torpor. Lifting his gaze and squinting against the glare, to spot a raptor soaring high against the sky's pale backdrop. Effortlessly spiralling on powerful thermal updraughts, the bird's short tail and easily discernible white underwing flashes confirmed it to be a bateleur eagle. Like any bird of prey, known to be opportunist hunters and occasionally taking small livestock, although protected from aggrieved farmers persecution by strict conservation laws. Pairing for life, this bird was most likely hunting to feed its chicks, perpetually ravenous eaglets waiting in a remote treetop nest, while their mate guarded against potential predators. Gracefully arcing from view behind the overhanging roofline, Craig's interest shifted to the edge of a cloud protruding further along.

Stickily hauling himself from the cushioned wicker to plod barefoot, enjoying the sensation of cool stone underfoot, before apprehensively descending three steps onto prickly dry grass. Away in the north, an immense cumulonimbus cloud hunkered atop the Drakensberg Mountain's majestically sweeping expanse. Rising above its darkly smudged grey base, white florets of vapour dazzlingly reflected the sun, bulging and pillowing upon one another high into the aether. Here, at the troposphere's upper limit, powerful winds tugged at the crown and forged an elongated anvil-like horn.

Afternoon storm clouds had frequently developed over recent weeks, only to disperse without a single drop of rainfall reaching the parched ground. Consequently unimpressed, also acutely aware of the sun's beating rays stinging his back's bare skin, Craig chose to observe only for a short while. It was far too hot to stand there any longer, affirmed by a warm trickle of sweat snaking between his shoulder blades, sparing the cloud a final contemptuous glance and returning to the porch.

Drifting into a fitful sleep, predictably plagued by snippets of all too familiar dreams, a blast of dust-laden wind stingingly woke him to a profoundly different outlook. The sun and sky were gone, only the narrowest band of blue left straddling the distant horizon, replaced by darkly spreading cloud that draped the landscape in murky twilight. Stirred by increasing gusts, surrounding trees and bushes swayed convulsively, adding unsettling animation to Craig's transformed surroundings. The atmosphere felt different too, charged by a sense of expectancy, foretelling something momentous in the offing.

Blearily rubbing a smarting face, Craig leapt to his feet and bounded onto the lawn, staring up into the looming underbelly of a massive storm. The distant cloud seen earlier had not only survived but grown, evolving into a monster; its roiling, charcoal underside ominously tinged with hues of green. Giving no warning, another violent gust struck from behind, windborne particles painfully thrashing his exposed back and legs. Paying no heed, attention instead drawn across the road, to where a stand of mature yellowwood's was taking the wind's full brunt. The trees' tough, thick-bladed leaves clattered in protest until the squall eased; a momentary respite, the wind regathering in greater ferocity, forcing them to heel and roar. Through the midst of this chaos a thought suddenly occurred. Craig wheeled and ran for the house, using one hand to shield his eyes against windblown debris.

Hurrying from room to room, shutting and latching all windows left open since morning, just managing to catch his own bedroom's sash as it was blown from the stay. Gathering both thoughts and breath in the lounge, a brilliant flash strobed outside, starkly illuminating the darkened interior and creating freakishly mutant, leaping staccato shadows. Briefly dazzled, in the interior gloom's return, Craig jumped at an ear-splitting crack that languorously rolled into a reverberating boom. Making his way into the open-plan kitchen when another flare forced him to blink, closer than the first, an almost instantaneous boom shaking the house and rattling chinaware stowed in wall units.

Right from when he'd been a little kid, growing up in an outlying suburb of Pietermaritzburg, Craig always found thunderstorms exhilarating. Sharing in his appreciation of "God's fireworks", the whole family would sit out on a part-covered porch whenever an especially spectacular storm struck. Overlooking the city from their hillside property, they braved the elements to watch lightning bolts and forks streak the sky, until the storm either abated, or wind-driven spray drove them indoors.

Stepping outside through the kitchen door to get a better view, a highly energised pulsating strike flashed on the crest of a nearby hillock. Looking directly at the strike, retinal sensory cells overloaded and forced his eyes to shut, leaving a temporarily etched purple replica image. An instantaneous pistol crack report morphed into a deep rumble, abruptly overwhelmed by the gut-shaking blast of another nearby discharge. In a timely hiatus, a single fat raindrop audibly plopped into a stone-edged dust bowl, once a carefully cultivated ornamental flower bed bordering the driveway. Another caught Craig's shoulder with a *smack* and spattered his cheek in cold droplets, then more began falling, releasing the scent of petrichor. A truly earthy African alchemy, stirred up by rain falling on aridly hot and sandy ground, uniquely interlaced with background notes of bushfire smoke. Without further ado, as though a giant bung had been removed, the heavens opened to unleash what could best be described as a biblical torrent.

The roof's overhang did little to offer shelter from such a deluge, instantly drenching Craig from the waist down. An inexplicably childlike urge overcame him, wanting to step forward and stand with arms outspread, allowing the downpour to wash away sweat and grime. A rash impulse, instantly dispelled when another bolt scored an explosively direct hit on one of the yellowwood trees. Singled out for being taller and slightly apart from the others, a searing plasma discharge struck near the crown, magically lighting up the entire tree from within. Several branches and a strip of bark, wider than a man's torso, exploded outwards amid a shower of leaves and javelin-like wood fragments. Common sense and self-preservation kicked in, Craig stepping backwards through the still open kitchen door and hastily slamming it shut.

Adrenaline pumping, he leant on the kitchen counter, now content to watch through the window, as this inundating monsoon turned the air opaquely grey-green and obscured everything beyond the road. A contrastingly white semi-sphere, twice the size of a golf ball, smashed on the paved driveway while two more bounced on the lawn. A loud *BANG* overhead made him jump, then more followed, as if a band of deranged percussionists were beating on the roof with baseball bats. Overwhelming the rain's roar, an ever-escalating up-tempo bedlam of hail beat down deafeningly. Despite the racket, Craig remembered his builder's recommendation of using corrugated iron sheets in lieu of his preferred concrete slates, acknowledging this to have been sound advice. Slap bang in the hail belt, right at that moment, fragile tiles would be getting pummelled into expensive rubble.

Throat parched from excitement, he reached into the fridge to grab a can of cola, popped the ring pull and downed half in one long chug. Belching loudly, he ambled into the lounge, seeing the same wild scene unfolding out back. Several long minutes passed before the hail's pounding gradually eased, allowing the rain's unabated roar to once more infiltrate.

Flopping down in his television chair to wait out the storm, since retaining the day's heat, the house's air felt closely humid and muggy. Lightning flashes were becoming less frequent and the interior's gloom felt oppressive, prompting Craig to click a table lamp's switch, cursing when the bulb failed to light.

Muttering, praying it was merely the power having tripped, he got up and went to the kitchen, opening a utility cupboard to check on the fuse board. Finding the main switch in the ON position, optimistically prodding a test button did nothing, the board was dead. Sighing stoically, he guessed the power outage to be widespread and most likely due to transmission lines getting hit by lightning or shorted out by a falling tree. In these remote parts, supply companies could take days or even weeks to rectify faults, and unfortunately for Craig, his property lay literally at the end of all utility lines. Although prizing the solitude and privacy this place allowed, living out in the sticks inevitably presented a double-edged sword. There was nothing for it but to return to his chair.

Hailfall stopped altogether and the rain gradually slowed to a steady patter, until a brightening outside stirred Craig. Glancing towards the fireplace mantel, his grandfather's antique carriage clock confirmed the storm to have lasted well over an hour. Since the mains power was out and only around two hours of daylight remained, he needed to act quickly to prepare for nightfall.

Exiting onto the porch, the outside temperature had dropped significantly and since wearing only a pair of shorts, he went back in to pull on a T-shirt discarded earlier. Created by lightning ripping apart oxygen atoms, faintly redolent of dilute pool chlorine, the scent of ozone perfumed and freshened the late afternoon air. Hail had devastated a usually orderly, mostly indigenous garden; leaves, twigs and small branches stripped from assorted vegetation borne by rainwater rivulets, then deposited in scattered and untidy sodden heaps. Surveying this disorderly scene, rain's tapping on the roof ceased altogether, the only sound now that of water dripping from the eaves and drenched vegetation. An ideal opportunity to head for the garage.

Negotiating scattered piles of smashed foliage and melting hailstones, he threaded a path around the house, checking for other damage en route. The roof had been liberally peppered with hail dents and one kitchen windowpane cracked by a hail strike, otherwise the place had survived its battering. Crossing the driveway turning area to reach a side door of the garage, Craig flipped a light switch and groaned when the interior remained dark. Returning to fetch a torch from the house, he briefly playing its beam over the four-wheel drive Isuzu before resting on a sleeker shape parked alongside. Snug under a custom-made cover, the '67 Chevy Impala held a special place in his heart.

When first working on the reef gold mines, Craig lodged with his dad's brother, Uncle Danny, happening to be a dyed-in-the-wool old car aficionado. Owning and constantly working on an enviable collection of fastidiously restored classic and vintage vehicles, it hadn't taken long for the same bug to bite

Craig. Back then, his sole mode of transport had been a second-hand 175CC Yamaha scrambler, riding it to work every day. Along his daily route, from a freeway flyover overlooking an industrial estate, he'd spotted the Impala's nose poking from a disused warehouse.

Curiosity got the better of him, deciding to go there on a day off and track down the owner, and to Craig's inexperienced eye the vehicle had appeared in fairly good shape. Sure, covered in dust, grime and bird droppings, but otherwise an object of potential automotive beauty. A big tick in Craig's naïve, novice car enthusiast box was not seeing much surface rust, plus the Impala came complete and all original. Falling hopelessly in love with the dilapidated car, after some haggling, he and the owner settled on what seemed to be a fair price.

Only once getting the old car back to Uncle Danny's workshop and stripping it down, did Craig uncover the true extent of body-filled rust, rot and general degradation requiring his attention. At this point, seconded by much sucking of teeth and disparaging grunts from Uncle Danny, Craig gained an inkling as to the enormity of his commitment. Not easily discouraged, a weekend's tinkering got the engine running, accompanied by spluttering, smoking and an indistinct knocking sound.

Further investigation identified a distinct milkiness in the crankcase's oil, inevitably spelling the tired old motor's fate. Not long qualified, Craig's graduate engineer's salary wasn't in the champagne and caviar bracket. Consequently, coughing up for a rebuilt, fuel-injected, high-performance V-8, new suspension and a recurrent plethora of assorted spares ate up most of that year's earnings. Constantly broke and a veritable social pariah, hadn't however bothered Craig and under the tutelage of his uncle, the Chevy became an all-consuming obsession.

Fortunately, Uncle Danny had plenty of contacts in the trade, so when it came to the all-important paint job, the Impala headed for a pro spray shop. Keeping the car true to its roots had been important to Craig; researching the manufacturer's original colours and opting for Nantucket blue. Getting a tub of paint airfreighted from Delaware in the US had cost him a small fortune and delayed the restoration's completion by a month. Nevertheless, parked on Uncle Danny's drive, distractedly poring over the virtually flawless finish, it had taken Craig an entire afternoon to refit all detailing and trims.

An aspect which never escaped him, at thirteen years his senior, the car should be treated with the kind of respect accorded an older brother. Possessing twice the horsepower of its original incarnation, pushing the Imp hard proved an irresistible temptation but Craig quickly learned when to tap off; lest, like that belligerent bigger sibling, it turned on him and bit back.

Returning from his lapse of nostalgic, Craig slowly wandered the torchlight around the garage, until satisfied the storm hadn't breached. Then, skirting around the back of both vehicles, he made for a separate work and storage room located at the opposite end. Serving as a repository for "stuff", items accumulated over the years, for which no space existed in the house but were either needed or he hadn't the heart to throw away.

Shoehorned in amongst knick-knacks and keepsakes were assorted gardening implements and DIY tools, work-related equipment and more recently acquired camping gear. Squeezing awkwardly between a workbench and stacked boxes of old vinyl records, swearing when catching his shin on the pointed leg of a survey tripod. Shoving a two-man tent and bag of waterproof gear to one side, uncovered a gas stove, pack of disposable canisters and two camping lamps. Extricating them from the clutter, some awkward balancing and more profanity ensued while negotiating his exit.

On his way back to the house, Craig was suddenly overtaken

by the rugged beauty of his surroundings, stopping and setting everything down to take it all in. The storm had moved away to the south-east and now straddled the plains, finding company in another further distant tempest. Appearing to have drawn strength in numbers, the first had rejuvenated, renewed flashes of lightning illuminating its bulk from within. Behind Craig, already impaling itself on Monk's Cowl's jagged peak, the sun painted the storms flanks in a descending progression of spectacular hues. Gleaming white peaks faded to orange, salmon pink into dusty red, then shades of purple and dark grey, all the while lashing the landscape below in rain and hail. Overhead, the earlier day's smoky pale sky now washed clean, cerulean blue deepening in shade towards the eastern horizon, a forewarning to twilight's approach. Somewhere upslope a bird warbled, and as if in response a baboon's strident bark resonated from rain-slicked cliff faces.

Craig's decision to relocate from the buzz and hubbub of Johannesburg to this remote Berg solitude had been driven by multiple factors. Top of this list, the divorce; leaving him despondent and embittered, compounded by stabbing pangs of remorse whenever visiting places he and Maria had frequented. Nowhere immune, shops, malls, restaurants, takeaways and cinemas all held the same painful associations. The only solution had been to put distance between himself and those all-pervading reminders; somewhere to take stock, rebuild and start over.

A self-imposed incident of soul-searching had stirred up fond childhood memories of holidaying with his family in these same mountains. Coincidentally, the same place where his fascination for rocks and minerals first ignited: shiny quartz crystals, complexly swirled agates, jaspers and other unusual stones, easily found strewn in dry sections of stream beds, or exposed in scattered hillside landslips. Their varied and complex beauty catching his youthful eye, he'd begun collecting, either when hiking mountain trails or on lazy days spent swimming and basking by clear streams and rivers.

Gathering and studying assorted rocks and stones, all the while yearning to understand their origins, how they'd been formed and where to find the best specimens. Purchasing books with pocket and birthday money simultaneously assuaged and fed his curiosity, further serving to feed an ever-growing fixation. Throughout a relatively untroubled adolescence, his interest and knowledge of the subject grew, although never compromising a love for rugby and awaking interest in girls. By his mid-teens, Craig had amassed a vast and varied collection of minerals, even several Triassic fossils picked up during a visit with family friends in Aliwal North. His parents would joke about buying the place next door, to house his ever-expanding hoard; nevertheless, steadfastly encouraging his pastime, one that would ultimately flourish into a successful career in mineral geology.

Once deciding to leave Joburg, Craig initially planned on moving to the coast; living in the mountains never entering his mind, until fate intervened. Stirred up by childhood reminiscences and in the process of booking a Berg holiday break online, a site advertising property for sale popped up. Something about the ad's pitch piqued his curiosity, spontaneously emailing the agent to arrange a viewing, without giving the matter further consideration.

The very next weekend, after a six-hour drive, Craig had fallen in love with the place. A mostly level, three-acre tract of land, its lower third gently sloped away towards the river valley, providing extensive views across the midland's plains, literally as far as the eye could see. The opposing vista equally breathtaking, an unbroken line of sight to the mountain's façades, sprawling like a procession of craggy ancient cathedrals. For Craig, the biggest drawcard had been the site's almost complete isolation, only one other inhabited property occurring within a kilometre's radius. An elderly couple with Border Collies lived halfway between him and the main road, although since moving in, neither seeing nor hearing much of them or their dogs.

Returning to Joburg late that night, doing the maths raised a quandary; the plot's asking price, with an estimated build budget added, was roughly equivalent to buying an established property at the coast. A well-maintained existing place in a suburb wouldn't entail as much hassle as building from scratch, although unlikely to find a spot with the same degree of privacy. Not content at leaving anything to chance, destiny intervened; Craig's phone ringing the next morning, with the agent calling to let him know the vendor had dropped her price.

It took several months for the deal to be finalised, have building plans drawn and approved, then find and engage a reputable local builder. A busy period followed, in which he had taken on several contract posts, travelling the country's length and breadth to work on these assignments. Thus distracted, time had flown, seeing Craig move into his new home shortly before Christmas, fourteen months after first setting foot on the property. Another year down the line and even in his wildest imaginings, Craig could never have foreseen how fate's influence would embroil him in a situation, forever changing his life.

CHAPTER 2

"We still do not know one thousandth of one percent of what nature has revealed to us." – Albert Einstein

Setting up his gas stove on the kitchen worktop, Craig lit both lamps, retaining one to cook by and placing the second on a lounge coffee table. Strong storm winds had blown the barbeque into the bougainvillea's thorny clutches, having to wrestle the thing free before setting it up on an outside paved area. Lighting a bag of charcoal to crackle on the fire grate, he went back inside to prepare hand-cut potato chips and a Greek salad. When finishing this prep, the barbeque coals were dressed in a fine layer of pale grey ash, signifying it was time to cook. An aged, thick-cut sirloin steak hit the hot grid with a satisfyingly aromatic sizzle and Craig flopped into a plastic garden chair, content to relax while contemplating the gathering cloak of dusk.

A grumbling roar from the hugely swollen, distant river drifted up from the valley depths, occasional *clacks* and *thuds* discernible from boulders overturning against one another in the raging torrent. Beyond that lay a sea of darkness, sporadically punctuated by pricks of light emanating from paraffin lamps and candles in homes scattered on the landscape below. A gentle breeze faintly carried the sweet scent of woodsmoke from distant cooking fires, telling of others like him, preparing an evening meal before settling for the night. Further away on the plains, where the tightly clustered lights of a large town would ordinarily twinkle, an impenetrably dusky void presented; compensated for by the muted flashes of far receded storms. Looming behind him, rendered in blackened silhouette, the unbroken mountain range underscored a skyline's rapidly fading radiance. Riding this pale band, a golden sliver of crescent moon hung, seeming as if suspended by an invisible thread from the bright planet Venus. Soaring above, embedded in twilight's deeper turquoise, emerging sprinklings of stars twinkled against the firmament.

While Craig sat eating at the garden table, a pair of territorially competing grass owls hooted somewhere way off downslope, then as if emboldened, a cricket began chirping nearby. Finishing the steak and wiping the plate clean with a last chip, he popped it into his mouth, shut off the lantern and leant back with a sigh of contentment. In the glittering blackness overhead, a shooting star flashed through the Southern Cross constellation, leaving behind a momentarily glowing residual trail of plasma. A good luck sign? Perhaps.

Getting up to take his plate in the kitchen, every hair on Craig's body suddenly stood on end and he instinctively froze in place, perplexed, until a flash of light and stock whip *SNAP* made him flinch.

"What the…?"

Remaining in his crouched posture, warily peering towards where the sound had come from and spotting a dull radiance part way across the yard.

His first thought: it could be the meteorite, surviving a fiery plunge through the atmosphere to land in his garden. To him as a geologist, this would be a fantastic prize and curiosity took over, sprinting towards the glow. After taking only a few strides, jarring foreboding slowed his pace, something about this didn't feel right. Slowing to a more measured gait, now able to make out a single glowing point on the ground with a sort of fuzzy radiance permeating the air above. Getting closer, it became apparent that the airborne fug was in fact steam, rising from a patch of gelatinous matter, then a putrid stench suddenly assailed his nostrils. Gagging, he halted, observing this weird spectacle with a growing sense of morbid fascination, noticing that as the foul-smelling matter vaporised, so the object's luminescence weakened.

Not wanting to lose whatever it might be to the darkness, Craig moved closer, intending to pick the thing up but withdrew sharply when it emitted a fine arc of buzzing energy. Urgently stabbing at surrounding ground, it seemed almost to be probing, blindly searching for something. Producing a final sharp static crack, its discharge ceased, the spot absorbed by darkness. Stunned into inaction, gobsmacked, Craig continued gaping at the thing's general resting place. Cognitive thought returned, along with an innate uneasiness at what he'd just witnessed, except that an all-consuming need to know what the hell he'd just seen immediately nudged sensibility to the sideline.

Realising he still held his dinner plate in one hand, thinking on the fly, Craig laid it down as a point of reference and ran to fetch the torch. Returning moments later, its beam easily found his plate and a short distance away, the object. When running to the house, alarm bells had begun ringing; warning that this thing could be toxic, possibly still highly charged or even radioactive. Rather than risk direct exposure to the unknown, he had also collected a snake catcher. Coming across several snakes on the property, some highly venomous, had prompted him to purchase the implement; an ideal tool for handling hazardous items with a degree of safety.

Keeping his torchlight trained on the thing, Craig guardedly circled, wanting to gain an understanding of what he might be dealing with. A little bigger than the first joint of his thumb and pitch-black in colour, identifying his target out here would be virtually impossible, needing to get it into brighter light. By then appearing completely inert and harmless, it would nevertheless be crazy to take any chances; the thing's earlier spontaneous display of electro-pyrotechnics had instilled profound distrust.

Reaching out to gingerly prod it with the catcher's jaws, nothing happened, the object remained unresponsive. Stepping to one side and poking at it from a different angle still provoked no reaction, although Craig's gut clenched and his hand shook. Fully expecting the worst, using the implement's wavering tip to flip the weird thing over, he immediately stepped back, but still nothing happened.

Inspiring a degree of confidence, he gently manoeuvred the catcher's jaws around the object and clamped down lightly, lifting it from the ground. Maintaining firm pressure on the hand trigger, all the while filled with anxiety, he took one wary step, then another, steadily making for the house. There was no way he intended taking this thing inside until gaining a better understanding; another bout of sparking and flaring could start a fire. Eventually reaching the porch steps, trigger hand aching from overstraining, he was immensely relieved to gently place his find on the uppermost tread. In that very instant, the porch and house were flooded in blindingly bright light.

Startled, he jumped back, until realising the electricity supply had been restored, glancing over one shoulder to see town lights sparkling in the distance.

"Idiot!" he scolded himself, chuckling in nervous relief. This whole episode had him absolutely spooked.

Ascending the steps, he headed directly to the kitchen to take a bottle of Scotch and tumbler from a wall unit, pouring a generous splash and shakily draining the glass in a gulp. Pausing to let the single malt warm his throat, wanting the calming hit of alcohol to take hold. Then, since still holding the open bottle, he poured another measure.

"What in heaven's name…?" he mumbled, shaking his head, half expecting to wake from an all-too-weird dream. Instead, present peculiar reality persisted, unchanging. Leaning on the breakfast bar, distractedly turning the glass in one hand, he stared across the lounge at the porch doors, where the mystery outside awaited answers. Taking another good slug of Scotch, he hesitantly paced across the lounge, mentally prepared himself for what was to come.

Standing in the doorway and eying the dark shape resting on the step, it seemed to emanate an unsettling familiar aura, as if drawing him magnetically. Nah, what utter nonsense, this whole incident simply had him rattled. Alcohol had steadied and settled his nerves, time to take the bull by its horns, before a warming surge of Dutch courage waned.

Using the catcher to place the object on a porch table, he fetched a thick pair of kitchen gloves and settled himself in the wicker chair. Leaning forward to scrutinise his find, becoming completely engrossed and oblivious to the frenzied buzzing of a fat moth fluttering at a bare light bulb overhead. Out in the yard the gizmo had appeared to be matt black, but there in the light it took on a gunmetal grey colour. Smoothly polished, elongated and subtly flattened, blunted at one end, it tapered to a point at the other. To Craig's thinking, the shape and size weren't dissimilar to that of a peach stone. Dizzied from besottedly circling the light, the moth dropped heavily to the table, briefly startling him, before sweeping the dazed insect away.

With the distracting insect out of the picture for now, he returned to inspecting his discovery. Manipulating it, while in the catcher's jaws and seated, proved cumbersome, eventually managing to bring the object up close to his face. Tilting it to catch the light revealed an indistinctly detailed, integral pattern of complexly swirling monochrome lines. Frustrated by the catcher's limitations, he freed the thing back onto the table, pulled off both rubber gloves and drained the whisky glass. Curiosity overrode better judgement, and not knowing what to expect, he picked the device up. Experiencing no immediately adverse effects, it felt metallic but surprisingly light and imparted a warming sensation to his hand.

As if responding to Craig's touch, the previously monotone detailing became enlivened, flushed with iridescent shades of bluey-green that were distinctly evocative of Polynesian paua shell. Viewing it from different angles, a wider colour spectrum emerged, bluey-green shifting to red, then orange-gold through shades of pink. Fearing this might signify another imminent eruption of sparking, Craig hurriedly dropped it to the glass tabletop and scooted his chair backwards. All colours immediately faded, the thing reverting to drab grey, rendering Craig even more perplexed and able only to stare. Perhaps a minute ticked by, and since remaining stable, he picked it up again and the colours returned. Having utterly no idea what this signified, although distrustful of the thing, he again set it down on the table.

Leaning back, his mind's analytical side whirred; most frustrating of all, this thing had him completely stumped. Not made of any readily identifiable mineral or metal, its regularity of form however pointed to having been manufactured. Unsure of its intended purpose, coupled with the downright peculiar circumstances of its arrival, further serving to compound the puzzle. One possibility cropped up, that it could have come from an aircraft, except he would have heard an overflying plane's engine noise. Besides, this scenario didn't readily account for the object's initial radiance, its electrical discharge, or the disgusting ooze and sickening stench.

The night had developed an unseasonal chill, prompting Craig to pick up his find and head inside, latching both doors and drawing the curtains. Dropping into his armchair and turning on the television, he flicked through channels, eventually finding himself staring unseeingly at one dedicated to telemarketing. Thumbing the remote to kill the set, he sat glaring at the maddeningly puzzling device resting on the open palm of his hand. In an innocuously coy manner, appearing almost as if challenging him to figure out its purpose or perhaps, more fundamentally, its origin. Everything suddenly caught up with Craig, the long and eventful day had left him dog-tired and distinctly frazzled, and his eyes closed.

In days to come, he would recall how comfortable the chair became, feeling a fleeting sense of balmy warmth but not the moment of drifting into sleep. Gradually slumping into the seat's softly padded leather, hours must have passed. A snore roused him when his head fell forwards and pinched the airway, instantly wide awake and opening his hand to find it empty.

Surmising the object must have dropped to the floor while asleep, Craig leant forwards, expecting to spot it on the floor. Except, there was no sign of the thing. Standing up and sliding the chair backwards left two furrows in the angora rug but revealed nothing else. Feeling around in the gap between chair arms and seat cushion turned up a clump of lint from one side, and a five-rand coin from the other. Experiencing a growing sense of frustration, he tipped the chair over to run a hand across its base, confirming the thing hadn't fallen through and become snagged in a fabric under-liner. Pacing away from the chair, shaking out his T-shirt and digging in both shorts' pockets also yielded nothing. This was getting darned ridiculous, no way had he dreamt the whole episode; it had to be there somewhere.

Slowly turning on one heel while scanning the room, Craig stopped at a heavy sheesham wood dresser, realising the gap below would quite easily have accommodated the thing skidding underneath. Groggy from sleep and light-headed due to probably one whisky too many, he had neither the inclination nor energy to begin moving furniture around.

"Ah, the hell with it. Have a look in the morning." It was time for a shower and bed anyway.

CHAPTER 3

"The saddest thing about betrayal is that it never comes from your enemies, it comes from those you trust the most." – Anon.

Suffusing through heavy cream curtains, morning's light bathed Craig's bedroom in a soft radiance, gradually stirring him from the night's slumber. Rolling onto his back and stretching, opening both eyes to slits and repeatedly blinking to clear lingering drowsiness that threatened to drag him back into Morpheus's fold. It suddenly came to mind that he hadn't woken to stomach-churning memories of his marital break-up.

Meeting his ex-wife when hosting a house-warming party, not long after moving into his first home in a middle-income suburb of Joburg. Maria had come along as a plus-one to his old friend, Margie. Not being entirely naïve, plainly obvious to Craig that he was being set-up, an observation quickly forgotten when they hit it off, right from the get-go.

Maria worked as a physiotherapist at Joburg General

Hospital, coincidentally also initially intending to become a geologist, an aspiration falling by the wayside when discovering she suffered from acute claustrophobia. She'd become hysterical during a high school trip to the goldfields, when her class was ushered into a mine cage and dropped to the workings. A career working mostly below ground would never have been a viable option, instead going on to study sports medicine.

As a couple, they shared diverse mutual interests, both enjoying travel, hiking the wilderness and eating out; all compatibilities serving to complement a budding relationship. At 5' 8", Maria was tall, only a few inches shorter than Craig, with an equally athletic build gained from years of ballet training. Her mother's Maltese ancestral heritage had gifted her with large, dark eyes, under sensuously curling lashes, olive skin and thick, gently waved chestnut hair. It wasn't only her looks and physical appeal that drew Craig to Maria; rather it was her sense of humour and instantly engaging, easy manner that captivated him.

Beginning to date right after the party, six months later Maria moved in, and Craig popped the question. Her father was a well-to-do national restaurant chain franchise owner and footed the bill of their society wedding. Since moving in rarefied social circles, her mother saw to it that the who's who of Joburg's hoi polloi attended the service and reception. If left to Craig, it would have been a small and intimate function, attended only by family and close friends. Not one for gadfly socialising, shmoozing and showcasing, this kind of superficial tokenism didn't sit well with him.

Returning from their two-week honeymoon in the Maldives, the newly-weds went back to work, resuming their regular lifestyle. A year down the line, Craig received an entirely unsolicited but lucrative offer for a six-month contract working on the Sierra Leone diamond fields. Once before, lured by the thrill of seeking out gemstone-bearing kimberlite, he'd left the gold mines to spend three years working in the Kimberley area. Making a name for himself, there in the Northern Cape, until gold and the big city lifestyle tempted him back to the reef. Time had marched on since then and despite priorities shifting, again finding work to be a boring drudge, he hankered after a challenge. Somewhere like Sierra Leone provided just that kind of potential, also the remuneration on offer was insanely too good to pass up.

If single at the time, Craig would have jumped at the deal but of course now had to factor in Maria's considerations. To the present day, his gullibility still rankled, thinking at the time how supportive she seemed of her husband's career opportunity.

Regarded as a major asset to the mine; a troubleshooter, possessing the unerring ability to follow high-yield gold-bearing seams three kilometres below ground, the mine manager was far less understanding. In the end accepting his resignation, the company offered to keep his position vacant until returning from Sierra Leone.

Flying out to the West African country a month later, once clearing customs, he'd been guided to a chartered flight bound for Koidu. With no specific reference or preconceptions, the place turned out to be a bustling city, grown up around one of the biggest, hard rock diamond mines in the country. Swelteringly hot and dusty, it sat high in the category of locations least likely to ever become a tourist destination. Nevertheless, Koidu harboured an other-worldly charm and was inhabited by some of the friendliest and most accommodating people Craig could ever have imagined. Checked into a comfortable suite at the Lion Mountains Hotel, he would be flown home every two months for a fortnight's break.

Working seven days a week, most evenings were spent in the hotel, either talking with Maria over Skype or working on his book. Destined exclusively for selective academic reading, a tome titled: *Intrusive Mineral-Bearing Rock Formations of Southern Africa*. Craig had spent several years researching his subject matter before beginning to commit anything to paper, a year before meeting Maria. Time and energy inevitably diverted from the project ever since, being away from home distractions provided the opportunity needed to resume writing.

During his first return home, Maria had been her usual self, engaging and fun with friends and family, otherwise devoted and passionately loving. That all changed on his second visit, finding her coldly offish and indifferent to his presence. Riding out a couple of frosty days, Craig could take no more and confronted Maria, who coolly ascribed her frame of mind to a new job role not panning out as hoped. They talked it through together and things went back to normal, leaving Craig with only minor lingering misgivings. Worries that escalated again during his final stint in Sierra Leone, when their virtual conversations became shorter and less frequent, Maria finding obscurely trivial issues to argue over. Koidu Mining's management team were eager to extend his contract, an offer Craig declined, knowing in his heart something to be going horribly wrong at home.

Landing on a late afternoon flight at Joburg's OR Tambo airport and discovering Maria wasn't there to meet him, anxiety turned to a lead weight in his belly. Her phone kept diverting to voicemail, so he called a taxi, that toxic mass in his gut becoming progressively heavier throughout the hour-long journey. Reaching their home, there was no sign of Maria's car on the driveway and the house lay in total darkness. Letting himself in, Craig quickly discovered that all Maria's belongings were gone; every material trace of his wife clinically removed, even a David Shepherd painting of lions, given to her as a thirtieth birthday present.

Propped against the kitchen coffee maker, a brief

handwritten note explained that she'd gone to stay with her parents. It went on to say things had changed; her feelings were in turmoil, needing time alone to think. Craig had enjoyed a great relationship with his mother-in-law from their first meeting, however this also summarily changed. Hearing his voice on the phone, Anita immediately became abrupt and dismissive, prepared only to say that Maria had gone out with friends. Although realising whatever the situation brewing two months before had festered, Craig couldn't begin to fathom the true nature or extent. At his wits' end, taking a bottle of Scotch into the den to reread Maria's note, until knowing it word for word. Alcohol certainly numbed the senses but provided no clarification as to Maria's stated need "to think", or what "things had changed". The bottle eventually two thirds empty, he remained none the wiser concerning her reasons for leaving.

It was late, and Craig extremely drunk but in need of a sympathetic ear, calling his best and most trusted mate, Paul Sturgis. They'd met at university while studying the same degree course, becoming virtually inseparable on campus and even going on to work together on the same mine. In a strange twist of fate at that long-ago house-warming party, Craig had introduced Paul to his friend, Margie, similarly becoming a couple, they often double dated. When Paul and Maria became buddies, this hadn't seemed out of place to Craig, blithely unfazed by their seemingly platonic bond.

Years passed, and in Craig's hour of need, Paul picked up the phone but sounded cagey from the outset. In his inebriated state, Craig missed the cue, although there was no mistaking Maria's voice overheard in the background, calling out, "Who is it babes?" Heart-wrenching, a term of endearment used exclusively for Craig when they were alone together, and in that instant the penny dropped; betrayed by the two people in whom he would literally have entrusted his life. How could he have been so stupid? Adding insult to injury, that chiselling rat and former friend still worked at the mine, rendering a return to his job untenable. The next morning, sober but hungover, Craig rang the mine boss to extend his leave of absence indefinitely. Some might have regarded this course of action as bowing out and losing face, cowardly even, but in truth, Craig couldn't trust himself being anywhere near the man.

Their divorce took six months to finalise, the settlement agreement stipulating all assets to be shared equally, effectively conveying half of Craig's house to Maria. By that stage, caring not that the market languished in a slump, he'd accepted a cheeky speculative offer for a quick sale and took a moderate equity loss. Needing another place to live, he rented a one-bedroom apartment in town and took to the bottle in a big way. Only, fate wasn't done dumping on Craig yet; his older brother, Ian calling one evening to inform him of their parents having been killed in a car accident.

A sizeable inheritance, shared equally between him and Ian, did little to temper a deepening sense of torment, so Craig drank more. The unfinished manuscript held no appeal either, spending most days in front of the television, glass or bottle in hand, floundering in an alcohol-induced stupor.

The turning point for Craig came one morning, after an all-night session, when he awoke slumped over the kitchen table, its surface glazed in his own vomit. Wishing the pounding hangover and dry mouth belonged to someone else, he got up and swayed unsteadily to the kitchen sink, treading on a jagged shard of broken vodka bottle. Stemming the bleed with a kitchen towel while clearing up broken glass, a sobering realisation hit home; if unchecked, this kind of aberrant behaviour saw him skidding down a slippery slope to self-ruin. It would have been all too easy to overlook such an unpleasant eventuality and dive headlong into an eighty-six-proof liquid breakfast, except that his body cried out for something more substantial. Shaving an indeterminate duration's beard growth, then taking his first shower in several days, Craig dressed and headed for a nearby café to order a cooked breakfast.

Seated in a corner booth to eat a fully loaded, three-egg omelette with chips and coleslaw, Craig confronted his demons head-on. Finally acknowledging that deliberately drowning himself in a mire of self-pity, while Maria and Paul were gaily oblivious to his self-scourging, was tantamount to defeatism. If perchance, either held any inkling as to his state of mind, they probably wouldn't care anyway. So, the hell with them! What goes around comes around. Their just deserts would inevitably arise at some point; a juncture deemed most fitting by karma. It wasn't for Craig to decide in what form, or timescale, such duly appropriate retribution occurred, judgements terms of penance lying solely in the hands of the gods. Something shifted in Craig's mind right then, and like a logjam clearing, his self-imposed penance ended.

The only thing for it was to make a clean break, disentangle and distance himself from that toxic environment, thereby securing the breathing room needed to restart his life. Funds from his inheritance provided the necessary catalyst, Craig initially picking the coast as a preferred location. Before immersing himself in the implications and minutia of uprooting and moving, a vacation was called for, ideally somewhere with happy associations. Connecting his phone to the café's free Wi-Fi, over a second mug of coffee, he searched for holidays available in the Drakensberg.

More than two years had elapsed since that pivotal day and now, with the final vestiges of sleep receded, he got out of bed and opened the curtains. Heading for the bathroom to relieve himself, Craig then shaved and took a shower, and it was while rinsing off under streaming warm water that the previous night's events began mentally replaying. Whatever the thing was he'd found, come hell or high water, that infernal gadget would be tracked down the minute he'd dried and got dressed.

Vanity never a significant aspect of Craig's psyche, even so, while towelling off in front of the bathroom's full-length mirror, he drew self-satisfaction at his own reflection. At thirty-eight years old and a whisker under an old-fashioned six foot tall, his eighty-three-kilogram frame remained lean and well-muscled. Years of playing high school and varsity rugby, also being all-round physically active, had served to strengthen both his frame and core. Temporarily sloughed during that year of misery, muscle and definition had quickly returned when put to weeks of hard graft establishing the garden.

Cracking a bedroom window open, the outside air held onto its nighttime chill, selecting a long-sleeved T-shirt and trackpants to wear. Suitably attired, Craig went in search of the annoyingly disappearing object, remembering thinking how it might have skidded under the dresser. An antique, constructed from solid Indian sheesham wood and bought at auction in the local town, it was an immensely heavy piece. Four burly delivery men had complained amongst themselves about its mass when carrying the thing in and setting it in place. No lightweight himself, Craig knew attempting to shift it alone wouldn't be straightforward, quite possibly resulting in a pulled muscle or thrown back. Coming up with a workaround, he fetched the snake catcher and torch, dropping to lie prone on the floor and peering into the unit's shadowed under space.

Even with one cheek pressed hard to the floor, the gap proved just that bit too narrow to get a proper view into the void; also occurring to him that the gizmo could have ricocheted in behind one of the dresser's stout legs. Reluctantly getting up from the floor, he grabbed one end of the dresser and heaved, emitting a straining grunt when it inched forwards. Repeating several times, at alternate ends, revealed nothing more than lacquered hardwood boards, bedecked in stray dust and scattered with balls of fluff. Hefting the antique back into place, he went to recheck his armchair, then rolled up and removed the rug, even going so far as to investigate each hem of the low-hanging curtains, drawing blanks at every turn.

"This is bloody ridiculous, it's got to be here somewhere," he assured himself, looking around the room for fresh inspiration.

Something about last night's incident wasn't adding up, there were only so many places the thing could have ended up, and all had been exhaustively checked.

Ticked off, Craig went to the kitchen and tapped his selection into the coffee maker's display, taking satisfaction from a concentrated whiff and satisfying grinding noise of dark roast beans tumbling through its mill. Returning to the lounge, leaving the machine to prepare his caffeine fix, intent on formulating a fresh strategy to find that darned thing. There was no way he'd dreamt the entire episode, confirmed by glancing through the window to see his dinner plate beckoning from the rear lawn. Without any new idea's forthcoming, he trotted outside to retrieve the plate, simultaneously rehashing the part when first seeing the object. Becoming so deeply engrossed in this recall that the same potent stench again overcame his senses, gagging at some bizarre kind of associative synaesthesia. Perhaps dredging at a long-evolved primitive intuition, instinct warning that introspective analysis of the disgusting accompanying sludge constituted a scab probably best left unpicked.

Wresting himself back into the present, Craig scanned the yard, hoping to spot anything fallen from the sky, something to put the object into context. Simultaneously, acknowledging himself to be clutching at straws, since already knowing there hadn't been any planes flying overhead last night. As if seeking to redirect his train of thought, a fuzzy half-memory emerged, tickling away at the periphery of subconsciousness; while sat in his armchair last night, something else had occurred. The details were however frustratingly blurry, probably from too much Scotch.

Lost in thought, but suddenly realising he was hungry, Craig ambled back indoors, just as a soft electronic ping confirmed his coffee was ready. Hunched on a stool at the breakfast bar, he ate a bowl of muesli while skimming through current news events on a tablet. There were several articles about widespread damage wrought by yesterday's storms and the ensuing power blackout, as suspected, caused by high-tension supply pylons sustaining a lightning strike. More of the usual political rhetoric and double-talk, a piece on a new trade deal brokered with Pakistan, then a short piece about several local people going missing. With many smaller farms crippled by the drought, unemployed and practically destitute workers were being forced to go further afield in search of paying manual work. It struck Craig how poignant these people's predicament really was, simply wanting an honest day's work to put food on the table, except finding themselves contending with some or other predatory menace.

A familiar clattering hum distracted, picking up his coffee mug and going outside to check out the source. Approaching at speed, a helicopter was coming up the valley from the south-east, Craig adjudging its flight path to miss him by around a hundred metres. Not an uncommon happening, the sight of helicopters out here usually signified rescue teams going in search of lost hikers or fallen climbers. Nothing about its presence struck him as anything out of the ordinary, continuing to watch as it flew in his general direction. One thing did however stand out; it wasn't the regular red-and-yellow rescue chopper, this one maroon with an indistinguishable gold logo on its side. Losing interest as the copter passed, he turned to go inside but stepped back when the rotor's pitch changed; in time to see the whirlybird bank sharply to starboard and return, heading his way. This time flying directly overhead and maintaining its course without deviation, Craig managed to catch a glimpse of the front seat passenger, a man wearing sunglasses staring down at him through footwell glass. Thinking no more of the matter, going to finish his breakfast.

After yet another fruitless bout of rechecking all the same places, Craig gave up the exercise as nothing more than a waste of time. One of life's weird little glitches, an event that would probably forever remain a mystery. Equally bothersome though, the half-memory re-emerged, itching away, just always out of reach. To distract himself, Craig amassed an assortment of gardening tools into a wheelbarrow, spending the rest of the morning raking up and clearing away the storm's mess. The property way too large to cover its full expanse, instead concentrating his efforts around the house, developed as formal garden. Nature would take its course for the rest, fallen vegetation either rotting down or being devoured by insects. This kind of labour proved therapeutic, the object fiasco gradually getting pushed to the back of his mind, replaced by the task at hand.

The day not getting anywhere near as hot as previous, even so, parched and needing a break from the hard slog, Craig packed up shortly before noon. Studying the lightning-struck yellowwood through the kitchen window while drinking a bottled water, the sound of approaching vehicles diverted his attention. A large, silver Japanese SUV hove into view, turned onto his driveway and drove part way to the house before halting. Identical to the first, another followed close behind but stopped at the open gates, reversing out to park facing down the road.

This sudden arrival set off a tingling at the base of Craig's neck, watching uneasily as three men alighted from the first vehicle and started towards the house. On his way to open the kitchen door, spotting two more exit the second and stay put.

Conveying the appearance of businessmen, all similarly attired in smart suits and wearing aviator-style sunglasses. Perhaps they were just lost and needed directions? On the face of it, their presence didn't represent anything immediately untoward, except something about their manner escalated Craig's sense of disquiet. Before he could call out a greeting, while still in full stride, the closest man spoke.

"You Craig Farrant?"

"Er, yeah, that's me. Why, what's this all about?"

Taken aback, wracking his brain for any rational reason that a total stranger should know his name.

"There's a matter of real importance we need to discuss with you, inside the house."

Clearly in charge of this crew, the first man's facial expression deadpan, giving Craig no clues.

The trio continued toward him determinedly, flustering Craig into unwittingly stepping backwards and allowing two to push past, the third remaining outside. Craig's bewilderment turned to annoyance at such an ill-mannered intrusion and was about to voice a challenge, when the boss man spoke again, his accent heavy, sounding of Russian origin.

"Okay, it's like this pal, you're coming with us."

Sudden pressure on Craig's neck, fractionally preceding a mechanical click and sharp sting, instantly regretting turning his back on the third man. The drug took effect before he could react, the kitchen spinning dizzyingly, until a sudden swooping blackness erased all consciousness.

CHAPTER 4

"Be so subtle that you are invisible. Be so mysterious that you are intangible. Then you will control your rivals' fate." – *Sun Tzu*

(Tuesday, 4th March 1941, 01:00 h. South Africa's eastern coast.)

Any moon in the sky would have been obscured behind a low-lying blanket of thick cloud, painting the night especially dark and ideal for their mission. Accompanied by the bridge helmsman, Kapitänleutnant Gunther Schneider stood gazing intently through a pair of binoculars. From the restricted deck space of *U-97*'s conning tower the sound of breaking shoreline surf was distinctly audible, from around three hundred metres off their port side. Unobtrusively silent, the helmsman remained steadfastly focused on keeping their vessel from being gathered into the clutches of backline breakers. Wallowing in these rolling swells made it tough to maintain the submarine's course, also hindering Schneider's ability to pick out his target on the dark and distant shore.

Schneider glanced down at the luminous face of his wristwatch, seeing the minute hand had already crept past 01:00 h. Scowling in annoyance; he was in position and on time, and they were late. Lifting the binoculars again, continuing to scan the unfamiliar coastline, his clenched jaw suddenly softened, allowing an uncommon smile to briefly tease the corners of his mouth. Seeing the faintest flare of a match being struck, igniting petroleum in one, two then a third steel drum; the arranged signal.

Turning away, he bellowed into the speaking tube, "Hoffmann, on deck!" before returning his attention to the signal fires.

Within seconds, the sound of boots on metal rungs echoed from below and Oberleutnant zur See, Werner Hoffmann came scrambling up the ladder from below decks, joining him on the bridge. At twenty-five, fifteen years Schneider's junior, Hoffmann was uncommonly young for a first watch officer, or second in command on a military vessel. Having graduated top of his intake class at Mürwik Kriegsmarine academy, three years previously, Hoffmann made no bones about being a ruthlessly ambitious career officer. On the other hand, Schneider hadn't enjoyed the privilege of attending the academy, instead rising through the ranks by dogged determination and his superior's recognition of both character and meritorious achievements. A born warrior, well respected by High Command for his Allied shipping kill rate in the Atlantic. He would have risen further, if not for a drunken scuffle with Admiral Doenitz's aide-de-camp, two months after the outbreak of war.

Clicking his heels smartly, Hoffmann announced himself.

"Kapitän."

"Our depth?" A man of few words and a stickler for formality at sea, Schneider's crew nonetheless revered the man.

"Seventeen metres, Herr Kapitän."

Acknowledged with an almost imperceptible nod.

"Good. Send the reply," indicating the glowing beacons ashore. "If we get the correct response, then we can unload our passengers and be done with this charade."

Hoffmann did as instructed, sending three short and three long flashes from the bridge signal lamp. A handheld torch immediately glinted out of the darkness of Isipingo beach, returning three long, then three short flashes.

"Launch the boats, ready the flak gun and have the deck cannon crew standby. If this isn't what it seems, we don't want to be caught standing around holding onto our cocks."

When his adjutant had disappeared below decks, Schneider pulled a pipe and tobacco pouch from an inside coat pocket, turning to lean on the deck railing.

A month earlier, on the last day of January, Schneider had been summoned to Konteradmiral Weisz's Naval Intelligence office in Berlin, receiving orders to sail for South Africa. His mission: to convey five specialist intelligence officers with an escort team of three, rendezvousing with agents of a Nazi allied partisan organisation. Aggrieved, taking this "soft" assignment as a personal slight and fundamentally beneath him; there was no glory to be gained in nursemaiding a group of civilians to a foreign shore. With the first leg now practically complete, every opportunity would be taken to hunt the Cape of Good Hope and West African coastal sea lanes during their return voyage to port in La Rochelle.

Another clatter of feet announced the flak gun crew's arrival. Grunting to heft a case of 20 mm ammunition on deck, the matrosen-obergefreiter in charge of the anti-aircraft gun emerged, followed by two subordinates, each lugging another box of shells. Working together with practised ease, they deftly readied and loaded the gun, swivelling it to bear landwards. A sudden freak swell forcefully lifted and rolled *U-97*, unbalancing and slamming the younger of the two matrosen into the bridge rail. Wincing he made no sound and immediately returned to station. The swell's passing yawed the sub hugely and broached her starboard dive plane, then slammed the fluke's broad flat surface against the water with bone-jarring impact.

Their twenty-nine-day voyage had covered seven and a half thousand nautical miles, including an unplanned six-day layover in the Breede River. When passing Table Bay at snorkel depth, the starboard engine's crankshaft bearing failed and seized; the huge diesel motor's immense torque shattering the bearing, wrecking its housing and scoring the shaft. With no option but to order the damaged engine shut down, Schneider had been unwilling to take the risk of continuing their mission on only one operational motor. Surfacing under cover of darkness an hour later, deeming them far enough from the busy enemy seaport, he instructed the navigator to plot a course for a place where assistance might be found.

The Union of South Africa was part of the British Commonwealth then, consequently also at war with Germany and her allies. However, a significant proportion of the country's population being of European mainland descent, were ambivalent to the distant war's outcome, some even supporting the Nazi cause. Shortly before midnight of the following day, the damaged sub limped into the Breede River mouth, Schneider's charts showing the waterway as navigable up to fifteen kilometres inland. Running on batteries for stealth and the crew at action stations, he directed the helmsman to steer upstream at walking pace. Schneider had silently offered up a prayer of thanks for a waning gibbous moon, fortuitously showing up the river's many sandbars and serpentine bends.

Eventually, rounding one of these sweeping bends, a cluster of lights came into view on the westerly bank. Ordering the anchor to be dropped, the sub's skipper dispatched a detachment of Kriegsmarine commandos to investigate. Fortune must have been smiling on the U-boat's crew, when the settlement turned out to be a remote and isolated farm belonging to an Afrikaner family. A burly boer [farmer], Hannes Britz welcomed them as if they were returning relatives; even proudly fishing out a framed photograph of Adolf Hitler and well-thumbed copy of *Mein Kampf* from a writing bureau. Having developed a brotherly rapport with the heavily armed commandos, he'd offered them food and home-made peach brandy. Officer in charge of the unit, Oberfähnrich Muller had been born and raised in South Africa to German immigrant parents, returning to his ancestral homeland two years before the outbreak of war. Speaking fluent Afrikaans, Muller declined the potent liquor on behalf of him and his men, going on to explain their predicament and request the farmer's help.

It had taken the sub's engineering crew the better part of a day to strip down the engine and load its damaged parts onto one of Britz's trailers. Wearing an ill-fitting assortment of the boer's eldest son's clothes, Muller had accompanied Britz in his clapped-out lorry, driving fifty kilometres to a friend's engineering workshop in the town of Swellendam. They'd returned the following evening, towing a fully rebuilt housing and crankshaft, fitted complete with a new bearing. Another day of reassembly had seen *U-97* restored, setting sail on the high tide to resume her mission.

A thousand kilometres further up the coast, three and a half days later, Schneider watched as three boats were launched from the port side aft deck. Muller and his men took the lead boat, while number two held the mission team and special-detail Sicherheitsdienst minders. The final boat, heavily laden with the men's belongings and several boxes, rode low in the water.

Breaking waves threatened to swamp the boats, making

rowing through the surf an arduous process, but the oarsmen were skilled, timing their strokes to ride each mustering swell. Off their starboard side, a metronomically flashing light served as constant reminder to Muller of their imminent beach landing's perilous nature. Holding sway over a projecting natural headland that protected Durban harbour from the Indian Ocean, Bluff Lighthouse also defined the position of a major enemy military encampment. Since serving as the principal staging point for the East African and Abyssinian campaigns, the heavily fortified port was guarded by fixed artillery pieces, all strategically sited along this vantage point.

Nearing shore and riding out a wave's surging crest, the beach came up fast, where shadowy figures could now be seen moving against a pale expanse of sand. All signal fires had been quenched and, aside from this indistinct and sketchy backdrop, their landing zone lay in complete darkness. Shivering in nervous anticipation, Muller imagined hostile eyes hidden in fringing coastal vegetation, following their progress, waiting for precisely the right moment to open fire and mow them down in a hail of gunfire. Clutching tightly at the StG-44 assault rifle's pistol grip, he braced for impact as their boat rode out the shore break, beaching with a gritty *whoosh*.

Training his weapon up the beach, towards where ghostly figures waited, Muller vaulted the raised bow. Landing on wet sand, he crouched and shouted.

"The sea wolf has landed!"

Seeming like an age, no more than a couple of seconds passed, when the desired response came. "The leopard awaits."

As if appearing from thin air, a veritable man-mountain abruptly loomed in front of Muller.

"Van Heerden," he exclaimed, grasping and warmly pumping Muller's hand in greeting.

"Oberfähnrich Muller," he managed, turning to see the second boat come ashore, its occupants awkwardly disembarking.

Without needing any orders, Muller's well-drilled squad established a beachhead, fanning out around the boats and covering the surrounding shore.

"Tell them to relax, Muller," Van Heerden's voice deep and gravelly, perfectly matched to his ursine stature.

Standing well over six feet tall and powerfully built, he projected the aura of a man accustomed to holding authority. In the Stygian darkness, Muller could discern a full, dark beard framing the man's broad face, although making the greatest impression were piercingly blue eyes, blazing with the intensity of a blowtorch flame.

"You're amongst friends here, ou boet [old brother], there's no rooinekke [British soldiers] to worry about," he rumbled. "You and your men are quite safe; we'll see to that."

Adrenaline still heavily lacing Muller's blood, despite this giant's assurances, on enemy soil, he wasn't yet ready to stand his men down.

From the second boat, a slight and stooped figure of a man fought his way through the clingingly thick sand towards them. Almost lost in a full-length leather coat and wearing a misshapen fedora that partially obscured his face, cutting an unlikely figure for a man in his position. Detecting his approach, Muller tensed.

Something about Reynhardt Koch made his skin crawl; first introduced and shaking hands on the day of departure, stimulating an overpowering urge to wash his hand. A weedy, fragile-looking man, afflicted by polio as a child, Koch had been left with an enduring limp and inability to quite stand up straight. Thinning, slicked-back, black hair, plastered down with pomade adorned a head appearing too small even for his puny frame. A meanly pinched, weasel-like face, given comical incongruence by the man's wide and thickly fleshy mouth. Self-consciously, his tongue incessantly darted at these lips; a repugnant accumulation of gummy, drying saliva perpetually collecting in each corner.

When in earshot, he barked shrilly, "Muller, why are we still on the beach? We are exposed out here. Get things moving, man."

Wheezing asthmatically from such unaccustomed exertion, he struggled the final few paces to where they stood. Close-set, piggy eyes darted erratically between Muller and Van Heerden, thickly lensed glasses doing little to disguise the man's agitation. Biting his tongue, Muller instead motioned to where Van Heerden's men could be seen helping to unload the third boat. Standing quietly to one side, having studied Koch's approach, Van Heerden refrained from extending his hand in greeting.

"And who might you be?" Neither voice nor manner carried the warmth extended to Muller.

Evidently unperturbed at Van Heerden's shortness, Koch responded without making actual eye contact.

"Hauptsturmführer Koch." Giving the Nazi salute and clicking his heels together as best the sand would permit, he immediately countered, "You must be Kapitan Van Heerden?"

Koch's demeanour transformed, face twisting peculiarly, thick lips curling and parting to expose small, irregularly spaced teeth. Evidently the man's best attempt at a smile, simultaneously thrusting out a hand in an ingratiatingly jocular manner. It was Muller's turn to spectate this interaction, seeing Van Heerden recoil ever so slightly, eyes flicking towards the commando they exchanged a tacit understanding.

It took mere minutes for Van Heerden's men to unload the boats, briskly toting everything up the beach and disappearing into dense coastal bush. Almost indistinguishable amongst wickedly thorned amatungulu bushes, a narrow footpath led to a cul-de-sac marking the end of a dirt road. Here, a lorry and three cars waited, guarded by two men crewing a belt-fed light machine gun trained up the road. When luggage and boxes had been loaded onto the lorry's flatbed, Van Heerden's men dragged a waterproof tarpaulin over, securing it in place with ropes. Back on the beach, the three signal beacon oil drums were tipped over then carried away and dumped, while the fire-blackened sand was kicked about to blend with the beach. Muller and his unit clambered into their boats and were gone, back to sea; simultaneously, the landward vehicles started up and drove off, leaving behind nothing but tyre tracks and footprints.

CHAPTER 5

"He who fights with monsters might take care lest he thereby become a monster." – Friedrich Nietzsche

In the lead car, a '38 Opel Admiral, Van Heerden sat up front with the driver, Koch and two others were squeezed into the rear. One being Werner Stein, a long-standing senior associate of Viktor Schauberger, the highly regarded Nazi scientist in charge of a top-secret project operating out of Mauthausen concentration camp. An undertaking of which Himmler and the Führer were convinced would assure certain victory over the Third Reich's enemies. Regarded by Schauberger as his best and brightest protégé, Stein had been entrusted with this top priority field assignment, pivotal to the Austrian death camp's success, or failure.

To avoid the potential risk of encountering military checkpoints, if taking a more direct route via the nearby city of Durban, they would instead travel down the coast before turning inland. A longer, more circuitous route but scrupulously planned to avoid main roads and bypass all major hubs. To mask appearing as a convoy, each vehicle would observe a two-minute interval between the next, stopping at prearranged locations to ensure they stayed together.

Deep in thought, Van Heerden took little notice of their route, the Opel's headlights illuminating a winding two-way, tarmac carriageway unrolling ahead. Harbouring a fiery loathing for the British as a younger man, now reaching the age of forty-five, time's passing had tempered hatred to mere smouldering contempt. Scorn borne out of reasonable cause, memories of nine months internment in a British concentration camp remaining clear as if happening only yesterday. During the Second Boer War, conditions in these tented camps had been atrocious at best.

Before these hostilities forever shifted the country's political canvas, his family held freehold title over an extensive tract of land roughly twenty kilometres east of Colenso. Predominantly cattle ranching, also growing enough fresh produce to feed themselves and their workers, selling any surplus at the town's market. On a cloudless summer's morning, not long after war had begun, Pa had left on horseback to join up with a local contingent of guerillas. Taking only his Mauser rifle, a revolver and saddlebag of essential items, he'd ridden out and not once looked back. Little had initially changed on the farm for six-year-old Andre and his siblings, daily chores were still to be done and Ma, Hannah, steadfastly oversaw the farm's operation.

Even with Pa away, life followed a degree of normality; that was until early autumn, when a company of British cavalry rode in. Hunting Boer commandos, they'd ransacked the Van Heerden's farmhouse and outbuildings, confiscating the rest of Pa's firearms. While the soldiers were loading appropriated bags of grain onto a wagon and rounding up the family's cattle,

Andre's eldest brother, Jannie had attempted snatching away his father's shotgun. The hussar holding it had struck him with the butt, breaking Jannie's nose and permanently blinding him in one eye. Marking a turning point in the Van Heerden's fortunes, two weeks later a British infantry unit turned up, this time torching the homestead and forcing the family to march thirty kilometres to Ladysmith's concentration camp.

Most abiding of Van Heerden's recollections of that terrible day was looking back from the crest of a distant koppie and seeing his family home engulfed in flames. Food in the camp had been scarce and virtually inedible, Ma stoically sharing her daily ration between him and his brothers. Consequently, rapidly dropping body weight, she became emaciated and weak, barely a month before their release contracting a dreaded illness. Feverish and wracked by a persistent cough, she lost all remaining appetite, all telltale signs of consumption, or tuberculosis. The bacteria spread like a windblown veld fire through the densely packed, tented squalor, until most families had at least one of their own stricken by this pestilence.

War ended and the Van Heerden's were freed, left to make the long trek home, or whatever may someday again be called home. Andre prayed that his Pa had survived the conflict and would be there, rebuilding while awaiting their return? However, this wasn't to be the case, discovering instead that what remained of their farmhouse and outbuildings were desolate, derelict and fire-blackened ruins. More fundamentally, no sign of his father.

Salvaging buckled lengths of rusting corrugated iron roof sheets and using charred roof beams as supports, they created a makeshift shelter inside the burnt-out house. Fearing her children would starve, Ma managed to scrape together spilled maize from their collapsed grain store. Badly spoiled by rain and rat droppings, she hand-picked the vermin fouling from what edible grains could be collected and rinsed them in the stream. Ground, mixed with water and cooked in a surviving pot to make a simple porridge, they had subsisted.

A few weeks on, Pa eventually returned on foot with only his rifle and the clothes on his back; deeply resentful at the war's outcome, nonetheless relieved to find his wife and children alive. Fortuitously, before leaving to fight, Piet van Heerden had buried a Mason jar of silver coins in a remote part of the farm. Their circumstances improved for a while, until three months down the line, when Ma eventually succumbed to the tuberculosis bacterium.

The final straw for Pa, hell-bent on leaving South Africa forever, he packed up their meagre belongings and took the three boys west. Four days, and as many different trains later, they'd arrived in a small fishing town on the coast of German South West Africa. Pa's older sister, Aunt Marita lived in Lüderitz and took them in like a fussing mother hen, without hesitation or question. Aunt Marita's husband owned and operated a small trawler, since fishing was the economic backbone of Lüderitz, taking Pa and Jannie on as deckhands. While the men were out trawling or handline fishing the surrounding coastal waters, for the first time in their lives, Andre and his second brother attended school.

Education proved no hardship for young Andre, even in a tough fishing village environment where men and boys usually settled disputes with their fists. An intelligent lad, quickly picking up reading, writing and simple arithmetic, whilst also learning how to handle others and look after himself. Being a German colony back then, he'd also learned the language, coincidentally a string to his bow that would serve well in later life. Despite overtly fitting in, he felt displaced and malcontent; plagued by dreadful memories which, in turn, fed darkly terrifying nightmares. Aggravated by Pa's increasingly drunken war stories and his own personal experiences, these chilling dreams ultimately fomented young Andre's hatred for everything British.

Leaving school at the age of thirteen, inevitably joining his older brothers and Pa on the boat. Soon after turning eighteen, he married his schoolyard sweetheart, Annalie Pretorius, regarded as the town's most beautiful girl and source of many a prospective suitor's brawl. A spirited young woman but demure, as required by society of that time, she worked as a packer in the fish-drying yards. Pooling their joint wages, the newlyweds saved up enough money to buy a plot of land and, with the help of family, built a modest wood and iron home on the town's outskirts.

Out of the blue, Archduke Franz Ferdinand's assassination set Europe ablaze, a new war, soon spreading to the colonies. In quick succession, British and South African troops invaded South West Africa, pushing hopelessly outnumbered colonial Schutztruppen northwards into an increasingly hot and barren desert. Uniting with other able-bodied men from Lüderitz and other remote settlements, the Van Heerden menfolk took up arms in support of the beleaguered German forces.

It had taken several days on horseback to reach the scene of conflict, at a place called Otjiwarongo. There, they located a ragtag, dishevelled, and demoralised gaggle of around a hundred German troops, catching a breather on the shady side of a rocky hill. After an early German victory at the Battle of Sandfontein, the tide of war had changed and running skirmishes on a hastily retreating front line proved the order of the day; simply staying alive took precedence over military rule of order.

Even bolstered by enthusiastic, albeit untrained locals, the small German military forces were no match for their enemy. Hopelessly outnumbered and outgunned, the rout continued, ever northwards. Fleeing towards Tsumeb, they'd joined up with General Victor Franke's command unit, better provisioned and equipped with several cannon and three Maxim machine guns. It was there that Andre Van Heerden spotted a heavily guarded wagon cart, its cargo concealed under a securely tied tarpaulin.

Whatever this payload might be, it was evidently important, and rank-and-file troops weren't allowed anywhere near the thing. Despite being allies, he and all other volunteers were considered as outsiders and more vigorously shepherded away. Realising the wagon had to hold something of appreciable value, Van Heerden ingratiated himself into an especially sullen clique of conscripted Schutztruppen. Plying them with witblits, a rotgut brandy distilled from winery leftovers, loosened their tongues enough for him to learn that the cart supposedly held a safe, containing a large sum of gold Reichsmarks.

Before sunrise the next morning and while most still slept, leaving several officers in charge, Franke and a hand-picked group of Kaokoveld and Ovamboland veterans were on the move. Commandeering all available horses, including Van Heerden's, hitched to pull the cannons and ammunition carts, they left the campsite at a gallop. Immediately noticing that the guarded wagon was gone, Van Heerden knew it had to be amongst the thundering melee. Heading north-west into scrubland, thick dust kicked up by horses' hooves rapidly enveloped the entourage's passage. Van Heerden watched until this cloud had been subsumed by an ever-intensifying heat haze. Kept busy all morning by an excessively attentive junior officer, it wasn't until mid-afternoon when the morning's assemblage returned, minus cannon, ammunition carts, and the gold-safe wagon.

Shortly before nightfall, all volunteers were called out and brought to attention by the morning's same overbearing young officer, extending their ensemble to Franke. The General had thanked them for their service and allegiance to the Kaiser; shaking each man's hand in turn, before going on to say that their service would no longer be required and that they should return home the next morning. Dismissed from parade, most were disgruntled, shaking their heads and complaining bitterly amongst themselves. Guessing at the German commander's next move, Andre van Heerden chose not to share these thoughts with Pa and his brothers, instead making plans of his own. Settling into his shell scrape, swaddled in a blanket to stave off the desert's night chill, a sleepless night of scheming had followed.

Signifying approaching daybreak, the blood-red horn of a crescent moon eventually poked over the eastern horizon, prompting Van Heerden to quietly get up. Informing the duty sentry of his intention to make an early homewards start, then walking his horse out of camp's sight and earshot, he mounted up and cantered away to the north-west. Cutting the previous day's wagon train path shortly after sunrise, he followed hoof and wheel tracks easily discernible in the red soil. After an hour, the trail met an exposed rocky table and all but disappeared, except for where steel wheel rims had left telltale abrasions and flakes, chipped from the dolomite's hard, irregular surface. Roughly a kilometre further on, the stone pavement disappeared below ground, and tracking became easier again.

Late morning, when rounding a dense patch of thorny scrub, Van Heerden's heart sank; a massive sinkhole stretched before him and at its rim the wagon train tracks ended. Dismounting and approaching the rim of a near vertical drop, he angrily kicked a fist-sized rock, its arcing trajectory ending in a watery splash. More than a hundred metres across and likely considerably deeper, murky water filled the sinkhole to within around ten metres of ground level. One of a network of caves and tunnels undermining the area, the overlying land here had collapsed in on itself, centuries earlier.

Known locally as Otjikoto Lake, it had been earmarked by General Franke as a final resting place for the German army's heavy weapons. Intending to surrender to the British at Khorab settlement but not wanting the guns seized, Franke had disposed of them in the sinkhole. It seemed that Van Heerden's dream of instant riches lay at the bottom of this lake, well and truly out of reach.

His only option at that point was a return to Lüderitz, the two-week horseback journey mellowing his disappointment and homecoming ultimately proving sweet. In quick succession, Annalie bore him a son, followed by twin daughters, filling their lives and home with both joy and responsibility. Annalie raised their children and minded the home, while Van Heerden returned to fishing the Atlantic's cold waters.

Following Germany's First World War capitulation, the League of Nations mandated South West Africa's governance to neighbouring South Africa. Not long after this political pen stroke, a Cape Town-based, British-owned fishing company exploited the open border and relocated most of their fleet to Lüderitz. Finding it difficult to compete against these larger commercial trawlers, local fishermen had seen their daily catches and livelihoods fall into steep decline.

At the age of twenty-five, tormented by mixed sentiments but seeing no future in the isolated desert enclave, Andre van Heerden uprooted his family and took them to the land of his birth. Word of mouth had travelled, telling of a place where anyone prepared for hard and dangerous work could make their fortune. Heading to the burgeoning South African gold fields, Van Heerden integrated with culturally kindred spirits, almost without exception retaining a similarly singular distaste for the British Crown.

There, he'd forged friendships and developed alliances within a quasi-secret society, known as the Broederbond. Its affiliation exclusively reserved for Afrikaner volk, a close-knit brotherhood seeking to usurp control of the country's governance. Becoming a fully-fledged member, intellect and strength of character propelled Van Heerden upwards through the ranks. Mutual associations along the way opened doors that became personally lucrative to him, and within two years he'd been able to leave the mines. Teaming up with two friends, they started up a security firm and secured an exclusive contract, transporting gold bullion for the mines.

During the mid-1930's, a chance meeting with a lawyer named Van Rensburg had seen Van Heerden instrumental in establishing the Ossewabrandwag (OB). Duly extending reverence to the Great Trek of their forefathers, this organisation's chosen name literally translated as "ox-wagon guard"; a radically fundamentalist organisation, with its roots firmly founded in the principles of national socialism. Advocating synergy with Nazi Germany's emerging ideology, an accord had been reached between the OB and Third Reich; culminating in an understanding that Hitler's imminent dominion over Europe would reciprocally bestow self-government to the Afrikaner people.

Relishing his foray into this world of shadow politics, Van Heerden became active in promoting hugely popular OB rallies. Chiefly targeting the heartlands of Afrikanerdom, the Orange Free State and Transvaal, these events had succeeded in swelling their ranks by tens of thousands of ardent devotees. At Britain's declaration of war on Germany in September '39, by default, so too did the Union of South Africa, prompting the OB to form a military wing; the Stormjaers [Storm Hunters]. Not having the military wherewithal to wage full-scale civil war, they instead ran interference, blowing up or sabotaging telephone lines, railway tracks and other soft targets. Due to his military experience and security background, Van Heerden had been assigned an active leadership role in this partisan paramilitary outfit. Summoned to the regional command office during the summer of 1940, he'd been given the responsibility of securing a construction project in the eastern Natal Midlands. Then a year later, ordered to meet a group of Germans arriving by U-boat, taking them to the same high-security facility.

Dawn approaching by the time their staggered convoy neared Pietermaritzburg; the provincial capital, comfortably nestled on a plain at the foot of World's View escarpment. Capped by a temperature inversion at that early hour, a wispy, grey veil of smoke from coal stoves of awakening homes wreathed the town in a hazy blanket. Directly ahead, a distant mesa known locally as Table Mountain appeared in dark relief, outlined by the glow of impending sunrise. Startled awake when their car hit a pothole, Van Heerden glanced over his shoulder, seeing that the other three occupants had been similarly roused.

Lifting the fedora from where it had tilted over his face, Koch hacked and coughed, winding the window down to spit before clearing his voice.

"How long still until we get there?"

Glancing quizzically at the driver who raised one finger, Van Heerden replied.

"About an hour, just in time for breakfast."

Grunting in acknowledgement, Koch turned away, aiming a look of evident distaste at the open countryside scrolling past.

"I hope the food here is better than on the submarine." It was the fresh-faced youngster, sandwiched between Koch and Stein.

Grinning at his open candour, Van Heerden replied, "Man, I can guarantee it! Eggs and bacon with pap and wors," emphatically referring to a dry maize porridge often eaten at breakfast with spicy South African sausage. "And as much good, strong coffee as you can stomach."

Suitably placated, the man smiled and nodded appreciatively but said nothing else, seemingly embarrassed at his own directness.

The remainder of their journey continued, cramped but uneventful, until a little way before Greytown, where they turned off onto a dirt road leading into untamed tribal lands. After five uncomfortable minutes of juddering on this seldom maintained, washboard track, they stopped, waiting for the others to catch up. The final planned rendezvous point and only around ten minutes from their destination, with negligible perceived risk of meeting a military blockade, from there on they drove in close convoy. Widely interspersed kraals of the Zulu people provided respite from a predominantly wild landscape of otherwise predictable sameness; undulating tall, blonde grassland, dotted with acacia thorn trees.

Traversing a treeless section, the road suddenly dipped sharply and gradually wound its way down one steep flank of a valley. Rounding an especially tight bend as they neared the gorge's floor, a structure came into view, one that seemed wholly out of place in such a remote rural setting. A large, modern factory-style building, partially dug into the valley's side slope and elevated to avoid flooding from a nearby stream when in spate. Roughly a third of the structure single storied and built of brick, the rest rising to double height, clad and roofed in corrugated asbestos cement sheets.

The double-storey façade's front had been left open, exposing huge industrial circular saws, conveyors and other heavy machinery, revealing itself to be a timber mill. Beyond, a smaller, open-sided structure held racks of air-drying cut boards. An imposing pair of wrought iron gates blocked their path, the Opel slowing, their driver raised his hand in greeting to a uniformed sentry stepping from a guard hut. Acknowledging, the gateman swung open one heavy leaf and stood to attention when they drove through. Flanking the entire brick gable end frontage, a neatly raked gravelled parking area enjoyed the benefit of a huge umbrella tree's shade. The day would become swelteringly hot later, and intent on taking full advantage of deepest shadow cast by the tree's widely spreading branches, Van Heerden's driver parked close to its stout, gnarled trunk.

Relieved that their five-hour long journey had finally come to an end, everyone climbed out of the cars, some making an exaggerated show of stretching stiff limbs. Emerging from the building and accompanied by another guard, an elderly man wearing a tan dustcoat over a dated three-piece suit headed their way.

Adopting a lopsided grin, the older man called out when close enough to be heard.

"Good morning, gentlemen. A warm welcome, one and all. I'm so glad to see you've arrived safely." First shaking Van Heerden's hand, he introduced himself to the rest of the group. "I'm Willem Koekemoer, but everyone calls me Billy."

In his early sixties, anyone could have been forgiven for adjudging him older, since coming from that stereotypical mould of intellectuals who dedicated their lives exclusively to the pursuit of academia. Chubby-faced, Billy's ruddy complexion stretched across a pinkly bald head, his amply proportioned frame giving clear indication of a man enjoying food and drink, whilst leading an otherwise sedentary lifestyle.

First taking the time to learn the new arrivals' names, Billy then led everyone into the brick building; through an unattended open office area and into a mess hall where the smell of cooking food enticingly laced the air. Around twenty men sat eating at long tables, some in workmen's overalls alongside others, like Billy, dressed in streetwear protected by lab coats. The newcomers were soon enjoying the promised hearty breakfast, although no conversation arose between them and the old hands. In the Germans' case, likely attributable to sheer fatigue, except that a perceptive individual may have detected a sense of unease amongst those already incumbent. Whether on account of the newcomer's presence, or due to something else entirely, would soon become apparent.

Suitably fed and watered, Billy showed the Germans to their living quarters within the brick building; a spartan, yet scrupulously clean, barracks-style billet. Single beds, each flanked by a locker for personal effects, with shelved metal wardrobes positioned in such a way as to afford some degree of personal privacy. Hovering attentively until their belongings were stowed, Billy invited the men to follow him for a tour of the facility.

Intended to live at the mill for the duration of their stay, cut off from the outside world, a cosy salon had been created for the new arrival's leisure time. Armchairs were arranged around coffee tables, a gramophone, snooker table, dartboard and fully stocked bar were complimented by a movie projector set up for nighttime entertainment. Ablution facilities were equally well provisioned, in a communal bathroom; on one side, a tiled row of open showers and washbasins, with separate toilet cubicles opposite. Suitably done showcasing available creature comforts, Billy's manner shifted; it was time to see their primary objective.

Leading the group through into the lumber mill and steering well clear of whirring blades, fluttering drive belts and other whining, roaring machinery, he made for a projection occupying the rear wall. A pair of doors there were signed "Storeroom", pausing to fish a set of keys from one coat pocket, he unlocked them and motioned for the group to enter. Inside, with the door shut, the mill's racket subsided to a level at which shouted conversation became just about possible.

Overhead, a single incandescent bulb provided adequate illumination to reveal a flight of stairs disappearing down into darkness on one side and an open goods hoist opposite, guarded by a metal gate. A devotee of the theatrical, Billy said nothing, allowing the men to take in their surroundings until all were drawn to the stairs. Flicking a second wall switch illuminated the stairwell's gloom, although proved somewhat of a teaser. Down at basement level, an enclosed lobby's opposite wall held another door, huge and made of steel, clearly intended to secure something of value.

Further muted at basement level, the mill's racket had softened to a droning rumble, allowing the men to talk amongst themselves. Billy struggled with the vault door's lock until it eventually turned and clicked. Swinging inwards to expose an enormous subterranean chamber, and all conversation instantly ceased in mid-sentence. Secretly relishing his companion's reactions, Billy stood to one side, a sly smile lifting the good side of his mouth. An entertainment sadly short-lived, when the group moved as one into the open vault.

CHAPTER 6

"Treasure is uncovered by the force of flowing water, and it is buried by the same currents." – Paulo Coelho

A little over two years before, prolonged late spring rains had waterlogged gently rolling savannah grasslands surrounding the valley. A vast catchment area, encompassing tens of thousands of hectares and funnelling all run-off into the little stream trickling past the mill. Initially upgrading to a vigorously flowing river, a massive thunderstorm had dumped another fifteen centimetres of rain in an hour, constituting the final straw. Transformed into a raging torrent, tearing through the valley and scouring out a broad channel that destabilised already saturated slopes, occasioning multiple landslides.

A pair of eleven-year-old Zulu herd boys were tending their goats on the adjacent plains a few days afterwards and ventured into the valley, searching for a number having strayed from the herd. While tracking down the wayward livestock, they'd come across something inexplicable, a sight that truly frightened them. Leaving the goats to their own devices, they had fled back to the village, only to have their story treated with abject ridicule. Adding insult to injury, then summoned by the elders to be chastised for abandoning the herd. Leopards still inhabited the region, and a much-prized goat would make an easy meal for such a predator. Duly reprimanded, the youngsters approached the chief's eldest son afterwards, managing to persuade him into accompanying them to retrieve the herd and validate their story.

Sceptical, but on the off chance they might be telling the truth, taking his spear and allowing the boys to lead the way. On reaching the place, the chief's son stood staring in bewilderment, while absently flicking away a persistent horsefly. A long swathe of valley slope had slumped, forming an extended, gradually sloping riverbank that diverted the stream's course. Exposed tree roots dangling from the sheer slope above created a gnarly curtain, overhanging a projecting arc of unusually smooth, silvery-grey rock. Below this peculiarly artificial looking ledge, a small, dark cave served as the chief's son's primary focus.

A steadfast traditionalist, his father's convictions were vested solely in long-established tribal customs and cultural lore. Disdaining European teachings, available to his many children through the local mission school, his son had consequently never received any formal education. Instead, like most Zulu children of that era, lessons comprised of legends and tales handed down from their ancestors and exclusively narrated by the elders. Nevertheless, intelligent and observant, the young man was certain about what he beheld having no place in their natural world, surely serving as a gateway to a vile witch's domain.

Trained from a young age to become a warrior and eventually take the reins of chief, decisively holding his umkhonto [spear] poised in both hands, he approached this evil portal. Imagining himself stalking a lion, intent on killing the beast with one well-placed thrust of the long, sharply pointed blade. The dark void entirely absorbing his attention, steadfastly intent on slaying the witch and saving his people from certain vexation. When no more than a few paces away, heart hammering in his chest, he knelt to peer inside and something caught his eye. Ghostly pale against the darkness, whatever it was lay too deep inside to be immediately distinguishable.

Eyes narrowed against the day's brightness, brushing aside a cluster of obscuring roots and using the spear's length as an extension to his arm, he reached in. Grown accustomed to the gloom, he suddenly scrambled backwards and leaped away, whirling in mid-air to land with spear poised in a defensive posture. However, despite displaying certain menace, the thing startling him stayed put. Perhaps his eyes had tricked him. Not wanting to appear foolish to his father and the elders, summoning the courage to take another look. This time, using the spear's tip to warily prise the shape from partially encasing soil, the skeletal bones of a hand abruptly broke free and clutched for the blade.

Wrenching his spear from its infernal bony grasp, long-dried cartilage connecting one phalange snagged on a tiny, raised metal burr and separated from the others. Slingshotting from the blade, it spun forwards to land at his feet; a terrible omen, certainly the doings of a spell, umthakathi [witchcraft]. Wide-eyed in horror and emitting a pitiful mewl of terror, the chief's son reflexively sprang backwards, all bravado evaporating. Peering from behind the flaking trunk of a nearby coral tree, the two herd boys had been spectating from what seemed a safe distance. Seeing what had happened, they broke cover to flee; similarly discarding his own tattered pride, the chief's son sprinted after them.

Managing to compose himself before entering the kraal's tight grouping of huts, then relaying his story in as calm and aloof a manner as could be mustered. Sitting on hard-packed bare earth around the central cooking fire's smoking embers, his father and assembled council reacted with predictable disbelief to this account. Sending the young man away after questioning him at length, more protracted discussion followed, eventually deciding to go see for themselves. Since there were only a few hours' daylight remaining, the chief postponed their excursion until the following day.

The next morning, chief and son had taken the lead, the kraal elite following in single-file procession, armed with an assortment of spears, knobkerries and fighting sticks. It is unthinkable in Zulu culture to show fear or reticence in the face of adversity, all the same, several among the elders hung back when nearing the site. Speaking in hushed voices, lest they anger the witch or dead occupant's sleeping spirit, they huddled together to gaze on this strange thing and debate how best to deal with its presence. Ultimately reaching consensus before hurriedly leaving that cursed place, collectively deciding to seek counsel and guidance from Pastor Merkel.

Head of the Lutheran Church mission, the local Zulu considered Otto Merkel to be a good and wise man. Periodically visiting their community, he often spoke with them about his god and that god's son, sometimes even discussing and advising them on happenings in their area and the wider country. Because the pastor clearly knew much about the outside world, he would be able to tell them what should be done about this strange and disturbing thing. The chief's son had been dispatched to track Merkel down, explain what had happened and invite him to their kraal.

Arriving on horseback mid-afternoon, the morning's entourage escorted the pastor to see their problem and were immediately gratified to see that they'd made the right decision. The pastor showed no fear, nor gave signs of being intimidated by the evil manifestation, in fact quite the contrary, becoming excited and enthused. Feeling suitably assured but questioning, wanting to understand how it could be that when faced with such a terrible adversary, this mlungu [white man] wasn't afraid. Merkel explained that his god was all-powerful and gave him protection, but they should never return to the valley; for them, these demonic spirits would be deadly. Before mounting up, Merkel promised to return in a few days and would bring someone specialised in dealing with this kind of evil.

Good to his word, the pastor returned after two days, accompanied by another smartly dressed mlungu, this one puce of face and perspiring from unaccustomed exertion. Introducing this man as his brother, the pastor explained how he had experience dealing with all kinds of witches and demons. First observing polite custom, they all sat around the cooking fire to drink umqombothi [Zulu beer], allowing the brother an opportunity to speak. It transpired that exorcising such a fiend would take a long time, possibly even years, emphasising that during this time nobody from the village should visit the valley.

Unbeknownst to these trusting rural people, a hive of frenzied activity had erupted in towns and cities around the country, right after the pastor's initial visit. Paradoxically, Pastor Otto's brother, Hans, was an economics lecturer and possessed no experience in the occult whatsoever. The brothers had been born in Germany, teenagers when their parents emigrated to South Africa, a year before the outbreak of the First Word War. Hans, the elder, had fervently clung to ancestral roots and been profoundly affected by the pillaging of his homeland under the Treaty of Versailles. When German National Socialism emerged years later, he'd become an avid supporter and joined the ideologically aligned Ossewabrandwag.

The Lutheran mission didn't have a telephone, Hans receiving word from his brother by way of a telegram, cryptically stating that he was needed to photograph something worthy to the cause. Suitably intrigued, albeit without any preconception as to what Otto meant by this, Hans had immediately driven out to the remote Hermannsburg church. An avid amateur photographer, he'd taken along a treasured Kodak Retina camera, secured in a leather carry bag and hung cumbersomely, bandolier-fashion around his neck.

Leaving the tribespeople to go about daily life, the Merkel brothers rode cross-country to reach the valley, where it took a while for Hans to process what he was seeing and ready himself. Hands trembling, fumbling to load the first of several film spools until eventually beginning to capture the scene, Hans rued not bringing along a tripod. Fortunately, having personal access to the university campus's art department darkroom, the films would never leave his hands, which provided a vital layer of confidentiality.

As it happened, shaky hands hadn't impaired the images' quality, all bar one developing with pristine clarity. Interleaving each print with tissue paper, then packing them into a thick manila envelope, he hand delivered this to the OB's regional commandant. A man with little comprehension of such phenomena, all the same canny enough to grasp their significance and realise that mere association would be a feather in his cap. Suitably securing the discovery was ultimately his responsibility, and summoned Van Heerden before departing for Pretoria. A squad of armed Stormjaers would be deployed to guard the site, day and night, under strict orders to shoot any trespassers on sight.

In the nation's spiritual capital of Pretoria, the Brotherhood's leadership had deliberated over the true significance of the Merkel's find. Unanimously agreeing that offering access to Hitler's Reich would be the perfect opportunity to cement and build on relations with the Führer. If properly managed, this could prove the gateway to fulfilling their aspirations of becoming an autonomous Afrikaner state. The thing must be safeguarded at all costs and kept secret from Jan Smuts' puppet British government at all costs, one sniff of its existence would certainly see such a prize snatched away.

A week to the day after Hans' unsteady hands gathered the OB's ultimate bargaining chip, Van Rensburg placed a telephone call to Heinrich Himmler's Berlin office. The Reichsführer had been indisposed at that time, and they'd had to endure a wait of several hours before an adjutant returned their call. After listening to Van Rensburg's pitch, the aide passed the phone to Himmler and from that moment cogs began turning in a complex and far-reaching wheel.

Deemed essential to develop the site in a manner unlikely to attract attention, wealthy and influential Brotherhood and OB members readily opened their wallets. Sawmills processing forestry for virtually unlimited commercial and industrial uses already dotted the region, another mill surely wouldn't raise eyebrows. Also, an economically viable facility, a mill would provide investors with compensatory income and offer ideal camouflage for discreet investigation and study. Hastily assembled from within the legion's ranks and sworn to secrecy, a team of designers, engineers and builders were put to work.

Complicated by its remote location and the discovery's size, construction of the new mill turned out being a significant engineering feat. A heavily shored excavation first had to be dug into the valley's steep and unstable flank, deep enough to fully expose their treasure. A basement was then constructed, essentially a subterranean concrete box, big enough to encapsulate the thing. Once completed, this complex substructure had been back-filled and then straddled by the observable above-ground mill. Finishing only a few months before the Germans' arrival hadn't left much time for other essential preparatory works, assigned to Billy Koekemoer.

A man destined to pursue a career in science since childhood, the universe's workings a fascination to Billy, eternally obsessed by what made everything mesh in synchronistic perfection and balanced harmony. An only child, his bemused working-class parents had been intellectually incapable of answering these questions, instead scolding their son over unfinished daily chores and telling him to get his head out of the clouds. Ignoring their rebukes had earned Billy many a tongue-lashing and cuffs to his head, although never blunted his thirst for knowledge.

Excelling at school academically, but since his parents lived by frugal means, they were unable to sponsor his further education. Instead, Billy became a teacher, following a second-choice career option, although scrimping and saving until managing to put himself through a part-time degree in physical sciences. A sharp and enquiring mind caught the attention of his lecturers, one in particular taking Billy under his wing and encouraging him along the extended road to attaining a doctorate in physics. Thereafter, invited by this former mentor to join the university's own research team, Billy relinquished teaching and through his own God-given intellect, determination and downright hard work, finally realised his dream.

Wholly absorbed into a world of theoretical physics, Billy never made time for romantic entanglements and at the age of thirty-two, remained a bachelor. Then, without warning, a massive stroke had impaired all right-side bodily motor function, his corresponding facial features perceptibly falling. Fortunately, these were to be the only long-term hallmarks of his brush with death, returning to the university after a period of convalescence. Inexplicably though, finding himself marginalised by colleagues, as if this cruel affliction were somehow contagious, only his former mentor remained resolutely unswayed by Billy's altered appearance.

They'd become close friends, since his mentor coincidentally being a cousin of the OB's leader, he'd been introduced to Van Rensburg at a memorial service. Never really adopting any political views or affiliations before then, more so out of a sense of duty to his friend, Billy enlisted.

CHAPTER 7

"Fishes live in the sea, as men do on land: the great ones eat up the little ones." – Pericles

Threads of chemically altered perception gave rise to a vividly coloured and warmly comfortable sense of floating weightlessly. From within Craig's stirring consciousness, a hypnotic and soothing voice emerged, reassuring and pacifying alarm bells stridently firing up in other parts of his mind. Speaking a foreign tongue, the words indistinct yet oddly understandable, until it suddenly disappeared, leaving him isolated and alone. A lurching jolt of waking pitched him forcefully forwards, dislodged from the aether of colourful hallucinations, falling towards a threateningly unfamiliar chasm.

Trying to shout but unable to make a sound, Craig woke with a start, lying on a cot in a small and brightly lit room. Disorientated, confused, head feeling as if stuffed with an impenetrably hazy fog that pounded in rhythm with a thudding heartbeat, a bitter chemical taste filled his mouth. Swinging both legs over the cot's edge and struggling into a sitting position, immediately overcome by dizzying waves of nausea, he gripped the mattress side tightly and dropped his head until it passed.

Remaining in this position, memories came flooding back; the helicopter and SUVs bearing suited goons, them coming into his house. The unexpected autoinjector must have contained some kind of fast-acting knockout agent, because he'd had no time whatsoever to react. Reflexively rubbing at the needle's entry point on his neck, it still felt tender. The drug was however wearing off, Craig's head clearing, allowing him to glance around and take stock of this place.

All four walls were blank and windowless, except for a featureless panel occupying one far corner, it had to be a door. On the concrete ceiling overhead, steel-meshed coverings guarded a single light fitting and two softly whispering, square vents bringing in fresh air. On the wall adjacent to his cot and completing the décor, a securely bolted stainless steel washbasin and toilet, reinforced Craig's emerging sense of being locked up in a high-security prison.

Cautiously easing himself from the cot into a crouched standing position, the room swayed disconcertingly awhile until gradually steadying. Looking toward the corner nearest the door, he noticed another fine-barred steel cage on the ceiling, this one containing a Perspex dome-enclosed camera. Going closer to get a better look, the surveillance unit's clinically cold, unblinking eye followed. Realising his every move was being remotely monitored, a sense of indignant rage welled up.

Turning, he hammered on the door with both fists, yelling, "Gothammit! Hey... Thumb'dy, c'mere!"

Another unpleasant side effect of the knockout drug, tongue and throat had been left feeling thick and numb, morphing his voice into a gruffly slurred whisper. Coughing from vocal exertion, he stepped back to wave at the camera and the door clicked, opening inwards. Even without sunglasses, Craig recognised both men in the open doorway as being two of those at his house earlier.

It took every ounce of control to stifle an initial reaction to run at them, punching and kicking; restraining himself when noticing that each held a Taser aimed directly at him.

"Whath in hell'th goi'g od here?" he began angrily, until the one who'd sounded Russian raised a hand.

"Calm down. Don't do anything stupid. There's no need to make this any more unpleasant for yourself." Pointing towards the cot. "Shut up and sit down."

Outgunned Craig complied, backing up and sitting without saying anything else.

"Here." Stepping inside, the Russian threw a plastic bottle of clear liquid onto the cot next to Craig. When he glanced at it suspiciously, the Russian continued. "Only water. It'll clear out that stuff we gave you. Drink it." Aiming a meaningful look at Craig, then they both left.

The door closed and Craig realised how incredibly thirsty he actually was, picking up and inspecting the bottle. A branded label identified it as containing still water, and since the plastic cap seal appeared intact, he cracked it open. Warily sniffing at the contents, smelling of nothing at all, he emptied the bottle in one long, chugging swallow. Irritated at his summary confinement and the two thugs authoritarian behaviour, he tossed the empty at the door, then leant back and clasped both hands behind his head.

Sounding more like himself, Craig spoke out loud. "This is bloody ridiculous. It can't really be happening."

Everything about his present situation had an unreal, dreamlike quality, a detached sense of altered reality. Knowing this trance-like state to be one of the brain's coping mechanisms, much like an airbag, protecting itself against sensory overload. Drawing a deep breath and forcing himself to acknowledge the reality of his circumstances, he began rationalising.

Whatever the object might, he'd found the night before had to be the reason for his abduction, way too coincidental to be anything else. Frustratingly, having pretty much vanished into thin air, he still had absolutely no idea what had become of the darned thing. Well, these people were barking up the wrong tree if this whole escapade had been the pretext for him returning it. Fortunately, they hadn't taken his wristwatch, seeing that it was three in the afternoon, around four hours since the encounter at his house. Everything happening in that timeslot would forever remain a complete blank.

At another click, the door reopened to the Russian and his mate, this time stepping aside and allowing a remarkably tall and skeletally thin Asian man to enter. Appearing a little older than Craig, perhaps in his mid-forties, he wore a long-sleeved white lab coat over regular clothing. Thickly lensed and oversized glasses adorned his narrow face, hugely magnifying the eyes and rendering his overall appearance praying mantis-like. A caricature which, under different circumstances, would have been farcically comical. Without so much as acknowledging Craig's presence, the mantis halted and began rummaging through bulging lab coat pockets. Eventually locating and extracting a small torch from one and a stethoscope out of another, turning his attention to Craig for the first time.

"I need to examine you." A matter-of-fact intonation, as if present circumstances were perfectly normal. "Stand up and remove your shirt."

Offering no introduction or explanation, the man's brusque manner set Craig's hackles rising.

"Ah, hell no, pal. First, you're going to tell me what's going on. Why am I here?"

The sharpness of Craig's response clearly startled the mantis, blinking in surprise and taking a few steps backwards. Taking a step closer, the Russian made a deliberate show of withdrawing a black pouch from his jacket side pocket, his sidekick circling behind Craig. As if summoned by an inaudible alarm, two more suited thugs appeared in the doorway.

When the Russian extracted an autoinjector from the pouch, Craig backed down.

"Alright, alright. Fine, have it your way." Reluctantly stripping off his T-shirt and allowing the mantis to carry out a superficial physical examination.

Apparently satisfied, the tall man turned away and left without another word, the Russian and his number two returning to station either side of the door. Arms folded and staring impassively at the opposite wall, although Craig knew any attempt made in going for the door would be met with force. Sitting on the cot's edge, he glared at them.

Nothing about this whole crazy set-up made any sense, seeming rather more like the weirdest kind of nightmare. Vainly wishing it might be just that, merely a dream, Craig dug his fingernails into the opposite hand; it hurt, this was no dream.

A few minutes passed before the mantis returned, this time accompanied by an attentive younger man with the subservient air of an assistant. Disregarding any socially conventional consideration of personal space, the mantis came way too close, towering over Craig. Evidently trying to appear amenable by cocking his head to one side.

"So, you want to know why you're here. It's really very simple, Mister Farrant, you have something valuable belonging to us. Of course, you know what I'm talking about." An enquiringly raised eyebrow confirmed this to be an indirect question.

In such close proximity, the man reeked of stale perspiration. Worse still, his breath carried an overpoweringly foul garlic odour which had Craig inching backwards, creating distance from this malodorous creature.

He could try bluffing. Instead, opting to play it straight, else heaven only knew how things might otherwise play out.

"Yeah, I think I know. Just to be clear, are you talking about a shiny metal thing, the size of a walnut? If so, then I don't have it any longer, it just vanished into thin air."

Craig wanted this fiasco to end without more needles, or whatever else the Russian and his cohorts may be capable of exacting.

"Yes, yes that's it, a shiny little metal thing," the mantis mimicked, without overtly appearing to patronise, before continuing, "Oh no, it's not gone anywhere. You may not be aware, but you most definitely still have it."

There was something unsettling about the man's insistence, more so in the way he now scrutinised Craig.

Sensing that this misconception might be heading somewhere unsavoury, Craig needed to set the record straight.

"Whoa, hang on. You're not getting it. I'm telling you; I don't have it. Yes, I found the thing but, like I said, it disappeared. Gone."

Grinning infuriatingly at Craig's insistence, the mantis smirked. The man's brazen condescension and outright disregard for his honesty rankled, turning to anger.

"Which part of what I've just said don't you understand? I haven't got your goddamn bauble!"

However unaccountably their trinket had ended up in his yard, Craig had ended up bearing the brunt of their blunder. Catching sight of the Russian edging closer and lowering his tone. Pointless getting himself drugged again, there had to be another way.

"Look, this is ridiculous. You can't get away with this. You need to let me go."

Ignoring his plea, the mantis' bearing shifted, becoming clinically detached.

"Mmm, that's not currently possible. Tell me how you found the item and all events leading up to the point when, as you say, it disappeared."

Further denial evidently pointless, Craig realised there was no alternative but to play along, a factually detailed account might get through to the man. Biting his lip and swallowing a rising sense of desperation, he related the previous night's events without glossing over a single detail, even sharing his frustration at being unable to identify the object. Motionless, the mantis listened intently, up to the point where Craig had woken to discover the thing missing, interrupting and insisting he repeat this part. While recapping that aspect in even greater detail, the mantis leant closer, absorbing every word.

When Craig's narrative ended, the man maintained this same stooped posture, face only inches away from Craig's, seeming as if trying to absorb further crucial details out of the air space between them. Reluctantly straightening up, he turned and beckoned to his assistant.

"Okay, take this down, word for word. Spontaneous autonomous Link assimilation occurred at the onset of sleep threshold consciousness. Subject had consumed alcohol, moderately intoxicated."

A tablet materialised from under the assistant's arm, obligingly setting about tapping at its screen.

Not wholly grasping the context of the mantis' statement, Craig was however savvy enough to get the gist and stifled a pang of horror. From his perception of what had been said, coupled with these people's obvious resources and the special forces' precision of his kidnapping, this whole set-up was geared around more than just recovering a lost article. He needed to find out precisely what that was, to stand any chance of getting out of there unscathed. The mantis' reference to "assimilation" held disconcerting literal connotations, instinctively knowing he wasn't going to like the answer to that part.

Either intuitively, or for reasons best known only to himself, unbidden, the mantis began offering up answers to Craig's unasked questions.

"What you referred to as a little metal thing… we know as the Link… and… well, let's just say that it has fused with you, assimilated into your being at an essential level." The mantis' eyes cast about uncomfortably; a darting tongue moistened his lips. "But be absolutely clear on this…" Pausing to choose his next words carefully, exaggeratedly wagging one finger admonishingly. "…it remains an asset of this facility. We intend to study its effects on you, ultimately recovering the Link. Better you come to accept being here during this process and understand that none of your friends or family have any possible way of ever finding you. Cooperate and the process will go smoothly, otherwise..." Allowing this sentence to hang, he shrugged awkwardly, leaving Craig in no doubt as to the implication of words unspoken.

Despite feeling physically sick at this realisation, Craig retained his composure, mind racing. Seeing as how the mantis was being candid, an opportunity presented itself to press the man for more details.

"Okay, I get that, but at least level with me. Who are you people and what's going on here?"

Considering for a moment, the mantis responded guardedly, "I am Doctor Govender, and this is a private research facility." Holding Craig's gaze unblinkingly, he continued. "As far as what's going on here… that's classified, and besides, it's highly technical. You wouldn't understand anyway."

The sheer dismissive arrogance of the man's response got to Craig.

"Oh right, and you're so smart that you've managed to lose the blasted thing, the Link, or whatever you want to call it. Now I've got it and suddenly it's my problem, huh?"

Regaining control, Craig regretted needling at the mantis, wanting instead to pump him for specifics.

Rather than taking the bait, Govender turned away, ushering his assistant to the door and getting the final word in, "That's all you need to know, Mr. Farrant."

Both minders followed, pulling the door shut and leaving Craig fuming.

Agitated at having blown the opportunity, Craig took his annoyance out on the door, hammering its steel skin with both fists, then turned and kicked at the cot. Realising venting his temper on the fixtures and fittings to be pointless, he turned and raised both hands to the camera, extending the middle fingers. An acrid smell like burnt sugar filled the air, its pungency stung Craig's nostrils and made his eyes water, feeling his legs turning to rubber, then the room swam disorientatingly. Realising what was happening, he managed to fall backwards towards the cot as the knockout gas took full effect.

There was no way of knowing how long he had been out, coming to lying as he'd fallen, only in a different setting. Assessing this place to be considerably bigger than the cell, an array of dazzlingly bright lights shone from above, forcing him to squint. A steady beeping caught his ear, glancing to the side and seeing a bank of monitors, the kind displaying a patient's vital signs in hospital. Craig tried to sit up, finding his arms and legs were held fast, craning side to side to see that both wrists and ankles were held fast by thick leather cuffs.

Disconcertingly, his T-shirt had been removed to facilitate gel pad electrodes adhered to his bare skin, wires running to the resonating monitors. By now accustomed to the overhead glare, the reality of his surroundings became evident and naked fear clutched at Craig's heart; he was strapped down in a surgical operating theatre.

Wanting to get the full picture, Craig tried to lift his head and look around but something unseen tugged back, resisting this movement. Unable to use his hands, Craig wiggled his scalp, discerning what could only be more electrodes stuck to his head. Struggling against his cranial restriction, managing to establish that he'd been strapped to a table, inlaid with a weirdly pulsating opaque surface. Rising out of this medium, a softly radiant honeycomb lattice framework of finger-width white plasticised filaments followed his body contour, a hand's width distant, effectively cocooning him. Even if managing to break free from the tough limb restraints, he would have to contend with essentially a cage, of indeterminate resilience. There was no sense in expending energy on a pointless attempt at freeing himself.

Remembering what the mantis had said about recovering the Link, Craig's imagination rocketed to the nightmare prospect of vivisection. Swallowing against a rising plug of nausea and stifling the urge to scream out, when he caught sight of movement. Govender and his assistant stood at the operating theatre's far end, quietly talking with a pair of shadowy figures seated behind an office-type workstation. Evidently engrossed in whatever was displayed on a computer monitor, none appeared to have noticed his wakefulness. From the screens' back-glow, Craig could just make out that both seated characters were women, one suddenly looking in his direction and saying something to alert the mantis. Peeling off from the group, he came Craig's way, poker-faced and unnervingly devoid of expression. Stopping beside the table, staring unblinkingly at Craig and appearing to relish his discomfort.

Eventually speaking, it was as though reading Craig's thoughts.

"Don't be afraid, Mr. Farrant, we don't intend cutting you open, not today." Smirking, apparently amused at his own dark humour, Craig realised this man to be a twisted individual.

Showing fear would only feed into whatever kind of power trip the mantis might be on, this also wasn't the moment for undue bravado.

"I'm really glad to hear that. So, what are you planning on doing with me then?" Holding Govender's gaze steadily, Craig wanted it to come across as if he were genuinely interested.

Inhaling noisily, Govender pursed his lips reflectively.

"Look, it's like this." He frowned and began talking slowly, manually engaging mental gears, striving to make his point unambiguously clear. "Like I said earlier, this is a research facility, a place where we're working on brand-new, highly classified technology."

Perceiving the mantis' evasiveness and hearing only waffle, Craig interjected.

"You're referring to the Link, right?"

Irked by this interruption, Govender hastened, "Yes precisely, the Link. Okay, so you thought it had been misplaced but to the contrary, like I said before the link has merged with you." Mistaking Craig's look of incredulity as confusion, the mantis reverted to speaking in a deliberate manner. "The Link has absorbed itself into your body, your essential being, to be exact." Pausing to nod affirmatively, unbeknownst to Craig, delighted by the fundamental significance of this statement and wanting it to sink into his own mind all over again.

Whatever self-enlightenment this provided galvanised the man, abruptly becoming animated and enthused at the import of his epiphany.

"You're a most remarkable individual, Mr. Farrant. None of the others survived as long as you have, following assimilation," this disclosure, conversely scuppering Govender's cheerful mood.

Slouching and dropping his eyes, lost to an internalised quandary, then shrugging off this downer and continuing, with Craig immediately wishing he hadn't.

"The others..." a regretful frown, "...disintegrated, pretty much right away." Another pause. "All except the most recent fellow who lasted a few minutes, then... disappeared."

Returning his gaze to the floor, left Craig processing an ever-escalating macabre spectre, grasping that no matter what twists and turns this helter-skelter took, he would end up totally screwed at the end of the ride.

Taking to pacing, the mantis finally stopped when nearest the head end of Craig's table. Seeming by this point to have worked through unsettling recollections of exploding people, he brightened.

"I'm going to show you something that will help you understand the concept."

Striding to the workstation, he spoke with one of the seated lab technicians. Unable to quite catch their dialogue, Craig watched as Govender returned, this time holding a small black remote control. At the touch of a button, a screen unfurled from its ceiling-mounted casing and a projector simultaneously whirred to life. An image of a human outline filled the screen, much like an intricately detailed full colour MRI or PET scan, showing skeletal structure and internal organs in exquisite high-definition, 3-D detail. As best the restraints would permit, Craig shifted to get a better view, seeing the projected form replicate his movements and understanding it to be of himself. Observing his reaction, Craig's surprise must have been plain to Govender.

"Yes, that is you, showing every internal structure in real-time." The mantis gave a signal, and the technician tapped at her keyboard. "Now, by varying proton frequency, the Link occupying you is exposed."

The monitor flickered almost imperceptibly, the scan's

outline blurred momentarily, and energetically sparkling flecks appeared, infusing all musculature and organs.

At first thinking this to be a glitch, Craig glanced at Govender, seeing him however staring in undisguised rapt fascination. Whatever the peculiar manifestation, it entirely saturated Craig's outline; tiny light forms remaining ever equidistant while subtly alternating in intensity to produce the effect of rhythmically complex, wave patterns. Morbid fascination took hold, as if hypnotised, Craig found himself unable to drag his eyes from the spectacle. Seeing himself infested by this weird foreign presence, Craig desperately wanted to feel violated, except for some reason unable to that emotion. In fact, other than prevailing circumstances, something about this revelation made him feel good; perversely riding the crest of a wave of unsolicited elation.

Shaking his head to disconnect, Govender returned to Craig's side.

"So, now you have seen the Link for yourself and understand what I have told you to be factual. When you were first brought in, we needed to be certain and ran this scan and other tests several times." While speaking, Govender picked up an empty syringe and inserted the tip into a tube protruding outside of the lattice frame. Craig followed his movements, noticing a cannula inserted into his arm.

"This might seem ridiculously simple, but it will effectively demonstrate the level at which the Link has assimilated."

Drawing off a quantity of Craig's blood, Govender slid the syringe through the lattice and onto the table beside him, its dark outline appearing on the projected image. Bizarrely, there were no dancing light forms showing from within the syringe. The mantis gestured dramatically, like a magician smugly completing a pièce de résistance conjuring trick.

"From this, it becomes obvious that the Link is not merely

circulating in your vascular system, instead fusing with you at a far deeper level. The link has become part of you, and you a part of the Link."

Obviously, an exciting concept to Govender, Craig however didn't share in his enthusiasm; everything about the man's revelation constituting sensory overload and way too weird.

"Yeah, whatever, except I'm not gonna be your goddamn guinea pig." No longer playing along, Craig snapped angrily, "You need to get this mumbo jumbo crap out of me and let me go. I'm not having anything to do with this, or you and your freakish Link."

Confident in Craig's restraints, Govender leant closer, his nose almost touching the lattice grid.

"Well then, that's where we share a problem, Mr Farrant, since we haven't yet figured out how to reverse the assimilation process, sans mortality. Being completely upfront with you here, we didn't develop the Link, someone or something else did."

This brutally frank disclosure came as a physical blow to Craig, hitting like a sucker punch to the breastbone. Pulling and kicking at the restraints, incensed, he let loose a torrent of profanities.

Calmly stepping back, the mantis made space for his assistant to step in and connect another syringe into Craig's cannula, sending him to oblivion.

CHAPTER 8

"I can calculate the motion of heavenly bodies but not the madness of people." – Isaac Newton

What had so captivated the German's attention held centre stage, virtually filling the subterranean chamber. Of course they'd known it to be there, since being the sole purpose for their perilous journey part way around the world. It was just that nothing could have prepared them for its sheer gravitas.

Shaped like a discus and roughly thirty metres in span, the curve of its uppermost apex extended more than six metres above basement floor level, although obscured by the spread of its sweeping underbody. Prevented from tipping over and stabilised in a horizontal plane by a sturdy steel support frame, a machine that had to have come from a different time or world beyond our own, a vehicle far surpassing the comprehension of most mere mortals.

The thing's observable silver-grey belly expanse appeared

seamless, without any visible amalgamation of panels, rivets or fixings of any kind. In fact, entirely smooth bar three concentric rings about two metres apart, which were regularly interrupted by protruding elliptical nodes. Despite its apparent simplicity, the craft's surface held a burnished patina, tantalisingly alluding to inexplicably mysterious origins. Simultaneously, projecting distinct melancholy; it had been fundamentally damaged, the nearest quadrant deformed by slamming into the ground. Here, all symmetry of curve was crushed and buckled, framing a long and wide split, peeled open to expose the craft's interior.

Built from the cavern floor a timber staircase rose to a high-level landing, where a gently inclined ramp projected to span the gap onto the opening's misshapen lower rim. Serving as an access bridge, the ramp had been strung with work lights that continued on inside, illuminating the craft's otherwise pitch-black interior.

Down at floor level, the basement had been purposed as both workshop and research laboratory; one wall taken up by a row of workbenches, already laid out with the contents of those packing crates accompanying the men. A variety of precision tools, some powered while others were manual, for pretty much any conceivable task, from cutting and boring, to probing and prising. An array of clamps, vices, verniers and gauges hung from hooks fitted on the wall behind.

The adjoining wall served as a backdrop to worktables that contained more sophisticated-looking scientific equipment. A multitude of technological electronic devices, some with projecting vacuum tubes, valves and indicator lamps, others had integral oscilloscopes for real-time analysis and interpretation of test outcomes. Half of the third side supported banks of rotating blackboards, the rest having been reserved for the world's most advanced piece of computing equipment in existence at that time.

One of only two Z3 machines ever built, created by Germany's leading electronics pioneer, Konrad Zuse; the second residing in a high security, reinforced concrete bunker somewhere below Berlin. Essentially a programmable, fully automatic digital computer, capable of performing complex floating-point binary arithmetic and considered optimal by high command for cracking the craft's secrets. Under Himmler's orders, two months before their arrival, the Z3 had been disassembled and shipped from Germany on two separate U-boats.

Looking around the basement, Koch's gaze settled on the fourth wall, blank except for two doors, one through which they had just entered, the other discreetly stuck away in the far corner. The concrete wall had been roughly finished around this second opening, as if formed as an afterthought, following the chamber's completion. Overhead, staggered rows of modern fluorescent lights glared from the walls' starkly whitewashed finish, making the basement altogether too bright for Koch's photosensitive eyes.

Billy had finished relating the backstory to the craft's discovery, and still nobody spoke, continuing to savour the moment. Eventually, Stein found his tongue.

"Magnificent, Herr Doktor. Worth enduring such a miserable journey, if only to witness such a truly marvellous spectacle." Grinning from ear to ear, he slapped Billy on the back before going on, "I'm sure I speak for everyone when I say that we are eager to see inside."

Without any further prompting, Billy obliged and led the way, but Koch deliberately lagged, self-conscious at how his deformed legs made climbing stairs an awkward and ungainly spectacle.

Out of breath, pausing on the top landing while the rest continued ahead into the craft, Koch was intrigued by the ragged tear in the craft's skin. Thicker than a man's wrist, the hull's metallic composition wasn't entirely solid, tiny pores irregularly dotted its exposed edges and sparked an obscure flashback.

Fleetingly, finding himself back in the dank and poky, woodworm-infested Cologne working quarter apartment where he'd been raised. Overrun by the tiny beetles, all visible timber peppered by their tunnels, and despite Mother's best efforts, every surface continuously blanketed in a fine dust of their droppings. He'd loathed that place, not only because of the infestation but for many, many more unpleasant reasons.

Hastily quashing the recollection, drawn instead to a tiny bead of clear liquid oozing from a larger pore and reaching out to touch, immediately recoiling at an intense burning sensation. As if having dipped his finger into a concentrated acid solution, he yelped and cursed in pain, frantically wiping the viscous goo off onto a nearby handrail. Instinctively sticking the burnt finger in his mouth turned out being Koch's second mistake, acridly bitter residue numbing his entire mouth. Aware that the others weren't far off, he looked about to ensure that no one had witnessed his folly, spitting vigorously before wiping his tongue on a coat sleeve. Glancing around again, satisfied that his moment's indiscretion hadn't been observed, he hurried after the others.

Disgruntled at his faux pas but intrigued by the craft, Koch discovered that the makeshift entrance led directly into a large open-plan cabin area. Well-lit by multiple work lamps, the interior surprisingly uncomplicated, yet somehow infinitely more fascinating by virtue of its simplicity. Smooth, off-white bulkhead panels overhead replicated the hull's flowing external arch, optimising available volume and creating a sense of spaciousness. Following the circular perimeter, powder-grey, matt-finished side walls were interrupted by four full-height, equidistantly spaced mirrors rising from a textured black floor. In front of each and unmistakable in their purposed form, ergonomically contoured, high-backed seats were finished in seamless, flock-like buff material. Waist-high consoles infilled the circumference between, except where one was conspicuously absent at the point of entry. The three remaining had glossy black, obsidian-like tops, each etched with arrays of unique symbols that could best be described as vaguely reminiscent of Egyptian hieroglyphs.

Studying the flight deck, Koch looked up and noticed an inverted black dome occupying the central apex. Roughly the size of a large beach ball, it appeared translucent and gleamingly reflected the work lamps' glares. For no immediately definable reason, this feature unsettled him, an irrational feeling of someone, or something watching their every move from inside. At deck level, the central area stepped down around a large arched, circular structure made up of interlocking and ornately fluted, amber crystalline segments. This had also been damaged in the crash, several missing sections created a gap, large enough that a man could easily fit through. It was there that the others had gathered, everyone staring at whatever might be inside. Billy was talking, so Koch went to join the group.

"From Doktor Schauberger's papers, it's my understanding that you intend removing this unit and taking it back to Germany. Correct?"

"Indeed, that is correct." Stein responded, nodding affirmatively. "Miraculously, the propulsion system appears to be completely intact and there are evident similarities to fragments recovered from the other one." He referred to an incident taking place in 1936, when a separate craft had crashed in the heart of Germany's Black Forest. That impact had however been catastrophic, the Nazis acquiring only fascinating but completely useless remnants of a technology far in advance of anything ever seen by humans.

Fanatically obsessed in the occult and alternative, paranormal pseudosciences, Himmler had enlisted aid from the All-German Society for Metaphysics, also known as the Vril. Their self-styled leader, Austrian-born Maria Orsic claimed to be a psychic medium, possessing the ability to channel off-world, alien civilisations. Appointed by Himmler to do precisely that, through a series of mystic seances, she had allegedly made contact; providing Schauberger and a select group of scientists with seemingly authentic details as to how the disintegrated craft's antigravity drive system should function.

Methodically following Orsic's guidance, the Nazis had partially pieced together twisted and shattered shards recovered from the wreck. Ultimately, a futile exercise, however succeeding in confirming the Vril leader's instructions regarding underlying concepts of such a propulsion unit. Consequently, Himmler had interpreted news of the South African discovery as a sign from Woden, an affirmation that the Third Reich's ascendency would be an irresistible inevitability.

Listening curiously and wanting to see what held their interest, Koch bobbed his head side to side, although since getting only glimpses of the device, he edged closer. The crystal structure enclosed a waist-deep pit, housing a multifaceted lattice frame, intricately spun with fine golden strands. Defying logic and gravity, at this elaborate matrix's centre, a basketball-sized, silver sphere hung suspended in mid-air. Not being an especially well-educated man, Koch was nonetheless smart enough to grasp the significance of such a physical impossibility. Discourteously pushing through the rest, he crouched at the pit rim and stared intently, trying to identify threads surely holding the ball aloft.

Distracted, he'd missed a question from Stein, although managed to get the gist from Billy's answer.

"Analysis of material removed from inside the craft showed it crashed into marshland, existing here long before the stream outside drained the area and eroded this valley. They couldn't determine the time span though, because the stream had worn away a lot of the overlying land required for an exact dating analysis. Also, due to its mass and likely velocity, the craft would have punched through saturated ground into older layers on impact, further complicating fixing a timeline. The geology lab instead compared soil profiles and tested other samples taken from the area. However, these could be only approximately dated, making the results inconclusive."

Not giving up easily, Stein was undeterred. "Your best estimate then. How long ago did it crash?"

Visibly flustered, Billy stammered, "S… s… somewhere around a hundred and fifty thousand years. Probably longer, more like two hundred, two fifty..."

A look of incredulity crossed Stein's face. He whistled softly and eyed Billy disbelievingly.

"A hundred to two fifty thousand years…!" Turning to the others, then back to Billy, he countered, "That can't be right, there must be a mistake. How can everything still be so immaculate?"

Tight-lipped, Billy squirmed uncomfortably, wanting to explain how he had questioned and even forcefully interrogated the geological report. Even if an estimate, the stated period seemed disproportionate, quite understanding Stein's scepticism. When assigned the task of overseeing the craft's preparation, the interior had been partially filled and spattered with impact debris, requiring extensive cleaning. Strangely though, uncontaminated surfaces had also looked like new, too well preserved to have lain buried over such an expanse of time. Billy had developed theories of his own during the clean-up, feeling compelled to share these.

"For one thing, most materials in here are of an entirely unfamiliar composition that simply don't deteriorate. Furthermore, none of the metals have any ferrous content, explaining why there is no rust evident. Different metallic compounds used inherently resist oxidation, which when considered collectively, explains why everything remains pristine. I acknowledge and understand your doubts, Doktor Stein, but the geologist's report wouldn't have been far off the mark." Backing down would have been a betrayal of his university peers; Billy set his jaw and looked Stein straight in the eye.

Although listening to Billy's explanation, Stein's expression remained critical. Rather than argue the topic, he changed the subject.

"In one of your weekly reports you referred to an accident. Will you please expand on what happened?"

A shadow crossed Billy's face and he sighed before replying, "When we were carrying out the clear-up, one of my men was killed." Taking a step forwards, pointing towards where the crystal structure had been damaged, he expanded, "Fragments had fallen inside the drive unit chamber, and when Marius went to retrieve them, he was electrocuted."

"Electrocuted!" Dismayed, Stein recoiled. "That's awful. How?"

Pointing at the overhead dome, Billy replied. "In the very instant when he reached inside, a powerful electrical discharge shot from that thing and killed him."

Stein's eyes flicked reflexively upwards, then back to Billy, with a look of disdain.

"Come now, Doktor, that's preposterous. You cannot seriously be suggesting that this craft still has a live power source? It must have come from somewhere else, perhaps a faulty lighting cable."

Undeterred, Billy again stood his ground. "I witnessed it happen with my own eyes, as did the rest of my men."

Conflicted but realising his refutation must have seemed offensive, Stein stared at Billy, grappling with the sheer outrageousness of the man's claim.

Much like the geologist's report, there had to be a mix-up, a misinterpretation of more reasonable facts. It was utterly inconceivable for that kind of energy to be stored, dormant for however many years the craft had actually been buried.

Recognising Stein's train of thought, the older man continued, knowing it to be essential that none of them should suffer the same fate.

"Again, Doktor Stein, I wholly understand your doubts. In all honesty, I can't definitively explain why everything here hasn't rotted away to dust. By the same token, I cannot clarify how that thing still works," extending his arm towards the dome, "but I am certain of one absolute; that if you are not extremely careful, Stein, this machine will kill all of you."

Beginning to back away, apprehension filled Stein's men's faces. Oblivious to the irony of self-prophecy and realising he may have overstepped the mark, Billy hurriedly changed tack.

"Gentlemen, I don't intend to cause undue alarm and in truth, I believe you to be perfectly safe at present. My men and I continued working in here, without further incident, for weeks after the fatality. What you must understand though, is that approaching and removing the unit will be a treacherous procedure, one for which you must be well prepared."

Regardless of Billy's assurances, an air of unease persisted, the group only partially mollified; evidenced by eyes periodically flitting towards the overhead mechanism.

Hearing of the fatality validated Koch's instinctive apprehension about the dome, now more so, perceiving an inherently sinister menace emanating from the thing.

Discreetly sidling to a spot nearer the exit, he manufactured an excuse to leave, abruptly interjecting, "Also in your documentation, you made mention of bodies found. I want to see them."

Ruffled by the Nazi's interruption, Billy experienced a flutter of irritation but managed to bite his tongue.

"Er... Of course, Herr Koch. Everyone will have the opportunity to view the crew's remains, once we are finished in here."

Taking a disliking to Koch from the outset, the patently ghoulish nature of his interruption served to heighten Billy's reservations. In his estimation, here was a bully, one without a single shred of academic or humanitarian interest, maintaining only a ghoulish fascination at seeing the dead crew. Running deeper than the man's superficial oafishness, he also detected a coldly calculating darkness, an insidiously ruthless creature who was well suited to his role in the SD.

Since the disclosure of Marius' death, Stein's men had become agitated, fidgeting like spooked cattle with a big cat circling the corral. Become engrossed in studying the console glyphs, Stein wasn't quite ready to move on, Billy having to insistently usher him out.

Down on the chamber floor, after unlocking the evidently retrofitted corner door, Billy turned and addressed the group solemnly. "Uncovering crew remains wasn't foreseen when this place was being built. Only once entering the craft to begin the clear-up did we discover… them. Needing a place to store the bodies, this room was more recently dug out and built, meaning that space inside is limited. Therefore, only two at a time please gentlemen."

Securing a spot nearest the door and making no effort to conceal his eagerness, Koch was first inside. Not quite so confined as imagined, the repository proved plenty spacious enough for its intended purpose. Stale air and the wan glow of a single low wattage bulb added a fittingly tomb-like ambience. There on the floor, laid out on a row of canvas stretchers were the remains of four bodies. Mummified by the passage of time, flesh and soft tissues had long since dried out, withering to acutely express musculoskeletal details. Tattered remnants of finely woven pale blue fabric clung in places, perhaps flight suits or uniforms worn on the day these beings had died.

Spectacles pushed up the bridge of his nose, Koch excitedly licked his lips, stepping forwards and leaning closer to see better; in so doing, unintentionally allowing Stein to squeeze through behind him. Eyes adjusting to the diminished light level, Koch began making out individual features; recoiling sharply, when realising they weren't human. Recovering from this initial shock, to resume his inspection. Autopsies would not have been required to establish the crew members' causes of death; a plethora of massive injuries plainly obvious to see. Crushed ribcages, shattered skulls and a multitude of fractured bones spoke to the severity of their craft's impact and certain suddenness of the crew's deaths.

Definitely not human, although physiologically the same, remains comprising of two symmetrically identical arms and legs, a torso and head. That's where similarity diverged. Standing well over two metres tall when alive, these creatures' limb, hand and foot bones were conspicuously longer and slenderer. It was, however, their heads that had so compulsively startled Koch. Disproportionately large, exhibiting elongated parietal and occipital bones which distended the skull's rear, creating a braincase around three times bigger than Homo sapiens. These beings would certainly have been intellectually superior to humans, a realisation that profoundly frightened Koch.

Huge and dark in death, recessed eye sockets accentuated the lower half of their faces; distinctly slighter than a man's, tapering into a less-pronounced jaw and chin. Cheek muscles withered and shrunken, their lips retracted into a humourless death rictus, exposing a continuous and dentally white ridge. This feature oddly distracting, reminded Koch of a botched filling, carried out a day before the submarine voyage. It had plagued him throughout the journey and the same accursed tooth still troubled him.

Stein suddenly interrupted, "Time to move on Herr Koch, the others also want to see."

Annoyed, he stifled an urge to curse at the man when something else caught his interest.

At the foot of each stretcher lay a clipboard, holding a sheet of handwritten notes and detailed sketch, depicting where each body had been found in the craft. Perched atop the clipboards was a small canvas bag, tied up with rough hemp string. Ignoring Stein's request, Koch knelt to pick up the nearest and felt a hard lump inside. Unknotting the string and peering inside, the crypt's dim lighting made it impossible to see the contents. Remembering his burned finger, he carefully folded the bag back on itself, until bringing the item into view. Short-sightedly pushing spectacles to his forehead, narrowing his eyes and scowling when discovering the find not especially interesting.

A drab grey lump with an unusual and symmetrically regular shape. Appearing harmless, he tipped it out into the other hand, finding it cold to the touch and to his surprise, the object immediately changed colour to an ugly muddy red hue. Something about the thing's contact with his hand made Koch feel uncommonly vulnerable. As if, in the most ridiculously contrived manner, possessing the sentience to assess and judge him.

"Ugh." Grunting in disgust and tipping the thing back into its bag, he tossed this onto the clipboard, stood up and left. The whole episode had been unpleasant, disturbing even, making a mental note to quiz Koekemoer regarding that verdammt thing at the first suitable opportunity.

Glad to be out of the bone store, he headed for a pair of researchers busying themselves by picking through pieces of the craft's shattered fourth console. These remnants had been removed by Billy's team during the clear-up and were arranged on a separate bench, conveniently placed in the corner furthest from the crypt. Entirely out of character, right at that moment, Koch found himself craving the company of his own kind.

Once everyone had been given an opportunity to view the

crew's remains, Billy called them together.

"Gentlemen, I trust you are satisfied with everything you have seen so far." Glancing at a pocket watch, he added, "It's lunchtime, then no doubt you will want to spend the afternoon resting." Beckoning for them to follow, he made for the basement exit.

Upstairs in the mess hall, Koch saw his opportunity and made a beeline to sit alongside Billy, casually eating a bowl of soup in silence before broaching the subject.

"I couldn't help but notice that there are small objects in canvas bags accompanying the bodies. So, tell me Doktor Koekemoer, what is their purpose?"

Up to that moment, Billy had been enjoying his meal and made little effort to disguise chagrin at Koch's opening.

Remaining steadfastly fixated on his plate, hesitating with a forkful of vegetables poised in mid transit.

"I have absolutely no idea, Herr Koch. All the bodies had one of those, er... tokens, usually at their feet. We recovered and catalogued them, but I'm sure your research team will be able to explain their purpose to you, in due course."

Without further ado, Billy shoved the food into his mouth, hoping to have dissuaded any further discussion.

Unfortunately for him, the tone of his response had aroused Koch's distrust, already suspecting the man to have exceeded the scope of his brief. Anyone, given such an opportunity, would almost certainly take the chance to poke and prod, perhaps even setting aside anything of value for himself. Undeterred by Billy's dismissal, Koch had no intention of letting him off the hook.

"Hmm, I see. When I inspected one of your tokens, it changed colour. Why do you think that might be?"

Desperately wanting to shut the man's further enquiry down, innately knowing this question to be a trap, Billy walked right into it anyway.

"That appears to be a common trait. They reacted the same

when my men handled them, but again, Herr Koch, I don't have an answer for you."

Detecting the makings of a sneer on his antagonist's face, realising he'd already said too much, Billy's face flushed hotly.

Blushes that confirmed Koch's initial suspicions, this time pressing harder.

"You are a learned scientist, Doktor. You must have an idea, if only a theory, as to how something like that would happen?"

Alarm bells were going off in Billy's head. Suspecting where the Nazi agent was headed with this line of questioning, he felt trapped.

Appetite thoroughly spoiled, he turned to face Koch.

"Look, Herr Koch, I don't wish to appear rude, but Doktor Stein and his men have been working with this level of technology for years. For me, it has been the first time I have seen such things, so forgive me if I appear ignorant. Now kindly excuse me, there are matters I must attend to." Leaving his meal unfinished, Billy left the table and hurriedly fled the mess hall.

Taking delight in the torment of others, Koch leered after the little man's scrambling departure, his intrinsic innocence made him an easy target. Then again, maybe he'd allowed Koekemoer to escape too easily, face hardening at this thought. Gnawing on a chicken drumstick, Koch's train of thought shifted to Stein, another character who needed cracking. Holding an in-depth knowledge of the man's failings and weaknesses would render that one's unpicking all too easy.

Proficient at laying bare the vulnerability of others, Koch had yet to encounter a human being who couldn't be broken; in a perverse manner, gaining immense satisfaction when inflicting either psychological or physical methods of torture. Formerly attached to the Gestapo and thus obliged to adopt the Nazi security police's interrogation techniques handbook, he had personally considered these officially sanctioned brutalities too tame. Privately, studying the *Malleus Maleficarum*, along with other medieval and eastern texts, he'd garnered an alternative and far superior suite of more radically effective methods for extracting information from tight-lipped individuals.

Retiring to their dormitory after lunch, the Germans spent what remained of the afternoon relaxing, most succumbing to the catatonic sleep of the profoundly travel-weary. Since having chosen a bed nearest the door, Koch could discreetly observe the other's comings and goings and their personal interactions, but for him, sleep never came easily. Half dozing on an overstuffed mattress, hands clasped behind his head, mentally recapping the day's events. One thing in particular stuck out, and it troubled him.

By early evening most of the men had begun to rouse, getting up and moving about. Not Stein however, who continued to snore softly, until abruptly opening his eyes and rolling into a seated position. Grabbing a holdall from his bedside locker, rummaging through its contents to eventually extract a crumpled pack of Juno's and a cigarette lighter. Standing and slipping his bare feet into unlaced shoes, he stretched and yawned, then lit up while heading for the door. Precisely the opportunity Koch had been waiting for, allowing a few seconds to tick by before following.

He found Stein outside, half turned to watch a group of antelope grazing on the far hillside, while urinating against the umbrella tree's bole. Koch approached nonchalantly, not wanting to make it blatantly obvious that he'd followed, opening conversation matter-of-factly.

"Doktor Stein, it would appear that you are going to have a problem in fulfilling your mission objective."

To avoid breathing in Stein's second-hand tobacco smoke, he kept a safe distance and made a show of casually kicking at a stone.

The Nazi Party was staunchly against smoking, but to Koch both cigarettes and alcohol were equally disgusting; repugnant vices, holding equally unpleasant and painful connotations. His father had been weak-willed, smoking and drinking heavily, although in truth, neither iniquity had been the absolute cause for his loathing of the man. Being a sickly child, Koch's father had regarded his only offspring as an embarrassment and would regularly find cause to beat him for no reason other than his physical disabilities.

Since most of his meagre steel mill earnings had been spent on drink and tobacco, Mama always struggled to keep home, pay the bills and put food on their table. Thoroughly soused most nights, Papa was a belligerent drunk to boot, needing little more than a perceived insolent look to tip him over the edge. To avoid aggravating arthritic pain in his hands, preferring to use a leather belt for young Reynhardt's thrashings. Mama would plead with him to stop. Taking little heed and often turning on her too.

Cigarette hanging from one side of his mouth, exhaling a blue-grey cloud of smoke, Stein coolly buttoned his trousers and countered. "Explain, what you mean by 'a problem', Koch?"

Smirking self-indulgently, Koch anticipated this being a rewarding encounter.

"Do you not remember the Afrikaner, Koekemoer telling us how the craft killed one of his men?"

Seemingly unperturbed at Koch's subtly needling manner, Stein appeared unconcerned.

"Of course, but you know as well as I that failure is not an option. Rest assured, Herr Koch, the drive unit will be removed and returned with us to the Fatherland."

Nodding thoughtfully, Koch was just getting started.

"You are of course a very learned and no doubt resourceful man, Doktor. So, tell me, how you intend achieving that objective, if you and your men can't get anywhere near the thing?"

Staring at the ground between them, Stein shifted his weight from one leg to the other.

"For one, I am not convinced Koekemoer is correct. It could

be a completely innocent mistake, believing they witnessed something they in fact didn't. Then again, maybe it's a tactic, trying to scare us off and wanting to keep the unit for themselves. If that is the case, then it will be for you and your men to assert superiority." Overhearing and correctly interpreting Koch's exchange with Billy over lunch, Stein wasn't above playing the Hauptsturmführer at his own game. "Besides, there's plenty of time and we'll soon establish whether there is anything to the man's story, or not."

His offhandedly dismissive response riled Koch, who stepped closer, tone thickening.

"You haven't answered my question, Stein, and I am beginning to think you're avoiding doing so. Let's say the Afrikaner is correct, what then? We have a strict deadline to meet, and I don't care about consequences, you do whatever is required to make it happen." Squaring up to Stein, the intent behind this challenging posture left no ambiguity, this insolent pup needed to understand who held the leash.

Stein had encountered his fair share of bullies in the past, unfazed by Koch's intimidation tactics. "I understand our directives perfectly, Koch, and the role you and your men are meant to play. Our mission schedule includes a period of study, to establish how the unit operates within the craft. It's not a simple matter of tearing the thing out and hauling it back to Berlin, unless of course, you intend explaining to Reichsführer Himmler just how antigravity propulsion works?" Maintaining an air of disdainful calm, Stein deliberately flicked a pale finger of cigarette ash to disintegrate on Koch's tunic front. "You focus on doing your job, Koch, and I'll do mine."

The man's unrelenting and blatant disrespect incensed Koch but he managed to restrain himself.

"Doktor, I will be closely monitoring you and your colleagues and on our return to the Fatherland, I shall file a detailed report regarding your behaviour, attitude and loyalty. Perhaps now you understand the role that I am here to play?"

Taking a long last draw on his cigarette, Stein blew smoke in Koch's face and bit back.

"We have all been vetted and hand-picked for this, the Reich's most secret programme, the loyalty of my men and I is above questioning by the likes of you. I too will be required to write a report and for your information, mine will land directly on the desk of Himmler himself!" Flicking the spent cigarette end away, he pushed past Koch and sauntered towards the building.

Things hadn't gone the way Koch had intended, Stein's final salvo scoring somewhat of a hit. Regardless, locked away in a safe back in Koch's dingy Prinz-Albrecht-Strasse office, he held the trump card. As required of any man in such a position of trust, Stein had become a Nazi Party member; homosexuals and Jews were strictly excluded. Before its enforced closure in '33, Stein had been a regular patron of Karls-Lounge, well known for being one of several exclusively queer clubs in Berlin.

Koch had been among a Gestapo raiding party that shut the club down, purely by coincidence acquiring irrefutable evidence of Stein's association and consequent guilt. During the ensuing chaos, he had secured the members' book, containing names and addresses that would ordinarily serve as a future Gestapo hit list; a manifest for the further prosecution, persecution or extortion of identified affiliates. Well aware of the value of such information, Koch had done the unthinkable and kept it for himself.

Never having fostered any desire for conventional romance, Koch's sole devotion towards people lay in ascertaining what made them tick, exclusively for the purpose of exploitation and domination. In the intervening years since the raid, he'd become professionally acquainted with many deviants identified by the members' book. It had been to his absolute delight when discovering that an otherwise obscure name, that of an eminent high-level scientist, would be the project lead of this assignment. While preparations were being made for their journey, as if Stein's homosexual predilections weren't damning enough, Koch had searched classified population records to unearth ironclad proof of the man's racial pedigree.

During the mid-1800s, fleeing ethnic persecution in Poland, Stein's paternal grandfather had adopted the present family name, changed from Goldstein. Even back then anti-Semitism had been prevalent, to an extent where many Juden chose this ruse, in search of sectarian anonymity.

Smiling self-assuredly at Stein's receding figure, anticipating their return to Berlin, where he would have the man arrested and shot for crimes of deception. High above in the tree's canopy, a bird broke into evensong, its sweet melody buoying his mood and laughing out loud.

CHAPTER 9

"The evil that men do lives after them; the good is oft interred with their bones." – William Shakespeare

A long-term, full-scale study and analysis of the craft in South Africa had been deemed too risky, and uplifting the entire craft back to Germany, logistically impossible. As Stein had explained to Koch during their previous day's run-in, his first objective lay in ascertaining how the propulsion unit's control systems worked. Only when once this key factor had been exhaustively established could the unit be removed. Secured in a packing crate, it would then be transported by lorry to Moçambique where they would rendezvous with a second U-boat.

When safely on German soil, the Nazis planned to replicate and mass-produce the machine; squadrons of practically invincible wunderwaffe assuring them of victory, and Nazi world domination.

A strict work schedule allotted two months in which to achieve their first objective, then a further week to remove the propulsion unit. Despite brazenly fending off Koch the evening before, Billy's disclosure had rattled Stein. Hardly sleeping that night, he'd risen before daybreak and dressed quietly so as not to disturb the others, then made his way down to the basement. Being the only living soul there, the place was deathly quiet, not manifested in a state of restfulness but rather a brooding still. Senses heightened, Stein found himself unconsciously withholding breaths, straining to pick out even the slightest sounds. The sinister overhead dome leeched on his awareness, stepping closer to look at it and halting when something moved inside.

Recoiling apprehensively but rationalising it to have been a trick of the light, or his sleep-deprived eyes. Rubbing both orbits with the palms of his hands while taking a deep breath, then shaking his head to clear the cobwebs. Whatever the optical aberration might have been, this simple therapy seemed to dispel it, observing no further activity within the dome. Opening his journal, Stein began making notes and sketching, drawing quickly with skilled precision. Everything in the craft would be photographed in extensive detail, even so, drawing aided him in visualising and grasping operational processes.

In another lifetime, he might have become an artist, gifted not only with an eye for plays of light and shade but also an inborn flair for exquisitely replicating shadow, form and detail. In the privacy of their apartment, dearest Rudi would pose for him, friends flatteringly asserting that he possessed Michelangelo's clarity of expression. Beginning to draw the dome, wistful fondness overtook Stein's conscious mind; it had been nearly a year since Rudi's conscription into the Sixth Army, last having received word from him when deployed somewhere near Zamość in Poland.

Backing up, to gain a wider perspective, he distractedly

stumbled and clutched at a fluted projection of the crystalline structure. A resonant hum immediately ensued from above, his blood freezing when realising what this must signify. Frantically pushing away, flinging himself towards the nearest console, then spinning about to face the threat. Panicked and losing hold of the journal, it flew flutteringly, ending up skidding across the floor. As suddenly as the noise had begun, so it stopped and peace returned, broken as quickly by the sniggering announcement of a more invasive menace. Stood near the entrance, Koch had followed the whole episode, face contorted in glee at Stein's terrified reaction.

Saying nothing and stooping to grab hold of the book that had slid to a stop at his feet, Koch sneered. Embarrassed, feeling compromised, Stein struggled to compose himself.

"You startled me, Herr Koch. I didn't realise you were there."

Uncomfortably aware of a discernible tremor in his voice, certain that his adversary would pick up on it.

Sure enough, Koch laughed caustically.

"It wasn't me that made you nearly piss your pants, Stein." Opening the journal and thumbing through a few pages, he glared from over his spectacles. Pointing the journal towards the dome, quizzically raising his eyebrows and adding, "I believe something else to have been responsible for the weakness of your bladder." Leafing to locate Stein's most recent entry, then scrutinising the page, he flicked back to the previous and huffed, "What is this rubbish, Stein? You're not here to draw pictures, man." Hobbling forwards and thrusting the book's tough leather spine into Stein's breastbone. "Now, Herr Doktor, you didn't give me a satisfactory answer yesterday, so tell me how you intend dealing with this, the true reason for almost fouling yourself."

Managing to pull himself together, Stein snatched his journal from Koch's grip.

"I've already told you, Koch I don't believe there to be a problem. Okay, so it made a noise, nothing more, and here I am, very much alive. Even if Koekemoer was telling the truth, in all probability there would only have been enough residual charge to kill one man." From Koch's expression, Stein knew his hastily contrived defence to be unconvincing.

"Very well, since you're a doktor of science, get inside with the machine and test your theory." Stepping aside, Koch waved him towards the ornate structure.

At this point, Stein lost his mettle and turned away, unable to find the right words, wanting to yell, telling Koch to get out and go away. He didn't have the answers and needed time to properly figure things out. Catching Stein completely off guard, Koch had won this round, grabbing the scientist's arm when he turned to leave.

"Select a volunteer from among your men and test it then. Either you nominate someone, or I will."

At this, Stein found his voice. "You must be mad! I could never do that to a colleague."

The idea of knowingly sacrificing someone, specifically one from amongst men who respected and trusted him, left Stein feeling physically nauseous. Koch, on the other hand, had no such qualms.

"Fine, it's the youngster then, the same one from yesterday's car ride. He's just a kid and doesn't have the level of experience or same value as the rest."

By now, Koch was openly enjoying this exchange. Stein on the other hand wasn't and quickly pulled away, heading for the exit, maddeningly knowing Koch to be correct.

Correct, only insofar as needing a means of testing to determine whether the dome had the capacity to kill again. An idea came to Stein, halting his flight. A solution, however in complete contradiction of his own morality, wrestling with it before returning to face Koch.

"Ask Van Heerden to find us a test subject from outside,

preferably a native."

At this, Koch started, then grimaced gleefully.

"Hah, you do have balls after all. Even so, you expect me to dirty your own hands?" In spite of his jibe, Stein's solution amused Koch, regarding the indigenous people as Untermensch of the lowest order and therefore suitably expendable. Nevertheless, Stein would not be allowed to wriggle free from complicity. "Very well, I will ask Van Heerden to arrange it so, but it will be you supervising the test."

Stein's horrified look of realisation provided all the gratification he needed.

Later that morning a car left the mill, its driver sent in search of a suitable volunteer. He didn't have to travel far either, happening upon two young men shambling along the gravelled road verge, one pushing a bicycle. Slowing to a crawl, Van Heerden's man called out, asking if they would be interested in a day's work. Without hesitation, both responded in the affirmative and, while one pushed his bike out of sight down the roadside embankment, the driver kept watch, wanting to ensure this pickup went unobserved.

Back at the mill, since only one man would be required for Stein's trial, the driver needed to split the pair up. Koos, the mill foreman, took charge of the taller and set him to work in the drying shed, stacking freshly cut boards, while the driver assumed the Judas goat role and led the test subject to the mill. Foreseeing the man becoming alarmed when entering the basement, Van Heerden's man spoke in Zulu, soothingly assuring him there was nothing to be concerned about.

On the craft's flight deck, Stein fiddled distractedly with his journal while Van Heerden, Koch and his two henchmen feigned conversation. Stepping forwards, Stein showed his victim to the crystal enclosure, explaining the Zulu's first task would be clearing broken glass remaining in the pit's base. An easy enough chore, the man compliantly squatted and lowered both legs into the pit, while Stein smartly stepped away. Advisedly so, when a searingly bright bolt of plasma immediately flashed, striking the man squarely at the top of his head and killing him instantly. Smoke filled the cabin space, carrying an acrid reek of ionised air, mixed with the stench of burnt hair and scorched flesh.

Stunned by the bolt's savage precision, ears ringing from an accompanying sonic shriek, the bystanders stared speechless until Koch began to applaud. Reacting angrily, Van Heerden grabbed his wrist.

"No, that's not right!" Glaring at the Nazi in disgust and thrusting the offending hand away, he addressed the others. "Boys, you are playing with fire. Mark my words, you will get burned by this thing." Face set in conviction, he backed up to the exit. "Gentlemen, I'm done here but wish you every good fortune."

That day's events did not sit well with Van Heerden.

Quaking, fearing he may pass out, Stein leaned his full weight on the nearest console.

Voice quavering, he pleaded, "Please, Koch, take… it… away." Unable to bring himself to look at the dead man's still smouldering corpse, he could only summon a faltering gesture in the body's general direction.

Reaching aggressively, Koch grabbed Stein by the coat lapels and snapped angrily, "For God's sake, Stein, behave like a man! This was your idea, and now you at least know what you're dealing with."

Unable to handle confrontation right then, Stein pushed him away and took off, following Van Heerden.

Allowing the scientist to escape, Koch instructed his men to dispose of the body then followed suit, heading for the exit and winking at his second in command.

"We won't be needing the other one. I'll deal with this personally."

Outside, the mill had shut down for lunch and the valley relaxed in temporary serenity, until the crack of a gunshot startled a flock of guinea fowl foraging on the stream bank. A brief pause, until a second report sent the birds cackling to hide out in nearby undergrowth. Koch had no reservations about summarily executing the second man; essential for no ties with the mill to be left open-ended.

Leaving his underlings to dispose of the electrocuted victim's body, he'd gone in search of the second man, finding him busy working in the drying shed. Drawing his pistol and holding it at arm's length, Koch stealthily approached his target from behind, until close enough to be certain of accurately placing his shot. Firing at near point-blank range, the man soundlessly crumpled into a kneeling position, head pushed to one side by the length of timber he'd been about to rack. Face devoid of expression, Koch moved in, straddled his kill and fired a wholly gratuitous coup de grâce, before holstering the Luger. Stepping away to cursorily check his clothing and boots for blood spatter, when satisfied there was none, he headed for the mess hall.

After filling his belly, Koch went to find Stein, fortuitously locating him alone in the dormitory, head disconsolately bowed and hunched over on the edge of his bed.

Storming in, Koch bellowed, "Get up, Stein! Stop behaving like a sulky child!"

The sound of his adversary's voice triggered in Stein something akin to a red flag. On his feet in an instant and ready to fight, it was precisely the reaction Koch wanted, pistol already drawn.

"Sit down, fool!" he brandished the weapon menacingly.

Solely an academic and never a fighter, Stein hesitated. Self-preservation cowed his temper, meekly slumping back onto the bed. Shifting his demeanour, Koch approached and sat opposite. Stein dropped his eyes to the floor, hating himself for such a display of cowardice and unable to face his tormentor.

Essential to his objective that the man remain calm, Koch spoke in a conciliatory tone.

"What happened could be described as unfortunate, Stein, but now you are left with no doubts as to whether that machine has the capacity to kill you and your men. Today's exercise was necessary, a small sacrifice to preserve your lives."

Stein looked up and Koch could tell he was losing the scientist again.

"We murdered that man. He had done nothing to deserve such treatment, absolutely nothing..."

Struggling to maintain an even temper and stifling an urge to lash out, slapping Stein, Koch cut in, "Inconsequential, they aren't the same as us and a choice had to be made, either that native or one of your own men. Surely you must see that. You have a job to do here, one vital to the Reich and there's no room for maudlin sentimentality." Appearing to become receptive, Stein nodded weakly, so Koch set about reeling him in. "Now you must ascertain how to turn that thing off, complete your research and remove the engine. Then we can all leave this gottverdammt place once and for all."

Stein's head sagged, his shoulders heaving. Thinking this to be the onset of more tears, Koch drew his hand back to lash out, when Stein laughed out loud.

Mirth ceasing as abruptly, he snarled, "You truly are an ignoramus, Koch. You think we can turn it off? Just like that? It could take us years of guessing at how to do that. Don't you get it? We're dealing with something maybe a million years ahead of our own time and technology. Imagine putting forward a monkey to overhaul an aircraft engine, well that's exactly how it is with us and this machine."

Startled, Koch could only stare dumbfounded. Returning empty-handed to Berlin, justifying their failure with Stein's monkey analogy, would certainly see them bound and blindfolded against a pockmarked wall.

"Then cover it up and protect yourselves. You have to do something, Stein, or we're done for!" All bluster and bullying gone, the scientist's admission of ignorance truly terrified Koch. Guilt and consequent punishment by association were an inseparably intertwined Nazi maxim.

As much as Stein detested the man, Koch's crude solution struck a note, although it wouldn't be quite that straightforward. In principle a sound notion, isolating the dome with a non-conductive material would theoretically eliminate the risk to him and his men. Wiping his cheeks dry, he faced Koch.

"That's in fact not a bad idea, Koch," he said, giving the man due credit. However, if ending in failure, then of course it would remain Koch's solution.

Leaving the bemused Hauptsturmführer to fret alone in their sleeping quarters, Stein went looking for Van Heerden and eventually tracked him down at the mill's bar, drinking beer with two strangers. Unsure quite where the unfamiliar pair fitted in, he apologised for interrupting and nodded for Van Heerden to come outside. After listening to Stein's plan, the burly Afrikaner agreed and sent for the mill foreman, instructing absolute cooperation in whatever Stein needed.

After that morning's confrontation with Koch inside the craft, Stein had gone outside to settle his nerves by smoking a cigarette. Whilst leaning against the tree, he'd watched the mill forklift unloading a brand-new conveyor belt, brought in to replace another on the log conveyor. The belt was manufactured from thick, fabric-reinforced rubber and Koch's idea had inspired Stein to repurpose it, potentially creating a suitable insulating barrier.

Under the foreman's direction, a special work detail cut the belt into pieces, then dragged the dismembered sections into the basement. Lashed together inside the craft to form a large composite square, the men then manoeuvred this over the crystalline structure and hoisted it up. The killing dome thus enshrouded, they propped the mat with posts and hastily built a strong timber framework to secure it in place.

It was late by the time the workmen finished and left, but Stein, Koch, Van Heerden and Billy stayed on, inevitably debating the likely effectiveness of such a "bush fix". Undeniably crude and makeshift, the dome had nevertheless been entirely obscured from view anywhere on the flight deck. There remained only one way to know for certain, each acutely aware how it would have to be tested. Before anyone else voiced that eventuality, Koch spoke up, making a crude joke about disposing of the second man too soon.

Already knowing in what direction the Nazi intended steering their debate, Stein slipped away from the others and made his move; nobody else would be put at risk, it was solely his responsibility. Before the others had chance to react, he crouched at the propulsion unit enclosure, sitting and sliding both legs into the void.

First to notice his actions, Billy gasped, "Stein, no!"

Simultaneously lunging, Van Heerden grabbed for the scientist but wasn't quick enough. Stein's momentum too great to be halted, he dropped into the pit. Everyone froze, including Stein, transfixed and expecting the worst, except only an eerie silence filled the flight deck. Van Heerden guffawed nervously.

"You've got some guts, Stein!" he roared. "I thought for sure you were a dead man!"

Ashen-faced, Stein smiled self-consciously, not considering his act any form of bravery rather mere partial redemption of recently corrupted personal values.

A crooked grin spreading across his ruddy face, Billy reached down to shake his hand.

"I salute you, Doctor Stein. You have nerves of steel." Enthusiastically clasping Stein's hand, he pumped vigorously.

Tight-lipped, seeming unmoved, Koch held himself detached from such puerile celebratory antics.

"Congratulations, Herr Doktor," he intoned coolly, as Van Heerden effortlessly pulled Stein from the pit. "Starting tomorrow morning, I look forward to observing you and your team commence working towards meeting the deadline."

Inured to Koch's derisive indifference, paying little heed to the Nazi and leaving him behind, the trio went to celebrate at the mill bar. Several hours were spent drinking beer and downing shots of schnapps, before Stein made his excuses and headed for bed. Such an indulgence was entirely out of character for him, and one ultimately paid for the next morning, awakening to a pounding hangover.

The research team's initial preparatory order of business, to remove what remained of the crystalline structure and expose the propulsion unit to proper scrutiny. All interlocking segments were held together at the apex by a complex mechanical ring, a puzzle in itself, taking several hours to figure out. When eventually disengaging this locking mechanism, each individual section became free-standing, proving to be lightweight and easily carried away. When the last had been removed, Stein's team took full advantage of their reward, for the first time getting an unrestricted view of the unit.

On a chair appropriated from the mill lounge and placed adjacent the craft's entrance, Koch lounged, following their progress with smug self-satisfaction. After all, if it hadn't been for his brilliant idea, Stein's men would at that very moment be contending with deadly accurate lightning bolts.

Unfettered access secured, Schauberger's primary objective for Stein's team was to assess and analyse the machine, gathering information required to replicate it on an industrial scale. It was presupposed by Schauberger, under the guidance of Maria Orsic, that the unit's antigravity capabilities were derived from manipulation of magnetic fields. More specifically, the interaction of electromagnetic fields generated by powerful magnets embedded in the pit's rim, with those produced by the sphere when in motion. Access to Zuse's computer during this analytical process paid dividends, facilitating calculation and modelling of theoretical directional flux amplification yield. During this phase, Koch seldom left the craft, nor did he engage in conversation with Stein or his team; steadfastly watchful and alert, seemingly biding his time, almost as if willing something to go awry.

This first task turned out being unexpectedly straightforward, the research team successfully gaining a fledgling conceptualisation of repulsive antigravitational force application. However, beyond this early victory they hit a brick wall, when attempting to determine and map out the craft's control systems. It appeared intuitively self-evident that the indecipherably marked consoles functioned as control panels; instruments for initiating and piloting the craft. To their mounting frustration, these cryptic glyphs remained unresponsive to either touch, electronic or magnetic stimulation. The craft clearly had a functioning power source, but their continued inability to engage with the system looked like being the proverbial death knell to this aspect of their research. Logic dictated that the absence of one console potentially inhibited interaction between the others, effectively shutting down the entire system.

A radical bypass option, the only way to save their hides; open the three remaining consoles, investigate the electronic circuitry and diagrammatically plot this onto blueprints. When back in Germany, teams of specialists would be able to unpick the wiring's logic, ascertaining and assigning functional designations, then infill the blank spaces.

Eventually managing to remove a console's cover, without resorting to brute force, exposed more questions than answers for Stein and his team. Replicating the craft's peculiar simplicity, there were none of the anticipated complex wiring looms or sophisticated electronics, instead something more bafflingly enigmatic. Behind the control panel's glossy façade, a layer of dense black, Bakelite-like material had been adhered and below that, the console cabinet was filled with a reservoir of viscous fluid. On the panel's underside, correspondingly opposing each glyph, egg cup-like protrusions fed softly gelatinous strands into the liquid. Glistening cords, each the thickness of a man's finger, quasi-organic, they resembled the exposed arteries of a living creature. Stumped by this discovery, and for the next few weeks, Stein couldn't overlook a sensation that they were merely treading water. During this time, he and his men became prone to a malignantly evolving tetchiness, spurred on by acute mindfulness of the clock's relentless ticking.

Crankiness, exacerbated by knowing that another entire level existed below their feet, one into which they had been unsuccessful gaining access. Simple analysis of the craft's proportions told Stein it was there, supported by the presence of a square access panel set in the textured deck. Sitting snugly flush with the surrounding floor and bordered by a gap so fine that even the slenderest bladed prising implement wouldn't fit, obstinately defying their every effort to broach.

Even after drilling and tapping lifting handles into the cover, with two men straining on a hefty steel bar slid through, it doggedly resisted. Collectively debating over cutting the hatch open, they had abandoned this idea, fearful of whatever potential consequences such drastic means might incur. Gallingly, Stein believed whatever existed down there would fundamentally fill the void in their understanding.

Muttered frustrations, occasional sharp exchanges and increasingly evident despondency amongst the research team didn't go unnoticed by Koch. Despite having little real conception of their undertakings, these tensions and a halt in noticeable progress served as clear warning signs of looming derailment. Simply getting to Lourenço Marques entailed an overland trip of almost seven hundred kilometres; understanding from Van Heerden that their route would be via predominantly dirt tracks, some scarcely meeting the basic criteria for a road. A journey likely to take two days, under ideal circumstances and driving non-stop, but since being the rainy season, rougher sections would prove treacherous going. Deeming it essential to allow an extra day for that reason and possible mechanical problems, Koch knew a time would come when he had to light a stick of dynamite under Stein's backside.

Appropriating a calendar from the administration office, he pinned it to a timber supporting the protective mat and began crossing off every passing day. Since they were due to rendezvous with the U-boat on 11th of April, it was essential to depart the mill no later than Tuesday the 8th, ringed in red pen. The sub would remain in port only twenty-four hours, affording scant leeway to accommodate any unforeseen hold-ups. Contemplating this impending journey stirred up mixed feelings in Koch, and while anxious at the prospect, nothing whatsoever would prevent their leaving this stinking rathole on schedule.

Wary of risking their prize falling into enemy hands, Himmler had selected the politically neutral Portuguese colony as the securest extraction point. A fast-growing and thoroughly cosmopolitan place, the capital city of Lourenço Marques had grown up around its bustling seaport. Home to more than fifty thousand citizens and boasting the country's first international airport, which had opened the previous year. While their intended route traversed sparsely populated countryside, the crossing of a tightly controlled international border presented high risk, a matter for Van Heerden and his contacts. It was an open secret that the man acquired rationed or otherwise unavailable commodities via Lourenço Marques, transporting them into South Africa and selling on at a hugely inflated profit. Black marketeering was a highly illegal enterprise, although one that Koch had no intention of rocking the boat over, so long as the Afrikaner got them safely into Moçambique.

To safeguard their departure by the appointed date, Stein needed to adopt Koch's way of thinking, the next morning providing a perfect opportunity. Forgetting his journal in the dormitory, Stein went to fetch it, and Koch followed; better to corner the man alone. Finding Stein knelt at his bedside locker, he entered silently and approached, stopping a few paces short of his quarry. Journal in hand, Stein rose to his feet and gasped aloud when realising he wasn't alone. In the next heartbeat, Koch was on the offensive.

"You have run out of time, Stein. That verdammt machine comes out today. Do you understand me?"

Caught completely off guard, Stein nodded meekly, acknowledging Koch's statement to be correct quenched an internal flicker of regret.

Despite learning so much about the craft's propulsion unit, more time and resource than available would inevitably have been required to fulfil the brief. Requesting an extension of time from Berlin simply wasn't an option, indeed likely to be construed tantamount to an abysmal failure on his part. An abhorrent brute, Koch would undoubtedly take immense pleasure from driving the nail home. His only way out, and pivotal to any form of redemption, would be a successful removal of the unit and its safe return to the Fatherland.

Flustered, but gathering his wits, Stein conceded, "I do agree with you, Koch, time has run out. My men will begin preparing for the extraction process."

Not good enough for Koch, thrusting his face to within inches of the other man's, white specks of saliva spattered Stein's face.

"You aren't properly listening, Stein. I don't want

preparations; it comes out today."

Wiping away the offensive spittle, Stein rejoined angrily, "For heaven's sake, Koch, it's not like removing a blown light bulb. If we rush this and cock it up, the machine could be damaged, or worse. Leave it to me, and I will ensure everything is ready by Tuesday."

Somewhat placated although not wholly satisfied, Koch scowled. "See to it that you do, Stein. If I don't witness immediate evidence of your commitment, then you and I will talk again," turning his back and swaggering from the dormitory.

Within an hour, Stein and Billy stood together at the pit rim, debating how best to lift the propulsion unit. Although snug within its pit, adequate space existed between the lattice framework and encircling wall for a slender man to squeeze in, crouch and reach under the gimbal support. Needing to understand how the whole assembly had been fixed in place, Stein clambered in, experiencing a sudden sense of heightened anxiety. A premonition, perhaps? Remonstrating with himself, ascribing these nerves to nothing more than natural apprehension at what they intended doing. Swallowing hard, he knelt and disappeared from Koch's ever-attentive view. From his post, the Hauptsturmführer watched Billy clamber onto all fours and peer in at whatever Stein was doing. A few minutes passed, when the latter re-emerged and the two scientists resumed talking. Deciding to eavesdrop, Koch got up and made his way over, in time to hear Stein explaining what he'd seen.

The lower assembly perched on five slender legs of elliptical cross section which were seamlessly fused into the pit base, appearing as though gimbal and floor had been made in a single casting. If the propulsion unit was securely rigged up to a block and tackle, then by severing the support legs the complete unit could be out of the pit. The timber framework holding their protective mat in place would require only minor alterations and additional stiffening to support a block, and be sturdy enough to take the propulsion unit's estimated weight. On the face of it, extracting the unit looked like being a remarkably straightforward process. Maybe a little too easy, Stein's intuition cautioned, remembering a favourite saying of Rudi's; "Act in haste, repent at leisure".

Not wanting another confrontation with Koch, Stein gathered his team together, describing how the procedure would be executed, while Billy left to organise logistical requirements. Separately estimating the propulsion unit and gimbal assembly's mass, then taking the average, they had arrived at a figure of around half a ton. Distrustful of chains for rigging and fearing these more likely to cause damage, Stein opted instead for thick canvas lifting strops, accessories used by the millmen for loading timber bundles onto dispatch lorries. Looped over the block's hook and fed under the gimbal's lower frame then back up to its hook, the block would be tensioned to ensure even weight distribution while severing the supports. Several hours of fastidiously measuring and remeasuring clearances, checking and rechecking strop placement, culminated in Stein's eventual satisfaction. The moment had arrived.

By default, Erich the team's junior, the same individual squeezed between Koch and Stein during the car ride got assigned cutting duty. Awkwardly manoeuvring himself prone in the pit, he blindly reached up to be handed a powered reciprocating saw. Gingerly feeding the tool under the gimbal subframe, while everyone else gathered to watch from topside. Partially obscured from view, Erich jostled the heavy saw into position, its cutting blade resting against the side of a supporting leg. Freeing one hand, Erich gave a thumbs up, signifying that he was ready for Stein to give the word.

Occupying an unobstructed ringside vantage point, Koch had intently followed the youngster's progress, glancing across the pit to see Stein pale-faced, looking as if he were about to be sick. Seconds ticked by, as Erich patiently awaited the order to start, when Stein's mouth twitched as if about to speak.

Balefully glaring at the weakling's hesitance, Koch harshly interjected, "Mein Gott! What are you waiting for? Just do it man!"

Billy's reassuring pat on the shoulder freed Stein's voice.

"Go ahead, Erich. Take it slow at first," pointedly ignoring Koch, to focus solely on the pit activity.

Down below, the saw started and chattered rhythmically, the fine teeth of its hardened steel blade effortlessly biting into the support leg, showering the pit floor with gleaming shavings. After a few seconds and to Erich's bemusement, the cut began resisting, as though the metal were binding, choking the blade's passage until not cutting at all. Drawing his knees up and wedging himself to apply more pressure, Erich sharply cried out in fright and released the tool. The heap of metal slivers had begun to liquefy, gathering into mercurial blobs that suddenly skidded together, merging and accreting into a quivering puddle. Shock turned to terror when a silvery tongue animatedly rose and snaked up the support leg, filling the cut and violently ejecting the blade.

Realising something terrible was about to happen, the young man wanted out, swearing and thrashing about wildly, desperately fighting to extricate himself from the confining space. Managing to scramble to his knees, just as a cloud of intensely bright specks of golden light silently emerged from the pit walls. Manifesting like a swarm of fireflies, they enveloped him, scything through clothing, tearing into skin, flesh and bone. More erupted from the pit and fell on the spectators, then chaos ensued. Screaming shrilly, Koch defensively waved his arms, vainly attempting to swat away the malevolent horde. Most similarly tried fending off these luminous attackers while others fell to their knees, instinctively covering their heads.

As quickly as appearing, so the fireflies were gone, and stunned incomprehension replaced frenzied hysteria. In dazed silence, glancing from one to another, the men's faces became etched in dismay and fear when seeing their comrades' exposed skin speckled by flecks of freshly oozing blood. A lull lasting mere seconds, when all simultaneously experienced a crawling sensation, like fire ants seething and burrowing under their skin. Screaming, they all bolted for the exit.

Unlike true fireflies, occasionally seen outdoors on balmy summer's evenings, these entities weren't a species of bioluminescent insect, in fact not even organic. Collectively autonomous energetic particles, minute defenders summoned by an unseen presence to protect the craft. Ripping into the soft-bodied intruders, the fireflies analytically determined their basic anatomical configuration, then entered the men's bloodstreams. Unerringly seeking out the darker, oxygen-depleted venous blood, they were already being inexorably propelled towards their ultimate objective.

Billy was first to succumb, when a cluster of fireflies passed through his great cerebral vein and triggered premature onset of a developing aneurysm. He died instantaneously, a mercifully painless death, although the rest would be less fortunate. Pumped into the right ventricle of each man's heart, their assailants clustered on the inner wall until attaining critical mass, punching through the tough muscle and tearing a marble-sized hole.

Futilely clawing at his chest, Koch experienced a vision, a mental vestige from a night forty years ago and eternally burned into his mind. His father's face, contorted in pain and rage, attempting to scream but only managing a wet glugging sound as he bled out on the kitchen floor.

Following a particularly savage beating, something in

eleven-year-old Reynhardt Koch had snapped that evening. When the leather belt slipped from Papa's drunken grasp, he'd stooped to retrieve it and drunkenly fallen face first into the bug-eaten floor. Without thinking, the boy had picked up a wickedly sharp kitchen knife from the table, grasped a handful of hair and wrenched his father's head back to expose the soft neck, then slashed, again and again. Despite forever ending the daily torment, slaughtering his own father like a beast had irrevocably cemented Koch's slide into a life of wickedness.

The image suddenly disappeared and unholy talons seized Koch's tainted soul, dragging his consciousness down into a place of eternal torment.

Oblivious to his damnation, the others' screams also eventually ceased.

Emerging from the lifeless husks of their victims, the fireflies grouped together in an innocuously twinkling swarm, drifting away until the next time.

CHAPTER 10

"When we are no longer able to change a situation, we are challenged to change ourselves." – Viktor Frankl

Taken unconscious to his cell and deposited face down on the cot, Craig came to an indeterminate time later, feeling decidedly woolly headed from whatever the mantis' assistant had administered. Lying motionless awhile with his eyes open, allowing for the return of lucid thought, then rolling onto one side and seeing a plastic food tray by the door. Flinging both legs over the cot's edge, he retrieved the meal and returned to examine the offerings; a bowl of meat stew with vegetables, two soft bread rolls and a bottle of water. Understanding that food in his system would help counteract the sedative's effects, also surprisingly hungry, he wolfed it down. Propping a pillow against the wall when he'd finished, Craig leant back and drank the water.

Perhaps an hour passed and a basic urge took hold, needing to go pee, he stood at the stainless-steel toilet, self-consciously glaring at the camera over one shoulder.

He muttered through gritted teeth, at whoever might be behind the lens. “Yeah, go on then, get your jollies, freak.” Zipping up and vigorously cranking the flush lever.

The cell had clearly been purpose-built to withstand potential escape attempts, even so, after rinsing his hands, Craig turned his attention to the door. It had no handle mechanism on the inside, only smooth-faced steel, snugly sealed by air-tight rubber gaskets into a matching frame. No way of prising that open, he was stuck in there, until they either let him go, or… A train of thought that didn't bear probing, instead selectively pushing it from his consciousness and returning to the cot. The hell with it, one way or another, he would get out of this place.

Over the foot of his cot, in the ceiling corner opposite the door, a spider busied itself, industriously building a complex web. Already having formed anchor threads and the radial structure, the arachnid now meticulously spun its capture spiral.

“You also stuck in here then, little buddy?” talking to the spider. Craig rolled his eyes in dismay when finding himself half expecting the creature to reply.

Being cooped up in this place had begun affecting his mind, surely losing it entirely, if not formulating a plan to get out of this place. Overcome by weariness, he yawned, then without any warning the overhead light dimmed to a night light's intensity. Glancing down at his wristwatch, it was ten o' clock, evidently lights out.

Stretching out on the cot and pulling a spare blanket over himself, Craig lay with one arm crooked behind his head, reflecting on the day's events. If the mantis was to be believed, then the Link had fused with his body in some kind of metaphysical fashion. Weirdly though, this supposed process hadn't left him feeling any different, and the projected images seen earlier could easily have been digitally fudged. But to what end? After all, what sane reasoning could there be, in concocting such a peculiarly elaborate fabrication? Ironically, such a scenario would ultimately explain why he'd been unable to track down that damned gizmo after falling asleep.

Thoughts turned to the previous evening, more specifically the fuzzy half-memory, existing from a fraction before nodding off. Frustratingly, all clarity of that precise moment remained elusively intangible, as if partially erased, even after rerunning it for the umpteenth time. Continuously darting, flittingly eluding the conscious mind's grasp and hovering always tantalising out of reach. Despite being unable to get a definitive fix on it, Craig knew with absolute certainty, something downright weird had happened in that instant.

Eventually, drifting off into the kind of fitfully restless slumber to which he'd become so accustomed in recent years, tossing and turning throughout the night, his rest bedevilled by progressively outlandish dreams. In one, at the seaside with Maria, sitting together on a shared beach towel and her in that same bright yellow bikini bought for their honeymoon. Fixedly staring to the distant horizon, over a continuously crashing shore break, she chattered excitedly, expressing just how happy she and Paul were together. Feeling profoundly uncomfortable, even in dream consciousness, Craig got the oddest sense she was talking with a girlfriend instead of him. Stopping in mid-sentence, Maria deliberately turned to face him, a transient air of disdain momentarily evident in those alluring hazel eyes.

Cupping his chin in one hand and shaking her head dismissively, she mocked, "Oh Craig, stop fighting it, you haven't got a snowball's hope in hell."

A huge wave broke thunderously, sending a churning maelstrom of fast-moving surf skidding up the beach; no longer party to the scene, Maria had disappeared. Desperately trying to get up, Craig found his legs to be held fast, encased in tightly packed sand, fancifully shaped to resemble a mermaid's tail. Stuck tight and unable to budge, shouting for help, he could only emit a guttural groaning that thankfully jolted him awake. Discovering his legs had become tangled in the blanket, he threw it off, it was too hot anyway. Relieved at the unnerving episode being merely a dream, he lay there half awake, until inevitably reclaimed by sleep.

Struggling, caught in a giant sticky web resembling a cargo net, fighting to escape its gooey strands, when a huge spider effortlessly scaled the web and advanced on him. As only possible in the realm of dreams, the beast suddenly transformed into a praying mantis with Govender's face. Held fast by the web's gummy threads and powerless to move, Craig could only watch as Govender-mantis loomed, grinning triumphantly. Sharply pointed mandibles snapped from the hybrid's mouth, extending and slashing at Craig's face. Somehow summoning the strength to free one hand, lashing out and punching at the creature's jaws. Darting agilely backwards, it grimaced a sickly smile, then spoke in Govender's voice.

"We're going to eat you alive, Craig."

Appearing from overhead, a swarming multitude of shrieking Govender-mantises descended on silken strands, all lunging at once.

Startled awake by his own scream, Craig sat up, finding himself bathed in sweat. The ventilation had been turned down, making the cell warm and unbearably stuffy. Checking his wristwatch and seeing it was a little after two thirty; this looked like turning into a long and fraught night, probably a side effect of drugs remaining in his system. It took longer to fall asleep this time and still the dreams persisted in a similarly disturbing vein; although come the morning, he would thankfully remember little of most nightmares. Except for one, coming to him shortly before waking, a dream that would stick hauntingly in his memory for years to come.

Without knowing how he'd come to be there, Craig sat astride the trunk of a fallen tree, deep in a strange and unworldly forest. Everything about this location appeared foreign and unlike any place occurring on earth but somehow unnervingly familiar, in a manner he couldn't identify. The trees were enormous, rivalling American western redwoods in stature, their smoothly shiny, grey-barked trunks towering into a dense canopy of broad-fronded, palmlike leaves. Through intermittent gaps in the thick foliage, snatches of a pale aquamarine sky could be seen. Heavily shaded, the forest floor was carpeted in a dark green vegetation that resembled sphagnum moss, imbuing the place with a softly serene ambience.

Looking around him, a pair of nearby trees stood out. Diseased, their bark had peeled away, allowing luminous yellow bracket fungi to develop and festoon exposed and darkened sapwood. Brilliantly lilac-hued insects, similar in appearance to hummingbird hawkmoths, flitted between the sulphurous growths to feed on a seeping amber liquid. From somewhere away in the distance, a melodic call resonated, perhaps the song of an exotic bird; tuneful, enchanting, and strangely recognisable.

At realising he wasn't alone, Craig started and scissored his legs on the log to about turn. A tall and slender man sat at the log's far end, Craig understanding that he'd been there all along. Although facing in the opposite direction, an air to the man's presence told Craig this stranger was very much aware of him. Dressed in a pale blue, close-fitting tracksuit made of an unusually finely woven material; the man's ash blonde hair reached midway down his back, its length and spread veiling any clues as to his countenance. Understanding that he was experiencing a lucid dream, the clarity and detail of the environment made it feel so real, and Craig found himself yearning for this to be his reality. Wanting to pinch himself but knowing it would end this dream, before finding out how the strange encounter would play out. As if sensing his dilemma, the stranger spoke.

"You must leave. Use the power of your mind, Craig. Go, before they do you any real harm." His voice, compelling and deeply authoritative, also reassuringly gentle.

A million questions whirling in Craig's mind, replying and amazed at hearing his own voice.

"What do you mean, why must I go? This is my home. I don't want to leave." The unexpected conviction of his own statement astonished Craig.

Ever more immersive and intriguing, he didn't want the dream to end.

Standing up and turning around, the stranger's facial expression conveyed universally unmistakeable seriousness. Craig gasped, not at the man's openly grave intent, but rather his facial features. Large, phosphorescently green eyes lanced across the span separating them, hypnotically demanding Craig's undivided attention. Those eyes were deep set below a broad forehead, his nose proportionally small with an upturned tip, poised over a fine-lipped mouth and underset by a slight, tapering jaw. An overall reminiscently elfin countenance, except in no way absurd, instead bizarrely conjuring an indefinable sense of kinship from within the recesses of Craig's mind.

At his evident surprise, the man's face softened, although continuing insistently, "Use your mind, Craig," urgency in his tone, unambiguous.

Uninvited, a blazing glare intruded, dissolving both stranger and forest, forcing Craig to shield his eyes against its brilliance. The cell lights had been turned to daytime level, killing the dream and bringing him back to the real world with sickening certainty. The time seven a.m., he began speculating at what the day might hold in store. Not left to ponder for long when the door clicked and opened, the Russian and his aide entering. The latter retrieved last night's dinner tray while his boss placed a fresh one on the cot next to Craig, both leaving without so much as a word.

"Morning jackasses, it's good to see you too," Craig muttered sarcastically, before scanning the tray.

Breakfast comprised a bowl of oatmeal, daubed with a blob of honey, two hard-boiled eggs and two slices of dry toast. Decidedly plain fare, even though quite edible, Craig would gladly have swapped it all for a mug of strong, black coffee. It was too soon after waking to have developed an appetite, but he ate the porridge anyway.

Last night's dreams already fading, limited snatches clinging to the periphery of his consciousness were being supplanted by wakeful thought processes. Feeling sticky and grubby, wanting to freshen up, Craig went to the washbasin and pulled off his T-shirt, splashing cold water over his face, arms and torso. A ridiculously small and inadequate towel hung from a rail below the sink, using it to dry off, he stood staring at a polished stainless steel wall mirror. The reflection returning his gaze shocked Craig, an unkempt and haggard, dystopian parody of himself; a day's beard growth accentuated dark rings encircling bloodshot eyes. Distractedly scratching at the stubble on his jawline, he made a face, ruefully yearning to be back home in his own bathroom.

"Hmm... a shave and shower would be nice, but what the hey," he grumbled, distastefully pulling the stale T-shirt over his head and returning to sitting on the cot.

Putting aside a not unreasonable desire for personal hygiene and grooming, to his surprise, Craig's mood suddenly lifted. It could be the food, he'd eaten but felt as if down to something else entirely. Whichever the case, introspectively knowing with absolute certainty that it had nothing to do with the onset of Stockholm syndrome. He had no intention whatsoever of forming any kind of bond with Govender or his cronies, unless feigning superficial rapport provided a means to escape.

Whatever this Link thingamy might actually be, the fact it held immense significance to these people was abundantly obvious. Therefore, by default, so too did he, just so long as they continued believing him to be in possession of the thing. In a peculiar way, this entirely unsolicited realisation afforded him an edge, leverage towards potentially bettering his circumstances. Even so, whilst entertaining no illusions this might extend so far as buying any degree of personal freedom, perhaps enough to barter against the use of sedatives and restraints. Of course, picking the right time to make a play at negotiating with Govender would be key. Heartened by this insight, Craig banged and kicked at the door.

"Hey! Anybody out there! Come here!"

The same sickly-sweet, burnt sugar smell filled the cell and realising what was about to happen, he staggered to the cot before blacking out.

Coming to, strapped to the same table as on the previous day, all earlier self-assuredness fell apart, dissolving into a mire of vulnerability. Fighting to stymie instinctive panic, Craig lifted his head to look around, spotting people at the workstation. The mantis, his aide and the same two technicians were busy at their monitors but now joined by three new faces; two women and a man, all engaged in conversation. One of these women right away reminded Craig of Miss Poole, a late middle-aged history teacher from his junior school. Also in the older age bracket, the man was a nondescript-looking individual, the type who never stood out in a crowd. Like the mantis, both wore identical white lab coats, yet more cogs to this establishment.

The second woman considerably younger, perhaps in her late twenties or early thirties and from the others' body language, Craig assessed her to be a key player. Wherever fitting in the hierarchy, she'd been blessed with a swimmer's build and dressed to subtly accentuate her physique. Wearing a white cotton blouse and tight-fitting navy midi-skirt with matching high heels, mid shoulder-length auburn hair had been severely scraped back and secured in a ponytail. Stood with her back to him, feet apart and arms akimbo, this woman projected an aura of undeniable dominance.

Keeping dead still, Craig discreetly observed the group's interaction, until the topic of their conversation had run its course. At this, Ponytail turned sharply and walked purposefully to his table, avoiding eye contact but staring critically, as if looking straight through him to ascertain the Link's presence. Feeling like a Petri dish specimen under this unwavering scrutiny, Craig expected Ponytail to say something, instead she remained mute. Eventually she looked into his face and Craig held the woman's gaze, seeing eyes that were unsettlingly devoid of any emotion, the colour of a cold, clear winter's sky.

A conventionally attractive woman, although masking natural good looks behind a lot of make-up, favouring an artificial, quasi-mannequin-like visage. An expensive but overpowering and cloyingly sickly-sweet perfume enveloped her, reinforcing Craig's immediately instinctual base-level dislike for the woman. Beyond the superficial, an indefinable element to the condescending arrogance of her overall persona irked him. Wanting to snap, demanding to know what the hell she wanted of him, instead conceding to an astute predisposition for survival by stifling this impulse. Besides, under present circumstances, it was more pragmatic to remain silent; shut up, listen and gather potentially useful information, rather than launch into an outright challenge.

The mantis and two other newbies had by now joined her at Craig's table.

"So, this is the one you spoke of Doctor. Remind me, what's the longest time span your previous subjects retained the Link?"

Half bowing, the mantis responded, "Number four lasted

two and a half minutes, Rebecca."

There it was, the first bit of information gleaned, Craig now knew this disagreeable creature's name. Govender hesitated before continuing.

"But, as stated in my report, this one's different in many more respects to earlier hosts: heart rate, BP and all vitals remain normal, even today. Also, there haven't been any significant psychotic episodes..."

Just getting into his stride when, without averting her eyes from Craig's, Rebecca cut in, "What do you mean by significant?"

Flustered at his evidently poor choice of words, Govender waved both hands appeasingly.

"No, no, what I meant was, while there's been the anticipated hostile reaction to restraint and confinement, these foreseeable responses have been successfully managed by reasoning with the subject."

Seemingly satisfied, Rebecca nodded, though Craig could tell her probe had rattled Govender, his hands more animated when speaking again.

"What I particularly wanted to highlight, is this subject's neural activity. EEG monitoring of baseline cognitive thought-waves is all perfectly normal for a subject of his age, socio-developmental status and physiological condition. However, the alpha and theta spectrums are quite remarkable, exhibiting a steadily increasing series of utterly anomalous spikes and dips, the likes of which I've never seen. It's as if he's in a perpetual state of deep meditation, although that's clearly not the case."

Belying his excitement, the mantis' voice had risen several octaves; whatever this revelation signified must carry fundamental significance, except going straight over Craig's head.

Maintaining an inexpressively blasé manner, Rebecca was either incapable of enthusiasm or shared in Craig's ignorance, he wasn't sure which.

"Send your data to Shane and tell him I want a full interpretative report by first thing tomorrow morning."

Craig's suspicion confirmed, clueless after all, she wanted it all spelled out in a user-friendly guide, although managing to disguise her ignorance flawlessly.

"I took the liberty of sending all monitoring data over last night, Rebecca. Shane's working on it, so you should get an email sometime today, I'll see to it that you do."

The mantis nodded, and his assistant made a note.

"So, on to today's programme," Rebecca continued. "Our guest has already arrived and he's with the CEO, being shown a demonstration of Lin's prototype. Anticipating the demo wrapping up by ten thirty, Daddy's bringing him up here straight afterwards. Make sure this one's sedated well before, I don't want any attempts to engage," her speech calmly matter of fact, obviously accustomed to calling the shots.

"Sedated, but conscious?" Govender raised an eyebrow enquiringly.

"Yes, of course, you won't be able to effectively demonstrate your EEG spectrum findings if he's out cold, Doctor." A biting edge of exasperation laced her tone, Govender should have known better than to ask such a stupid question.

Turning away, she seamlessly switched persona to velvet and honey.

"Very good. Thank you, Doctor. You may carry on with your planned routine until they arrive."

Crossing to a vacant bay at the workstation, Rebecca set about logging into a laptop, while Govender directed his attention to Craig, except displaying none of yesterday's personability.

"Now then, Mr. Farrant, how are you doing this morning? Our monitoring team tell me you had a restless night."

Deliberately, Craig wasn't going to make it easy for the man in front of his boss and erupted, "Really, how would you imagine I'm doing? I can tell you; I'm cheesed off is how I am. You've drugged and locked me up in this stinkhole, all because you've got some idiotic notion that I've got your precious Link!"

At his outburst, Rebecca slammed the laptop shut and came straight over.

"Sedate him now," she snapped, mouth set in a tight line that accentuated fine, dark hairs riding both bows of her upper lip.

Tentatively raising one hand, signifying the situation to be under control, Govender addressed Craig.

"I do understand your frustrations, Mr. Farrant. I was only asking how you're feeling, in a physical sense. A restless night could be symptomatic of an onset adverse reaction to the Link." His voice had become unmistakably patronising, and Craig desperately wanted to swing a punch into the man's hawk beak nose.

Instead, taking a breath before playing his card.

"Yeah, I'm otherwise fine, but you can't realistically expect me to sleep like a baby when I'm locked up in this place. Putting that aside, we need to talk. Yesterday, you said I would need to cooperate with whatever you're doing. Well, as I see it, I've been that, so how about cooperation working both ways, for our mutual benefit?"

About to interrupt, Govender appeared annoyed but Craig pressed on.

"Hear me out. Seeing as how I've got your Link and you need my cooperation to achieve whatever you're doing, then I'm going to need lots of straight answers and no more drugs, gas, or cuffs."

Craig's kept his focus directed on Govender, sporadically flicking to Rebecca, seeking to gauge the reactions of both. Govender opened his mouth to speak but Rebecca cut in, addressing Craig directly.

"Let's be perfectly clear about this, Mr. Farrant, the Link belongs exclusively to us. No matter how you came to acquire it, we will study you on our terms and eventually retrieve it, one way or another. Your cooperation isn't an absolute requirement, but it will facilitate more humane treatment during the process. That is the straightforward reality of your situation here, so make no mistake, you're in no position to try negotiating with us." Not prepared to entertain any potential response forthcoming, she marched back to her laptop.

The astringency of Rebecca's tirade confirmed Craig's expectation that Rebecca didn't appreciate being challenged. Regardless, the woman's hostility hadn't intimidated him, calling after her. By all accounts, having nothing to lose.

"Hey, Rebecca, what did you mean when you said you'll retrieve the Link one way or another?"

Shooting Craig a look of warning, Govender stepped into his sight line.

"Rebecca was merely referring to us finding a way to recover the Link from you once our research is complete."

Govender hadn't the stomach for brutal honesty, but Rebecca had no such misgivings. Coming to within an arm's length and smirking sadistically.

"No, that's not what I meant at all. I'm sure the good doctor means well, but the simple fact is that your having survived this long provides us with a unique opportunity. However, when my research team have achieved their objectives, you will be terminated and the Link recovered. Any more questions?"

Clearly delighting in ruthlessness, Rebecca's put-down highlighted the overall certainty of Craig's predicament. Stark reality emerging: any chance of ever getting out of this place alive was slim to non-existent. Unmoving and maintaining a poker-faced expression, Rebecca stared Craig down, daring him to another challenge. Losing interest in the game, she checked an expensive-looking wristwatch.

"Our guest will be here in an hour, sedate him now. I've got work to do and don't need any distractions."

Ashen-faced, Govender wouldn't look at Craig when administering a cocktail of sedatives.

A wave of numbing antipsychotic agents quickly washed away Craig's cares, although remaining aware of everything going on in the theatre, nothing fazed him any longer. After an indeterminable period, the door opened and an older man, who could have been Rebecca's father, ushered another into the lab. Tall, ruggedly handsome and smartly dressed in a tailored cashmere suit, their guest exuded the disdainful self-confident cockiness of an untouchable.

A pair of less sartorially suited men followed close on his heels, their attire obviously having come "off the peg"; they carried the carefully cultivated, hard disposition of bodyguards. Fanning out, eyes ever-scanning, evaluating the environment and hunting out potential threats to their charge. Quietly closing her laptop this time, Rebecca smiled broadly and hurried to welcome the visitor, extending her hand in greeting. Craig's altered consciousness observing her mannerisms as overtly unctuous, fawning and devoid of any sincerity.

"Minister Radebe, how wonderful to see you again and thank you for making the time to come see us," she gushed, as the man took her hand in both of his.

He responded boomingly, "Rebecca, it's so good to see you again, my dear. Every time, you're more beautiful than the last."

Throughout their cringingly disingenuous exchange, the man likely to be Rebecca's father mostly stood with his back to Craig, drug-bleared vision simply unable to get a fix on the man's image.

Blocked from view, someone else half opened the door and caught the possible father's attention, excusing himself and leaving the theatre. Ignoring his departure and demurely looking at the floor, Rebecca bobbed girlishly at the minister's reciprocal flattery.

"You are too kind, Mr. Minister. I do hope my father has taken good care of you so far?" With the requisite niceties over, not waiting for an answer before redirecting the conversation. "So, what did you think of the prototype demonstration?"

Clearly a stickler for etiquette, the minister nodded politely.

"Answering your first question, yes, your father always takes very good care of me. As for our machine, what can I say? Incredible. Everything I have come to expect of you two."

Coyly cocking her head to one side, Rebecca's tone turned syrupy.

"Excellent, we do like to show our appreciation of your continuing support, and I am so pleased to hear that you are satisfied with our progress. It's a pity Minister Shabalala couldn't be here today, I'm sure he would be equally satisfied."

Unable to catch everything being said by this point, it occurred to Craig that there was something familiar about the visitor.

At first unable to place where from, then it came to him, remembering a recent television news item covering a trade and technology fair in Cape Town. This character had been featured in his official capacity as government Minister of Science and Technology, making the opening speech. Therefore, by indirect association, the name Shabalala likely referred to the minister of defence; a fiery and abrasive individual, probably not best suited to controlling the country's armed forces.

A scandal had erupted a few years ago, the press implicating Thomas Shabalala as the kingpin in an illegal foreign arms deal, supplying heavy weapons and ammunition to rebels in a war-torn Middle Eastern country. Unsurprisingly, the very next day, the same newspaper had printed an unreserved retraction and apologised grovellingly. The journalist responsible for the exposé had summarily disappeared under mysterious circumstances, rumours abounding over her fate going unpublished by any tabloids.

From what he'd overheard, Craig's addled brain began putting two and two together; seeming as if the national government and Rebecca's people were unholy bedfellows. An irony surfaced, being that only time would prove which side would ultimately be determined as having done a deal with the Devil.

Bowing his head in simulated contrition, Radebe lowered his voice. "Yes, unfortunately Thomas had important matters of state to deal with today. He of course extends his sincerest apologies and is looking forward to me bringing him up to speed. I must also tell you that everybody within the inner circle was delighted to receive news and the video of our working prototype."

Beaming fawningly, Rebecca touched his arm. "That's wonderful to hear, thank you Minister. Time and schedules permitting of course, my father and I would be honoured to host further demonstrations for everyone else." Waving towards Craig, seamlessly changing tack, "We've also had an exciting, even if unexpected, breakthrough with the transference modules. But the unique and unforeseen circumstances surrounding this subject have attracted an unfortunate problem. I understand my father has already discussed this with you?"

Despite lolling in a drug-induced stupor, Radebe's reply left Craig feeling physically sick.

"There's no problem, Rebecca. I personally cleared this with our chief this morning and it's covered. Any reports regarding his disappearance will never be officially investigated. To all intents and purposes, this man no longer exists."

It wasn't uncommon for people to go missing without trace or eyebrows being raised in South Africa, whether through accident, misadventure or homicide. In most cases, these disappearances were deemed inconsequential, generally being indigents or ne'er-do-wells. Institutional apathy even applied to ordinary folk of limited means, those finding themselves in the wrong place at the wrong time. The police simply didn't have resources available to tackle and investigate the sheer volume of crimes committed daily, let alone look for absentee persons, in many cases discreetly removing themselves from difficult situations. Craig, on the other hand, didn't fulfil any of these categories. Ordinarily anyone fitting his socio-economic standing going missing would attract some degree of attention and airtime, unless intentionally blanketed in official secrecy.

"Thank you, Minister. We really do value your assistance in this matter. Things could otherwise become very messy, if this ever got out into the public realm." Beckoning to a loitering Govender, Rebecca appeared relieved at returning to their agenda. "I am going to hand over to Doctor Govender now, and he is going to talk us through the principal differences between this individual and previous subjects. Over to you then, Doctor."

Immediately launching into a patently well-prepared speech, the mantis soon had the government minister's attention drifting. Likewise detaching himself from the droning patter, irrespective of a government cover-up, Craig already knew it would take weeks or even months before anyone noticed his disappearance. Following the divorce-initiated dissolution of his and Maria's shared social circle, he had opted for self-isolation, avoiding any solicitations to form new friendships. His brother Ian might think it unusual not getting an annual birthday call later that year: then again, maybe not. They'd never been especially close as siblings, since Ian was seven years older than him. Strangely enough, Gladys Nkosi, the ever-cheery local Spaza shopkeeper would probably be first to notice his absence, when not stopping to buying fresh eggs and other sundry supplies.

Painting a truly sobering prospect, one that didn't sit well with Craig; forcibly wrenching himself from morose prospects to half following Govender's monologue. It was becoming highly technical, glancing at the visiting VIP and correctly guessing the man to not be getting much of it either. Not wishing to appear ignorant or churlishly disinterested, everyone had gathered in a semicircle, while Govender expounded on intricacies of Craig's body scan; thankfully, as it turned out, the mantis' grand finale.

Evidently satisfied at how enthused the minister seemed when Govender's oratory ended, Rebecca caught hold of Radebe's arm. Resisting momentarily, he paused to stare directly at Craig, who for a millisecond understood how a plump lobster in a restaurant tank might feel when under a discerning diner's scrutiny. Sensing an unspoken interaction taking place, Rebecca took charge and insistently steered the man away, suggesting they go for some refreshments.

A visibly relieved Govender sighed when the door closed, sinking heavily into his desk chair and dabbing a handkerchief at perspiration beading his brow. Giving speeches to politicians and the boss's daughter wasn't to his liking, Craig deriving little pleasure from this socially awkward creature's obvious discomfort. The morning's charade had left him with far bigger problems of his own to contend with.

At some point, the sedative and accompanying brain fog began wearing off, sharpening his senses, everything seen and heard merging into an alarming summation. This freakishly sordid business had full backing from the country's top political players, thereby extending Govender and Rebecca's reach well beyond the confines of this place.

Whatever the government's stake may be, the connection with Radebe's science and technology portfolio was plainly obvious. However, any tie-in with military and defence presented a complete mystery, Craig surmising it must centre around the prototype. Then again, having no idea as to the kind of prototype or its application, there was no way of validating this supposition.

Frankly, holding no interest whatsoever in these people's shenanigans, he wanted only to be rid of the Link and set free. Experiencing a lurch of angst, when remembering Rebecca gleefully explaining their fail-safe way of extracting the Link, at whatever point his usefulness came to an end. Even if by some miracle managing to escape, the resources they could collectively deploy to track him down were almost unlimited. From everything seen and heard so far, they had no intention of letting him go alive; whichever way the coin landed, he was utterly screwed.

Inexplicably, last night's dream about the tall, odd-looking man interjected into the forefront of his thoughts, and a crazy notion grew. The stranger's instruction, an improbable reference to his situation and no matter how he tried to dismiss the absurd correlation, it kept returning. Recalling snatches of the nightmares, all making perfect sense, subconscious reconciliations of events and circumstances, whereas the weirdo in a strange forest carried no apparent relevance. Ludicrously abstract and without any basis in logic, yet there existed an enticingly obscure significance to the man's words.

"Use your mind."

Dammit, it held meaning, but what? Already using his mind to think up naïvely desperate ploys, seeing them shot to pieces by Rebecca and left floating dead in the water. Looking at it from any angle, Craig couldn't conceive of another use of his intellect or cunning that would get him out of this situation. Probably just a weird dream after all, yet another side effect of the drugs being used on him. Still the tall stranger's words persisted, becoming an irrepressible earworm.

The day wore on; bouts of prodding, probing and even mild electrical shocks administered through the electrodes stuck to his scalp, eventually ended by Govender's assistant pumping a syringe of clear liquid into his cannula. The ensuing routine was much the same as the previous night's, coming round on the cot to a tray of food waiting on the floor. Sat cross-legged on the cot, he ate then propped a pillow against the wall and leant back, drifting in a sea of mind-numbingly repetitive dead-end thoughts.

The actuality of cabin fever and life-term convicts' apathy had by now become wholly understandable, bleakly seeming as though he were living on death-row. As to his allotted time quota remaining, there was no way of knowing with any degree of certainty; wholly dependent on how long it took Govender to conclude whatever he was trying to achieve. Perhaps days, weeks or months... or his life could be brought to an abrupt, hopefully humane, end tomorrow.

Suddenly, blindsided by the forest dream again, distinctly clear, as if reliving it.

"Enough, dammit!"

Leaping from the cot and butting his forehead against the opposite wall's cold masonry, Craig wanted to batter the irritation from his mind.

Regardless, even more insistently, something purposefully prompting him to consider the content differently.

"Nah, that's impossible... crazy," responding to his own internalising, probably another side effect of the drugs, or... "You're losing your freakin' mind."

Disconsolately nursing a throbbing head, he returned to sit on the cot. Although, the torment wouldn't let up, demanding his undivided attention. Relenting, Craig shut his eyes and thought of being at home.

Elsewhere in the building, a technician sat eating his dinner at a security control desk, simultaneously keeping an eye on a double-stacked bank of high-resolution monitors. Distracted and not enjoying the meal, he was annoyed at not having been relieved in time to dine with his workmates. All because of some lazy idiot running late. Scowling at the array of screens while attacking the food, further exasperated by knowing his state of mind would only lead to heartburn and reflux. Monitors to the left ran a live feed from externally mounted cameras, those on the right covered key internal areas, including views from inside each of six holding cells. One of these images suddenly flared brightly, then degraded into static.

Cursing, fork clattering to the plate and shoving it aside, he pulled a keyboard across to type in a reset code, hoping to clear the fault. It worked and the picture returned, only instead of returning to his meal, the guard swore again when noticing the cell's occupant to be out of view. Punching more keys, he took hold of an integral joystick and panned the camera, checking default position blind spots and seeing the cell to be empty. The occupant had simply vanished.

CHAPTER 11

"A thief is a thief, whether he steals oranges or diamonds" – African Proverb

A towering storm cloud threatened to blot out the mid-afternoon sun by the time Andre van Heerden returned to the mill, annoyance creasing his brow when noticing the main gates wide open. Displeasure quickly became concern at clearly panicked workmen throwing their belongings onto the mill truck and scrambling aboard its open load bed. Eyes wide in fear, Koos the foreman occupied the driver's position, head out of the side window shouting at them to hurry. Realising something must have gone terribly wrong, Van Heerden accelerated the Opel, stopping in front of the truck to block its passage. Striding over to the cab, he grabbed hold of the mirror arm, and in one fluid movement pulled himself up onto the running board.

Reaching in to grab the foreman's coat front in one huge fist, he bellowed, "What the donder [thunder] you playing at,

Koos? Who said you can leave?"

Startled at Van Heerden's offensive, the foreman's face fell, fear replaced by shame until panic reasserted itself.

"Boss, that thing's killed them all," he blurted, before a vice-like grip constricted his throat, choking the next words to a hoarse whisper.

Recognising the man to be genuinely terrified, Van Heerden released his hold.

"Turn it off and get out. Tell me, what's happened?"

Reluctantly the man obeyed but became uncharacteristically defiant when clambering down.

"There's no way we's going back in that place, Boss," he said, desperately needing to convince Van Heerden, then losing his nerve again. "It's that devil machine in the basement what's killed them. They's all dead for sure, honest, Boss. We's getting the hell outta here."

Van Heerden was a big man, quite accustomed to using his physical strength and fists if required, when subduing those seeking to challenge his will. Needing to get the full story from this gibberingly incoherent fool, he stifled an overwhelming urge to pound it from the frightened man, instead grabbing hold of both coat collars and shaking violently.

"Pull yourself together, Koos. Tell me what happened?" he roared, pulling the foreman towards him until nose to nose.

"I… I don't know, Boss. Please… we didn't see nothing," he wheedled, frantically looked over his shoulder for the other men's support, but they had all fallen silent.

Letting go, Van Heerden changed his approach.

"Okay, okay. Calm down, I'm here to fix this. Tell me who's dead and who found them?" lowering his voice, although still adopting a no-nonsense tone.

"Everyone, Boss. Koekemoer and the Germans, all the boffins. They didn't come up for lunch like they usually done, so

I used my key and went down below to check." Recalling what he'd seen, Koos shuddered, eyes widening before continuing, "They's all over the place in there. It's horrible, Boss."

Reaching inside the cab, Van Heerden pulled the ignition key.

"Right, you're going to show me," grabbing the scared man's arm and forcibly pushing through the others, parting without protest.

Both the mill level and lower chamber doors were wide open, as Koos had left them when fleeing the scene. In the basement, precisely as described, a trail of bodies lay strewn across the floor and up the craft access stairs, all posed in gruesome definition of their attempted flight from something. An expectant silence filled the place, broken only by the sound of their footsteps, and Van Heerden couldn't shake an inescapably eerie feeling that they were being watched. Taking stock of the harrowing scene, suppressing his own apprehension by telling himself it was only the foreman's palpable fear spooking him.

Nearest to the entrance, one of the researchers lay face down, arm outstretched where he'd been futilely reaching for the door. Going further, gingerly treading through the trail of bodies, Van Heerden had seen enough dead men to know there was no point in checking for signs of life. Coming across Koch at the foot of the timber stairs, fallen to his knees then toppled backwards, arched face up, lower legs folded under his thighs. Both lifeless hands still gripping his tunic front, fingers tightly intertwined in the material as if trying to tear himself open. Van Heerden could find no remorse at the Nazi's death, although something in the man's facial expression chilled him; glazed eyes wide open, mouth agape, Koch had died screaming in terror.

Initially passing by and missing Stein, half turning and picking the man out by a pair of high-fashion shoes he wore. Managing to make it a few paces closer to the exit, the lead scientist lay sprawled on his belly, face buried in the crook of an elbow. Even in death, he retained greater dignity than Koch. A pang of regret tugged at Van Heerden's heart, albeit having guessed at Stein's relationship preferences and regardless of contemporary social stigma, he'd grown fond of the man.

Whatever had gone down in that place quite clearly scared the men witless before overcoming them, excruciatingly evidenced in their rigor mortis death poses and anguished facial expressions. Something strange caught Van Heerden's attention; every one of them without exception, their faces and any other areas of exposed skin flecked in spots of blood. Covering his mouth and nose with a handkerchief, he stepped over and around dead men to climb the craft access stairs. Pausing when reaching the upper landing, increasingly attuned to a sense of being under constant scrutiny. Survival instinct kicked in; this wasn't a good place to be, time to leave. Retracing his steps to where Koos waited, he led the man into the basement lobby and placed a reassuring hand on his shoulder.

"We can't do anything for them. Give me your keys and go wait outside," he said, scanning the basement one last time before extending an open hand.

Fishing the keys from a trousers pocket, only too glad to be rid of their associated responsibility, the foreman handed them over and raced off up the exit stairs. After locking the basement, Van Heerden followed, finding the workmen waiting restlessly at the truck.

"Right, you all go home and not a word about any of this to your families. I want every one of you at Venter's mill tomorrow and the same goes there, you keep shtum about everything you've ever seen or heard here. Mouths shut, got it?" staring at every man in turn, until nodding their assent.

Returning to the building when they'd left, he checked every room for stragglers before finally locking up and heading for the Opel. Although glad to get away from that accursed place,

Van Heerden dreaded his next task even more so, beginning to mentally compose an explanation to his superiors. There was no sugar-coating what had happened, a truly awful incident; something had to have come from that machine, the only rational explanation for the entire research team and their minders being wiped out. Relaying this much would be the easy part, as for the inevitable what that could be, he had absolutely no way of answering. Thankfully, the unenviable task of passing on the news to Nazi High Command would fall to someone in Pretoria.

Predictably, phone calls made that evening were not well received and before sunup the next morning, under orders, Van Heerden returned to the mill. Predawn luminescence brightened a thick fog settled across the region when reaching the dirt road. A treacherously thick, ground-hugging cloud, noticeably denser in low-lying areas, forcing him to crawl the car at walking pace into the valley.

Cold, damp vapour settling on both halves of the windscreen compelled him to turn on the wipers, sweeping condensation from the inside with the cuff of a coat sleeve. Eventually reaching the mill, he was relieved to find the gates still locked shut, opening both leaves wide and driving in. Parking up under the umbrella tree and killing the engine, silence fell, broken only by fat water droplets randomly tapping on the car's bodywork. Getting out and heading around back of the building, the densely dank air felt cloying and heavy to breathe.

The generator started at first crank and ran smoothly, pushing in the choke toggle, he engaged the load lever to power up the building. When the big diesel engine revved up to confirm current was being drawn, he closed the front cover and made for the building. Hesitating at the main entrance door, his imagination worked overtime, although not due to trepidation occasioned by memories of yesterday's dreadful scenes. He'd been toying with an idea overnight and hadn't slept well, the significance of his intentions hitting home in that moment. There would be no turning back, mind made up, he let himself in and went directly to the men's dormitory and Stein's bedside locker.

Sitting on the dead man's neatly made bed, trying the drawer and unsurprisingly finding it locked; the storage cupboard below providing the same outcome. Knowing the keys to be with Stein, he grimaced at the thought of returning to the basement but took a degree of assurance from a pronounced bulge under his left armpit. Knowing full well it would prove completely ineffectual against whatever had killed the researchers, it still provided a sense of comfort. Tucked into a shoulder holster and concealed by his coat, the Ruger .44 wasn't intended to defend against whatever creature resided in the craft, instead brought along as insurance against any of the mill men getting drunk and speaking out of turn. The war had brought out the best and worst in people, and a hardy opportunist would certainly jump at the prospect of enrichment gained by stealing a trophy from the craft. It crossed his mind that the craft would ironically prove a far sterner adversary to any mal-intentioned trespasser than himself.

The mill-level stairs door was still locked, dispelling the prospect of coming across the bodies of any such trespassers, the basement's grizzly spectacle remaining exactly as remembered from the previous day. While nothing seemed to have physically changed overnight, the basement's atmosphere had become tainted by the unmistakably foul odour of death. Covering his nose and mouth with a fresh handkerchief, Van Heerden picked through the tangle of corpses, going directly to Stein's body. Pushing aside feelings of guilt while delving through the dead man's pockets to locate a set of keys, he hastily returned to the dormitory. One key on the bunch opened the locker drawer and another, the storage cupboard.

The drawer yielded nothing of any real interest, holding mostly personal effects; several photographs of a handsome young man, a part-used letter pad, toiletry bag and half a roll of peppermints. Opening the cupboard below, Van Heerden was immediately rewarded with Stein's leather-bound journal peeping out from amongst other paperwork. Tugging it from between a stack of cardboard folders and opening the swastika-emblazoned cover, he flicked through the first few pages, skimming over their contents. Since the Germans' arrival, his early life's command of the language had quickly returned and even expanded. Sitting on the bed, he continued leafing through the book, reading excerpts from Stein's detailed and neatly handwritten chronicle, skipping pages of bafflingly complex calculations and annotated sketches.

Eventually setting the journal next to himself on the bed to rifle through the folders, there were letters and reports from Schauberger, among them reference documents from research carried out at Mauthausen. Selecting three of these Manila folders, he closed and locked the unit then got up from the bed, pausing to listen for any sounds coming from outside. Satisfied at being alone, he tucked all selected documents inside his coat and exited the dormitory.

Stopping on the front step, the only audible sound was that of occasional water droplets falling from nearby vegetation, his surroundings otherwise cloaked in pregnant silence. Eerily, the thick fog blanket created an illusion of being the only remaining living soul on the planet. Hastily crunching across the gravel expanse to open the Opel's driver-side door, he slid the journal and folders out of sight under the seat and slammed the door, just as the muffled sound of approaching engines became audible; the clean-up party were approaching.

Emerging from behind a dazzle of headlights, the first vehicle was a black Daimler driven by Bernardus "Boet" Meyer, his boss of the last eight years. The Brotherhood's provincial commandant and recipient of Van Heerden's unpleasant telephone call the night before. Aside from holding a senior position within the OB, Meyer was also a presiding provincial court judge and well connected throughout government's upper echelons. A Boer War veteran, decorated for meritorious gallantry at the bloody Battle of Colenso by Paul Kruger himself. Despite advancing years, Meyer was a good man to have on your side, and conversely the worst kind of adversary.

Until that morning, never having any cause to visit the mill, instead relying on Van Heerden's weekly progress updates to stay abreast of noteworthy developments. A thoroughly direct man who harboured little patience for small talk, after a perfunctory greeting, Meyer demanded a recap of everything that had gone down there the previous day. Interrupting a few times to probe, until his understanding had been satisfied, then instructing Van Heerden to show him the scene.

Stood side by side in the basement-level doorway, Van Heerden knew well enough to say nothing, leaving Meyer to solemnly take in the grim spectacle. Raising his attention to the craft, the commandant spoke in an uncharacteristically humble tone.

"Photographs don't do this thing justice. Where do you think it came from, Dee?" an amicable nickname bestowed on Van Heerden years before, and only ever used informally.

Sighing reflectively, Van Heerden could only shrug.

"Honestly, I haven't got the faintest idea, Boet. Maybe from the Moon, or even Mars, like in that book," referring to Jules Verne's epic, pointing skywards to where he imagined the red planet might be.

A faint smile creased the corners of Meyer's mouth.

"Huh. I suppose we'll never get to know the whole story."

Unsure whether Meyer was mocking, Van Heerden didn't reply, staring fixedly at the craft instead.

Detecting his charge's discomfort, Meyer slapped his shoulder.

"Never mind, hey? Now show me around inside." Meyer

managed a few steps before Van Heerden grabbed his arm.

"Boet, wait! With all due respect, whatever killed these men had to come from inside that thing. It's not safe to go in there yet. Let me send some of my guys in first, to check it out." Immediately the words left his mouth, realising from Meyer's contemptuous look that his entreaty had been a complete waste of breath.

Firmly removing Van Heerden's hand, Meyer continued apace, calling out, "Come on, Dee, you're getting soft in your old age."

Wholly exasperated at the older man's insistence but genuinely concerned, he obeyed, following his superior up the stairs and into the craft. They came across Billy Koekemoer at the entranceway, slumped in an ungainly, half-seated position against the nearest console. Only one other body remained inside, that of the unfortunate Erich, lying face down a few paces from the pit. The man's frantic but futile struggle to escape the fireflies, spelled out by a long shred of his lab coat hanging from the propulsion unit's lattice frame. It had evidently been snagged there, until managing to tear himself free.

Clearly fascinated at getting to see the craft's interior first-hand, Meyer took his time in circuiting the flight deck, scrutinising everything in detail; incongruously, taking on the appearance of a speculative auction bidder previewing the lots. Tight-lipped and vigilant, Van Heerden followed a few paces behind, right hand gripping the revolver's butt. Stopping abruptly, Meyer pointed at the conveyer belt mat held aloft.

"So, behind that is what killed these men, right?"

Being unable to answer with any degree of certainty irked Van Heerden.

"I can't say for sure, Boet. Probably, although what happened to the German's isn't like when we tested that thing on the Bantu. It killed him on the spot, except this time... for sure, they were running away from something."

Electing not to respond right away, nodding thoughtfully

instead, Meyer leant forward from the waist and stared into the pit.

"And this is what all the fuss and bother is about, huh? Were they close to figuring out how this machine works?"

Turning to redirect his gaze at Van Heerden, Meyer's face hardened, eyes seemingly boring into his adjutant's skull.

Van Heerden knew that look, a good time to tread lightly.

"Stein was undoubtedly a very clever man; he shared some things with me but would have been under orders to keep his mouth shut about the important stuff."

Nodding again, Meyer pointed at the power saw, lying in the pit where Erich had discarded it.

"Look, Dee. The machine killed them because they were trying to steal its engine." Van Heerden's turn to nod; Meyer had hit the nail squarely on its head. "This thing is priceless and belongs in our country, to our volk, not the Germans. If we had their kind of know-how, we wouldn't be selling ourselves short and giving it away. Think about it, we'd have the kind of power the Germans do, maybe even the Yankees. All this nonsense, for a promise that might come to nothing."

Recently arriving at a personal understanding of the craft's potential worth, Meyer's reference to its value made Van Heerden uneasy. Taking a tentative first step towards garnering what may be a route to virtually unlimited self-enrichment, he had no intention of jeopardising that emergent plan. Despite being unquestionably patriotic, he felt no prick of conscience, solely an awareness of needing to measure each word spoken, and every move made. Knowing Meyer to have an unerring ability to read deception, he pushed these thoughts to the back of his mind. Better in fact to steer their conversation along the same route Meyer had begun taking.

"Do you think Hitler might back out of his agreement with us?"

Shrugging noncommittally, Meyer frowned.

"Who knows? He may prove a man of his word, but anyone

entirely trusting him is a fool. Stalin is his ally for now, but sources tell me he's planning an invasion of Russia, wanting their land for German expansion. If that's true, then what's the odds of him honouring our understanding?" Pausing to chuckle dryly, "Of course, first he would have to win the war anyway." Absent-mindedly stroking his chin, Meyer smiled at an internal musing, then became serious again. "Right, I've seen enough here. Nothing we've spoken about is ever to leave this place, understood Van Heerden?"

Informal chumminess at an end, the order of hierarchy had returned.

"Yes, of course, Commandant. I'll get this place cleaned up and secured. More guards are being placed around the perimeter."

Both making for the exit, Van Heerden remained ever a pace behind Meyer.

"Very good. Just so you know, Van Rensburg informed Berlin last night, so Himmler knows what's happened, but we haven't heard anything since. I'll keep you informed regarding any further duties."

Making their way topside and discovering that the risen sun had burned away most of the early morning fog, to leave ragged tufts of cotton wool drifting lazily across a brilliant blue sky. Van Heerden breathed a sigh of relief when Meyer drove out of the gate, feeling as if a physical weight were lifting from his shoulders.

CHAPTER 12

"You have power over your mind, not outside events. Realise this, and you will find strength." – Marcus Aurelius

A state where tangible reality and space-time ceased to exist, stripped of physical substance although consciously aware, Craig felt weightless, floating in all-encompassing nothingness. A singular sentience enduring; intense heat, roaring viscerally and instilling a strangely pleasurable sensation, as if becoming the very essence of potently superheated plasma. Any measurable constructs of time annulled, several millennia could have passed, or the merest fraction of a second before reality resumed. Sensation and sound instantly ceasing in the moment of his reconstitution, cast into a dark and tranquil setting.

Conscious thought couldn't keep up, unable to reconnect with physical self, his mind a complete blank and lacking any ability to process either thought or manage physical coordination. Neural continuity between brain and limbs still disconnected, he dropped like a discarded marionette to land in an uncomposed heap. Lying motionless, awareness, thoughts and returning sensations were immediately overridden by uncontrollable waves of nausea.

Gagging and dry heaving, Craig struggled into a crouching position on all fours when, somewhere amidst more immediate discomfort, confusion kicked in. Glancing around the unlit space, frantically needing to understand where he was, panicking. Then, abruptly as it had taken hold, his imbalance sickness subsided in the same moment as bewildering realisation of present whereabouts. It was the living room of his own home. Staggering to his feet and swaying momentarily, then falling backwards into a chair, he sprawled there, gasping to gather both breath and wits.

Glaringly lucid, events of the last two days came racing back: being abducted by the Russian and his mob, the containment cell and that weirdo, Govender, Rebecca and others in that freaky surgical theatre. The cell, for goodness' sake! He'd been locked in his cell seconds before, and now here he was, inexplicably back home. Nothing about this physical transposition made any sense in the addled time and spatial continuum of his consciousness.

Perhaps they'd sedated and brought him back here, but for what reason? After all, they'd still been running various experiments on him that same afternoon, without any apparently significant breakthrough. Something violently traumatic could have happened during subsequent procedures, giving rise to amnesia and accounting for a blank spot in his memory. It would also explain that overwhelming sense of displacement and disorientation experienced when waking up at home. Having a rudimentary understanding of the mind's overload prevention feature, its capacity to erase periods surrounding harrowing events, this concept held a ring of plausibility.

Then Craig's imagination took over, painting a more

worrisome scenario; possibly having imagined the whole thing, some sort of elaborate mental aberration, brought about by... Anxiety escalating when envisaging a developing brain tumour, exerting increasing pressure as it grew, generating delusional false memories. Like a punch to the gut, this made more sense. More logical than the fanciful recall of a peculiar artefact landing in his yard, foreign thugs with needles, knockout gas and mad Frankenstein doctors in a laboratory controlled by Rebecca.

In the comfortable familiarity of his unlit lounge, that entire section of supposed recall took on the hue of ridiculous fiction, not unlike the contrived plot of a poorly produced B-movie. It had to be a tumour after all, his brain sending an elaborately coded message, alerting him to something going wrong in his head... otherwise, he might just be going stark staring mad.

First thing tomorrow, he would call the doctors' rooms and make an appointment to get a check-up. Grim, yet calm acceptance took hold; such an outcome could be dealt with, whatever the consequences. Having recovered his breath, feeling steadier and in better control of his limbs, Craig got up and turned the overhead light on, revealing the porch doors wide open. Passing by the sofa to shut them, a scattering of dry bougainvillea flowers spread amidst windblown dust caught his eye. Confusion returned and he yelled aloud in despair. What the hell was wrong with him? How long had he been sat there in a state of catatonic stupor?

Locking the doors and drawing the curtains, he went into the kitchen where another surprise awaited, providing a more tangible corroboration. Sat on the kitchen countertop, a half-empty bottle of water, Craig distinctly remembering drinking from it when the SUVs pulled in. A thought arose, raising his left arm and recoiling when seeing bruised needle marks speckling the elbows' crook. Legs threatening to give way, he placed both hands on the countertop to steady himself.

In a bizarre twist, evidential comprehension of initial memories being valid proved infinitely worse than dealing with the prospect of a tumour. Neither facing a potentially terminal illness, nor going mad; he had indeed been abducted, imprisoned and experimented on, and yet still had no idea how he'd got home. Feelings of both relief and dismay welled up; he may be healthy and sane, but this meant facing the even more daunting prospect of dealing with an unquantifiably complex peril.

Determining how he'd got home became the next primary focus, knowing with certainty that the answer would only raise more potentially unresolvable questions. The last thing coherently remembered before waking up in the living room, he'd been in the cell, thinking about that dream, when everything transformed into weird bright heat. A vague notion darted in from beyond the fringe of sound reasoning, summarily dismissing it as utterly ridiculous. Swiftly overriding such a whimsical concept, a more pressing reality emerged; no matter what had transpired, they would by now be looking for him by now. Ergo, staying put wasn't a sensible option.

Inevitably, using whatever means they had traced him with in the first place, the Russian and his heavies would turn up in force. Also, there was no way of knowing where he'd been held, or how long it would take them to reach his place. The facility could be on the other side of the country or close by. For all he knew, they might be racing up his road right at that very instant. A moving target would be more difficult to pin down; he had to get out of there right away.

Pulling an overnight bag from the wardrobe in his bedroom, Craig set about stuffing it with clothes, all the while conscious of having no idea how long he might be on the move. While packing a washbag with assorted toiletries, the urge to take a shower became irresistible, deciding to risk it. Reaching inside the glass cubicle and turning the mixer control, a spray of invitingly warm water jetted from an elliptical, chromed shower head. Stripping off and stepping in without hesitation, he briskly soaped and scrubbed himself all over before rinsing off.

Feeling immeasurably better, revitalised and cleansed, it had been worth sacrificing three minutes to feel human again. Towelling himself dry, Craig simultaneously launched the pre-packed toiletry bag one-handed, to land on the bed next to his waiting holdall. Threading his damp towel over a heated rail and returning to the bedroom, he suddenly became acutely aware of being stark naked in full view of the window. Living out in the sticks such a thing ordinarily never bothered him, now circumstances had changed and tonight seemed different. Feeling exposed, he yanked the curtains shut.

Dressing hurriedly, Craig slung the travel bag over one shoulder when a thought came to him and dropped it back on the bed. Kneeling to pull aside a bedside mat exposed a concealed flush-set floor panel, inlaid with brass pull rings. Lifting this out, he reached down to a recessed safe built into the concrete subfloor and worked the combination. Grabbing a wad of banknotes, kept there as an emergency cash reserve, he stuffed the money into a jeans' side pocket, passport next. Hesitating, then withdrawing a Glock 40 bought while living in crime-ridden Joburg, back when he and Paul had been friends. They'd signed up at a shooting range and spent many a Saturday afternoon on either target practice or combat shooting. He'd selected that particular handgun for its stopping power, becoming thoroughly proficient on the range, and kept it loaded with hollow point rounds.

Dropping the magazine and pulling the slide back to half-cock, spying the brass rim of a casing peeking from the ejector port confirmed there to be a round in the spout. Releasing the slide and reinserting the mag, he also packed two full boxes of ammunition into the overnight bag. Closing and locking the safe, he replaced the floor panel then slid the obscuring mat back into place. Tucking the Glock inside the pants' waistband at the small of his back, he pushed a spare mag into the passport pocket.

"Just in case, you never know," he told himself.

Grabbing the bag, Craig headed for the back door, picking up his wallet and both sets of car keys from a fruit bowl on the kitchen counter. About to grab his cell phone but stopping himself, knowing that his pursuers probably already had the number and would likely listen in on any calls made. Leaving it behind, he ran to the garage where heart overruled common sense, going straight to the '67 Chevy.

Pragmatism would have advised taking the 4x4, but Craig's preference lay in speed, something the Impala had aplenty, easily leaving the heavy Isuzu and most regular vehicles in its dust. Withdrawing the Glock before sliding behind the wheel, he placed it on the passenger seat and keyed the ignition. The car hadn't been driven for around a month, its 5-litre V8 at first spluttering, until firmly depressing the accelerator pedal elicited a gutsy roar.

Meeting tarmac at the lane's end, a dilemma arose; which way to go, left or right? In the chaotic scramble to get ready and leave, Craig hadn't taken time to consider where best to head for, mentally kicking himself for not figuring this out beforehand. Then again, with only one way in or out of his place, he would have been a sitting duck there when the Russian and his goons turned up.

If turning left, the road wound through open country to Elandskop, then on to join the national road that would him to Joburg. Straight away his emotively less favoured option, although still knowing people living in the city's suburbs who would take him in without hesitation. Going right would take him through Nottingham Road, and onwards to Pietermaritzburg or Durban, with old friends and acquaintances in both cities. Instinct took over, turning right and gunning the engine.

Being late, the backwoods road held very little traffic,

meaning Craig could push it, putting distance between him and the house. Turning on the stereo system for distraction, a disc left in resumed playing and he smiled wryly when AC/DC's 'Highway to Hell' boomed out. The speeding Impala's upgraded xenon headlights cut a brilliant swathe of contrast between road ahead and unlit country verges either side. Dimming the beams, so as not to dazzle drivers of occasional oncoming vehicles; each passing raised his anxiety, thinking any of them might be the Russian and his men. To his detriment, contrast between darkness and glaring headlights made it virtually impossible to identify onrushing vehicles, other than big trucks. Nevertheless, so far as discernible, none had been SUVs. Reaching the town of Nottingham Road, he elected to stay on the old main road in favour of cutting across to the faster and more direct freeway. It seemed less likely for the hostiles to use this slower and more tortuous route; however, this would turn out to be his first big mistake.

A few kilometres on, rounding a blind bend, Craig saw a blinking light in the sky ahead, flying low and unmistakeably coming his way. Heart skipping a beat, he spotted an overhead road and rail bridge coming up a few hundred metres ahead, plenty wide enough to provide cover. Still coming out of the bend, he floored it aggressively and had to quickly correct when the back end snaked wickedly. Gut-wrenching seconds passed before streaking under the structure, braking sharply to a halt and killing the engine. Winding down the window confirmed his worst fears, hearing the unmistakable chatter of helicopter rotors reverberating in the semi-enclosed space. Berating himself for choosing this route, Craig fought to suppress a surging sense of fear; just possibly, it might not be them. Holding his breath and listening intently to place the sound, willing the chopper to fly over and keep going.

The rotors' noise shifted, coming from behind now and continuing onwards, not deviating from its course. Craig sighed in relief and went to restart the engine, then the resonance's pitch altered, the chopper was turning around. A long straight lay ahead, the sudden glare of vehicle headlights rapidly rounding a distant bend made him wince and blink. Two, no three vehicles driving nose to tail and coming fast, it had to be them. Deciding to make a run for it, Craig cranked the motor to life, wound the steering wheel to full lock and booted it. Spinning tyres shrieked on asphalt, the Chevy swinging across both lanes to rocket back the way he'd come.

At the exact moment of straightening up, the helicopter dropped below the far bridge span, appearing like a giant predatory dragonfly descending. Any optimistically harboured doubts evaporated, they'd caught up with him. Settling in the road, the copter's whirring blades threw up thickly billowing clouds of dust from adjacent embankments, completely obscuring his view. The choking haze parted momentarily, long enough for Craig to make out the nearest road edge; looking like he could squeeze through the gap.

Still accelerating, the approaching dust cloud closed in again, drawing a veil that masked a steel crash barrier framing the bridge abutment. At the last second, the dust dispersed enough for him to see it, too late; the speedo's needle hit ninety, a fraction before the Impala ploughed headlong into the hefty barricade. A brutal impact, flipping the car end over end to land right way up but precariously canted on the steep embankment.

Craig must have blacked out momentarily, coming to and smelling petrol vapour mixed with engine coolant and hot oil. Stunned and winded, dazedly moving one arm dislodged broken glass shards, chinking and rattling to the central console. Vision swimming, head pounding in time to a ringing noise from getting slammed against the side pillar. Only the sound of running footsteps and approaching voices dragged him back from the brink of further unconsciousness. Fumbling ineffectually with the four-point-locking seat belt, eventually locating the release button to free himself. Desperately feeling around for the Glock, he leant over into the passenger footwell, groping blindly until his hand brushed something hard.

Grabbing hold of the pistol by its slide, Craig was about to sit up when the driver's side window that had somehow survived the crash abruptly shattered, showering him in more beads of glass. He froze when a sharp pop ensued, unaware of two fine wire strands falling across him until glancing a cheek and delivering a searing shock.

Out of Craig's line of sight, when smashing in the side window his attacker had reflexively discharged a Taser; both darts passing over him and embedding themselves in the passenger door card. A balaclava-clad face lurched into view, someone was trying to force the door and Craig's adrenaline surged. Awkwardly half rolling, simultaneously correcting his grip on the Glock to take aim at the man's shape, finger tightening on the trigger. Instead of the pistol's concussive report, a surging sense of calm overtook survival instinct. All anger suppressed, mind inexplicably shifting to a place last seen in childhood and the car's dark interior flared, his assailants and wrecked Impala gone.

The same uncanny phenomenon as before, heat and light, Craig emerging to find himself knelt with one hand in a patch of damp moss, the other on stone paving. This time the transit played out differently, its aftereffect markedly less debilitating and without any state of disconnected confusion or ensuing nausea. Becoming aware of a vaguely familiar stink of rotten eggs, he looked around and immediately recognising this as the same location from that uninvited but insistent memory, mere seconds before. Suddenly, it all made sense, finally dawning on Craig what the stranger in his dream had meant when telling him to use his mind.

Built in the 1920s as a well-being retreat, Lilani Hot Springs Spa & Hotel had catered exclusively for the well-to-do, but poorly maintained access to this remote location saw the business's demise after thirty years. Neglected ever since, the roof had fallen in which allowed strangler figs to take hold, sprouting from fruit seeds dropped by birds and monkeys. Growing vigorously into huge trees, their roots had torn apart the building's walls and even lifted heavy adjacent flagstone paving.

Unaffected by the adjacent structures' dereliction, the foul-smelling geothermal springs continued flowing through man-made pools. Few knew of this crumbling folly's existence and only a handful of local folks ever visited, among these had been friends of Craig's parents. Owning forestry plantations and a mill, they'd introduced his family to the place back when he'd been around eight years old. Coming to take the waters here had left happy memories, although tinged by poignant melancholy at witnessing the disintegration of a once so imposingly grand place. Even at such a young age, if detaching himself from fun and frivolity, the old buildings gave off a disturbing atmosphere.

Years later, in the here and now, this creepiness was exponentially amplified. Decaying remnants of door and window joinery clung in the surviving façade's apertures, appearing not unlike corrupted flesh hanging from the gaping mouths and eye sockets of rotting corpses. Saturated in brooding inkiness, the building's interior features were indistinguishable; something moved in there, scuttling, darting to escape an invisible predator or seeking out a better vantage point from which to spy on him.

Instinctively jumping at the sound, Craig stepped backwards a few paces, putting distance between him and the gloomy building while turning to scan the near surroundings. Scarcely having reached first quarter, the moon cast feebly watery light; not sufficient to properly detail his environs, although enough to deepen shadows cast by encircling undergrowth and overhanging trees.

Cooled by night's embrace, the air had condensed a fine

blanket of steam that draped over the main bath and adjoining shallower children's pool. Further away, but made invisible by impenetrable darkness, a mud bath incessantly *bloop*, *bloop*, *bloop*-ed. Whirling at rustling dry leaves stirred by a breath of wind, that also created swaying shadowy tree bough outlines on the ground; parting for an instant, just long enough for Craig to catch sight of a geometric shape. Retrieving the Glock, he checked it over, relieved to find that other than a scuffed handgrip it hadn't sustained any damage. Clasping at his thigh and touching the pocketed spare magazine's distinctive shape, he suddenly felt less exposed.

Fallen from the ruined hotel's second floor, a large slab of masonry made for a suitable, albeit hard perch to sit and ponder the situation. His captors would doubtless already have redirected their hunt, meaning that sticking around here wouldn't be feasible for long. Essential that he keep on the move, going somewhere else, but where? Head in hands, stewing on his predicament, when a glimmer of positivity elbowed its way to the fore. Since being instilled with the Link, if bestowing him with the uncanny ability to do what he had now begun to believe, then it would be safe staying put awhile. Miles from anywhere and desolately quiet, any approaching vehicles would be a dead giveaway, long before posing a threat.

Through whatever means he had escaped both cell and car wreck, must hold a correlation to the Link, similarly explaining why Govender and Rebecca wanted it back so badly. Having gained a speculative appreciation of the thing's application, Craig could only reason it being some kind of top-secret technology. Rebecca had referred to it by another name during Radebe visit… a "transference module". However, something about this black op's supposition didn't add up and it bugged him.

Govender had openly admitted they hadn't developed the Link, flippantly referring to someone or "something" else being the creator; reflecting on inferences to the latter truly creeped him out. Whatever the mantis might have been alluding to, and whichever way Craig viewed it, they must have acquired the thing through illicit means. Probably stolen from one of the superpowers, they had the device but no access to its software, which clarified Govender's caginess and inability to properly run the thing. This eventuality also explained how they had come to lose it, ending up in his yard.

If he'd pinned a tail on the donkey, the ability imparted to him would be mind-blowing; except logical thinking swooped in here, cautioning that such fanciful wizardry simply wasn't realistically feasible. No matter how much funding may have been poured into research and development, teleportation remained solely the stuff of comic books and sci-fi films. Although, based on Craig's recent experiences, no matter how implausible, it genuinely seemed as if he had acquired precisely this freakishly outlandish capability.

Another thing mentioned by Govender also concerned Craig; he wasn't the first to have assimilated the Link, previous recipients dying horrifically during the mantis's bungling experimentation. According to him, the Link had then reconstituted, compounding the conundrum as to how it ended up in his yard without the recipient. Or had it, indeed? Remembering first seeing the thing surrounded by a foetid mess of organic appearance, gave Craig a queasy feeling.

Preferring to abandon that train of thought, skipping instead to an anomaly glaring at him out of such hideous conjecture, one raising yet more befuddling questions. If the device had killed all the others, then why was he still very much alive and what made him different to the others? Had the thing really stabilised, or was he a time-delayed bomb, ultimately doomed to share in Govender's previous victims' fate?

More unresolvable suppositions, speculation and questions

swirled in his head. Of only one factor was Craig entirely certain, wanting rid of the damned thing and returning to his untroubled and straightforward lifestyle. Running simply wasn't a sustainable option, they would be looking for him no matter where he went, even if going to the opposite side of the world.

An uncomfortable conclusion kept bobbing to the surface, that the only way of ever getting shot of this accursed thing, paradoxically meant handing himself over to the very people pursuing him. The old saying of being 'caught between the Devil and a deep blue sea' rang in his head. Then again, surrendering without first establishing suitable terms would be akin to suicide. To circumvent that unfavourable outcome meant devising a backup survival strategy.

Govender and Co currently held the upper hand, knowing his identity and likely every personal detail, probably via government-sanctioned access to the revenue service's database. Towards levelling the playing field, Craig needed to identify them and establish exactly what they were all about. Since not having the slightest inkling, meant starting his investigation at the place where he'd been held.

Not really understanding how the Link's transference capability functioned, superficially appearing as if visualising a location initiated the process. Herein lay another poser. Craig had no clue where the research facility might be situated, being familiar only with the confines of his cell and the operating theatre. This wasn't going to be easy. Returning to the cell would be futile, potentially making him the proverbial fish in a barrel. The theatre, on the other hand, would probably be unoccupied at this time of night and could be the ideal place to turn up something useful.

Yet another problem. Remembering the key card ID around Govender's neck probably signified the place being secured by an electronic security-locking system. Going to the theatre would therefore restrict his search solely to that space, impossible to leave that area and explore any further. Still, sitting on a chunk of old bricks and procrastinating while the Russian closed in wasn't getting him anywhere either; it had to be worth taking the risk. Shutting his eyes, Craig focused on remembering every detail of lying on the procedure table.

CHAPTER 13

"Amicus certus in re incerta cernitur
[A friend in need is a friend indeed]" – *Quintus Ennius*

Initially experiencing a panicked sense of déjà vu, Craig emerged lying on the table, except this time not held fast by leather straps or confined by a lattice cocoon. The theatre was unoccupied as hoped, with every monitor fortuitously left turned on and bathing the space in a wan radiance. Sitting up and slipping from the table, it occurred to him that transiting no longer incurred any unpleasant after-effects whatsoever. In fact, the only sensation experienced felt like when he'd fallen asleep holding the Link.

Suddenly drawn into that recall, a trance-like state took hold, everything in the theatre faded to grey sepia and brain fog blocking detailed recollection of that moment abruptly lifted. As if viewing an old black-and-white movie, Craig relived that moment again, reclining in his chair and aware of drifting into sleep state. Stirred by a tickling in his closed hand, opening it to see the object changing from its solid state, liquefying to become mercurial and absorbing into the skin of his open palm.

Pseudo-daydream vanishing, Craig was back in the theatre but wanting to return to the vision, needing to know what had happened next. Frustratingly, access had been withdrawn, except now making absolute sense of that moment and dropping another part of the puzzle into place. Pushing this newly acquired recollection aside to centre on his more immediate objective of scouting about the room. Predictably, the silently glowing computer monitors drives had been logged out, each screen displaying an identical idyllic tropical beach scene. Touching the keyboards would no doubt bring up a password request, trying it all the same and met by an inevitable login prompt. Repeatedly stabbing the enter key in exasperation, he made a sour face at the uncooperative devices and gave up.

There wasn't much more to go on at the workstation: wireless mice and keyboards served each monitor, a heavily stained, empty coffee mug, stationery odds and ends and a hairband, fuzzily entangled with strands of dark and grey hair. Angling one of the monitors to cast its light across the room, he went over to the opposite wall; fitted out with base and wall storage units, a thick acrylic work surface topping the lower tier.

The units' carcasses had been made from a tough, commercial-grade composite board material and were fronted by sturdy, high-gloss white lacquered doors, all predictably locked. Pulling hard at the upper corner of a lower unit door, Craig managed to work his fingers in behind, attempting to force it open, but letting go after ineffectually grappling awhile. Looking around for something to use as a pry bar, a theatre trolley near the examination table rewarded him with a variety of options.

An array of gleaming stainless steel surgical implements, all precisely laid out on a white cotton sheet. Shuddering at the sight of these sawbones' stock in trade tools, simultaneously experiencing a sense of relief at not being subjected to their deployment. A tongue depressor was his first choice, but it felt flimsy, instead opting for a wickedly pointed pair of serrated shears.

Selecting the same stubborn cupboard door, he jammed the shears' tip in behind and heaved, popping it open with a loud crack. The broken locking mechanism flicked away, clattering noisily across the hard resin-coated floor. Regretting using brute force, Craig froze, listening for any alarm or sounds of running footsteps, but all remained quiet. Releasing a smell of new lacquer, the open cupboard turned out being empty, as was the next, giving up after forcing a third. Having drawn a blank with the workstation and finding the storage cupboards unused, all available avenues to search had been exhausted. Exasperated at striking out so soon, he tried the theatre's exit door, finding it secured by an electronic mechanism as anticipated; a validated key card would be required to disengage the lock.

Cursing under his breath and giving the handle an optimistic tug, to no avail. It was beginning to look very much like this had been a complete waste of time, until noticing an emergency break glass panel sited slightly above the card reader. Hitting this apparatus would unlock the door and simultaneously trigger the building's fire alarm system, likely stirring up a hornet's nest of activity. In the ensuing pandemonium, he might be able to slip through and explore other parts of the building unnoticed. On the other hand, late at night, the only building occupants would be security guards, who he didn't want to encounter. Nevertheless, it was essential to get an outdoor view of this place, a building or street name, anything to provide him the opportunity of identifying these people.

To hell with it, deciding to go for it and take the risk of bumping into guards on the way out, he was about to hit the button when something protruding from under the door caught his eye. Stooping to pull it free, he'd found a business card, maroon-fronted with a gold-embossed company mandala and the letters VHP in stylised script. Something about this logo seemed familiar, although unable to quite place where he'd seen it before. Flipping the card over and angling it to catch the monitor's light, a plain font read: *Doctor Ruben Govender – Principal Researcher*, nothing else, no phone numbers or email address, nonetheless something concrete and a quantifiable lead.

Slipping the card into his wallet, two options presented; think himself out of this place to another location or hit the break glass panel and try identifying the building. Reasoning that, if leaving right away and managing to get his hands on a computer, should an internet search of the card's scant details draw a blank, then he would have to return anyway. Conversely, if he struck the break glass panel and ran into trouble, he could mind jump away and would have lost nothing for taking the risk. Pulling the Glock from the rear of his jeans and habitually rechecking to see a round chambered, he stuffed the pistol inside his front waistband for an easier draw. Using a small metal hammer dangling on a chain, he smashed the glass, hearing the door latch disengage and a whooping siren at once begin sounding.

Gingerly pulling the door open revealed a passing corridor. Craig inhaled deeply and poked his head out, glancing both ways. To the right, a solid door was signed *Authorised Access Only* and blocked any view of what or who might be on the other side, not a good idea. Opposite, empty corridor stretched away, ending in a right-angle turn where a green-and-white escape arrow pointed the way out. Only one relatively safe choice, hooking left, he sprinted down the passageway, passing by several closed side doors; fully expecting one to be flung open and a burly security guard to leap out.

Halting a step before the turn, he furtively peeked around the corner and saw another door a few paces ahead, this one partially glazed with a tall vision panel. Its glazing would minimise line of sight to anyone on the other side, so he hugged the opposing wall and approached stealthily. Peering through the glass, his caution warranted when spotting two men casually sauntering away from him, both in black uniforms with *SECURITY* shoulder flashes.

Watching anxiously until they'd disappeared through yet another door, he followed, passing by an elevator. Regardless of the alarm's deafening racket, Craig found himself inadvertently moving slowly and treading softly, lest his footfalls be heard over the wailing din. Reaching the next door, also fitted with a vision panel, rewarded him with sight of a blank wall opposite.

The corridor apparently turned left at this point and the slender glass pane restricted his view of whatever might lie in that direction. Hinged away from him like the one before, opening it would be risky, as the guards might be just around the corner and notice the door move. With no alternative but to take this risk, he cracked it open a chink and pressed the side of his head hard up against an oak veneer, managing to steal a glimpse before quickly withdrawing and easing the door shut.

Roughly a dozen paces along the corridor, it opened out into an opulently chic, high-ceilinged entrance foyer, potentially heralding the final stretch of his escape route. Only one thing now stood between him and identifying this place, both guards seen before were in the foyer, talking with two more. Craig had noticed one wearing a brocade-adorned peaked hat, probably the guard's supervisor. Uncertain of his next move, imagination working overtime, it dawned on him that modern fire alarm systems usually have a master panel, indicating which sensor had triggered the alarm. This being the case, the surgical theatre would be identified, and the guard commander would probably dispatch at least one of his underlings to investigate, almost certainly coming Craig's way.

For a few heart-pounding seconds Craig procrastinated, considering doubling back to hide in a side room and wait until they had passed. Flustered, retracing his steps to find the first side door fitted with an ordinary keyed mechanism and locked, so too the next. Cursing himself when realising this frantic dithering to be time-wasting, he'd end up getting caught at this rate.

"Get a grip, dammit. Stop being stupid." Being so close to the exit, he decided to brazen it out.

With a gut-swirling sensation, mouth and throat suddenly turned dry as dust, he opened the door and calmly strolled through, angling straight towards the foursome.

"Hey guys, what's happening? Another false alarm?" he quipped, having absolutely no idea where this impromptu bluff came from.

All four started then relaxed, fooled by his casual approach. The supervisor appeared as if about to reply when Craig noticed, too late, all eyes collectively falling to his midriff, he'd neglected to pull his T-shirt over the Glock. Right away, the nearest guard began fiddling to disengage a press stud securing his own holstered sidearm. Recognising his mistake gave Craig a fractional edge, enough to draw and cover the group, just as the first guard managed to free his pistol.

"Hold up! Steady guys. No need for trouble. I'm leaving anyway."

Fighting an urge to run for the exit, he knew that would almost certainly be a fatal mistake.

Gradually edging towards where he'd seen the building's glass frontage, Craig risked a quick sideways glance, pinpointing a set of revolving glass doors and a pivoting delivery door midway between. So temptingly close. In this instant of distraction, guard supervisor man hoarsely whispered something to firearm-drawn guard, who vehemently shook his head. Unable to catch the words spoken, no need anyway, Craig guessed at the order given and obstinately disregarded. Overhead lights accentuated sweat forming on the man's forehead; he wasn't prepared to risk dying for minimum wage.

Keeping the Glock steadily trained on the watchmen, Craig paced backwards towards where he reckoned the single door ought to be. Reaching behind with one hand and touching glass, he shoved firmly, feeling it gave way and swing wide. Continuing to back up through the open door, detecting the presence of stairs out the corner of his eye. Briefly halting to menace the guards with the Glock, he spun around and ran. A firearm report boomed in that split second, instantly drowned out by a cascade of shattering glass, then a volley of shots from all four guards opening fire.

Craig had exited into a large parking area with space for at least a hundred cars, empty at this hour except for two marked security vans. Covering the stairs in one bound and veering left, he instinctively ducked at the salvo of gunfire. Blindly reaching over his shoulder at full stride to squeeze off three shots in quick succession, knowing this to be pointless but hoping to buy time. It worked, when all four guards bursting through the smashed door immediately dived to ground.

Not daring slow his sprint or look around, ignoring pounding heart and burning lungs, he desperately needed to put distance between him and them, as more shots rang out. When first turning to run, he'd caught sight of an illuminated overhead sign spanning the building's upper frontage but been too preoccupied to discern what it said. Unwilling to risk distracting himself a second time at the risk of taking a well-aimed slug, he would still need to identify the place. At that point, the best option was to find somewhere quiet and mind jump out of danger, coming back another time to check it out.

Perceiving where the driveway exit ought to lay, he sprinted headlong, paying scant regard to a landscape architect's skill in softening an otherwise utilitarian parking area. Tastefully fringed with ornamental shrub hedges and dwarf trees, the parking's perimeter was interspersed with ornate lighting bollards. Not quite as well lit, the entrance road's gradient gradually steepened and Craig's legs bore the brunt, feeling like in one of those nightmares, fleeing from something unseen and terrifying but seeming as if wading through waist-deep treacle. Coming from behind, the sound of vehicle doors slamming and engines roaring to life spurred him on; the guards had regained the upper hand.

Thankfully the entrance appeared and not a moment too soon, as headlights scythed the vegetation to his right side, glaring beams of photons probing for their prey. Up ahead, a lowered red and white vehicle boom guarded the property entrance, beyond which all formal landscaping and artificial illumination ended. Darkness offered the prospect of escape, and Craig dug deep, arms and legs pumping. The lead security van's headlights abruptly caught him squarely, also revealing a drop-off to one side.

Realising any attempt at outrunning the vehicles would be suicidal, he vaulted the boom and swerved blindly away from the road. Underfoot the ground fell steeply, and his eyes quickly adjusted to distinguish the facility's tall, razor wire-topped boundary fence on his left side. Directly ahead the partial moon had settled on the horizon, back-lighting indigenous veld to his right, open grassland interspersed with trees. Easy going downhill, he stuck to a hard-packed margin strip adjoining the security fence, until the valley bottom came into view, where moonlight reflected from a small stream. On the road, by now well behind, the guard team were out of their vans, raised voices affirming that he wasn't out of danger.

A little way ahead, a tight thicket of trees and brush out in the open would provide him with sanctuary, turning sharply to go for cover. Ploughing blindly through waist-deep grass, Craig had almost reached the grove when a loose stone underfoot threw him headlong. Landing hard and winded, lying motionless when the beam of a powerful handheld searchlight turned the grass flaxen gold around him. Shielding his eyes from this sudden brilliance, knowing with certainty that they would have spotted him, if not for stumbling. Hovering a few seconds, the torch beam moved away, its operator sweeping the veld.

Worming through tough stands of grass, Craig inched over the stony ground, hands burning from grazes received in the fall. Worryingly, his twisted ankle throbbed, hoping and praying it wasn't fractured, acutely aware this would be a handicap he couldn't afford to carry. Managing to keep hold of the Glock when falling, he was glad to have brought it along; being armed had extricated him from a very sticky situation back there. Crawling around a tree's wide bole to take refuge in the thicket, he got to his haunches and tested the injured ankle. Twinging somewhat, it took his weight; not broken, thank God. Carefully working himself deeper into the thickly grown copse, taking care not to snag projecting low-lying branches that might give away his position.

At the sound of hushed voices approaching, he froze; spotlight turned off, the nearing guards would be keenly alert to the slightest movement. Pressed tightly against an acacia's knotty trunk, Craig cautiously parted leafy eye-level twigs, wanting to know how close they were and get a heads-up if detecting his trail into the grove. Two men, adopting stalking postures and barely ten metres away; almost level with his position, neither appeared to have noticed the disturbed grass. Craig surmised the other two had stayed with the road, anticipating him ultimately looping around and intending to catch their quarry when emerging. Whatever the case, they were out of the picture and Craig watched as the nearby pair passed on by, way too close for comfort.

Frustrated at being unable to get a better look at the all-important building signage, he took comfort in the gamble of coming here not turning out a complete bust. Unsure what he'd expected to find in the surgical theatre, although anticipating at least unearthing something more substantial. While not much to go on, Govender's business card did provide a solid lead to follow up and hopefully learn more about VHP. Worst case, if drawing a blank, he would have to come back another time. Situated outside the building's landscaped perimeter, this spot provided an ideal and secluded location close to his objective with little risk of him being detected.

First and foremost, he needed somewhere to catch his breath; a bolthole with internet access, to enable researching Govender and VHP while also figuring out his next move. Before leaving the hot springs, Craig had thought this through, knowing where he might find such a place, and a solid ally. Despite having relatives, a few long-standing friends and acquaintances scattered throughout the country, only one person could be trusted and relied upon, no matter the circumstances. Memorising minute details of the thicket, he left that place.

CHAPTER 14

"He will win who knows when to fight, and when not to fight." – Sun Tzu

Unaware of Craig's own marital problems, Margie had phoned Craig, the day after being dumped by Paul; seeking solace and weeping bitterly about what had happened. Without any prior inkling, she'd returned home from a work assignment to discover her belongings packed into boxes on the front patio. Initially thinking they were being burgled, she went to go inside and challenge the thieves, then discovered her key no longer worked the lock.

While struggling with the door, Paul had opened it from inside, blocking her entry and getting straight to the point. Apparently, their relationship had run its course and was over. At first thinking this to be some kind of cruel joke, until realising he was serious and demanding an explanation. Paul wasn't interested in discussing his decision, prepared only to say that he'd met someone else and it was time to move on, slamming the door in her face.

Overwhelmed and beside herself, she'd left, returning later that evening with her brother to collect her things. Paul had been there, words predictably being exchanged between the men and tempers flaring, they'd ended up fighting in the front garden. A concerned neighbour must have called the police who turned up within minutes. To the seasoned cops, this was just another domestic dispute, sticking around only long enough for Margie to finish gathering her belongings and leave the premises. Accompanying Keith to his one-bedroom flat, where she'd slept on the sofa until managing to sort out another place to stay.

Marguerite Brooks, known to friends as Margie or Mags, worked as a freelance private investigator, marital infidelity cases ironically the cornerstone of her business. Inevitably paralleling the bitter satire of her profession with personal circumstances only rubbed more salt into the break-up's raw wound. A betrayal further compounded, when establishing that it was Craig's wife, Maria who had been carrying on with Paul behind their backs.

In a clinically businesslike manner, Margie then set out to pinpoint when their treachery had begun; determining this to be while working a case in Cape Town, and right after Craig's first return to Sierra Leone. Their mutual cuckolding initially drew Craig and Margie closer, paradoxically driving a subsequent wedge into their friendship. Neither blamed the other for their partner's deceit, this rift instead developing from the ache of painful memories evoked when in one another's company.

Like Craig, Margie had chosen to leave Joburg, relocating to Durban and staying with her older sister for a month. Thereafter, renting an apartment until re-establishing her business in the city. Putting the past behind her, she'd then bought a two-bedroom simplex in an outlying suburb. Craig had occasionally stayed over at Margie's place, while researching for his book at Durban University's library. It was during one of these stopovers that they'd managed to thrash out the past, burying the hurt and rekindling their friendship. Even so, other than occasionally chatting and catching up over the phone, it had been almost a year since last getting together.

Fast-forward to the here and now, standing across the road from Margie's place, a pang of conscience gnawed at Craig. Torn between needing help and the potential consequences of exposing Margie to the Russian and his sidekicks, intuition however assured Craig, he had no other alternative. In justification and to minimise the risk, he would stay just long enough to explain what had happened, use her laptop, then get the heck out. His next destination entirely hinged on whatever insight could be gained on VHP, but right at that moment had no inspiration whatsoever.

Presuming to jump directly inside Margie's home would never have occurred to Craig, instead choosing a spot in an adjacent pocket park. The trailing branches of a weeping willow growing there reached to the ground, casting an oasis of shadows that made for the ideal arrival site. Situated within a gated complex and guarded by a private security firm, Margie's understatedly smart, semi-detached unit lay behind a low-level brick wall, topped with hooped metal railings. By then well after midnight, other than widely interspersed streetlights, the entire neighbourhood slumbered in silent virtual darkness. All the same, not wanting to bump into a vigilant patrolling sentry, Craig stood listening and checking both ways along the road.

Emerging from cover to a neatly trimmed grass verge, he crossed the road, passing by Margie's parked Jeep to reach her garden gate. Quietly unlatching its mechanism to let himself through, then briskly covering a block-paved path, he bounded up two steps to the front door. Pushing the doorbell, a delicately melodic tone resonated within and set an alert dog barking a few doors away. Giving it a few moments, about to depress the button again, when the hallway light came on and an approaching figure became discernible through peacock-patterned stained glass. Slippered feet on carpet made a muffled swishing sound, then Margie's voice, throaty from sleep and carrying an edge of anxious annoyance.

"Do you know what the bloody time is? Who is it?"

That niggle of guilt returned. "I'm so sorry, Mags, it's me, Craig. I need your help."

At a solid clunk of the lock being released, the door pulled open.

Wearing lilac satin pyjamas and purple slippers, Margie appeared in the doorway, wide-eyed, her face framed by a mass of sleep-tousled, blonde hair.

"What the hell, Craig. What's happened?" she asked, taking a step back and tiptoeing to glance over his shoulder. "Come in. Where did you park?"

Seeing the panicked look on Margie's face, Craig stepped forwards to catch her hands in his.

"It's okay, I'm fine." Maintaining as calm a voice as he could muster, the look on her face confirmed his dishevelled appearance indicated otherwise. "Really, I'm alright, Mags. Just that there's something going on and I can't go home."

Her demeanour changed subtly and a faint, knowing smile crossed her face.

"Oh, I see. Who is she, and what've you gone and done?"

Shaking his head, Craig nodded towards the empty hallway behind her. "No, nothing like that. Anyone else here?"

He received a sarcastic look.

"No, only me. Come on in, I'll make us some coffee." Reaching past him to push the door shut, she turned and headed for the kitchen.

After filling the kettle and taking two mugs from a wall cupboard, placing them on the counter, she looked him up and down enquiringly.

"Go on, do tell. What's happening then, Craigy?" Self-consciously running her fingers through tangled hair before he could answer, she added, "Damn, I must look such a mess. But that's what you get, turning up uninvited at this time of night." Giggling self-consciously, she shrugged. "Oh well, whatever." Leaning across the breakfast bar, becoming serious. "Right, mister, speak to me."

His cue, except Craig didn't know where to start. Words and sentences forming seemed nonsensical and affectedly contrived; the whole story absolutely absurd. Perhaps it was better if he condensed everything into a few sentences, after all, the less Margie knew the safer she would be.

"I've, um… unintentionally got hold of something that these people want to get back. They've been chasing me around, even know where I live… which is the actual reason I can't go home," he ended, wanting to clarify any misunderstanding. Pointedly holding his gaze, Margie waited for him to continue, but here he floundered. "Er… The problem is I don't really understand what this thing I've got is all about. I can't explain it properly, everything about it's all too weird and you'll think I've lost my mind… Hell, I'd even begun wondering if I'd gone loco too, developed a brain tumour or something…"

Faltering and lost for words, worse still, all the while acutely aware that she knew him to be skirting the facts. Getting an exasperated look of frustration confirmed as much; he swallowed, mind racing, desperately trying to find the right avenue of approach. Fortunately for him, the boiling kettle's whistle provided a distraction. Purposefully pushing away from the breakfast bar, Margie turned her back on him, removing the lid of a crockery jar to extract a tin of instant coffee. Seizing on this, Craig changed the subject.

"Ah, come on, Mags. Tell me you're not still drinking that same disgusting stuff. What happened to the machine I got you last Christmas?"

Visibly stiffening, her response was unmistakably curt.

"Still in the box, Craig. I've been busy and haven't found the time to set it up," dismissively, spooning granules into each mug.

Filling them with still steaming water, she placed one at his elbow and gave him a frosty look.

"Don't try changing the subject, Craig. Stop waffling and just get to the nitty-gritty, for goodness' sake. If you want my help, then I need to know what's actually going on. And I mean everything."

Thrown by her forthrightness, Craig knew her to be correct, owing at least a suitable explanation.

So far, things weren't going to plan, best to spill the beans.

"Okay, but there's lots to tell and I mustn't stay here long, so I'm keeping it as short as possible."

While Margie settled herself on a stool opposite, Craig collected his thoughts and started from when he'd found the object.

Listening without interruption, Margie got up midway through to refill their mugs, holding her peace even when he'd finished. Absently reaching into a cupboard below the breakfast bar, she took out a first aid box, moving her stool around the counter to place it beside Craig's. Brow furrowed in concentration, she used saline solution swabs to clean grit and grime from the cuts on his hands. Craig knew his friend's reticent silence to be her way of processing and followed suit, out of respect, flinching when a stubborn piece of grit was picked out with a fingernail. Finishing up, she patted his knee.

"No need for dressings, its only grazes, but be a good boy and keep them clean. Stay there. I'll go get my laptop."

Slipping from the stool, she disappeared down the hallway, returning moments later with a black carry bag.

Setting up her laptop on the counter, Margie typed in a password, prompting Craig to extract Govender's business card from his wallet. The silence was however getting to him.

"So? You haven't said a word about what I've told you. D'you think I've lost it, gone mad?" he found himself blurting out, partly not wanting to hear the answer.

Swivelling on her stool, Margie took his hand and squeezed gently.

"Honestly Craigy, it does all sound like the ravings of a lunatic, or druggie, but you're neither. Now, if anyone else came here in the middle of the night with that same story, I'd write them off as a complete kook, but not you. It's confusing and a lot to take in, although yes, I believe everything you've told me."

A wave of relief flooded over Craig, not only for Margie's acceptance, also because of his own lingering niggling doubts.

Smiling sweetly, she motioned for the business card.

"Let me have that, your hands are all cut up. Besides, it'll be quicker if I do it, I've seen you tapping away at a keyboard like an arthritic snail," she teased.

Reaching over to take the card, she propped it against the screen and began typing prompts into a search engine, angling the laptop for Craig to see.

"There's a few hits for VHP, but only two here in this country. One's a polytechnic in the Western Cape, buuut… this one's more local," she exclaimed triumphantly, stabbing the touchpad to bring up the web page of Van Heerden Pharmaceutica.

A privately owned manufacturing and medical research facility, and according to an inset location map, around eighty kilometres distant. Established in 1953, VHP produced pharmaceutical medicines and other commercial products for both domestic and international customers. A panoramic photograph, appearing on a scrolling slide roll, made Craig choke on a sip of coffee. A glass-fronted office building, set behind a large car park that was fringed with trees and shrubs.

"That's it, that's the place!" he managed through a fit of coughing, overcome by sudden uncontrollable anger and swearing profusely. Then, remembering his company. "Sorry, Mags, but that's where those bastards had me locked up!"

Stoically ignoring his outburst, Margie continued flicking through the website tabs, occasionally muttering.

"Leeet's see then. History of the company, no not that. Awards, who cares? Board of directors, bingo!" Clicking, the touchpad brought up a collage of faces, and before he could interject, Margie jabbed a finger, pointing at one of only two women's photographs. "That's her, Rebecca, right?"

Evidently having changed her hair colour, since whenever the picture had been taken, there was no mistaking Rebecca's unsmiling countenance. Gazing haughtily at the camera, as though simultaneously catching a whiff of an unpleasant odour. Her full name Rebecca Hannah van Heerden, listed as the group sales and marketing director.

Biting his lip, Craig nodded.

"Yep, that's her, and these are the two from when the government bigwig showed up," pointing at an older woman and dowdy-looking man on the bottom row. "I don't recognise any of the others. No, wait a minute."

Scowling at the ensemble, his eyes settled on another, double taking to be certain, just as Margie spoke.

"This must be her father then," one long fingernail tapping on an isolated image, strategically larger and positioned at the top.

The name read, Bruno van Heerden, CEO.

"Yeah, it's got to be. I was out of it and couldn't get a good look, but I'm sure he's the same bloke who came in with Minister Radebe." Aside from sharing a surname, familial resemblances between Rebecca and her father were undeniably obvious.

Late middle-aged, the chief exec had greying hair, receding

at his temples but kept cropped short, and sported a neatly trimmed beard. A prominent indentation disfigured one side of his forehead, likely the result of serious injury, accentuated by an inverted V-shaped scar that ran from adjacent temple to a finger's width above his right eye. Notwithstanding other facial similarities, their eyes were an absolute give away, father and daughter sharing the same soul-piercing, glacial stare. Studying the man, Craig grunted.

"Most definitely Rebecca's dad. Like I said, didn't get a good look, but that's him for sure. Is there anything else? What about Govender?"

Leaning closer, his arm inadvertently pressed against Margie's smooth warmth, evoking a fleeting flash of recall.

First meeting in the lift of an apartment block where they'd once both lived, Margie had literally taken his breath away, except instantly deciding she was out of his league. A petite 5'1" with the lithe build of a gymnast, it was her eyes that held him transfixed. Holding to Shakespeare's adage of eyes being windows to the soul, hers the colour of Sri Lankan sapphires, told of a warm and intrinsically gentle soul.

Besides, she'd been seeing someone else then, nevertheless striking up a friendship and occasionally getting together in social groups. Some weekends were spent waterskiing and braai'ing [barbecuing] at the Vaal Dam or picnicking at outlying nature reserves. During these occasions, coming to know Margie as a friend, her face lit up whenever she laughed and Craig couldn't detach himself from the same feelings experienced when first meeting.

Fair-skinned and blessed with perfect oval facial symmetry, she had the cutest nose over a sensuously alluring mouth, undoubtedly the most gorgeous woman he'd ever known. In spite of repressing his true feelings, they shared the kind of relationship where the passage of weeks, or even months of not seeing one another never compromised the easiness of each other's company.

Not withdrawing from his touch, Margie glanced sideways, giving a slightly quizzical smile.

"Haven't found any references to your buddy, Govender yet, but we might still dig him up on social media. I'll have a look when I'm done here." Flicking between tabs, she suddenly exclaimed, "Hey, it's nearly half four, where does the time go?"

Realisation hit Craig hard; he'd been at Margie's place for almost four hours. Far too long! Already compromising her by being there in the first place, he should have left hours ago but one problem remained, having absolutely no idea where to go next. Sudden apprehension dried his mouth and without replying, hurried to the living room where approaching dawn's faintest grey tinge could be seen through a chink in the curtains. Parting them with a finger to glance out into an empty street, about to turn away when blue flickering on the white gable of a house diagonally opposite caught his eye.

Cautiously inching forwards, face pressed as close to the drapes as he dared, Craig peered slantwise up the street and cursed out loud, risking a quick look the other way. Sealing off the road at either end, cordons had been set up and behind one, a dozen or so paramilitary-looking figures were formed up next to armoured transports. It was only the frenetically blinking roof-mounted flashers of these vehicles that had given away their presence. Too late, they had caught up, this time employing silent pincer tactics.

There was no polite way of saying it, he'd screwed up and got Margie involved, now needing to deal with the situation before it got out of hand. From the streetlights' soft glow, Craig had also noticed the assembled military types all carrying assault rifles. Neatly lined up abreast, appearing as a highly trained and potentially ruthless special forces unit or police SWAT team, not the kind of partisans making up the Russian's mob. Taking another furtive look, just in time to see a group of six or seven suddenly peel off from behind the right-side cordon, coming directly for the house at a steady crouched trot. Leaving this scene to unfold, Craig raced back to the kitchen, finding it empty.

"Margie!" Fear lifted his tone, not sounding like his own voice.

"I'm here, Craigy. Don't come in, I'm getting dressed." Her reply came from up the hallway.

Disregarding personal modesty, he was going for the door when it opened. Margie emerged, hair hastily brushed back into a ponytail, she'd changed into a pair of trackpants and sweat top.

"Right, I'm decent," the beginnings of a cheeky grin, then from the look on his face, she realised something had gone amiss. "What?"

About to continue, Craig blustered, "They're here, blocked off the road and coming in. We've got to go now!"

Making no attempt to hide her alarm, Margie cried out, "Dammit! Just go, Craig, while you still can..."

Sharply cutting her off, "There's no way I'm leaving you here, you'll get hurt." Ignoring her anguished look and stepping forwards to enfold Margie with both arms. "I don't know if this is gonna work, but..."

A splintering crash of wood and breaking glass came from both ends of the house simultaneously; assault teams breaching the doors, they were seconds from being caught.

The onslaught's sudden violence distracted Craig a fraction, then two stun grenades detonated with concussive force.

CHAPTER 15

"Violence, even well intentioned,
always rebounds upon oneself" – Lao Tzu

Deep in thought, distractedly gazing at a polished chunk of tiger's eye purposed as a paperweight, Andre van Heerden hunched over the desk. Suddenly grunting, he chuckled softly, either at an amusingly abstract thought or personal memory. Waxed, dark kiaat heartwood panelling lined the walls of his study, alternately interspersed with bushveld-themed oil paintings and hunting trophies, shot over a span of many years. Directly opposite where he sat, strategically placed to serve as a poignant reminder of his own mortality, the unblinking glass eyes of a huge warthog boar's head belligerently stared back at him.

Pushing his padded suede chair backwards, wincing when getting up; the enduring consequence of an injury inflicted by the same warthog. Three years before, he and a friend had been on a week-long hunting safari in the aridly hot and inhospitable veld straddling the Limpopo River. Shortly after sunup on the second day, they'd been tracking a leopard's spoor when the warthog emerged from a thorn scrub spinney around a hundred metres ahead. Spotting the animal first, Van Heerden signalled and settled himself on a stubble grass knoll, taking aim through the open sights of his father's old Mauser. Seeing what was unfolding, his companion and their bearer both crouched silently to one knee.

Drawing a bead slightly behind the animal's fore-shoulder, Van Heerden slowly exhaled, but a bird's alarm call startled the warthog in the very instant of squeezing the rifle's hair trigger. The 7.65 mm round found its mark, although hadn't mortally wounded the wild pig. Squealing and kicking up a cloud of dust, it tore back into the dense thicket. Passing his rifle to their bearer, Van Heerden drew a .44 revolver and went after the injured animal, intent on ending its suffering. On reaching the brush line, the enraged beast burst from thick undergrowth, charging and knocking him to the ground. Weighing one and a half times as much as a man, the warthog was on him immediately, one razor-sharp tusk flaying open his right thigh to the bone. Tussling in fine grey sand, made red by their blood, he'd grappled with the maddened hog and eventually got off a shot, ending the attack but leaving him to carry its legacy for the rest of his life.

Reaching down to drawers occupying the lower quarter of a glass-fronted bookcase, he withdrew a thick roll of land survey drawings. Unfurling, then spreading them out on the desk, he set the tiger's eye on one end and a silver letter opener at the other. Poring over the old plans, done countless times before, using a finger to trace a convoluted red pencil-highlighted boundary, he grinned in self-satisfaction then straightened up. Acquisition of a final tract of land, completing the highlighted area, had not only tested his patience but also come at considerable personal expense, and a fair degree of bloodshed.

Comprised of four consolidated farms, the outline

represented an agricultural expanse of more than thirty thousand hectares: mostly suitable for crops and grazing land, elsewise forestry. Intending to feed an ever-growing population after the war, whilst also stimulating a flagging economy, the government had carved up vast expanses of tribal land and designated these areas for agriculture. Tens of thousands of traditional inhabitants were thereby disenfranchised and displaced into shanty towns, fomenting a groundswell of resentment towards the country's white rulers.

Around that time, the Ossewabrandwag had been absorbed into the ruling National Party which disillusioned Van Heerden, regarding this move as capitulation to an abhorrently toadying puppet government. Abandoning previous ambitions of pursuing a career in politics, he'd bought one of the four farms, although feeding the masses never formed part of his game plan.

Shortly before this newly assigned farmland became available, Van Heerden's wife had been diagnosed with an especially aggressive form of breast cancer. Wasting away over a period of three months, while in a morphine-induced sleep on a cold winter's night, Annalie mercifully slipped away into the afterlife.

Since remaining steadfastly at her bedside throughout the illness, Van Heerden had missed out on acquiring the farm incorporating the old mill's site. As a compromise, settling for the adjoining farm, even though knowing it to be of poor agricultural quality. Predominantly sloping ground that bordered a sheer drop-off into the adjacent krantz, its shallow soil overlaid sandstone bedrock. A patient and resourceful man, undeterred by this setback, Van Heerden was accustomed to ultimately getting what he wanted.

Before the owners of newly christened Old Mill Farm set about the process of building a farmhouse, he'd paid the Levins a visit at their current home in the backwoods town of Kranskop. Going there with the wholly honourable intention of making a generous offer to buy their land, this meeting had not gone well and sealed his future neighbour's fate. Manny Levin turned out being a taciturn and unconscionably rude little man, his far heftier wife, Martha, offensively abrupt and outspoken for a woman of that era.

Holding to established male-centric beliefs, Martha Levin's behaviour completely unbefitting of Van Heerden's views on matrimonial hierarchy. After cursorily hearing out his pitch and without thinking to gain her husband's approval, the woman had rebuffed Van Heerden and ushered him to door, while the emasculated husband resumed reading his newspaper. Smarting from the humiliation of such an outright and discourteous rejection, Van Heerden left, vowing he'd see to it they paid for such abject rudeness.

A self-made man, hell-bent on empire-building throughout his adult life, Van Heerden had never been encumbered by scruples. When shifting priorities to politics and selling out his stake in the security business to the other partners, he'd unilaterally awarded himself a golden handshake. Achieving this by orchestrating an armed hold-up of the bullion transport.

Their company used armoured vehicles when transporting gold ingots, smelted at the mine works, to Pretoria's Reserve Bank. It had been easy, too easy in fact, since knowing the timetables, routes taken and how many guards would be in escort. During the heist, one guard and two hijackers had been killed, ensuring Van Heerden kept a larger share of the spoils. Relentlessly driven by an obsessive desire for wealth, going on to increase his fortune during the war years by masterminding and operating a nationwide black marketeering enterprise.

Nearly a decade later, having amassed a considerable fortune from various illicit dealings, there was no real need for the farm to produce any income. Building a modest farmhouse, he ranched a token herd of cattle to fulfil obligations under the government's land ownership scheme. From his front porch, Van Heerden overlooked the Levins' gently rolling, lush grazing land and precisely aligned maize fields. If using a pair of binoculars, he could even see the old mill's valley rim.

Never able to shake memories indelibly acquired at the mill, it seemed to Van Heerden as though events taking place there had happened only yesterday. Starkest of these memories was overseeing the clearance and disposal of Stein and his men's bodies. Predictably enough, following a month's interlude, word had come of the Nazis dispatching a replacement research group. Two months to the day from when Van Heerden had walked among the dead bodies of Stein and his team, this fresh contingent arrived by U-boat.

Picking up where their predecessors had left off, tasked solely with recovering the craft's drive unit as a matter of utmost urgency. Due to this enforced haste, a mere two weeks passed before a second clear-up operation became necessary. On this occasion, the craft responded with greater violence, creating a truly harrowing aftermath that saw Van Heerden's men shovelling unidentifiably grizzly organic remnants into wheelbarrows. Quite what maliciously hellish force had shredded those unfortunate men remained a consideration on which Van Heerden preferred not to dwell.

German high command demanded answers, and a detailed plan from the Brotherhood, stipulating how subsequent teams would be protected from the craft's demons. In Van Heerden's estimation, the project's Nazi handlers were becoming suspicious of information relayed to Berlin. Consequently, Hans Merkel had been recalled to capture the second event's lurid scenes. Entering the basement, he fainted and despite Van Heerden's cajoling and eventual outright threats, refused to continue. Angrily snatching the man's camera away, Van Heerden went to the basement, snapping horrifically graphic photographs for dispatch to Himmler's office.

In a similar fashion to the first, Van Heerden had systematically pillaged the dead men's records, although this group's mission objective had been notably less refined, with nothing worthy of retention. Word of the fate befalling both research parties must have reached others working under Schauberger, and almost six months elapsed before the next team arrived. Acknowledging the foolishness of rushing the Sudafrika Projekt, this final group were allocated a three-month window in which to complete Stein's work and remove the propulsion unit.

Four heavily armed escorts had been hand-picked from within the elite 1st SS Panzer Division to accompany six scientists, all bar one visibly nervous; evidenced by strained, tight-lipped expressions and virtually no interpersonal communication. Clearly dispatched under duress, Van Heerden could only guess at the kind of intimidation measures employed to secure their compliance.

The only researcher seemingly unperturbed by the craft's reputation had been the project lead, a zealously fanatical tartar who instilled fear into his subordinates. An obnoxious bully, Doktor Walther Bruck perfectly fitted the model of archetypal genius and mad scientist, all rolled into a stocky bundle of volatile energy. To the man's credit, much like his earliest deceased predecessor, Bruck kept extensive notes and detailed diagrams, in a leather journal identical to Stein's.

Nearing the end of their three-month stint, seemingly making remarkable progress, Bruck and his team had been "taken" by the craft. A loose term, but the only plausible explanation because there'd been no mutilated bodies, not a single drop of blood or torn shreds of clothing to hint at what became of them. Purely consequent to Bruck's authoritarian temperament, and all the men's personal belongings remaining in their billet, were considerations of a mass desertion discounted. Regardless, an extensive manhunt had been ordered, more for the sake of appearances than in any real hope of ever finding them.

In consideration of previous events occurring at the mill, the conclusion was drawn that something far more puzzling and disturbing had taken place this time.

Taking advantage of the ensuing chaos, Bruck's journal and other paperwork were of course added to Van Heerden's collection. If he were ever to be caught and interrogated about the fates of all three research teams, Van Heerden would have freely admitted that the final group's disappearance had most rattled him. Without any mortal remains for the living to make sense of, something fundamentally insidious hung over their disappearance.

The Afrikaner culture, being inherently God-fearing, his own personal beliefs were inevitably deeply influenced by religion, even if sometimes questioning what appeared as inconsistencies in the doctrines on good and evil. A like-minded friend had once lent him a copy of The Book of Enoch, translated from ancient texts attributed to Noah's great-grandfather. Enoch's accounts of the Watchers, their interaction with God's children and an alternative Garden of Eden narrative had left an enduring impression.

Hitched to personal experiences with the craft, everything gelled; a divergent, albeit not religiously sanctifiable notion emerged, one in which other-worldly and ungodly forces must have been at play. At some point in the not-too-distant future, he would pooh-pooh these beliefs as nothing more than absurd overimagining's; after all, nothing would ever be allowed to interfere with grandiose plans in the making.

Shortly after Bruck and his team's evident demise, the war took a turn for the worse against Germany, starting with a crushing defeat at Stalin's hands on the Eastern Front during the severe Russian winter of 1941/42. Woes profoundly exacerbated by ever-escalating Western bombing raids, levelling the Fatherland's cities and crippling the armaments industry, beyond which point Berlin's priorities shifted exclusively towards plugging the failing dyke of Nazidom.

Out of dire necessity, Himmler postponed any further advancement of the Sudafrika Projekt, possibly indefinitely. Subsequently a permanent abandonment, when British and American forces stormed Normandy's beaches in 1944; a vengeful Soviet Bear ferociously tightening the noose. When Berlin eventually fell to this simultaneous onslaught, the victors rounded up, tried and executed as many surviving Nazi protagonists as could be cornered. Ironically, a purge that played right into Van Heerden's hands, since those in a position to exploit the craft's existence as a bargaining tool were amongst the numbers hanged, shot, or committing suicide. A few within the hierarchy did however manage to escape, fleeing Europe, along with many from the rank and file.

In May of 1945, Van Heerden had been ordered to raze the mill to ground level, thereby eradicating and sealing off all evidence of the craft's existence. The basement stairs were filled with rubble then concreted over, although not before the basement's adjoining wall had been strengthened and sealed against water ingress. The craft, thus safely entombed until a future Afrikaner-controlled nation gained the wherewithal to harness and develop its power. Years passed, a period of political changes and shifting power, during which Boet Meyer succumbed to a heart attack and others formerly associated with the OB were sidelined, an outcome ostensibly leaving the coast clear for Van Heerden to begin implementing his master scheme.

More time would pass before Van Heerden acquired Old Mill Farm; an eventual milestone, costing not only money and resources, but almost certainly the sanctity of his soul. After the Levins' refusal to sell, he'd hired an investigator to check out their backgrounds and, to his chagrin, their characters were scrupulously clean. Attending synagogue every week, paying their taxes in full and on time, they were even patrons of several benevolent foundations.

Frustrated at not achieving any leverage over his neighbours, Van Heerden paid local tribesmen to cut fences at night and drive out their cattle, spread herbicide on newly shooting crops, even setting fire to barns and outbuildings. Doggedly weathering this harassment, the Levins had simply restocked, replanted and rebuilt. Neither of the other adjoining landowners had been so pig-headedly stubborn, acquiescing and selling up to Van Heerden without hassle. Only the Levins resolutely stood in his way.

Most Saturdays, while the family were at worship, he would mount up and ride across their land, accompanied by two favourite hunting dogs. Making a beeline for the valley where the sawmill had once stood, he sought reassurance of the site enduring undisturbed. Sometimes finding the Levins' cattle grazing the slopes, on odd occasions a herd of antelope, although generally only birds and insects frequented the valley. Save for seasonal variations in flora, the place perpetuated, unchanged; Manny Levin seemingly having no intention of exploring or removing the mill floor.

That was, until a particular summer's day when Van Heerden saw that a headward section of vegetation had been stripped, the exposed soil scraped into an earthen embankment spanning the valley's width. The offending bulldozer sat parked atop this neatly graded levee and upstream the recently dammed river had already broken its banks, beginning to flood the surrounding land.

By sheer good fortune, the old mill's remnants hadn't been incorporated, the Levins' irrigation dam set further upriver, nevertheless demonstrating the little man's intention to exploit the valley. In Van Heerden's estimation they were parochial and insignificant people, if ever discovering the craft, wholly lacking the vision or means to conceptualise its worth. Time had come to act and reclaim what should rightly be his; in a sense, safeguarding those simple folk from having to deal with such a dilemma.

Martha Levin had borne Manny two children, the eldest

a surprisingly pretty daughter, around twenty at the time of first approaching the parents. Their son, a spotty teenager, had drawn the short straw, afflicted by his mother's heavy-set jowls and stout physique. Since then, the daughter had married and moved out, their son going off to college a few weeks before the dam incident. Van Heerden could never in good conscience have addressed the situation while both children lived at home, although these moral reservations didn't extend to the parents.

To solve the Levin problem, he'd enlisted the services of someone with the same military background as himself, knowing this individual to be capable of perpetrating any manner of outrageous acts for money.

Similarly encumbered by few principles, Rennie Haart had been one of Van Heerden's most staunchly loyal foot soldiers during the war years. Familiar with many such individuals, selecting Haart not just for the man's unreserved allegiance, rather knowing the man to have no family, a lone wolf. Resurrecting old network connections, it had been simple enough to locate Haart, working then as a welder on Durban harbour's dry dock. The man stayed at a men's hostel in Point Road, a seedier part of the city and notorious for its "ladies of the night". Arrested several times, on charges of assaulting prostitutes and for dealing in marijuana, the epitomal all-round unsavoury character. For all of these reasons, the ideal candidate to carry out Van Heerden's plan to deal with the Levins.

A few days after the dam incident, around mid-afternoon, Van Heerden parked his Mercedes opposite the harbour entrance and waited, easily picking out Haart from amongst other workers leaving at the end of their shift. Sauntering in groups, laughing and joking amongst themselves, Haart walked alone, head down, shunning their company. Beeping the car's horn, Van Heerden called him over and they spoke awhile, before going to a nearby working men's café for a meal and some beers.

There Van Heerden spelled out his offer, a simple arrangement; provided that Haart fulfilled his side of the deal, a cash payment equivalent to a year's wages would be forthcoming. Finishing his third beer, Haart calmly accepted without question or barter, and they left together. The contract would be fulfilled that same evening, Haart getting to stay in a vacant farmworker's cottage overnight, with Van Heerden driving him back to the city the next morning.

Their two-hour journey had been in silence, not in any way awkward, just that outside of a shared history there was little commonality between the two men. Arriving at the farm, everything ensuing went smoothly, just like their military operations of old. Shortly after sunset, Haart set off on foot with a 12-bore shotgun and pocketful of 00 buckshot shells, the firearm reported stolen by Van Heerden earlier the same day. Having gauged the lay of the land while still light, Haart chose a circuitous route, benefitting from thick vegetation that afforded good cover.

Unusually for farm folk, due to Martha suffering from allergies, the Levins didn't own any dogs which might have alerted them to his approach. Reaching their farmhouse, Haart furtively peered through each window in turn, until locating the man and woman seated at opposite ends of a dining table, eating an evening meal together. Picking his way around the house, stopping outside the kitchen to recheck that both barrels were loaded, he let himself in through the unlocked door.

Wearing soft-soled veldschoens and following strains of Handel playing on a gramophone, Haart crept silently to the dining room. The Levins had been completely oblivious to his presence, right up to the moment he kicked the ajar door open. Consequently, neither had time to react before both barrels fired in quick succession. Pellets from the first shot hit Manny squarely between the shoulder blades, punching a fist-sized hole that severed his spine and shredded the man's heart. Instantly dead, he slumped face first into his dinner plate, but Martha wasn't to be as fortunate. Traversing the gun from Manny to her, Haart snatched the trigger a fraction early, low and slightly off target.

Pea-sized balls of lead caught the table's edge, splintering dark veneer from a cheaper softwood base and only a few struck her in the belly. Stunned into staring at Haart in wide-eyed disbelief, she instinctively clutched at the wounds, lifting one reddened hand as if accusingly showing what he'd done. Realising this to be her end, Martha's mouth moved as if about to speak but having already reloaded, Haart raised the gun and fired again. Shot from both barrels struck Martha between the breasts, the impact flipping her, still in the chair, backwards to the floor.

To make the murders appear like an indiscriminately violent burglary, Haart then ransacked the place, taking anything of value and stuffing it into a suitcase taken from a wardrobe. Heading for the back door, case in one hand and shotgun in the other, military weapon's readiness training paid dividends when an unforeseen outcome arose. A short distance away at the workers kraal, the Levins' induna [headman] had gone outside to relieve himself and heard gunshots coming from the house. Arming himself with a panga [machete], he'd gone to investigate.

At the instant of stepping out onto the kitchen porch, Haart was confronted by the farmworker's swinging blade, instinctively ducking and simultaneously firing at point-blank range. Leaving the third casualty where he fell, Haart quickly slipped away into the night, retracing his same route back to Van Heerden's farm.

Waiting outside the worker's cottage, Van Heerden grinned broadly when seeing the man approaching.

"Any problems?"

Handing over the shotgun and coolly shaking his head, Haart replied.

"Nah, easy," looking up expectantly.

Pulling a thick fold of banknotes from an overcoat pocket,

Van Heerden handed over the agreed blood money.

Without counting, Haart stuffed the wad into a trouser pocket, while Van Heerden propped the shotgun against a wall and directed him to enter the cottage. The man's back turned, Van Heerden dropped a skinning knife from concealment up a coat sleeve into his hand. The first inkling Haart had of being set up was his hair being grabbed, head yanked backwards and the cold burn of a razor-sharp blade slitting his throat confirmed the deceit.

Strong and wiry for his size, Haart struggled fiercely, desperately trying to free himself, but Van Heerden maintained his advantage and forced the man to his knees. Holding on until the man's struggles gradually weakened and all flailing stopped, eventually becoming still. Pulling his limp body inside the cottage, Van Heerden kicked its ill-fitting door shut, a lit paraffin lamp guttering in the sudden draught.

He truly regretted killing Haart, since the man would in all probability have kept his mouth shut, however, the risk of him blabbing had been too great. Alcohol had a way of loosening men's lips and Haart, well known for his liking of strong liquor, also had a propensity for getting himself into trouble. Pulling off his long overcoat and draping it over Haart's corpse, Van Heerden held the lamp aloft, swaying it side to side while checking his own clothing and shoes for blood spatter. Satisfied at avoiding Haart's arterial spurting, returning to the farmhouse and resuming his birthday celebrations.

When the family had left in the morning, Van Heerden gave the cook and housekeeper the afternoon off, then dispatched all farmhands with a tractor and trailer to fetch firewood dropped off at the farm entrance. Thus, giving himself a clear window without interruption or witnesses to assume an odious task, disposing of Haart's body, shotgun and stolen items into a sludge pond behind the cattle sheds.

Later that afternoon the local police paid a visit, and he'd feigned shocked outrage when hearing of the Levins' murder. Knowing both officers on first-name terms, he invited them in and plied them with brandy before enquiring after the Levins' children. Evidently, they had been notified of their parent's deaths and would be coming out to Old Mill Farm the following morning. Just the opportunity Van Heerden needed, there to meet them, pay his respects and offer any assistance needed.

According to custom, the Levins were buried in the Jewish cemetery the very next day; naturally, Van Heerden attended, sombrely suited and wearing a borrowed yarmulke. Not wishing to appear so insensitive as discussing business immediately after the funeral, waiting the prescribed seven days before making his approach.

Neither sibling had any intention or desire to take on the farm, each asserting the intent of never returning to a place where their parents had been so senselessly killed. Lawyers concluded the deal swiftly, Van Heerden finally taking ownership of Old Mill Farm, along with the carefully preserved basement. Despite once agreeing with Boet Meyer that the craft should rightfully serve to enrich their volk, his own plans for its exploitation would be exclusively one-sided.

CHAPTER 16

"...to go look for a needle in a meadow." – *St. Thomas More*

Everything falling neatly into place, Van Heerden possessed the financial wherewithal to pick up where the Nazis had left off, yet a fundamental obstacle stood in his way. A stumbling block of which he'd been cognisant all the time and had worked behind the scenes to resolve, long before fixing the Levin problem.

The kind of expertise required to initiate and advance the project couldn't be engaged by placing an advert in the newspapers. Run-of-the-mill engineers simply wouldn't cut it; besides, he needed the kind of control that ensured perpetual discretion. Managing to track down Viktor Schauberger, he'd gone to Europe and met with the man, only to have his overtures flatly turned down. Imprisoned after the war, interrogated by American occupation forces and coerced into divulging his secrets, Schauberger had become disenchanted with humanity. Spirit broken by the time of his release, he retreated to retire in the forests of Austria, vowing never again to toil under the yoke of a master.

The man's outright rejection baffled Van Heerden, he'd made a generous offer, providing the ungrateful man an opportunity to crack the craft's enigmas and vindicate his life's work. Many working alongside Schauberger had been killed or captured, the latter spoken for and drafted into service of either the Americans or Russians. A third category however existed, those escaping and fleeing the country; these were the people Van Heerden intended finding. During his association with the Sudafrika Projekt, he'd engineered off-the-cuff conversations with researchers, learning the identities of key players. He also derived further references from the stolen paperwork, compiling a list of names. Cross-referencing this with information gleaned from contacts made in Germany, he struck off those confirmed as deceased or indentured. Ultimately left with the names of seven men, scarce and valuable individuals needing to be tracked down.

Locating persons having no desire of ever being found wasn't going to be an easy process, a hitch Van Heerden grasped only too well. However, by fortunate coincidence, he had another acquaintance with precisely that skill, a former Stormjaer intelligence officer by the name of Walter Manning. After the war, Manning had taken up a mid-level position at his father-in-law's Port Elizabeth-based insurance company. Catching a commercial flight there to meet with Manning, Van Heerden had been circumspect about his intentions, wanting to attract the man's interest before drawing him in.

Artfully concocting an intricately woven collage of intrigue, in a roundabout way disclosing the craft's existence as top-secret war project remnants. The man was interested after all, so he switched to full disclosure, laying it on the line; Manning's uniquely bloodhound-like abilities were required in finding specific people to progress the stalled research project. While selling insurance provided a steady pay cheque, Manning's lustreless career move provided no real job satisfaction, shaking Van Heerden's hand at the end of their meeting and flying out of Joburg a week later on a Viscount airliner bound for Buenos Aires.

It was no secret that many South American countries, predominantly Argentina, became relatively safe and welcoming havens for displaced Nazis. Taking advantage of "ratlines", they fled headlong from justice being meted out at the Nuremberg war trials; an exodus well known to Mossad, the CIA and KGB. The secret services of many foreign states were actively seeking to capture these fugitives, generally with intentions less altruistic than those of Van Heerden.

Travelling throughout Central and South America, Manning learned to tread wisely, developing his own network while amassing an ever-expanding dossier of information. Fluent in several languages, including Spanish, German and Hebrew, taking full advantage of this linguistic gift when integrating himself into the subcultures of both post-war fugitives and their hunters.

Meeting with one such associate at a cantina in the business district of Guadalajara, Mexico, he'd struck pay dirt for the price of a few Coronas. Introduced to a clerk from the city's police department payroll office, the woman claimed to know of a detective going by the alias Tino Rodriguez, whose true name topped Van Heerden's list. Manning had heard this line too many times to count and probed her story, coercing the woman into providing proof. Agreeing, she left the restaurant and returned a while later, sliding a grainy Xerox copy of a passport across the table.

Even though of poor quality, the photograph almost indistinguishable, there was no mistaking the eagle-and-swastika emblem part stamped over the man's image. An identical endorsement at the page's footer recorded the travel document as being issued to Manfred Wagner in Berlin, on October 16th of 1939. Retaining the sheet, he handed the woman a tight wad of US dollars and a slip of paper on which the name of his hotel had been written. The female clerk departed, leaving Manning inevitably wondering if he'd been artfully played.

Misgivings that grew until three days later, about to check out of the hotel, when the front desk Conserje passed him a handwritten note. Untidily scribbled in cursive script was the name of a nearby public park and the time 14:00, which he could only assume meant that same day. Situated within easy walking distance of the hotel, it turned out being a small urban oasis, surrounded on three sides by busy streets and bordering a nursery school on the other. Neatly cut grassed paths wound through equally well-kept beds planted with shrubs and flowering perennials, all afforded refuge from the hot afternoon sun by the spreading boughs of a massive jacaranda in full bloom. A confetti-like litter of the tree's lilac blossoms carpeted a cobbled area adjacent to the two busiest roads' junction. Here a semicircle of benches surrounded a fountain dedicated to a local saint.

Arriving a few minutes early, Manning took in the lay of the land and selected a bench, sweeping the fragrant flowers to the ground before taking a seat. Leaning back and tilting his trilby to shield against the sun's reflected glare, also permitting discreet scrutiny of passers-by. The bench he'd chosen angled in such a way as to give clear line of sight across the park and an unobstructed view of adjacent streets. A few minutes passed, when a marked police car pulled up at the nearest kerb, its uniformed driver sounded the horn, and a back-seat passenger waved to catch his attention.

Approaching the cruiser, unable to help but notice that the waving occupant bore a striking resemblance to Clark Gable. Without any pleasantries, in broken English the film star lookalike asked Manning for identification and what he wanted with Tino Rodriguez. After explaining that he represented a foreigner, wanting to do business with Rodriguez, the passenger climbed out and told Manning to get in. Something felt off but he complied anyway, discovering another passenger occupying the furthest space, too late to back out. This casually dressed individual, uncommunicative and reeking of body odour, sat with one hand concealed inside a cloth bag. It was immediately obvious to Manning what the bag disguised.

Sandwiched between both new acquaintances they drove off, heading south out of the city and into predominantly unpopulated countryside. The journey continued in silence, Manning's fears ramping up when they suddenly veered onto an unpaved side road. Dusty and rutted, the cart track wound up a gradually steepening hillside until rounding a sharp bend near the summit, where a lay-by appeared. Serving as a lookout point offering spectacular views over Lake Chapala, here a rusted cream Dodge pickup waited, parked facing their approach.

They pulled in nose to nose and while the dust settled, Clark Gable clambered out, the enforcer motioning for Manning to follow suit. The pickup's driver had similarly alighted and came sauntering over, a snub-nosed .38 casually hanging in one hand. Jet-black hair greying, deeply tanned and dressed in a handwoven, embroidered huipil shirt over pleated trousers and suspenders, the man looked every inch a local. No way could this be Manfred Wagner; the payroll clerk had duped him after all.

This had to be a set-up, and Manning began praying to his sorely neglected god. Stopping a few paces short, the armed Mexican brusquely identified himself as Tino Rodriguez and demanded that Manning state his business. Openly hostile, the man made no bones about being suspicious of the gringo's intentions, raising the revolver and thrusting its gaping muzzle in his face. Life hanging in the balance, Manning's heart nonetheless skipped a beat when detecting an unmistakably Germanic undertone to Rodriguez's accent.

Swallowing against a mouth and throat feeling as if packed

with talcum powder, Manning relayed Van Heerden's brief, referencing the Sudafrika Projekt. At this mention the mean edge left Rodriguez, hostility turning to curiosity, they talked awhile until he came clean and confirmed he was indeed Manfred Wagner. Not once though, did he express any interest in the recited proposal, instead asking for Van Heerden's contact details. Breathing a sigh of relief, Manning would later privately reflect on just how badly this encounter could have ended.

It transpired that Wagner had indeed been interested, for two key reasons: losing his actual identity to that of Rodriguez, more pressingly however, being fed up with constantly looking over his shoulder. The hunt for Nazi fugitives had escalated, with Soviet operatives recently arriving in Guadalajara and asking questions. If tipped off, as Manning had been, the KGB would doubtless take him without negotiation, probably to a bleak, off-grid research facility somewhere in the Siberian tundra or endless reaches of the taiga. A prospective outcome giving him sleepless nights, Mexico no longer a place of safe asylum and circumstantially appearing as if his chequered past may finally have caught up.

Manning's arrival had been a timely lifeline, South Africa a country largely off the radar of those seeking out proclaimed war criminals. A place he would never have considered before then, it now presented as an appealing alternative, a vast and largely untamed land with the prospect of disappearing for good.

On opposite sides of the equator and Atlantic Ocean, Manning's news served as a spark to ignite the next stage of Van Heerden's scheme. The catalyst to hire a contractor, tasking them with clearing out the old mill's basement stairs and building a concrete block structure that would secure the entrance. Enthused by this modest progress, he engaged an architectural practice, appointing them to draw up plans for a far grander facility. Not content at leaving it there, the design team were given the additional brief of detailing an imposing new farmhouse. Ever since Haart's visit, the Levins' modest home had stood empty, bearing silent witness to the depths of depravity to which he had stooped. An uncomfortable reminder, it had to go; all reference to that night must be permanently eradicated.

The deceased owners had however chosen its location well, sited on an elevated plain and offering a sweeping view over pretty much their entire original farm. Consequently, making for the best spot to build a more fitting replacement. Since not being privy to Van Heerden's insights, his builder couldn't understand the rationale in demolishing a perfectly sound and well-built house, nevertheless following the client's wishes to level the place. Gracing the front lawn, a pair of semi-mature, Natal mahogany trees were to be retained; intended to provide shade and natural gravitas to a future envisioned outdoor entertainment space.

Influenced by his early life in Lüderitz, the farmhouse would be built in classical Cape Dutch-style and feature an open-beamed thatched roof. Placing a personal stamp, Van Heerden then rechristened the consolidated farm Rooiessenhout, electing to name it with reference to the retained trees. Holding great admiration for Paul Kruger, like many of Dutch descent in that era, he'd toyed with the name Boekenhoutfontein, thinking to echo the Boer leader's own farm's name. Discounting this notion, considering some may deem it sycophantic, besides, his eventual choice more befitting to one following in the great man's footsteps.

The day after meeting Manning, Wagner had contacted Van Heerden, a month later leaving Mexico for South Africa. Landing at Durban's newly opened Louis Botha Airport, he was greeted by Van Heerden and taken to stay at Rooiessenhout. After breakfast the next morning, Wagner had been presented with the stolen documents; later in the day, saddling a pair of horses, they rode cross-country to the old mill site. Hooked by everything seen so far, that evening Wagner agreed to take on the project, subject to specific provisos. The first of which,

Manning must locate two former Mauthausen colleagues, who would be required to work alongside him.

In a covert facility, secreted within the concentration camp's industrialised killing machine, the trio had become more than mere colleagues and forged a bond of friendship. They escaped Germany together when the war ended, going to Panama where they made a pact to never disclose one another's identities and split up, thereafter following separate paths. Six years had elapsed since then, leaving Wagner clueless as to the other's whereabouts, whether remaining free men, or if even still alive.

Given no more than the pair's original aliases, Manning's best chance of picking up on this long-cold trail lay in Panama City, first heading south to meet with contacts in Casco Viejo. Here, he eventually came to learn that Alfonso Martinez, once known as Werner Krause, hadn't travelled far since arriving in the country. Living in a former fisherman's shack on a narrow peninsular of Chiriquí Lagoon's Bagui Island, Krause proved more hostile than Wagner when first approached.

It was July, the rainy season, and an especially sodden day when Manning hired a fisherman to take him in search of Krause's reclusive hideout. Being on an island and cut off from the mainland by around a kilometre of open water, the only mode of getting there was by boat. Manning's open hull charter reeked of spilled petrol and putrefying fish guts, a stomach-churning concoction slopping around his shoes. Set in a clearing and flanked by coconut palms, the clapboard shack turned out being as unkempt and decrepit looking as its heavily bearded inhabitant. Hearing the approaching outboard engine, his figure emerged to a lagoon-side porch, watching from the cover of its rusting corrugated iron overhang.

Once within hailing distance, Manning called out a greeting, getting no reaction until they pulled in alongside a projecting jetty. Galvanised into motion, Krause came hobbling along the wooden boardwalk, waving a machete and bellowing threats at these prospective intruders. Seemingly unperturbed, Manning's skipper gunned the engine, swinging the boat out into deeper water and putting distance between them and the deranged madman. Glad of the watery expanse separating them from an evidently unhinged Krause, Manning raised his voice to explain the purpose of their visit. An expletive-laden dismissal made it perfectly clear that no meaningful dialogue would be happening on that occasion.

Not put off by this rebuttal, hiring the same boat and skipper two days later, Manning returned to find Krause fishing from his jetty. A pair of freshly caught juvenile roosterfish hung by their gills from nails driven into a solitary sturdy post, midway along the dilapidated structure. Either worn down by Manning's persistence, or more likely tempted by a bottle of seco held out as a peace offering, the former Nazi allowed them to moor up. Accepting the sugarcane spirit and listening to Manning's pitch, Krause grew increasingly agitated, eventually asking him to leave and never return. The analogy of taking a horse to water crossed Manning's mind, giving up and returning to the mainland, although managing to leave Van Heerden's particulars with Krause. From his hotel room in Panama City, Manning sent word to his employer, detailing the blank drawn with Krause but softening the blow with information of a solid lead regarding the last man.

Leaving Central America to traverse the globe, Manning landed in Australia, spending a night in Adelaide before catching a single-engine plane into the hinterland. Touching down on a soft, sandy airstrip that served the outback settlement of Coober Pedy, he hitched a ride into the unimaginably hot and dusty mining town. Like many buildings there, the solitary hotel had been partially dug into the ground, a subterranean environment providing some moderation to summer's blistering heat and bitterly cold winter nights.

Like Wagner in Mexico, Hermann Maier had never been able to entirely settle in the Americas, travelling around itinerantly until upping sticks and shipping out to Australia. According to Manning's Panama contacts, he'd gone with the expressed intention of getting into the opal trade. A somewhat sketchy lead, with nothing to lose, Manning had thought to begin his search at the heart of the country's biggest mining region. Attending rough stone auctions held in the town, trekking to outlying claims and frequenting the bars, after three weeks, still no closer to finding Maier.

Washing the day's dust from his throat in a stale beer-perfumed tavern, he'd struck up conversation with a rheumy-eyed old soak. Over a few lagers, the old-timer recounted once doing business with a German stone dealer, broadly fitting Maier's description. This fella had worked the area a year or so back, until suddenly upping and leaving around the time news broke of a lucrative black opal strike at the more recent settlement of Andamooka. The old prospector's best guess being that Maier, or whoever he was, had followed the money and gone there. The following morning, Manning bribed passage on a supply plane, flying south-east to an even more desolately remote outpost.

Andamooka's airfield proved a misnomer, little more than a long-evaporated lakebed situated north of the ramshackle tent, wood and iron colony. At the pan's edge, waiting to collect provisions from the plane, the local trading post owner chattily explained to Manning that there weren't any hotels in those parts, although lodgings might be found at the town's solitary guest house. For helping the shopkeeper load fresh stock into the back of his desert-worn Holden ute, the trader gave Manning a ride into town.

On their way, the man didn't stop talking; a returning Anzac, he'd lived in Andamooka for five years and knew pretty much everyone who'd been there over that period. He did recall a German opal trader coming to the area a few months before, except the fella had gone by the name Fischer, not Maier. By an odd quirk of fate, Fischer had lodged at the guest house they were heading for, then came the bombshell. Pulling up outside the place, the merchant turned to Manning and finished his story, relating how Fischer had gone out to a claim a few weeks back, been bitten by an eastern brown snake and died.

Alone on the roadside outside his new digs, ankle deep in soft, pale sand, Manning's heart fell. He'd run slap bang into literally another dead end. Since already there in Andamooka, it made sense to stick around and find out whatever he could about the recently deceased. Ted and Betty, the guest house owners were warmly welcoming salt of the earth outback folk, coincidentally assigning him the same room Fischer had occupied. It had of course been serviced since, carpet swept and fresh linen on the bed, a sparsely furnished room with a comfortably homely ambience.

The dead man's belongings had been cleared and packed into a disused wooden tea chest, stored in an outbuilding. Under the pretence of being a displaced family friend of Fischer's, Manning talked Betty into showing him to the storage box, where hope returned. Opening the dead man's passport, its thumb-sized photograph depicted a dark-haired, slight and bespectacled Ernst Fischer, an image bearing no resemblance whatsoever to a snapshot in his possession of stocky, ginger-haired Maier.

Late that afternoon, Manning joined Ted on the back porch to enjoy the sunset and chat, while downing a few beers. The landlord became progressively more talkative with every drained bottle clattering into a metal bucket between their chairs. Taking advantage of the man's mounting insobriety, Manning steered their conversation around to Fischer, asking whether he'd mentioned other friends or associates living in Australia.

Ted appeared as if ignoring the question, entranced by the sun's shimmering orange disc sliding behind distant mullock heaps. Manning had been about to repeat himself, when Ted snapped out of his reverie; telling how, a few weeks before his death, Fischer had set off for Melbourne on business. Something to do with meeting a fellow Kraut in the city, he couldn't remember more than that, but Manning's sixth sense told him, he'd scored a direct hit. Staying in Andamooka until the supply plane returned, Manning departed the hurly-burly backwoods settlement, tempering growing excitement by reconciling that this could turn out being yet another wild goose chase.

Considered to be Australia's business and cultural capital, even in 1950, Melbourne was a big city and home to one and a half million people. Spending several weeks following one dead end after another, until late on a Tuesday afternoon when Lady Luck took pity on Manning. Lost in thought and at his wits' end, he'd crossed to the Yarra's west bank via a bridge not used before, finding himself in an unfamiliar neighbourhood. Figuring that cutting through a busy shopping quarter should come out in the general vicinity of his hotel, when something down a side street stopped him dead.

Across the road from an Oriental market, a jewellery store had caught his eye and, having nothing to lose, he crossed over. Just as reaching the place, so the proprietor came to the door, flipping a twine-hung sign to indicate the shop had closed for the day. Somewhere in his late fifties, a strongly built man, square-faced below a shock of cropped white hair that could once have been ginger. Despite years passing since the photo had been taken, the jeweller was instantly recognisable as Hermann Maier.

Expecting distrust and hostility on introducing himself, Manning was taken aback when Maier extended his hand in warm greeting. Ushering him inside and directing his visitor into a back-room workshop, all the while chattering away as though they were long-lost acquaintances. Pointing Manning to a pair of armchairs, he poured vodka into a couple of cordial glasses, handing one over and offering a cigar from a lapis lazuli-inlaid humidor. Politely declining, Manning took a sip of neat spirit while his host selected a slender cheroot, returning the cedar-wood box to its space on a wall shelf. Running the gnarly hand-rolled Colombian under his nose while inhaling deeply, Maier sneezed, excusing himself before lighting up with a chunky silver table lighter. Taking advantage of the man's distraction, Manning began telling of his travels through Southern and Central America, describing how he'd found Wagner and Krause, moving on to the period spent in Australia.

News of Ernst Fischer's death saddened Maier, having known the man, raising a toast and draining his glass before slumping back into the chair, absent-mindedly stroking its fabric armrest with his free hand. Staring up at the nicotine-stained ceiling, he took a long draw on the cigar and blew a succession of fragrant smoke-rings to enhance the once white paint's discolouration. Sighing nostalgically and dropping his gaze to Manning, he wanted to know more about Van Heerden's intentions for the craft. Disclosing what he knew, Manning could only reiterate his employer's proposal without embellishment, then sat studying Maier. The man, by that stage lost in contemplation, perhaps weighing up the offer's pros and cons.

More vodka had to be drunk, then half a small bottle of schnapps, culminating in both thoroughly soused men puffing on fat Cohiba's. Eventually, time came to bring their soiree to a close. The jeweller wanted to think things over, suggesting that Manning return in a week's time. Sensing an imminent brush-off, insisting on scribbling his city centre hotel's name and Van Heerden's information on the back of a cash receipt pad. The hour was late when Manning left the store, decidedly sozzled, and discovered it had begun raining; a steady drizzle that quickly soaked through his light day coat, sobering and chilling him to the bone.

Days ticked by without word from Maier and come Friday, Manning went to pay a visit, discovering the shop empty and locked. The next morning, when going downstairs to breakfast, a clearly nervous Maier waited for him in the lift lobby. At first unable to ascertain whether his jitters were due to anxiety or excitement, Manning invited the man to join him. Sat across from one another, eating in silence, until midway through a plate of scrambled eggs and devilled kidneys, Maier couldn't contain himself any longer and blurted; telling Manning how he'd contacted Van Heerden and spoken with Wagner. Getting this much off his chest, enthusiasm subsided, replaced by a wistfully pained expression. Turning to look out over Lonsdale Street, paying no heed to a steady stream of people hurrying to work, he continued, revealing a movingly sad tale.

When first arriving in the country, he'd gone to the White Cliff Opal Fields and made friends with several local miners, among them one called Pete, who had a sister, Janet. He'd fallen for her in a big way, romance quickly blossoming and not long into their relationship, Janet fell pregnant; doing the right thing by getting married, they rented a place in the town and set up home. Sadly, he'd then screwed it all up one day by going for a few drinks with Pete, before fetching his wife from work. "One for the road" had been his undoing, losing control on a bend and crashing into a blue gum at speed. Flung from the wreck, Janet was badly hurt and miscarried their baby boy at four months.

The parents had rightly laid the blame squarely on Maier's shoulders and in the following months, his and Janet's relationship spiralled into an ever-deepening well of acrimony, ending in divorce. Shaken to the core by the death of their unborn son and dissolution of his marriage, Maier had left town and gone on to Coober Pedy. Ironically finding good fortune and making a lot of money there, enough to leave the sweat and dust of the opal fields behind and move to Melbourne. Acquiring the shop, even ongoing financial success had done nothing to alleviate Maier's conscience, he simply couldn't move on from what had happened at White Cliff.

Desperate to close that dark chapter, Manning's appearance seemed to herald just such a prospect, then the motivation behind Maier's personal disclosure emerged. A month ago, at the time thinking it nothing more than pure fluke, he'd bumped into the former brother-in-law on a trip to Melbourne. A thoroughly laid-back character, Pete bore no animosity, and they'd stopped at a nearby watering hole for a drink and catch-up. When hearing all about Maier's shop, Pete had shown real interest and asked to see the business, taking a shine and asking for first option if Maier ever decided to sell up. With the premises' lease coming due for renewal, he'd gone to White Cliff the day before, where Pete had made an offer which Maier accepted.

Maier's solicitor had been instructed to draw up a deed of sale and once the paperwork had been endorsed and lodged, he intended leaving Australia to go work with Wagner.

CHAPTER 17

"A risk is a chance you take; if it fails you can recover. A gamble is a chance taken; if it fails, recovery is impossible." – Field Marshal Erwin Rommel

Losing track of time in the easy familiarity of Margie's company, lowering his guard and allowing the hours to fly past had been a careless mistake. An unforgiveable blunder, putting them both in mortal danger. In the heart-stopping moment of spotting the approaching SWAT team, all faux sense of unassailability had dispersed, any scant remnants shattered by the brutal force of their attack. In those frenzied moments, Craig kicked himself for neither being more vigilant, nor figuring out his next move, which by that stage had been far too late.

The assault had come quickly and with rehearsed precision, in the subsequent turmoil only able to envisage the most obscure of locations. Quite why his shock-addled mind had picked this spot, bemusement quickly fell by the wayside when rematerialising to find himself holding onto a dead weight. In the instant of the attack, he'd instinctively grabbed hold of Margie, and she'd clung to him just as fiercely but now flopped lifeless in his arms, like a rag doll. Desperately clutching her tightly, overwhelming waves of dread were amplified by this place's virtual darkness; the jump had surely killed her. What in God's name had he been thinking? He should have known better, she wasn't infused with the same unworldly stuff and hadn't stood a chance.

Without warning, Margie's body stiffened and arched rigidly against him, clenching hands painfully driving sharply manicured fingernails into his lats. Abruptly doubling over, she retched and coughed, gasping for air.

"You absolute asshole, Craig!" she wheezed, pulling herself up to glare at him, before dropping her face into his chest, body trembling.

Margie's vitriolic outburst, and the burning discomfort below his armpits, gave Craig all the reassurance he needed; she had survived their transference after all. The warming sensation of her breath on his chest an added comfort, tilting his head back to give silent thanks. Pulling her close, he leant forwards until resting his face in her hair. A fresh shampoo scent melded with Margie's unique body chemistry, creating a sensually beguiling fusion, reminiscent of baking biscuits and flowers on a warm summers' day. Sensing an unfamiliarity to their closeness, Margie let go and went to step back, her legs buckling and giving way.

Grabbing hold before she fell, Craig cautioned, "Whoa, steady, Mags. Give it a couple of minutes and you'll find your feet."

Without resisting, slipping both arms around his waist, she leant in and embraced the support.

In this enclosed and scantly lit space, the floor hard, uneven and gritty underfoot, their slightest movements echoed crisply. The air stale, holding onto a dry, distinctly sulphurous odour from explosives used to hew and blast the chamber from solid rock. The same place Craig had visualised a split second before stun grenades detonated, they'd ended up in an abandoned prospector's workings. Scarcely able to see well enough to move about but recalling the layout in detail, Craig guided Margie to sit on a protruding rock ledge. What little faint light permeated into the space, came from the tunnel's entrance which was obscured by the horizontal shaft's curvature. Illumination barely enough to see his own feet, yet sufficient to reassure Craig of nothing changing, nobody else had been there since last being in this place.

Sitting next to Margie on the ledge, he slipped a supportive arm around her shoulders.

"How are you doing, Mags?" It sounded lame, but he couldn't think of anything else to say right at that moment.

Nodding meekly, feeling along both arms and legs, she touched her face shakily, replying in a small voice, "I'm okay, I think."

Craig sympathised, remembering how disorientated and thrown he'd felt after the first time.

"That was freaky and horrible, Craig. I don't want to do that ever again," turning to look at him, her eyes expressive. "I mean it, never again. Okay?"

It probably wasn't the time to start explaining the absence of alternatives they would face, whenever needing to leave this place. Instead, he responded with what felt like a suitably placatory nod.

"Completely understood, Mags. I know how it feels, but it was the only way of getting you out of there. Those guys meant business, and I didn't want you getting hurt." When Margie dropped her gaze, Craig guessed her to be reliving those final moments at her place and changed the subject. "I experienced the same kind of after-effects the first time I, err… travelled, but honestly, it eases off when you've done it a few times," he said, doing his best to reassure, getting a sceptical look that confirmed she wasn't buying into his pep talk.

Shaking her head then looking around, she got up and took an unsteady step.

"So, where are we? What is this place?" looking at him enquiringly and reaching on tiptoes to touch the rock face's curvature.

Outside, an unseen sun had begun rising, steadily brightening and intensifying light levels in the chamber.

"Easiest to explain, is if I show you."

Getting up and guiding Margie into the tunnel, Craig explained how he'd come to know of this place.

Two and a half years before, he'd been contacted by a friend of a friend and partner in a Pilgrim's Rest-based mining conglomerate. Holding a gold prospecting license over a moderate-sized tract of land north of Tzaneen, they commissioned Craig to undertake a geological survey of the area. Their permit included a stretch of near vertical escarpment face, marking the transition between high and lowveld. Until then, they had been following promising traces of the metal in exposed quartz veins, only for these to repetitively peter out. Rather than risk throwing good money after bad, they wanted a professional assessment of the stake's mineralogical potential.

Craig had spent two weeks tracking the metal, taking and field-testing rock samples from accessible gold-bearing strata. Eventually identifying a spot showing good potential, the prospectors had blasted out this shaft and chamber. Ultimately, even this location had been determined commercially unviable, the prospectors' venture a route to likely bankruptcy. Disheartened, they had abandoned the pursuit and returned to mining the moderately paying reefs of Pilgrim's Rest.

Nearing the twenty-metre-long tunnel's opening, cloying mustiness steadily replaced by fresher air, Craig and Margie emerged to find day broken. Squinting against the sun's glare, they were greeted by the sight of a far-reaching canopy of indigenous mopane, bushwillow, wild fig and knob-thorn trees. Lushly verdant, subtropical vegetation stretched away, virtually unbroken, to where wilderness and farmland butted heads on the lowveld plains. From where they stood, any immediate view of the sky above was blocked by a projecting overhang, a wide canopy of weathered Archaean granite. Exposed roots of trees growing above dangled from its extensively oxidised, umber fringe, forming a ragged primeval curtain that imparted a sense of seclusion. Set halfway up the vertical back face of an expansive, open cave, the tunnel's mouth offered an unrestricted view across its rocky floor several metres below.

Out of sight, an unmistakable tinkling of falling water carried from somewhere beyond the cave's confines; a seasonal spring bubbling from the plateau above, then cascading over a sheer cliff face. A timber scaffold remained in place at the tunnel's mouth; it had been erected by the prospectors to access the rock face. Also abandoned when leaving the site, off to one side, an eight-berth caravan rested on the undulating and gradually sloping cave floor.

At the outset of their quest, the mining company used an old Land Rover to tow the thing up a convoluted and deeply rutted erosion channel. Proving too much for its ageing chassis, the caravan's fatigued support frame succumbed on one side and sheared. Undeterred, the hardy and resourceful miners had winched their mobile home the rest of the way, jacked its broken section up and stacked rocks below, inserting timber wedges to prop it level. Creature comforts secured, they got on with their day jobs, drilling and blasting out the tunnel. Dents in the roof and a shattered window bore testament to ejecta flung out by charges of ammonium nitrate gel, exploding deep within bores drilled into the ancient rock.

Coinciding with the planning stages of his Berg home, Craig's time spent here had been pretty much carefree, feeling more like an adventure holiday than paid work. Stiflingly hot days of intense exertion, hiking through thorny bush and rope climbing perilous rock faces had been rewarded by nightly barbecues. Known as braaivleis [meat roast], these feasts were washed down with as many chilled beers as he could handle. Working as a team during the days, at night everyone lounged in camp chairs arranged around a roaring wood fire, joking and sharing tales late into the night. Worn dog-tired from the daily slog but with a full belly and thoroughly inebriated, buoyed by good company, Craig would crawl into his sleeping bag to fall asleep the instant his head hit the pillow. The group's camaraderie and banter had been cathartic, a welcome interval from less convivial happenings still weighing on his mind, a reintroduction to the positive side of human interaction.

Momentarily absorbed into these memories, when a thought intruded, and Craig quickly stepped back inside the tunnel. Just possibly, he might be undetectable in this place, shielded from whatever tracking mechanisms the Russian's men were using. Hard, dense and high in mineral content, the overlying rock formation could block electromagnetic surveillance systems from pinpointing his position. If able to remain undetected, so long as sheltering in the tunnel, it would give them respite and the opportunity to plan, strategise and formulate a way out of this mess. Of course, only time would tell whether this notion held any merit.

Oblivious to his thoughts, Margie had wandered out onto the timber-boarded scaffold deck. Peering out over the edge, she asked.

"Hey, what's with the old caravan? Do you reckon someone might be living in the thing?" Even though the prospectors were long gone, the possibility of a homeless person taking advantage of the shelter provided hadn't occurred to Craig. "We'll find out soon enough."

Before he could answer, Margie picked up a fist-sized chunk of rock, tossing it to land on the caravan's roof with a loud *DOONK*, reverberating off the cave's planar surfaces. Dropping to her haunches, she peeked through gaps in the wooden boards, waiting to see if the din had roused anyone. Straightening, after what seemed like a suitable interlude, she leaned against the handrail, frowning.

"If anyone's in there, they'd have to be stone deaf. Yeah, looks to be deserted. Come on, let's go have a look-see, there could be some useful stuff in there."

Already starting towards the scaffold stairs, Craig called her back, explaining his theory.

Listening, she shrugged non-committally.

"Makes sense, I suppose. Okay, you stay here, and I'll go."

By now halfway down the stairs and too late for any further protestations, watching through board gaps, Craig followed her progress until disappearing behind the caravan.

From a squeaking noise, he knew her to be working the door handle. A muffled curse followed, then sounds of her yanking at the thing.

"Damned door's either locked or jammed shut."

Stepping back into view, she began scouting the floor, looking for something to use as a lever.

"Yeah, it was always awkward, from when the chassis got twisted," he quipped, by way of explanation. "Hey, Mags. Have a look behind that big rock in front of you. They kept toolboxes and other equipment over there; might've left something you can use."

Feeling a pang of guilt at Margie having to deal with the stubborn door, Craig reasoned it wiser to stay put.

Sure enough, from amongst a pile of clutter, Margie uncovered a long, bent screwdriver.

"Got something!"

Re-emerging and waving the thing triumphantly aloft, she disappeared again, resuming battle with the stuck door.

Mere seconds passed, when a splintering crack confirmed her success. Stepping back into line of sight long enough to give two thumbs up, she was about to enter the caravan when Craig called out.

"Hey, be careful. Look out for snakes!"

Making a contemptuous face, she was gone, the old caravan rocking unsteadily on its improvised supports, the wooden packing having dried out and shrunk in the cavern's perpetual drought.

An age seemed to pass, although probably only a few minutes, when the caravan ceased swaying and Craig began fretting.

"How are you getting on?" There was no answer.

Instead, Margie's head suddenly reappeared, gradually followed by the rest of her, evidently hauling something which turned out to be a mattress. Dragging it across the rocky floor and fighting it up the stairs, eventually dropping the thing on the landing to stand with hands on hips, panting from her exertion.

"If you're right about being out of sight here, we might end up staying a while." Pointing at the bed and wrinkling her nose, "This one smells but it's cleanest of them all, the others were absolutely disgusting. Oh, and forget about the pillows. Ugh!" feigning gagging, before continuing. "There's also a stack of folding chairs and other odds and ends. I'll get them when I've had a breather."

Grabbing hold of the mattress' corner, Craig began pulling it inside the tunnel and caught a whiff.

"Actually, think I'll leave this here a while, so it can air out."

With a "told you so" look, Margie turned to go.

Making two more trips, fetching a pair of camp chairs and lastly returning clutching a packing box labelled *Baked Beans*. Having eaten the canned pulses, with chopped fresh onion, tomatoes and chillies as an accompaniment to most braais,

Craig remembered only too well the effect they had on those sharing the caravan's confines. Repurposed, the box now held assorted items Margie had scavenged.

"Look."

Offering the box up for him to see, it held an unopened pack of candles, a half-used book of matches from an Italian restaurant, two unopened jars of brined franks, a folding knife with one broken blade and two empty, plastic cola bottles.

Clearly pleased at her haul, Margie laid the box down, taking out an empty bottle and tapping it for emphasis.

"I was thinking, if I rinsed these out at the waterfall and filled them, we'd have water. Do you think it's alright to drink without boiling?" She looked at him questioningly.

"It's the only water we drank when I was here with the prospectors. There's no settlements or farmland anywhere beyond the krantz above for miles, it's all wilderness reserve." Pausing, he couldn't stop himself from teasing, "Only thing to consider would be whether monkeys have been pooping in the stream."

Grimacing and shaking her head, Margie turned to go, not wanting him to see her smile but managing to get the final word, on her way down the stairs.

"That's disgusting, Craig, you men are such pigs. Speaking of which, the state of that caravan is revolting. I can't believe you, of all people, lived in that thing for two whole weeks. Now, make yourself useful and get this place organised."

Setting up the camp chairs while Margie was away, Craig placed them towards the timber platform's back edge, pausing to study this arrangement. On reflection, moving them further backwards, until flanking the tunnel's mouth. There was ample space to sit next to each other, while still leaving enough room to squeeze through into the shaft. It had been over an hour since their arrival, probably too early to gauge whether his invisibility idea held water. Unlike back at his house, in the car and again at the hot springs, where a sense of imminent peril had endured, he felt more at ease here, as if intuitively knowing they were safe. Only an element of conscious doubt endured, and he found himself muttering out loud.

"Please, just give me a break."

A faint sound from behind made him jump skittishly, spinning around.

Oblivious to her approach, Margie stood there, grinning at his startled look.

"Well, that's gratitude for you. Okay then, I'll go and leave you to it." A look of mock contrition crossed her face and Craig flushed, realising she'd overheard.

"No, no. Just thinking… I really hope I'm right about this place and we do get to catch a breather here."

Lowering herself into a camp chair, Margie offered him one of the filled bottles.

"You go first. I drank some at the waterfall. Tastes fine."

Cool, fresh water, Craig drank deeply before returning the bottle.

"It's good. Doesn't taste of monkey poop either."

Rolling her eyes, Margie took a swig, then stretched her legs out.

"Right, so we've got to figure something out. You got any ideas?"

Easing into the adjacent chair, its metal frame squeaked in protest when Craig leant back.

"Dunno. It's all been one crazy muddle after another. Honestly, Mags, I really need to clear my head before I can even begin to think straight. We'll figure something out, not right away though."

Distracted, incapable of appreciating the beauty of their plains' subtropical view, they sat in silence until a dark look crossed Craig's face.

"I should never have come to your place; this is far too dangerous for you to be involved. You saw what they're capable of. Those guys were well armed and meant business. I don't want you getting hurt, Mags, so best if I take you somewhere safe. What about your mom's place?"

Knowing his intentions to be honourable, Craig's voice took on an edge of urgency, wanting Margie to get the severity of this situation. Besides, he would never be able to forgive himself if she got hurt.

Margie leant forwards while he spoke, absent-mindedly picking sparkling, pea-sized granite crystals from the sandy floor to gather a palmful. Rolling them crunchingly between both hands awhile, she dropped them and leant back, grimacing.

"Okay, now listen to me, Craig. You need to understand that I'm perfectly capable of looking after myself, so I'm not going anywhere. Alright? You came asking for my help and that's exactly what you're getting, until this whole nonsense has been sorted. You're not ditching me that easily, mister."

From a sharpness to her voice, Craig knew there was no sense in arguing the point right then, he'd deal with it differently another time.

In truth, Margie certainly could take care of herself. A softly feminine demeanour belied years spent training in a jiu-jitsu dojo, a highly technical martial art, which she had proven herself proficiently capable of deploying. When still married to Maria, Craig and Margie had met up for coffee and a catch-up at a Joburg shopping mall, an ordinary and uneventful social occasion, until time came to leave. Out in the mall's open car park, Craig got to his 4x4 first and got in, watching Margie head for her vehicle when two wannabe hijackers emerged from behind a stationary minibus. They immediately confronted her; one threatening with a long-bladed knife and grabbing for her handbag, while the other thrust a handgun in her face.

Before Craig could move a muscle, Margie had the pistol out of the second man's hand, dropping him with a short punch to the larynx and roundhouse kicking the other, right at the sweet spot of his jaw. Stood over them, covering both with the stripped away Czech-made pistol, Margie had been coolly nonchalant by the time a rattled Craig reached the scene. Neither would-be mugger made any attempt to get up until mall security guards arrived, dragged them to their feet and marched both away to a custody office.

Despite Margie's jiu-jitsu prowess, Craig still didn't feel comfortable exposing her to the wholly evident risk of being anywhere near him. Stalemate, glaring at each other, eventually he sighed and turned away. She could be infuriatingly stubborn, and any further debate would only end in a blazing row. A simpler solution presented itself; whenever back in civilisation and in a place of relative safety, he would simply jump away, leaving Margie behind. Annoyingly, an interfering counter-thought told him this wasn't the best way of dealing with the situation, she would never forgive him. Oh, whatever! He'd rather incur Margie's displeasure than see her get injured, or worse.

Staring unseeingly at the scenery, a maelstrom of thoughts and emotions whirled in his head. How could life take such a freakish and disturbingly weird turn? One minute enjoying an idyllic life of tranquil solitude, in the next taken prisoner and now a fugitive. The hell with it, he had to do right by Margie, might as well have it out in the here and now. First off, adopting tact.

"Look, Mags, I honestly can't see this ending well. These people are well resourced and won't give up until getting what they want. Even assuming I'm right about being off the radar in this place, we can't stay here forever. Somewhere along the way, we're going to make a slip-up and that's when they'll get us. If you're with me when that happens, they'll take you too, but since you're…" Hesitating, struggling to find the right words before continuing. "You've got no intrinsic worth to them; it's only me they want. What d'you think they might do with you?"

Leaving this question hanging, staring at Margie imploringly, desperate for her to see reason.

"Okay, think about it another way, Craigy. Alone, you're a sitting duck. You've got to sleep sometime and that's when they'll get you, but together we can watch each other's backs until figuring out a solution. Besides, where would I go? Think about it, if I went home and tried carrying on as normal, d'you think they'd leave me be? Hell no, as far as they're concerned, I probably know too much for their liking, and they'd take me out anyway. We've got to stick together; it's the only way we'll get through this alive."

Nodding begrudgingly, her argument giving Craig a completely different perspective, an uncomfortable awakening.

"Dammit!" was all he could manage.

Leaning back in the chair to scowl frustratedly at the rocky soffit overhead. Reaching across, Margie patted his knee.

"Hey, listen, I've got an idea. It's a bit out there but still worth considering. So, I got to meet the *Daily Star*'s editor when I went to their Christmas party last year, and I'm pretty sure he'll remember me." Stifling a frown at memories of the event, she continued. "If we went to see the bloke and got your story into print, the Van Heerden's people would have to back off. If it was all handled right, public interest would make it very difficult for them to carry on like they have up to now."

Margie had no intention of telling Craig the reason behind being certain of the newspaperman remembering her; events that would only make things awkward, possibly even messing up a meeting of the two men. Margie's sister and her husband had an ink supply deal with the paper and, with Eddie out of the country, Kim had asked Margie to go along as her plus-one. Mike Winter had been drunk by the time they were introduced, thereafter zoning in on her; making progressively more inappropriate and salacious advances as the evening wore on. Purely out of deference to her sister and brother-in-law's business deal, she had politely fended the man off, as opposed to handling the situation in a more vigorous manner.

Managing a smile, Craig agreed. Margie's suggestion held a ring of promise but, remembering the newspaper building sitting slap bang in the busiest part of the city, he expressed reservations.

"It's a good thought, but hopping into the city centre during the day would draw the kind of attention we don't need."

Unmissable due to its gigantic, revolving rooftop logo of a red star crossed by a quill pen and supported in a semicircular cradle, the paper's motif bore a striking resemblance to the Soviet crest.

Back in the mid '70s, when the tabloid first went to print, this emblem had caused uproar, exacerbated by the publication's liberal editorial leanings. The paper's offices had accordingly been the target of many and frequent raids by the Bureau of State Security, seeing suspect journalists and the incumbent editor whisked off for questioning.

"It's not in the metro centre anymore, they moved out to that new business park opposite the wildlife sanctuary several years ago." At his blank expression, Margie expanded. "You remember when we found that sick mongoose, the time we went hiking in Burman Bush?"

At this prompt, recall flooded back. Usually a pack animal, they'd come across the cat-sized predator alone, deep in a remote part of the nature reserve. Clearly sick and consequently abandoned by its group, they bundled the fiercely hissing and scratching animal into a backpack, returned to Craig's pickup and took it to the sanctuary. Both duty vets had been busy when they got there and while hanging around in the car park waiting to be seen, they had discovered an overgrown trail. Killing time by exploring the path, finding that it led to the Umgeni Riverbank, opening out into a grassed area where a memorialised bench overlooked the water. A heavily laden guava tree grew at the clearing's far end and, since the place was deserted, they'd sat eating the ripe fruits.

Evidently seldom frequented, it would be an ideal spot to go, and only a short walk from there to the newspaper building. Smiling at the memory, Craig nodded.

"Yeah, I remember now. Best of all, the mongoose survived and got rewilded."

Emerging from his murk of pessimism, sensing a glimmer of hope.

One downside remained, being that if the story did make the news, he'd inevitably become an object of interest to mainstream science and the general masses. An intensely private person, this outcome appalled Craig, the thought of being likened to a proverbial fairground freak and spotlighted for ghoulish public entertainment. Nevertheless, an outcome infinitely preferable to a life of relentless pursuit, hunted like a prey animal. Events of the previous day's suddenly caught up with him, feeling utterly exhausted and it must have showed, when Margie poked at his knee.

"Hey you. Help me haul the mattress inside. I'll keep lookout while you get a couple of hours' shut eye."

Craig wasn't about to argue, they'd been there a few hours and still no sign of the Russian and his men. Maybe the cave really had become their safe place.

"Thanks, Mags, that sounds good. Only a couple of hours though, then wake me, unless of course anything else happens," he quipped, mouth set in a humourless grin. "We'll go see your editor chappie afterwards."

Pulling a candle from its wax paper packaging, Craig lit the wick, cupping the flame with one hand while making his way along the tunnel. Locating a crevice on the chamber's rock ledge, he wedged the taper and returned to help Margie with the mattress. Kicking away loose stones, they laid the mattress out on a semi-level section, while the candle's flickering flame cast monstrously distorted shadows of their moving outlines on the chamber's walls. Slipping the Glock from his waistband and handing it to Margie, she took it without question, heading off into the tunnel.

Left alone, Craig flopped backwards onto the mattress, prompting the release of a renewed pungency of intensely stale odour. Some of the springs had gone, overall a foul-smelling and irregularly lumpy bed, but none of these qualities bothered Craig in the slightest. Within seconds, gone, into a deep and dreamless sleep, well before Margie had even reached the tunnel mouth.

Weirdly, feeling as though he'd just shut his eyes, Margie's voice intruded.

"Come on, mister. Wakey-wakey. Time to get up."

Sleep befuddled, for a moment imagining himself to be staying over in Margie's spare bedroom and being woken with a morning coffee, until stark reality returned. The candle long since burned out, Margie carried a fresh one, face illuminated in its soft glow as she leant close.

"Mmm. Everything okay? What's the time?"

Voice hoarse from sleeping with his mouth open, Craig's tongue felt like a dry wad of thickly folded rags. Seeing a look of alarm flit across his face, Margie was quick to reassure.

"Everything's fine, all quiet out there. It's gone five, so you've been out for around seven hours."

Rubbing his face, Craig sat up.

"Ah, heck. Sorry, Mags. I was completely shattered, but did say only a couple of hours..."

Crossing her legs to sit on the mattress next to him, cutting in.

"Yeah, well you obviously needed it, and in the meantime nothing's happened. No harm, no foul, huh?"

Yawning aloud and stretching, Craig felt rested and refreshed.

"Okay, good. Looks like there might be something to my theory after all. I must be obscured by the rock here, otherwise they'd have been crawling all over this place by now." There was no smugness to his observation, only a sense of relief. They'd found a safe den. "Only problem though, it's too late to go see your editor friend now."

Stiffening and not quite catching herself in time, Margie retorted, "He's not my friend." Coming out way too brusquely. Realising the gaffe, she attempted a cover-up. "He might still be there, the presses do run through the night, but it's probably better to stay here overnight and go in the morning. What I mean is, if we went now and those people turned up, they'd have the advantage of darkness."

A sensible counter, since the outside cavern and this tunnel were easily defensible. Even if Govender's thugs had managed to get a fix on Craig's location, it would be him and Margie holding the upper hand. The slightest movements in the thick bush surrounding their cave would make noise, giving away the stealthiest approach and providing ample time for them to escape. Craig's mind eased, a more basic human need leaping to the fore.

"I'm starving, what about you? Let's check out those franks you found. Hopefully they're still good to eat."

Chuckling, Margie teasingly poked his stomach.

"You'll never change, Craigy. Here we are in the middle of God knows what, and you're thinking about your belly."

"Hey, even in war, soldiers still have to eat," he returned, scrambling to his feet and pulling Margie to hers.

Dropping into a chair, Craig leant forward and fished both jars from the box, squinting at each label in turn.

"They're a few months out of date but probably still okay, if we cook them. You collect some dry wood, and I'll make a fire."

Keeping watch, as Margie scavenged the treeline and cave

floor, it didn't take long to collect as much as she could carry. Handfuls of dead grass tufts made for ideal tinder and bone-dry lengths of dead tree roots served as kindling, while chunky scaffold board offcuts provided a primary solid fuel. Fire going, they roasted a whole jar of sausages on skewers, fashioned from sticks by Margie, using the broken penknife.

Satiated by the meal, they sat talking about everything and nothing, anything but their present situation. A few hours after sunset, time came for Margie's turn on the mattress. Craig was glad of the stack of firewood, in part for warmth but mostly because of the glow it reflected from the rock overhang. Casting sufficient diffuse illumination around the cave to give away any uninvited visitors, it served as an early warning system. Comfortably settled to hold sway over a panoramic view of cave floor, out as far as the treeline's perimeter, he relaxed into the camp chair.

Hours passed, with only the sounds of nocturnal wildlife providing distraction: crickets chirping in the undergrowth were accompanied by the *ping-ping-ping* echolocation of insectivorous bats, occasionally darting close to snatch moths drawn by the fire's glow. A little after midnight, an animal wailing in the darkness startled Craig from the brink of slumber; either defending its territory and warning off an intruder, or prey caught by a stealthier predator.

Despite freshly heightened senses, Craig's mind soon began wandering. Margie's strategy sounded good in principle and provided perhaps the only way of extricating themselves from this nightmare. On the other hand, it contained potential pitfalls; this editor bloke could quite conceivably dismiss Craig's tale out of hand, as the babblings of a delusional and attention-seeking fool. Hell, if not having personal insight to the backstory, a total stranger giving him the same account... More so, the risk of going into a public place; in a matter of hours, an entire special forces team had mobilised and pounced on Margie's place in an outlying suburb. Where they were going, on the city's immediate outskirts, would likely be a lot closer to where a SWAT team or police station existed.

All the same, sitting around here doing nothing wasn't a sustainable option, nor did it address the root of their problem. Similarly, Craig didn't intend spending the rest of his life jumping from one location to another, purely to avoid being captured. For no apparent reason, Govender suddenly intruded into his thought processes. Strangely enough, seeming that the man bore Craig no personal malice, just happening to be part of his day job. Although party to Craig's abduction and confinement, the mantis was basically your textbook scientist; a bumbling and disconnected oddball, whose dealings with Craig were purely academic, albeit of a darkly macabre nature.

Yet another swooping bat interrupted Craig's musings, checking his wristwatch and startled at seeing the time approaching half four in the morning. Wide awake, sleeping during the day had thrown his body clock completely out of sync. Opting to leave Margie to sleep but deciding to check in on her, he lit a candle and started into the tunnel. Treading carefully, so as not to startle her awake, suddenly recoiling at a ghostly, pale shape looming from the inky blackness.

"I need to go pee. What's the time?"

It was Margie, feeling her way along the rock wall, and despite last-second realisation, prickles on the back of his neck persisted.

She chuckled throatily. "Sorry, didn't mean to make you jump, Craigy."

Caught completely off guard, he did his best to front it out.

"It's half four and the ladies' room's that way," pointing exaggeratedly, attempting to disguise his embarrassment with humour.

Waiting until Margie had disappeared down the steps, Craig

returned to the fire's smouldering embers, stacking more wood on the coals. By the time she returned, crackling bright orange flames had begun licking hungrily at the fresh fuel.

"Good morning, sunshine." Managing a cheery grin, she flopped into the other chair, pointing towards a grey band outlining the horizon. "It's nearly daybreak, why didn't you wake me?"

Busy lifting an escaped piece of wood back onto the fire, using Margie's screwdriver, he shrugged.

"I kinda lost track of time." A white lie. "Besides, I wasn't feeling tired and you also needed to rest. You sleep okay?"

Leaning back, she stretched her legs out and scowled.

"Eh, not the best night's sleep, that mattress really stinks and it's lumpy." Frowning at the memory, then announcing, "Breakfast and coffee would be nice, please."

Holding up the second jar of franks, Craig offered a rueful look.

"Breakfast I can just about manage, but I'm afraid we're out of coffee. As I remember, it wasn't me who organised the catering."

Sticking out her tongue, she made a face.

"Ugh, no thanks, not for breakfast. Maybe later. It's too early and I'm not hungry anyway."

Sitting together, they watched the stars withdraw into a sky gradually rinsed in blue. A sombre mood settled, each contemplating the uncertainty of this new day's prospects. Craig eventually broke the silence.

"Any idea what time the paper's office opens?"

Stirred from her own internalising, Margie sat forwards.

"Hmm, not sure. I'd guess probably either eight or nine."

Craig mulled over this snippet, then recalled Margie's reaction from the night before, wanting context.

"What's his name, your editor fellow?"

Curiously, a twinge of jealousy tugged at that part of his

psyche, believed long since buried.

"His name's Mike, Mike Winter, and the only time I've ever met him was at that Christmas party," picking up on a subtle undertone to his question and not taking the bait. "Apparently he's been with the paper his entire working life, started out as a compositor and worked his way up the ladder, as they say," smoothly, deflecting the line of conversation away from where she suspected Craig to be heading.

"Ah, right. So, what's he like then?" he wasn't letting go so easily but genuinely also wanted to gain a mental image of the man.

"He's a total jackass, Craig, if that's what you want to know." There was no point in beating around the bush anymore and Margie got straight to the point. "Married with kids, and yes, he did try hitting on me at the party, drunk as a lord and just couldn't help himself. Kim says he's like that with all the woman who work there too, but he's extremely good at his job and gets away with it."

There, out in the open, and the look on Craig's face confirmed this was what he'd been angling at. Finding Craig so easy to read, she could tell that more unasked questions lingered. Pausing to allow the first revelation to sink in, she went on.

"Mike's in his early, maybe mid-forties, sharp as a razor and apparently very switched-on, workwise. Got a bit of money and likes showing it off, being one of the boys. He's basically your average, middle-aged, waning alpha male type."

"Aha," Craig managed in response, still absorbing Margie's disclosure and not much liking an evolving image of the man. "So why didn't you kick his arse?"

Giving him a terse look, she finally put everything into perspective.

"Believe me, he was pretty darned close to getting a slap, but Kim and Eddie's business supplies all their printing ink, along with other materials. Need I say more?"

Realising the time had come to stop picking at that particular scab, Craig changed the subject.

"Right then, let's leave at around half nine to go see him. That way, by then everyone working there should be busy and out of the way. It'd be a kicker though, if he's out at a meeting or away on holiday…" They had no way of knowing the man's whereabouts, one way or the other.

This prospect hadn't occurred to Margie.

"I could call Kim to get his number, if I had my phone. You got yours?" Craig shook his head.

"No, didn't bring it along. Besides, it would be a bad idea, either of us having a phone. They could probably listen in to calls and use the GPS locator to track us. Believe me, they'll know everything about you by now, and almost certainly be monitoring our phones."

Staring wide-eyed, Margie frowned.

"Oh, I hadn't thought of that. Well, we'll just have to hope that he's there, we don't really have any other choice."

Craig raised his eyebrow's, nodding resignedly; Margie was correct, there were currently no other options available to them. A case of roll the dice and take your chances.

Seeming as though time had slowed, waiting for their planned departure slot, the minutes ticked by at an agonising crawl. Clearing the treeline, the sun chased shadows across the cavern, ultimately bathing them in its warmth. Around the same time an excitedly chattering troop of foraging vervet monkeys appeared in the treetops below. A pair of hornbills eating wild figs were scared away by the primates' noisy arrival, immediately claiming the tree and gorging themselves on its ripe fruit. A ceaseless commotion of screeching and tussling ensued amongst those seeking to claim the best branches. Serving as a distraction to what lay ahead, Craig and Margie watched until the vervet's had eaten their fill and settled down; the adults sedately grooming one another and their infants, leaving adolescents to play amongst the canopies. Eventually, after what had seemed like an extended eternity, the minute hand of Craig's watch reached the allotted time, and they got up.

Margie had been doing her utmost to conceal a steadily growing sense of trepidation at the prospect of jumping again, although Craig had seen straight through her.

"It's going to be fine, Mags. You came through alright the first time. Trust me, today will be better."

Trying to settle her anxiety, despite having absolutely no idea how this Link thing worked, a nagging doubt nevertheless gnawed at the back of Craig's skull. A flashcard doubt had presented itself yesterday, in the instant of grabbing hold of Margie, half-expecting to arrive here alone and Margie left behind to deal with the SWAT team. What would happen a second time? He had no way of knowing.

Exaggeratedly rolling her eyes, stepping forwards and reaching into his embrace, Margie's steady gaze held no fear, rather something far more complex.

Since reconciling the repercussions of their break-ups, an unquantifiably subtle shift in their friendship had begun taking root. Initially embryonic, a swing neither dared voice for fear of spoiling what they already shared. It might have been yesterday's perilous experience serving as the spark, kindling in each a realisation of mortal existence's impermanence and the folly of wasting opportunity. Whatever the source, a new and brighter flame had begun to ignite. Reaching up in the same moment as he leant forwards, they kissed fleetingly. Sighing softly, Margie leant against Craig in a moment of closeness, each enjoying this new intimacy. After a while, Craig spoke, voicing what they already knew.

"Mags, with what's that's going on, it's just not the right time."

She nodded; taking that next step now could serve to distract, even impair a crucial split-second decision in whatever lay ahead.

From his vantage point high in a knob-thorn tree, the bull monkey had spotted them, barking a warning and glaring at the humans. About to repeat the call when he stopped, mouth agape in an unmistakably simian expression of disbelief at witnessing what unfolded in the cave.

CHAPTER 18

"Chance rules our lives, and the future is all unknown. Best live as we may, from day to day." – Sophocles

Construction progressed to schedule, despite costs spiralling beyond all original budgets, over-expenditure however not constituting a pressing concern to Van Heerden. Time posed the biggest significant factor, an aspect others involved in the build had come to understand only too well. A habitual early riser, Van Heerden would arrive on site every morning shortly after sunrise, much to his contractor's vexation. With no alternative but to accept such an imposed degree of client's participation, the builder never suspected this attentiveness as masking a more clandestine investment. Throughout the entire process, Van Heerden retained an obsessive paranoia of the workmen inadvertently stumbling upon the hidden basement.

Rebuilding the sawmill or anything remotely agricultural had never entered his mind, the structure instead serving to facilitate a joint venture between him and his son. Oscar owned an ever-expanding and highly successful pharmaceutical manufacturing business. Operating out of leased premises on the outskirts of the nearby capital, in a way falling victim to his own success when the business outgrew this facility's capacity. Rental rates and taxes on bigger commercial properties around the city were exorbitant, an obvious solution presenting itself; a modern, purpose-built, state-of-the-art factory to suit both their needs. Logistically, Oscar's operation required more space than his father's, an ideal compromise then, since essentially serving as a cover to Van Heerden's enterprise.

At the age of fifty-nine, despite having the physical strength and endurance of most men half his age, lately finding himself ever more acutely aware of his own mortality. Grown from a seedling concept, fulfilment of the project had taken far longer in bringing to fruition than initially anticipated, fortunately blessed with the means to comfortably absorb these delays. Now that the specialised expertise required to realise this vision had been secured, his patience began waning. If the project weren't completed in his lifetime, then everything else achieved along the way would be for naught.

Scarcely a month after Maier's arrival from Australia, Van Heerden received a telegram from Colombia, sent by Werner Krause. Cryptically worded but essentially stating that due to changing circumstances, he'd reconsidered and wished to join Wagner. Sure enough, a few days later the man placed a reverse-charge call to the farm, asking to be collected from the airport. Coming without luggage and wearing only the clothes on his back, over dinner with Van Heerden and the other two, disclosing how he'd been forced to flee Panama.

Friendly local fishermen had tipped him off to Mossad agents combing the archipelago, specifically searching for him. A concern potentially corroborated the following morning while sat on his porch, seeing strangers passing by the island in an unfamiliar boat. It would be only a matter of time before someone pointed the finger his way.

Krause went on to relate the tale of his flight from Panama. Not owning a boat himself or entirely trusting the fishermen in not delivering him to the Israeli intelligence service for bounty had put him at a disadvantage. At dusk, he'd sealed a forged passport and what money and valuables he had in a small waterproof bag, securing this package around his neck with string. Swimming with the current to reach mainland, he then negotiated perilous mangrove quicksand's until reaching solid ground. Several days were spent trekking through mosquito-infested coastal reed marshes and tropical bush, bartering or buying food from settlements en route. Severely dehydrated by the time he reached Chiriquí Grande, there paying an unknown fisherman to ferry him to Colón, where he'd stowed away on a freighter bound for Cartagena. The price of a single air ticket to South Africa exceeded what money he had left, sleeping in a park while labouring to earn the difference.

Having three employees as resident house guests wasn't in keeping with Van Heerden's custom, relocating himself to Rooiessenhout's practically complete new farmhouse. The researchers would remain and live in his original home; a new cook and housekeeper employed, seeing to their daily needs. An adjacent barn was converted into an office and workshop for interim use, until the basement facility became fully operational.

Despite both undertakings operating from the same building, each would be kept scrupulously independent of the other; Oscar must never be exposed to any risks, occasioned by association with his father's affairs. Two separate entrances were accordingly created, strategically sited on opposite sides and levels of the facility: staff, deliveries and the like, never to mingle. Oscar's pharmaceutical business occupied the upper section and was accessed via the main façade, thereby taking front of house. Conversely, the research facility lay around back, where entry through a gated and fenced off section of the valley could be strictly controlled.

Inevitably, Van Heerden had to bring Oscar into his confidence, disclosing the craft's existence and his intentions. At first incredulous, thinking the old man to have taken leave of his senses; doubts concerning his father's sanity, greatly amplified when shown the craft first-hand. Paradoxically, identical misgivings that would return to haunt Oscar in years to come.

Functioning like a complex Swiss clock, everything clicking into place, until an unforeseeably tragic event almost brought the project to a dead halt. It happened after breakfast on a Sunday morning, during a weekend family gathering at Rooiessenhout. They had stayed the night and would return home after lunch, but before that, Van Heerden wanted to take his grandson on a tour of the farm. No better way than on horseback, first saddling his bay Boerperd, then a pony given to Oscar's eldest son, Bruno on his eighth birthday.

Riding out to the property's southern perimeter, the pair stopped awhile at the Mvoti River gorge rim, taking in spectacular views from the kloof. From that angle, the snaking river was only sporadically visible through flanking indigenous forest, ducking in and out of sight on its course. Moving on, they hugged the sheer canyon edge before changing course and veering towards where the older man would show Bruno the nearly completed laboratory. Predictably, the rambling structure's significance had been lost on the youngster, his grandfather hoping though that memories of this day might influence the boy's future decisions.

Midday approaching, they turned towards the farmhouse and young Bruno challenged a race, pitting pony and youthfully burgeoning horsemanship against the more experienced pair. Cantering madly across open veld, Van Heerden allowed the youngster to take the lead, following close on his heels. A large, flattened boulder stood in their path, when nearing a stand of acacia trees; atop this, a forest cobra sunning itself suddenly reared up, spreading its hood. Bruno's pony spooked, throwing him headlong against the boulder, to crumple well within the snake's striking distance. The boy lay deathly still, in a way serving as a blessing when the highly venomous cobra stood its ground.

Frantically dismounting, Van Heerden picked up rocks, throwing them to drive off the snake and going to Bruno's aid. Turning the boy over, he immediately feared the worst when seeing his face plastered red, a gaping forehead wound oozing thickly dark blood. It wasn't so much the blood that alarmed him, rather how significantly the boy's skull had been crushed by the savage impact. The farmhouse in sight, he gently lifted the badly injured child, cradling his head between shoulder and chin, then ran the rest of the way.

Refusing to relinquish hold of the boy while climbing into the back seat of Oscar's car, they had raced to Greys Hospital in the city. Bruno was admitted straight away and taken into surgery, however not before doctors cautioned the family to prepare for the worst. Utterly distraught, weeping uncontrollably and blaming himself entirely, Van Heerden lamented ever getting that accursed pony. Besides which, he should have known better than to take up the boy's challenge. This must be God's divine judgement, punishment for past sins; the gold heist, stealing the journals, the Levins' assassination and Haart's murder, everything defiled and surely damned by his own sinful acts.

No longer especially religious, although still a believer, Van Heerden went to the hospital chapel and implored the Almighty to spare his grandson's life. If it were His will, then Van Heerden would willingly exchange his own untimely demise against Oscar's survival. Five hours later, a grave-faced surgeon emerged from the theatre, informing the family that everything possible had been done and only time would tell. All accessible foreign objects and bone splinters had been removed from Bruno's braincase, but it was impossible to be certain of having removed every minute foreign body.

Over the days, weeks and months that followed, any fragments left behind could migrate into the brain, causing either sudden death or a bleed that might render the boy a mental invalid. Subsidence of localised brain tissue oedema and other associated trauma, together with the body's capacity to heal itself, would determine the eventual outcome.

Refusing to leave the hospital, Van Heerden chose to remain in the waiting room until days later, when the matron permitted him a chair at Bruno's bedside. Motionless and in a deep coma, fragile body nourished by tubes passed through his mouth, a ventilator providing artificial breath; days and weeks passed, with no sign of improvement. Until one evening, exhausted from his vigil and teetering on the verge of sleep, when Bruno's voice roused Van Heerden.

Disoriented, at first thinking it had to be another of the many dreams bedevilling his fitful stolen naps. Some had been of happier times spent with Bruno; hunting, camping and telling far-fetched stories by the fireside, late into the night. Others were terrifying nightmares, one ominously recurrent, where Van Heerden stood alone in a cemetery in pouring rain, staring down at Bruno's small coffin resting in an open grave.

"Oupa, wake up. Oupa! Oupa!"

Bruno's voice ever more insistent, Van Heerden rubbed at his eyes, needing to be certain of being awake. Then joyful realisation, Bruno had awoken.

The family's elation would be tempered by the surgeon's further warnings; although Bruno had regained conscious, a relapse could happen at any time, too soon for celebrations. Despite these cautions, Van Heerden's intuition whispered that his prayers had been answered, and Bruno would make a full recovery. Seeming also portentous, a divine indication that the project had His blessings.

After a further week's observation, Bruno's speech and mental reasoning appeared normal, subsequent X-rays coming back clear and allowing for the boy's discharge. Over the coming year, more surgical procedures were required; including a metal plate screwed into his skull, covering a gaping hole remaining in the frontal bone. In time, the only discernible evidence of Bruno's accident, a wide V-shaped scar over a subtly sunken section of his forehead. Otherwise, Bruno continued to develop as a normal child should, except never again riding a horse.

Earlier contrition fallen by the wayside, Van Heerden threw himself headlong into the project, rationalising this terrible event to have been a test of his resolve. The pharmaceutical laboratory had been completed and Oscar put the place into full production, generating much-needed revenue. All contractors had left site, signifying to Van Heerden that time had come to regain access into the basement. Undeterred by a saturating drizzle, he led Wagner and the others into a freshly painted workshop, where the temporary block structure had stood. At the lower basement lobby, they took turns, using a sledgehammer to smash through the bricked-up doorway.

Fired up by anticipation and adrenaline, they quickly broke through, exposing the long-hidden door. The men's excitement was palpable, probably not unlike that of Carter's team when first broaching Tutankhamun's tomb. Knocking down final pieces of precariously hanging loose masonry, they practically fought one another to get at the uncovered door. After more than ten years interment, rusted hinges creaked in loud protest when swung, their flashlights immediately piercing the gloom. Other than a fine layer of dust settled on every surface, the scene remained unaltered, just as Van Heerden remembered.

Whooping like big kids, Van Heerden allowed the three scientists to rush ahead but held back, either since already knowing what was there, or from reluctance at all too lurid memories of experiences in that place. Playing his torch over the craft's sweeping form, it wasn't his imagination; like on the day when seeing Stein's men dead, the craft exuded a menacing presence, as if recognising him without fondness. Like a wholly unexpected slap across the face, flashbacks to past events replayed in his mind. Rocked by an overwhelmingly unaccustomed sense of guilt, unable to shrug this feeling and quailing momentarily; he recalled the prayer, his deal done with God, instilling definite awareness that he would not see the project's completion.

In the ensuing weeks, Wagner's team spent days cleaning, scrupulously removing dust and grime accumulated during the basement's quarantine. The electrical system needed upgrading and they installed an automated hoist to facilitate installation of new hi-tech equipment. In the spring of 1953, the day after Van Heerden's sixtieth birthday, a final coat of fresh paint signalled the basement's refurbishment as complete. Wagner and the others could dedicate themselves to studying the craft, probing and verifying Stein and Bruck's records, then delve deeper into the craft's secrets. Unrelenting, the very same obstacle stymieing their predecessors' progress stood firm, the lower deck entry hatch refused to budge.

A few weeks down the line, Wagner and Krause were busy configuring a recently installed piece of equipment on the basement floor, while Maier worked inside the craft. Assigned the task of determining correlations between the consoles' etched runes, he worked alone. Intrigued by two separate "yin and yang" lookalike icons, he touched each simultaneously and experienced a tingling sensation surging through his fingertips. A soft hiss from behind startled him, turning around to see the hitherto unresponsive floor panel disengage, drop fractionally and slide into a concealed recess. Acutely aware of stories about the craft's fickle propensity for killing meddlers, he stood rooted to the spot, fixated on the hatch while shouting for the others to come.

First on deck, Wagner took one look at the open hatch. Instructing the others to leave well alone, he took off, running to the farmhouse. Bursting into Van Heerden's study, out of breath and unable to speak coherently, simply gesturing for their employer to follow. Carrying the mantle of Provincial Farmers Association chairman, Van Heerden had been writing a letter to the Minister of Agriculture; indicative progress of this task, a waste bin brimming with crumpled and blotted folio pages. Wagner's evident agitation stalled his pen in mid stroke, needing little encouragement to abandon yet another half-written draft and go after the man.

Reaching the basement together, finding Maier and Krause had plucked up the courage to crouch on all fours and were peering suspiciously into the opening. Hastily scrambling to their feet, making way for Van Heerden and Wagner, then all four men stood staring into the aperture. Big enough for a man to easily climb through, to Van Heerden this breakthrough seemed otherwise altogether anticlimactic, until noticing the space wasn't completely dark. An unseen source down there emitted only a low-level of luminescence, making it difficult to discern features of whatever might be there. Getting to his knees and leaning forwards, Van Heerden strained to identify the light's origins, however the flight deck's floor make-up obscured whatever it might be, eventually giving up.

"Well, what are you waiting for? Let's get down there and see what you've found."

Unable to contain himself any longer, this could turn out being the single biggest breakthrough since the craft's discovery. Nervously glancing from one to another, none of the researchers were prepared to make the first move, until Wagner found his voice and sent Maier to fetch a ladder. Lowering a set of wooden steps through the opening, all three reverted to pillars of stone, inert and uncommunicative. Making no effort to conceal his contempt at their spinelessness, Van Heerden pushed Krause aside and grasped the ladder's rail, stepping onto a deck-level rung and descending.

Head drawn level with the upper deck, he ducked to look around, eyes growing accustomed to the lower ambient light levels. At heart, a man of the open veld's relative predictability, nothing could have prepared him for what he beheld, things beyond even his most fanciful imaginings. Around the deck's outer circumference, a continuous waist-high console mimicked that on the upper level; suspended in mid-air above its surface, a wafer-thin sheet of blue-white light. Punctuating this radiant layer were a proliferation of intricately differing and ethereally translucent forms, many static, while others continuously shapeshifted.

Mind blown, Van Heerden shakily negotiated the final rungs, to begin cautiously circumnavigating this unworldly spectacle. Feeling somewhat like an unarmed man encountering a beast of prey, so engaged with the holographic array that he jumped when his shoulder struck a solid object. It was the ladder, realising he had completed an entire circuit. Turning to look inwards, the weirdest spectacle of all came last. Wider than a man's outstretched arms and occupying the deck's centre, filled with luminously glowing liquid, a clear circular column rose from floor level to meet the deck above's underside. Suspended at eye level inside this cylinder, a shape moved ever so slightly, making the hairs on the back of his neck stand on end.

Whatever it might be, Van Heerden suddenly became aware that this thing had been monitoring him since entering the level, observing his every move made. Then realisation broke, this was the same presence felt on the day they broke into the basement, also years before, when finding Stein's lifeless team. Heart pounding, his legs moved of their own accord, powerless to resist being summoned to meet the entity.

His nose a mere hand's width from the transparent column, looking in and seeing a roughly spherical, cyan-coloured mass the size of basketball. Striated by deeply riven clefts, rhythmically pulsating in time to flaring waves of incandescent blue and red streamers, erupting from its surface like solar prominences. A gelatinous nub, the size of a man's fist perched at the thing's crown, tapering into a snaking umbilical that disappeared up into the tank's murky apex. Suddenly, its hold over Van Heerden released.

"Mein Gott, es ist unglaublich. [My God, it's incredible.]"

Entirely focussed on the thing, Van Heerden hadn't heard Wagner enter the compartment, startled by the man's voice.

"What is it?" he managed, more surprised at hearing his own voice.

"My guess, something akin to a brain. A biomechanical intelligence, responsible for every function of the craft: flight control, navigation, crew's atmosphere… maybe, even self-defence."

Engrossed, they watched as the mass throbbed and shimmered.

On a primally intuitive level, it occurred to Van Heerden that this so-called brain had been probing, assessing his own mind, determining his strengths and weaknesses; conceivably, even how best to deal with him should the need or whim arise. An intensely unnerving train of thought, leaving him shuffling uncomfortably and interrupting their silent observation.

"What of these other… things?" Vocabulary failing him, Van Heerden indicated the noiselessly floating shapes encircling them.

Affectedly rubbing at his chin, Wagner paced to the nearest array.

"I would say these are some kind of hologram; essentially, three-dimensional projected light images, although there doesn't appear to be any obvious source. Quite remarkable, as if existing independent of any means of generation and, scientifically speaking, purely theoretical. We don't currently have the capability to produce anything like this." Raising his eyebrows, Wagner continued speculatively. "I would hazard a guess, they're a display of the craft's functional status, like gauges on the dashboard of an automobile or aircraft's instrument panel. But that's purely conjecture, we won't know for sure until properly studying this section."

Comprehending only snatches of Wagner's lecture, Van Heerden remained impassive, not wanting to display ignorance.

"That's for you figure to out then, Wagner. Knowing everything about this machine will help you and your men build a working replica."

Perceiving the end goal to be in sight, Van Heerden permitted himself an internal surge of exhilaration, conceivably sitting on the cusp of holding the key to mankind's next great leap forwards. The wealth and global influence this success would bring him, inestimable.

Interpreting the look on his employer's face, Wagner had seen this before when Himmler visited Mauthausen, the power lust of a megalomaniac. In the aftermath of the Reichsführer's "progress compliance audits", colleagues deemed unfit or not pulling their weight were frequently made to disappear.

An insatiable appetite for absolute dominance could be an insidious corruptor of men's virtue, and Wagner feared a tempest in the offing.

"I must caution, even though gaining entry into this section is an incredible breakthrough, we must still learn how to walk before ever hoping to run. What you see in here is of a technology infinitely more advanced than ours, and it will take time to ascertain functionality and operational methods. It could be months, even years, requiring significant investment before we're anywhere close to successful replication."

Understanding the motivation behind Van Heerden's fervour, the sheer complexity of their undertaking made Wagner uneasy. A very real possibility existing that they may never succeed in duplicating the craft's intricate complexities, such science proving to be beyond mankind's technological capacity or intellect.

Clearly not completely satisfied at Wagner's response, Van Heerden frowned and nodded tersely. Having little grasp of this machine's workings himself, certain of but one aspect, Wagner's team were his only option.

The relationship between him and the scientists constituted a brittle symbiosis, neither able to survive nor prosper without the other. A delicately loaded interdependence, however intended to foster a long-term and stable relationship, functional for now, although no kinship would ever arise from of their association. In the event of one party not fulfilling the other's implicit trust, inevitably leading to mutually assured ruin. The three German scientists were intensely aware of the potential fragility of their tenure but, with limited options available, collectively resolving to throw themselves into the endeavour's ultimate success.

Years before, when studying a subsequent batch of Hans Merkel's photographs, taken of the propulsion unit, Schauberger had assumed credit for theorising the machine's capabilities to be derived from flux manipulation. More specifically, a merger of weak fields generated by the propulsion unit's spinning sphere, interacting with those of strategically placed powerful electromagnets.

Invited by the Nazi leadership to address a closed gathering of the party, he'd gone into detail; describing how these unified fields could be harmonised by varying current applied to the magnets, until achieving synchronicity. Craft and crew, enveloped within a "drawn bubble" of highly magnetised energy, would then undergo a fundamental particulate shift. Vibrationally elevated, everything within the cell imbued with the capacity to transcend established laws of physics, attaining the holy grail of stable and sustained antigravitational state. Schauberger had been lauded by the Nazi elite for his intellect and vision, although Wagner had cynically pondered whether this concept should more authentically be attributed to private time spent in the company of interplanetary medium Maria Orsic.

Either which way, Schauberger never offered any theories regarding the control and direction of his unified energy field, leaving Wagner to figure out this aspect for himself. Compounding this poser, he shouldered the infinitely more complex quandary of ascertaining the craft's seemingly infinite power supply. Almost certainly located in the rubber mat-enshrouded death ray dome, the element Wagner singularly most dreaded probing.

At Mauthausen, he'd read Max Planck's 1900 paper on zero-point energy capture and a more recent work on the subject by Hendrik Casimir. However fanciful these esteemed physicists' theories on quantum vacuum extraction may seem, they neatly fitted the bill. There simply wasn't another known mechanism or process by which the craft could derive perpetual power, other than through literally sucking energy from thin air.

Schauberger's neat but incompletely packaged principles defining antigravity propulsion were a coup more akin to child's play, in comparison to defining how the power source functioned. Yet more finer detail overlooked by his former boss, were the craft's flight control systems. Since not having any apparent movable flight surfaces, pointed to something far in advance of man's own crude system of ailerons, flaps and rudders. Internally wrangling with this challenge, Wagner kept coming back to a belief that the propulsion unit fulfilled a secondary function. The thing sat on a gimbal, suggesting that by manipulating the unit's orientation, impetus' bearing would correspondingly be shifted, essentially creating omnidirectional thrust and manoeuvrability.

Somewhere, somehow, control of this capability had to

be designed into the craft's operating systems, enabling either crew or biomechanical intelligence to pilot the vehicle. First and foremost, they needed to identify and differentiate these controls, establishing means of access and manipulation. Much painstaking research would be needed, just like he'd told Van Heerden. Indeterminable time and expense were required, knowing his impatient master likely reluctant to concede. Throwing the man an occasional bone would be prudent, a placebo to distract and buy time while they progressed the important stuff. An intuitively contradictory reality, the simplest of all the craft's operating systems appeared to be the propulsion unit; a relatively straightforward electromechanical device, one they may be able to reverse-engineer within a year.

Moving away, lost in thought, Van Heerden stood staring at a cluster of holographic shapes; a series of multi-tiered, magenta columns, striated with regularly ascending multicoloured bands. Further along, a huge projection caught his attention, reaching from console to the deck above and considerably wider than his motor car. Its geometric rendering reminiscent of a modern art piece; albeit not the kind of nonsense he'd only last week acquiescently wasted an afternoon viewing with Oscar and his wife. The thing's central focal point comprised of a luminous orange disc, roughly the diameter of a teacup, surrounded by a complex web of regular patterns.

Staring at the circle, it took a few moments before understanding this to depict the craft; symmetrical adjacent lines representing the basement walls, even the stairs and hoist precisely positioned. Taking a step back to gain a wider perspective, his vision adapted to the display's representation and an abundance of three-dimensional detail suddenly popped. The pharmaceutical building wing overlying the basement emerged, then to one side, an organically meandering outline denoted the stream outside. Overall, representing an area of perhaps a hundred metres square, an uncannily detailed and comprehensive map of their immediate surroundings. Astounding quite how this display, interred in a concrete coffin, could produce such an accurate map of the basement and external environment.

The longer he studied it, so more elements became evident, until noticing a row of four glowing blue dots within a rectangular space adjacent to the basement.

Excited by an idea, he stammered.

"W-Wagner, quick, c-come here. Look at this."

Rushing to his side, Wagner glanced from hologram to Van Heerden and back again, not yet getting it.

"You see, Wagner? It's everything and look, look..." Becoming uncharacteristically agitated, struggling to maintain composure.

Unable to drag his eyes from the image, Wagner's mouth began moving, although not getting the chance to reply before Van Heerden cut in.

"Go fetch one of the bags from the skeletons," sending Wagner obediently hurrying off.

Van Heerden stayed put, watching the display, until one blue dot suddenly jiggled and began tracing a route towards the craft; he'd read it correctly, bellowing gleefully and punching the air. While the science may be incomprehensibly foreign, he'd interpreted a significant aspect and scored a small victory. Calming himself before Wagner's legs appeared on the ladder, he resumed staring into the holographic map. Seeing no harm come to either of them, both Maier and Krause chose to follow close behind their leader. Ignoring them, pointing first to the display then the hessian bag, Van Heerden's voice even and measured.

"Now, do you see what this means? Those things in the bags are important, Wagner. You's need to figure out why, and what they're supposed to do."

Wanting to emphasise this point, he reached to tap the

display as if it were a blackboard, drastically altering the image. The craft icon shrank to pea size, corresponding view panning out to cover an area of several hectares. The house and garden had been incorporated, as were adjacent fields and veld, barns, the farm roads, even a new tractor parked beside the workshop. Like in an aerial photograph, every minute detail of the immediate landscape perfectly represented.

Bewildered, Van Heerden inadvertently flinched; ingrained in him, the upbringing of parents from a generation where such things would be considered witchcraft. Modern times had of course ushered in more rational and enlightened thinking, but those learned reservations assailed him with a vengeance. The lower deck space suddenly felt oppressively confined and all too weird, needing the sun's warmth on his face, to touch a blade of grass and be surrounded by nature's comfortable familiarity. Striving to appear calm, all the while fighting an ever-escalating sense of claustrophobia, he set foot on the ladder's first rung.

"I've seen enough. You've done well today, boys. Come over for dinner tonight and we'll talk more."

Misinterpreting their employer's hasty exit as polite discretion, Wagner grinned boyishly, stood to attention and saluted.

"Thank you, sir. Your invitation is accepted, and we must insist on champagne, it will be a celebration."

Several toasts were indeed drunk that evening, before, during and after their meal, everyone's mood becoming increasingly buoyant. Late into their meal, Van Heerden flinched at a sudden painful twinge stabbing deep inside his chest, so acute as to make swallowing a mouthful of food impossible. Clutching at his sternum, the others were fortunately so deeply engrossed in debating a topic of discussion as to not notice. Leaning back in his chair and breathing deeply, forcing himself to relax; it had to be indigestion, the meal too lavish and excessively rich. Driving the discomfort from his mind to rejoin the conversation, then finishing his meal with a slice of rum-soaked fruit cake, topped with whipped cream.

Retiring to his study after they'd left, pouring a snifter of cognac and lighting a cigar before settling on the sofa with a well-thumbed first edition of *Jock of the Bushveld*. Halfway through the book for the umpteenth time, he never tired of Fitzpatrick's iconic tale of his relationship with the dog and their adventures together. That night, for some reason though, Van Heerden found it impossible to immerse himself in the story.

Despite the pain having subsided, memories of his deal with God had returned, nagging away in the recesses of his mind. Witnessing that thing in the craft today had resurrected the intrusive certainty experienced when they broke in, laying bare repressed doubts as to whether he would live to see this undertaking come to fruition. Trying to shrug it off by topping up the crystal for a third time didn't help either, that infernal badgering became relentless. Cursing out loud, he closed the book, slammed it on a side table and swigged the brandy's dregs. Leaving the cigar to smoulder and die in its ashtray, he got up and headed for his bedroom.

CHAPTER 19

"Success is not final, failure is not fatal: it is the courage to continue that counts." – Sir Winston Churchill

Little appeared to have changed on the Umgeni River's bank in the intervening years, except fruiting season had ended, the guava tree's convolutedly mottled branches bearing only leaves. Wasps' wings intermittently buzzed in the undergrowth, as the combatant insects competed for dominance over the last rotting fruits. Alarmed at the humans' sudden appearance, a mynah bird flew off an uppermost branch, squawking in loud protest. This time Margie didn't come as a dead weight, her arms wrapped tightly around Craig's waist, but keeping hold of his arm when stepping back.

"Okay, that's better. Not so bad this time round, but I can't imagine ever getting used to this thing of yours."

Letting go of his arm with a squeeze, she turned to look across the river.

Despite the thick riverside vegetation's concealment, Craig was acutely aware of being in a public area, glancing around and ducking when spotting a pair of fishermen on the opposite bank. Around a hundred metres downstream of the sluggishly flowing river, remaining steadfastly intent on a pair of drifting floats, neither gave indication of noticing anything out of the ordinary. A hum of traffic on the nearby busy road, clearly audible through a screen of otherwise impenetrable greenery, provided the sole indicator to their being slap bang in the heart of civilisation.

Reassured at the anglers' apparent disinterest, Craig relaxed.

"See, I told you. It gets easier every time. I wouldn't lie to you, Mags," winking at her conspiratorially.

"Yeah, you wouldn't dare, Craigy. Not if you know what's good for you," she shot back, pretending at a dirty look.

"Come on, let's get going." Motioning for her to follow, Craig nodded towards a gap in tall reed grass marking the pathway.

The trail was narrow and more overgrown than on their previous visit, having to push through growths of blackjack plants, seeds hooking onto the legs of their clothing. Reaching the animal sanctuary's parking area, most bays were empty and lettering protruding beyond a handful of parked vehicles indicated these belonging to staff. Margie paused to brush and pick at the fine, black seeds sticking to her trackpants.

"Come on, we haven't got time for that."

Striding ahead across the tarmacked area, Craig had sensed she wasn't keeping up and turned, mild frustration furrowing his brow.

"Speak for yourself. I'm not going in there like this, it looks like we've been rolling in the bushes. You'd do well to get rid of them yourself," pointing at thick, bristling clusters stuck to Craig's jeans. Margie trotted to catch up, while he distractedly picked at the offending clumps.

Heading through the parking lot, then over a palm-fringed

grass verge planted with beds of flowering canna lilies, they reached the roadside. Waiting for a gap in traffic, crossing at a jog until a speeding minibus taxi emerging from behind a double-parked lorry blared its horn, forcing them to run the last few paces. Bounding onto the far sidewalk, immediately ahead of them were hewn stone-topped stairs, leading up to a glass curtain wall-fronted, warehouse-style building. Its otherwise repetitious monotony of commercial fenestration broken by an ostentatiously imposing concrete-columned entrance canopy, crested with an updated version of the *Daily Star*'s infamous logo.

About to start up the steps, Margie caught Craig's arm, holding him back. His face had become set with the expression of a lag up for murder, and about to appear in front of a notorious hanging judge.

"Not so fast, mister. Let's be clear about this first. I'll lead in with Mike, since he sees himself as top dog and doesn't know you from Adam. When, and only when, I give the nod, you tell him everything, and I mean absolutely every detail, just like you told me." Releasing her grip and encouragingly patting the back of his arm, she added, "Don't look so stressed out. Just remember, we've got nothing to lose."

"Yeah, got it," Craig's face softened. "That's fine, exactly how we'll play it. And yes, I'm gonna tell the whole story, whether he believes it or not, even though I'm sure he'll think I'm nuts." Shrugging, he gave a wry smile.

Framed by large concrete planters, automated glass entrance doors parted with a *whoosh* when they approached, allowing sight of an imposing, triple-volume foyer. Stepping aside, Craig let Margie go first. Immediately adopting a business persona, she headed to where a solitary man sat at a centrally positioned reception booth.

"Hi, I'm Marguerite Brooks and I need to see Mike Winter for half an hour," her voice transformed, clipped and no-nonsense.

A pinned tag on his pristine white shirt told them the receptionist's name was Raj. The man's unfalteringly deadpan countenance unchanging, when reaching for a wireless mouse below the counter's recessed worktop. Seemingly impervious to this kind of approach, he looked up, responding perfunctorily.

"Do you have an appointment, Mrs. Brooks?"

Although not perceptibly rising to Raj's indifferent nonchalance, Craig knew Margie well enough to guess it had galled her.

"It's Miss, and no, I don't, but Mike knows me, and it's essential we see him right away." Gesturing towards Craig at her side, she continued, "We've got what's likely to be the paper's biggest ever story."

Having probably heard that opening more times than he cared to count, Raj continued languidly clicking at his mouse while coolly peering at a computer screen.

"He's in a meeting right now. I'll try his line anyway, Ms. Brooks."

Unblinking, Raj abandoned the mouse, picked up a desk phone with practised ease and tapped in an extension number.

After several seconds, he replaced the handset.

"I'm sorry, he's not taking calls right now. Please take a seat and I'll see if his secretary is available to come down," at the phone again, simultaneously pointing to couches arranged in a signed waiting area.

Instead of complying, Margie grabbed Craig's hand.

"Come on, I know the way." Almost unbalancing Craig, towing him behind, she took off towards a pair of glass doors leading to a lift lobby.

Obviously not a stranger to pushy folks, Raj leapt from his swivel chair protesting loudly, voice taking on a pronounced nasal twang. Ignoring the lifts and shoving through a glass door, Margie led Craig up a flight of stairs with Raj pursuing hot on their heels and stridently insisting they return to the waiting area. Still dragging Craig by the top of the stairs, Margie went left and followed a long passageway running parallel to the building's glazed façade. Raj, at this point beside himself, managed to skirt around and impose himself in their path, arms outstretched. When Margie continued to push onwards, he backed up a way and stood his ground.

To their right, people who had up till that point, been busy working in brightly lit, glass-fronted offices got up to stare at the ensuing commotion. Seeing her adversary momentarily distracted, Margie jinked left and forwards. Raj countered, so she went right and forwards. In this fashion, they successively duelled along the walkway, shepherding the growingly irate receptionist in an ineffectual backwards dance. Eventually they reached a conference room, where an enormous meeting table was surrounded with likewise startled faces. Lit by an overhead projector, a screen at the far end held a slide containing several pie charts, with corresponding text boxes. Hesitating for a second, then spotting the man they'd come to see, Margie yanked Craig towards the meeting room door.

So far as Raj was concerned this would be the end of their road, Margie's indecision providing an opportunity to firmly wedge himself in the door frame, letting go only to fend off her reach for the handle. Abruptly opening from the inside, Raj staggered backwards and would have fallen, if it weren't for the man stood there catching him. Quickly recovering, he was back up and ready to carry on the fight, until a firm hand on the shoulder checked him. Spinning round indignantly, an angry outburst cut short and replaced by reflexive apology.

"So sorry, Mr. Winter. I told them you were busy, but they came up anyway, and I tried to..."

Margie hastily cut in.

"I really must apologise for our interruption, Mike. We need to see you, right away. Remember me? It's Marguerite, Margie Brooks, Kim's sister, from last year's Christmas party."

Deciding a more physical approach was needed to eject these intruders, Raj spread both arms wide and launched at them, desperately trying to shove both away from the open door.

"Raj! Stop, Raj! It's okay, I'll deal with this. You can carry on at reception now. Thank you."

Evidently, Mike did remember Margie, that captivatingly sexy lady at the Christmas do, the tease deftly managing to elude his charms. Wearing an inquiringly mystified expression, extending his hand in greeting.

"Of course. Hi, Margie, what's going on? Kim and Eddie okay? What's up?"

Shaking her head, Margie accepted his hand, without returning the smile.

"No, it's nothing's like that, they're fine. This is a completely different matter. Can we talk? Alone, please." Then, sparing a glance for the curious faces, "I… I, we're really sorry to burst in like this," acknowledging the room with a contrite nod.

Mike's puzzled look had by now been replaced with one of open curiosity.

"Yeah, sure. Why not? Nandi, you carry on please. Go over the ad accounts, like we discussed yesterday, and focus on generating repeats." A petite, smartly suited, younger woman in the chair next to that he'd recently vacated nodded and smiled. "Nandi's my deputy. She can take this one," he offered by way of explanation, ushering Craig and Margie out, before leading them to his office.

Opening the door, signifying they should enter with a sweep of his arm, Mike's office turned out being nothing like what Craig had expected. An excruciatingly small and cramped little coop, for the boss of a national paper. Set in the opposite wall, a full-width window overlooked the presses, the newspaper's beating heart, the glass festooned with Post-it notes and sellotaped memos. What could only be Mike's desk occupied the far end, groaning under box folders and stacks of papers, leaving no visible workspace. A single nod to Craig's imagination, an antique brass Anglepoise lamp poked out through the mess. Nearer to the door, a small, round table set with four chairs hadn't escaped the mayhem, an open lever arch file and several stacks of papers at its centre. Behind, one entire wall, fitted with floor-to-ceiling secure cabinets, presented the only concession to order and tidiness.

Seemingly unabashed, Mike scooped up the file, skilfully launching it to land dead centre of his desk and moving paperwork from the table to one chair.

"Please, have a seat. Can I get you some tea, coffee?"

At the mention of coffee, Craig glanced at Margie who caught his look and nodded.

"Please, that would be lovely, thanks. Strong and black for both of us. Oh, excuse my manners, Mike. This is Craig Farrant, an old friend."

They shook hands, in the mechanical way that men do when meeting for the first time, then Craig and Margie took a seat at the table. Turning away and reaching across his desk, Mike stabbed at a hidden phone's intercom button. A woman's voice answered and, after requesting refreshments, he came to sit directly opposite Craig.

Without further pleasantries, Margie launched into outlining their reason for being there, although left out the salient details. Throughout her intro, Craig could feel the newspaperman's gaze boring, sizing him up. Choosing to ignore Mike's scrutiny, he steadfastly focused on a swirl of woodgrain in the ash-veneered tabletop. The end of Margie's narrative approaching, Craig looked up, his turn to check Mike out. A little taller than himself and quite handsome, in a rakish sort of way, silvering hair that had probably been blonde on a younger man was kept cropped short at the back and sides. Blue-grey eyes, slightly sunken below prominent, yet neatly trimmed brows, his skin exuded the permanent tan of a lifelong sun worshipper. Since wearing a lemon-yellow Lacoste T-shirt, Craig took an educated guess that the man's bronzed tone originated from leisure time and business meetings held on the golf course. Mike had remained unmoving, listening attentively to Margie's intro, likely making a clinical assessment of the potential authenticity of whatever Craig had been feeding her.

A tap on the door heralded the arrival of their coffees, right on cue, just as Margie finished her overview. Without waiting to be bidden, an older, rather frumpish woman pushed the door open with her elbow. Carrying a tray, she bustled in with a fussily maternal manner, smiling warmly at the ensemble; three steaming newspaper logoed mugs introduced the aroma of freshly filtered coffee. Setting their drinks and a pack of chocolate digestives on the table, she asked Mike if there was anything else, then discreetly let herself out when he shook his head.

Later, when alone again, Margie shared with Craig that this had been a cousin of Mike's wife; the incumbent Mrs. Winter seeing to it her relative got the job. At first such an imposition seemed unusual to Craig, since employment of an assistant would surely be at Mike's own discretion. Margie then went on to explain that the wife had, on a certain occasion, come to Mike's office when he'd been ostensibly working late, catching him and his former PA *in flagrante delicto*. Consequently, he'd had no say in the matter.

Now it was Craig's turn, taking an appreciative sip of coffee and biting into a biscuit before beginning. Using this interlude to his advantage, Mike got up to fetch a compact digital voice recorder from a desk drawer, switching it on and placing the device centre of their table.

"I always record this kind of meeting. Memory's not as good as it used to be. You don't mind?" Not waiting for Craig's answer, he sat down. "So, now what's this all about then? Give me the whole spiel, whatever it is you've got yourself into."

Leaning back in the chair, he folded both hands together and propped his chin on projecting index fingers. Mike's tone came across overtly enquiring, amicable even, although a subtle flippancy lacing his tone riled Craig. There was a smug smarminess about the bloke's manner, besides, he'd hit on Margie. Right there and then, deciding that he didn't much care for Mike.

Regardless of festering sentiment, Craig related every detail of the past few days, all the while scrutinising Mike's face, alert to the inevitable telltale signs of scorn and derision. Either an excellent poker player, or perhaps accepting Craig's narrative at face value, whichever the case, he didn't interject and remained impassive. Slouching casually, Mike fixated on the recorder, occasionally looking up to acknowledge prominent highlights of Craig's story, or spare Margie a lingering glance. When Craig had finished, he sat unmoving a few moments longer. Shifting forwards to place both elbows on the table, raising both eyebrows and inhaling deeply, he switched from listener to inquisitor, like a detective questioning a suspect.

"Wowzers, that's quite a story. So, what evidence have you got to back it all up?"

Taken aback, Craig fished Govender's business card from his wallet, laying it on the table between them.

Mike glanced at it without reaction.

"Nah, that won't do. You could've picked that up anywhere, it's worthless. What I mean is, surely you took pics when you went back to the pharmaceutical's place? Right?"

Craig had to shake his head.

"I didn't have my phone. There was no point, I knew they'd be monitoring and listening in if I made any calls. Besides, I wasn't thinking about going to the press at that time. It was only when Margie suggested…"

Lifting his hand, Mike interrupted, "Not good. Not good at all. We're going nowhere like this. You've got to understand that these are serious allegations, concerning very powerful and influential people. There's no way I could run that kind of story without solid proof, and I mean irrefutably ironclad evidence, the kind of stuff that would stand up in a court of law. Without that, our credibility would be shot to pieces. I mean, in all honesty, I don't even know whether or not to believe any of this myself, so what's the chances of our readers believing it? Even worse, when it all went legal, and I can absolutely guarantee you that would happen, we'd get our arses handed to us on a plate."

Getting up, agitated, he prowled to the window overlooking the press floor, head clutched in both hands.

"Look, it's only because you're here with Margie that you got to sit in that chair, anybody else telling me a story like yours would've been escorted out of the front door by now. Yes, we do have security."

Getting that much off his chest, becoming less animated, he flopped back in the chair, scowling at the audio recorder.

Giving Margie a look of resignation, Craig began getting up, but she smiled and winked, nodding for him to remain seated.

"Fine, you want proof, Mike, we'll give you proof. But somewhere completely private, a place where there's no chance of anyone walking in on us." Realising where she was going with this, Craig began to object until she raised a hand. "I know this all sounds crazy and far-fetched, but I promise you, it's true, Mike. Craig's going to give you a demonstration," shooting a look at him and nodding affirmatively.

Mike had already checked out and shrugged non-committally, opting to call her bluff.

"Well, we could go to the staff canteen. It'll be empty until lunchtime. You must appreciate, though, my time's valuable and this had better not be a load of bullcrap. Sorry, with all due respect, Margie, even if this bloke can do what he says, witnessed with my own eyes, I still can't run a story without a whole lot more solid evidence. Seriously, I wouldn't be able to get a job pushing a broom in this city." Widening his eyes, he nodded at the door. "Ah, what the hell. This has got to be good for a laugh. Let's go."

For Craig, desperation had taken hold, only the tiniest spark of hope lingering.

"Film it, then. You film it and run the clip on your digital edition; you can even leave out the government VIPs' names. We really need this to go public, so we can both stop running," he entreated, frustratingly powerless to mask the anguish in his voice.

Smiling sardonically, Mike pulled a smartphone from his trouser pocket, waving it mockingly.

"Oh yeah, way ahead of yah. Make no mistake, I'll be filming whatever it is you think you can do, pal."

The man's familiarity galled Craig, but he didn't bite back. A scathing look from Margie instead, got Mike to park the sarcasm.

"You also need to understand that I'm not making any promises or sticking my neck out. I'd have to go to the board first." Mike's get-out had just emerged. If Craig's claims turned out to be valid, it would be a huge scoop for him and the paper, with personal safeguarding coming via the publication's shareholders' say-so.

Leading the way, Mike retraced their earlier route, down the stairs and into the lift lobby. At this point, instead of heading out to the reception foyer, he took them through a side door, opening into a short passageway that followed an internal glass façade, overlooking reception. The corridor terminated at the canteen, an austere but spotlessly clean staff mess room, vacant as Mike had promised it would be. Ordered rows of white Formica-topped tables were surrounded by stackable, padded chairs, tea and coffee vending machines occupying the far corner. Along the adjacent wall, a matched pair of fridges served to frame a prep counter, holding a pair of microwaves and inset with a large integral double-bowl sink. Stacks of gleaming white plates were piled next to boxes of assorted cutlery. A large potted ficus occupied the adjacent corner, providing the only modicum of relief to the canteen's otherwise clinical severity.

Heading straight to the furthest fridge, Mike stood scrolling through his phone, selecting and activating its video function.

"Okay, ready when you are. Show me what you've got, big boy. No, wait, wait. I want you to do your thing from right where you're at now, over next to the coffee machine. Think you can manage that?"

Frowning intently at the phone, clearly relishing his directorial role, he was interrupted by Raj's raised and unmistakably whiny voice coming from outside. Evidently structured reception area protocols were being flouted for the second time that day, something he wasn't at all happy about. To Craig and Margie, this could mean only one thing.

Cracking the canteen door open a fraction, Craig peeked out, seeing through the adjacent glass wall that the foyer swarmed with activity. Sure enough, five men in suits were accompanied by several uniformed police officers, two holding Raj unceremoniously pinned to the ground. Spotting the Russian amongst the suits, brushing past the altercation, he was heading for the lift lobby and toted a squat rifle. A week or so back, Craig had watched a nature programme about rhinos being relocated to Kruger Park, realising the weapon to be a tranquilliser dart gun. Pulling the door shut, he gave Margie a grim look.

"It's them, we've gotta get outta here."

Flustered, Mike cursed.

"Dammit, wait. Let's do this first."

Ignoring him, Craig stepped forwards and reached for Margie.

A seasoned editor, Mike had pretty much seen and heard it all before, but years of exposing scandal, murder and corruption could never have prepared him for what happened next. The consistency of air in the room changed, every hair on his body standing on end when Craig and Margie embraced, then everything turned really weird. Their outlines blurred, fusing, enveloped by a translucent bubble, warping and folding in on itself to an infinite point until disappearing. Anxiously approaching the spot they'd occupied only seconds before, nothing remained, no residue or clue to their ever having been there. Outside, the foyer commotion had subsided, leaving the canteen seeming eerily silent.

Fingers trembling and fumbling excitedly at his phone, Mike had begun filming several seconds before Margie and Craig vanished. Finding the most recent video clip, he selected the play icon and watched as those incredible events began replaying in high-definition colour, all to the accompaniment of Raj's indistinct but enraged voice. There was Craig opening the door, looking outside, then closing it, speaking with Margie, now they were hugging. Suddenly, static filled the screen, nothing but worthless bloody static, even when rerunning the clip several times. Howling in anguish, Mike flung the useless device to smash on the white ceramic-tiled floor.

CHAPTER 20

"If you gaze into the abyss, the abyss gazes also into you." – *Friedrich Nietzsche*

Waking later than usual the next morning, Van Heerden's head pounded, his belly queasy from the previous night's overindulgences. On a positive note, the chest pain experienced over dinner had vanished, experiencing only the usual age-bestowed morning aches and stiffness. Knowing the best way of easing morning's waking discomfort was to get moving, he sat up and swung both legs over the bedside, chiding himself.

"Stupid old man. It was nothing, you're still strong as a bull."

Getting dressed before making his way through the house to find breakfast already laid out on the dining room table. Cookie knew her employer well; a steaming bowl of maize meal porridge and next to it, a strategically placed tumbler containing effervescent antacid pain relievers dissolved in water. After eating alone while reading the morning newspaper, it was time to go see how Wagner and the others were doing.

Heading for the door, Van Heerden stopped at the living room fireplace where split, black wattle logs had burned away to smouldering slithers and balanced on a bed of glowing embers. Taking a brass poker and prodding the coals to life, he selected four fresh logs from an adjacent wrought iron basket, arranging them to burn evenly. Well-seasoned, they wouldn't take long to catch, keeping the house warm until his return later that morning.

The weather had turned bitterly cold overnight, clear skies leaching warmth from air and ground to the point where frost and ice had formed, creating beautifully fernlike patterns on all south-facing windowpanes. Snow had also blanketed the Berg, an uncommon occurrence so late in the spring and worth taking advantage of, intending to drive the grandchildren up to the mountains the following day. Pulling on riding boots and a heavy coat at the front door, he donned a woollen flat cap and went to fetch his horse from the stables.

A steady ride to the valley brim usually took around five minutes; although, still feeling decidedly hungover, he opted for a slower pace. Accustomed to taking it at a canter, Shaka chewed impatiently at the bit, warm breath steaming from the stallion's flared nostrils. A brilliantly azure sky stretched from horizon to horizon and even in direct sunlight, the early morning air carried an invigorating chill. Either side of the road, wraiths of ground mist persisted in scattered hollows, frost sparkling from shaded patches when infiltrated by the sun's rays. Up ahead, a tenacious pillow of fog filled the valley, its dazzling glare forcing Van Heerden to avert his gaze, looking to either side and taking in the countryside's gently undulating beauty.

Following the vehicle track, horse and rider reached the decline's brow and stopped, staring into the foggy valley; a darker, dank and wholly different landscape lay below. Readying

Shaka to start downslope, the needle-sharp talons of an iron claw viciously tore into Van Heerden's chest. Pain so intense, breathing became virtually impossible, gasping and doubling over, managing to grab the saddle's pommel in one hand. Resting his head against Shaka's neck, dizziness took hold, desperately clinging to consciousness. Sensing his master's distress, the horse snorted and whinnied, stamping his feet while turning in a semicircle to face the farmhouse.

Clutching at the pain in his chest with one free hand, when all sensation left the other arm. Losing his grip and sliding forwards, toppling across Shaka's shoulder and falling heavily to the ground. One foot had caught in the stirrup, Shaka dragging him from the road into grass when instinctively stepping away. Summoning strength from within, he managed to kick the entangled foot free, leaving Shaka free to bolt. Rolling over onto his back and lying motionless, staring dazedly at the sky when the strangest thing happened. Annalie suddenly appeared at his side, kneeling and smiling tenderly; young again and so beautiful, just like when they'd met at school all those years ago. His mother and father were there too, seeing them over Annalie's shoulder; Ma, as he remembered, prior to the ravages of tuberculosis and Pa from before the Boer War. Gradually, everything became hazy, the day darkening, visions fading; realisation dawned, this was it, his time had come.

Later, a farmhand carrying a pail of milk to the house spotted Shaka standing riderless beside the stables. Thinking it unlike the baas to leave his Boerperd untethered, he became concerned and called for Cookie, who confirmed that their employer wasn't indoors. Checking the stables and scouting the yard, the workman realised something to be amiss, going to find their headman. Taking charge, the induna rounded up all hands and began splitting them into search parties when a cattle herder spoke up. He had seen the baas riding towards the valley earlier; spreading out, the workers followed this route, finding Van Heerden where he had fallen.

A week later, the funeral of Andre Lodewijk van Heerden took place at the Dutch Reformed Church in Pietermaritzburg. Attended by over a thousand mourners, consequently standing room only for most well-wishers and mourners. There to pay their respects, dignitaries from local and national government got to sit up front with the deceased's family. Those knowing or having had dealings with Van Heerden either loved and admired, or hated and feared him, albeit begrudgingly respecting the man.

If he'd been able to give voice at the ceremony, Van Heerden would probably have declared attendance of those in the latter category, as being there purely to ensure he was indeed dead. According to wishes expressed in his will, laid to rest a short distance from the spot where he died; a favourite location, overlooking the valley and in sight of Rooiessenhout.

Returning to work a few days after the ceremony, Oscar was met by Wagner and the other two, anxiously wanting to know what impact his father's demise signalled for the project. Because his father had so doggedly ensured both sides of the business remain separate, the son presented as a virtual stranger to them. Nevertheless, needing to know of his intentions; would the project continue, or should they begin preparing for an uncertain future?

Not yet in the frame of mind to deal with this shady trio, or begin probing into that side of the business, he'd sent them away. Although, acknowledging this conversation couldn't be postponed indefinitely, suggesting they carry on as normal until a proper meeting could be scheduled. In some respects, much like his father, Oscar held as an honourable man and went to see them at the basement workshop the next day.

He was, of course, aware of what lay secreted in the basement, a thing which to Oscar's religious side represented an outrageous and fundamentally wicked abomination. Never verbalising these opinions, all the same deeply disturbed that his father should choose to dabble with such an unnatural thing. Holding Pa in the utmost esteem and not wanting to incite affront or incur his resentment, he had politely feigned interest whenever his father raised the subject.

Retaining a set of keys for just such an eventuality, Oscar used them for the first time, wholly intending to inform Wagner that the operation would be shut down. Wanting no part in this dangerously distasteful business, the accursed thing would then be left to rot in this hole for all eternity. Entering the ground floor workshop, Wagner and the other two were gathered around an outlandish, although highly sophisticated-looking machine. Taking Wagner aside, Oscar broke the news, except hadn't reckoned on the man's wily resourcefulness.

Not long after coming to the farm, Wagner and the old man got drunk on a bottle of apricot mampoer one night. Pa's tongue progressively loosened by the fiery spirit, reservation flew out of the window, and he confided a hitherto buried secret. Despite being in a similarly inebriated state, hearing tell of the Levins' assassination and their killer's subsequent murder had elicited waves of revulsion in Wagner. Openly bragging, Van Heerden even spoke of where he'd personally disposed of Haart's body, the Levins' valuables and a shotgun used in their murder. Somewhere not far away in fact, the exact spot, Wagner of course chose to withhold.

Feeling sick, Oscar left but despite not wanting to believe a word of it, Wagner's tale had awakened memories, things he recalled inadvertently overhearing as a child. Pairing these long-repressed memories with Wagner's revelation, coloured a picture of Pa as an utterly ruthless man. If such a heinous tale ever came to light, not only would it besmirch Pa's memory, but also stigmatise the family name and potentially compromise his own flourishing business.

Smiling tersely when the heavy steel outer door closed, Wagner rejoined Maier and Krause, safe in the knowledge of holding the trump card. Although harbouring no real regrets at outright blackmailing Oscar, Wagner recognised his slate to be indelibly marked. This aspect gave him cause for discomfort, knowing first-hand that there were virtually unlimited places where a body could be secretly disposed of on the farm. Seeing little point in sharing details of this exchange with the other two, believing it would only lead to needless uncertainty and worry, even impairing their progress.

While making an enemy of Oscar might well end badly for him, it made sound sense to set out their stall in the manner of a business proposal to the man. Wagner also appreciated that good fortune had a way of slipping from the grasp of any man foolish enough not to seize advantage and hold tight. Gleaning from informal chats with Van Heerden that the man's only son was in truth a shrewd entrepreneur, a deal must be cemented quickly so as to maintain their advantage. Working late into the night, he prepared a detailed report of the project's results and status, including projected future funding requirements.

Presenting himself uninvited at Oscar's office the next morning, Wagner found his new boss unsurprisingly stand-offish, reticent and tight-lipped. It would have been crassly naïve, if expecting an unsolicited sheaf of papers to break the crust of ice arising from his extortion of the man. Scarcely acknowledging Wagner's presence, Oscar cursorily leafed through the document, not once offering comment or inviting discussion. Surmising that he was being humoured, and not wishing to further antagonise, Wagner waited till Oscar had finished. A final roll of his dice, Wagner suggested a tour of the basement workplace, to which Oscar reluctantly agreed; a play, ultimately serving as the proverbial ice pick.

Retaining only the horror stories and thus acquiring a

superficially emotive impression of the project, Oscar had appreciated none of its prospective commercial worth. That all changed, his mood and outlook shifting when seeing first-hand what the research team were engaged in. While still finding the craft's presence unnervingly supernatural, those hours spent in the basement opened his eyes to the craft's intrinsic value. An entente cordiale of sorts established, Wagner and his team's tenure would continue for the foreseeable future.

The day after Andre van Heerden's passing and already foreseeing a luke-warm response from Oscar, Wagner had prioritised accelerating the construction of a prototype they had been developing. Unable to verify the original unit's diverse metallurgy, for fear of fireflies, their choices had to be guided by the principles of performance approximation criteria. Most difficult to gauge, the sphere, Wagner suspecting this to be either of rhodium or iridium; both highly conductive, extremely rare and expensive metals, known for being notoriously unworkable.

Solely in consideration of manufacturing constraints, he had substituted; opting to fit an annealed sphere of silver, filled with mercury, into an aluminium frame surrounding by electromagnets. Progressively increasing electrical current to this test rig, an hour into the experiment, when the entire assembly lifted from their workbench and hovered. They had done it, creating a simple antigravitational device.

Not resting on their laurels, the team set about upscaling, building a mechanism capable of controllable flight characteristics. Wagner adopted his previous anticipation, that the propulsion unit's gimbal assembly provided a means to control; by shifting its orientation, thrust would be correspondingly vectored and provide manoeuvrability. Regardless of adopting every conceivable angle of investigation, the researchers had made no real headway in determining how the original craft's crew would achieve these functions.

An overriding fundamental comprehension gap persisted, leaving little alternative but to compensate, instead using a car battery for power and fitting multiple radio-controlled servomotors between the gravity drive system and its supporting frame. A rudimentary workaround to something far more complex, still, one allowing the unit to be remotely tilted in any plane.

Two years down the line, a new decade arrived, the '60s; an age of financial boom and global social change, ushering in an era of purported enlightenment. Around Easter time, Wagner's team were putting the finishing touches to their fourth model, previous attempts not getting off the bench, let alone the ground. Exhaustive design improvements had been made and integrated, with further material substitutions fine-tuned into this latest version. Tethered workshop tests had gone well, and they were optimistic, the next step being a field trial which was where another problem arose.

There was no way of predicting what to expect from the prototype and despite their remote location, surrounding farms and settlements had to be considered. If losing control of the machine, subsequent recovery by an outsider would constitute a massive security breach. Bringing Oscar in on this dilemma, he concurred, suggesting they take the machine deep into the hinterland, to a place he knew.

It had taken fourteen hours to reach the long-abandoned sheep farm, thirty kilometres due north of Graaff-Reinet. A setting where Oscar and his pa had once hunted Cape grysbok, on that occasion the small antelope proving elusive. They had returned home empty-handed, Oscar's only keepsake an enduring memory of the region's brutally desolate isolation.

Taking a wrong turn en route landed them in the town of Middelburg, eventually finding the right place around midnight, too late and dark to pitch tents. A region of rocky and mostly barren scrub wilderness, this semi-desert veld still held significant wildlife perils for the unwary. Reluctant to deal with nocturnal snakes and scorpions, Wagner and the other two unrolled their sleeping bags atop the lorry's canvas canopy and settled for the night. Not content at such a bourgeois notion of sleeping under the stars, Oscar elected to spend an uncomfortably cramped night on the back seat of his Mercedes.

Their excursion hadn't been planned as an extended camping trip, consequently bringing limited provisions. Watching the sun emerge, straddled by a blazing orange band of cloud, the four men staved off morning hunger pangs on tins of bully beef and dry bread. Sat around a fire, drinking Camp Coffee out of tin mugs and warming up after the night's frigid cold, time came for Wagner's team to ready their prototype.

Slightly larger than a modern washing machine, the apparatus was patently devoid of any concessions to the original's gracefully engineered geometry. Appearing incapable of flight, the thing wobbled alarmingly on stubby support legs when Maier set the sphere running. To one side, Krause prayed silently as Wagner adjusted the radio-control unit, working levers to increase the sphere's rotation. Defying its appearance, the ungainly contraption leapt effortlessly from the ground, soaring higher than a nearby sweet thorn tree. Here, Wagner paused its ascent, and all four men whooped gleefully, unaware that their excitement would be short-lived.

The hovering machine was suddenly enveloped by a transparent bubble, gradually darkening within, where charged incandescent blue threads arced and crackled like a Tesla coil's discharge. A calamitous clattering heralded the end, their machine falling like a stone and everyone scattering to get out of its way.

Crashing to the ground, it ejected a shower of scalding hot, shiny mercury globules, spattering the men and surrounding stony land. Skidding off unforgivingly angular planes, the sphere's lifeblood ran in silvery rivulets that coalesced in quivering puddles. Sustaining catastrophic damage, the machine's aluminium frame was twisted and bent, its integral lattice frame fractured and collapsed. Their carefully crafted, arbored silver sphere had split in several places, longitudinal tears mimicking the symmetry of orange segments.

Tripping and falling headlong into the spikily thorned clutches of a Karoo aloe, Oscar extricated himself painfully and stood stony-faced, breathing heavily. Puncture wounds and lacerations streaked his face in red, blood steadily dripping from a deeply gashed forearm. From his tight-lipped glare, Wagner gathered the inaugural flight's unfortunate outcome had not been well received. Ignoring his injuries, Oscar spared the researchers a final murderous scowl and stormed to his car. Clouds of dust and a shower of grit churned up by the Mercedes' spinning tyres, confirmed Wagner's conclusion; they had better get it right the next time. Staying there only long enough to scoop up as much spilled mercury as could be trapped; after loading the wrecked prototype onto the lorry, they also took to the road.

Occupying the window seat, although paying scant attention to the passing landscape, Wagner stewed over potential causes behind the test's failure. The prototype's construction had certainly involved a fair degree of assumption and compromise, although in their defence, any derogations were due either to technological limitations, or a justifiable fear of tampering with the original.

Regardless of today's outcome, everyone should take heart from the unit's initial performance; all the same, Oscar's hostile reaction worried him. Temperamental and increasingly impatient, the man might well pull the plug on their return, prepared to suffer the consequences. Leaving the test's outcome to fester in Oscar's mind would only making matters worse. Unfortunately, it was too late to meet with the man by the time they got back, it would have to be tomorrow. A frank and open conversation around the maiden flight's shortcomings serving as an introduction, he would then sweeten the situation with an emergent olive branch solution.

Night had fallen when reaching the lab, Wagner enduring a fitful night's sleep. The next morning, Oscar evidently still smarted, arm supported in a sling and swathed in bandages, deep scratches streaking one half of his face, as if drawn by a big cat. Only half listening to Wagner, prior disclosure of Pa's wrongdoings ringing a bell in his head. The obstacle to following this cue, being that he didn't have the stomach to follow through in the manner his father would.

Gut instinct should have prevailed at the outset, except caving to Wagner's blackmail, then falling for unsubstantiated gains centred on bewilderingly complex science and technology. Distractedly mithering over allowing himself to become ensnared in this ungodly alliance, Oscar's focus suddenly sharpened when snagging on Wagner's plan for future-proofing subsequent testing. Incredibly risky and certainly foolhardy, the consequences of interfering with the craft's propulsion unit could however be just the key to release him from their deal. Feigning shared enthusiasm at the man's proposal, Oscar gave his blessing and ushered Wagner out, citing an imminent meeting.

Deliberately working late that evening, it had gone eight o'clock when Oscar packed up and left his office, going directly to the basement. Finding the outer steel door unlocked and letting himself in, finding the workshop to be empty and silent. Dry mouthed, belly fluttering, he descended to the basement lobby, hesitating briefly before opening the doors. Lacking in Pa's constitution and bloodlust, he'd been secretly repulsed by shared hunting trips, to Oscar the taking of any life was abhorrent. Therefore, scared spitless at the prospect of what gore might lie in the basement, he turned the handle and shoved, involuntarily gasping in relief when the was place deserted.

Convincing himself that perhaps Wagner and his men had finished up for the day and returned to their house, forgetting to lock up, he suddenly felt foolish. Deciding to check inside the craft anyway, just to be sure, he'd then head home for a late dinner with his wife.

Bounding up a newly installed metal staircase, Oscar abruptly lost his appetite; a few paces inside the craft, Maier lay face down and unmoving, a little way beyond him, Krause. Crumpled in a foetal position against the nearest console, the second man's hands were drawn up as if shielding against an attack. Unaccustomed to the sight of cadavers, Oscar instinctively knew both men to be dead but was left wondering what had become of Wagner.

Covering his mouth in distaste while edging around the first two, he started when spotting the man opposite, sprawled in a mirror-backed seat. Wagner's eyes were wide open, staring at him from across the flight deck, alive after all. Oscar's heart skipped a beat, in the next, feeling shame at a momentary sense of disappointment. Hailing Wagner but getting no response, he rounded the deck, to crouch in front of the man, perceiving not so much as a flicker of recognition. Reaching out and slipping two fingers below his jawline to feel for a pulse, then abruptly recoiling at speckles of dried blood dotting the dead man's face.

Heavy silence filled the craft, oppressive, as if an enormous invisible hand were trying to crush him to the flight deck. Fearing he may faint, until realising his dizziness was due to hyperventilating, on the verge of a panic attack. Steadying himself and looking around, a hasty glance confirmed they hadn't succeeded in dismantling the propulsion unit. Their intentions however clear from assorted tools arranged around the pit, the craft must have pre-emptively reacted to deal with their threat.

A sudden comprehension overcame Oscar; to the best of his knowledge, he remained the only living person aware of the craft's existence. Therefore, having sole discretion, the capacity to end this madness and forever draw a line under further dabbling with the evil thing. Rising delight at this epiphany abruptly quashed by a sickening lurch, realising he was ethically behoved to dispose of the dead men's remains, alone.

It took every ounce of strength and nerve Oscar possessed to drag all three bodies down the staircase and into the goods hoist. Going topside to raise the platform, he hauled them through the workshop, hefting their dead weights aboard the same lorry used on yesterday's test excursion. Driving it to a remote corner of the farm, three long hours were spent digging then refilling a single mass grave. Hands blistered, splintered and cramping painfully from such unfamiliar physical activity, it was a struggle just grasping the steering wheel on his return drive.

A little after one in the morning, drenched in perspiration and filthy from his grizzly task, Oscar parked up outside the goods forwarding depot. Leaving the transport's keys in the ignition, he got into his Mercedes and sped off, yearning for the familiarity of home comforts.

CHAPTER 21

"Foul cankering rust the hidden treasure frets, but gold that's put to use more gold begets." – William Shakespeare

A sharp upswing in the world's economy had coincided with the 1960s; immigrants flooding into South Africa saw to it that the pharmaceutical industry boomed. An age of prosperity fortuitously offset past profits burned on the business's failed alternative investment. Project abandoned, the basement would remain locked up and mothballed for good, only occasionally plaguing Oscar with unpleasant memories or nightmares. Over the ensuing years, wild vegetation growing vigorously in the valley's richly fertile alluvial soil, choked and obscured the basement's dirt access road and gravelled clearing. Sometimes sitting on a bench next to his father's gravesite, Oscar drew relief at witnessing all evidence of the workshop's existence gradually disappear; in a sense, therapeutically cleansing his psyche, out of sight, out of mind.

Forty years would elapse, until merely six months before Oscar's own end, when his eldest son returned to begin assuming control of the family business. Bruno had left the country two decades earlier, taking his wife and infant daughter, their departure a bitter disappointment to Oscar. Not content with the idea of suckling off the family fortune, he had gone to Europe, intent on carving out his own path in life.

Entering the volatile realm of futures markets and successfully built a separate empire, growing his own fortune on the world's stock exchanges. Ultimately becoming weary of the cut and thrust surrounding international commodities trading, his father's failing health came at an opportune point. Nearer the time of departure, a kind of delayed nostalgia set in, and Bruno found himself truly longing for the old country, hankering after its wild open spaces and slower, simpler way of life.

Younger brother François had also foregone all benefits of the Van Heerden name; similarly, displaying no interest in the pharmaceutical business, but that's where all likeness ended. Oscar's two sons could not have been more polar opposites. In sharp contrast to Bruno, François was entirely devoid of motivation and ambition. To his father's chagrin, the stupid boy had taken up employment at a hardware retail chain, then packed up in the early nineties and moved his own family to faraway New Zealand. Never close as siblings, the boys had seldom spoken, until a few days before Bruno's return when he'd called to inform little brother of their father's ill health. Separated from his wife and out of work, François wasn't interested, opting to maintain his prodigal lifestyle.

Leaving their Luxembourg penthouse fully furnished and taking only suitcases of clothing and personal effects, Bruno and Zelda moved in with his parents. In truth, even with a retinue of servants and carers, the farmhouse was just too big for the old folks to rattle around in alone. It made for sound sense, they'd help run the place and keep an eye on the elderly couple, without displacing them from their marital home of nearly fifty years. Staying behind at London's Imperial College, Bruno's twenty-three-year-old daughter would follow once graduating a marketing and business management degree.

Allowed to fall fallow by Oscar, the farm had reverted to grassland, interspersed by indigenous thorny scrub and maturing trees. Formerly eking out a tenuous existence on surrounding working farms, wildlife had also returned, coming to take refuge in this immense natural reserve. Not long after taking up residence, Bruno purchased a quad bike, riding out across the rewilded veld and sometimes disappearing for days at a time. Taking a rifle and camping gear, seeking out all the places he and Oupa had been or simply camp at the old man's gravesite.

On just such a day, sat in tall grass while casually surveying the laboratory from across the valley, something caught Bruno's interest. Through a pair of binoculars fetched from the quad, he noticed how the building's riverside level had fallen into disrepair, peeling paint exposing plastered masonry. Partially obscured by a limb fallen from a knotty old umbrella tree, it took a few passes before locating what had drawn his eye. Eventually capturing the target in his field of view, adjusting the focus wheel minutely sharpened the image and gave definition to a large steel door. Once white, the passage of time and cloying dust had given old flaking, lead-based paint a pale pink hue.

At first, seeming odd that this lowest part of the building should have a door but no windows, until a distant memory returned and stimulated his curiosity. Aged around eleven at the time, sat in pretty much this exact same spot, Oupa had told him a fantastical story about a special secret hidden below the laboratory. Oupa had all kinds of stories and, even as a child, Bruno understood these to be generally mere tales; the kind of yarns grandfathers tell impressionable grandkids. Except, something about that particular story stood out as different, being neither gratuitously scary, nor containing any moral. Why would Oupa concoct such an offbeat fabrication, unless holding an element of truth?

An enduring chord resoundingly struck, right there and then, absolutely having to know the facts overcame Bruno. Straddling the quad and locating an overgrown but still discernible trail, he followed it, angling cross-contour to reach a level patch surrounding the umbrella tree. Fighting his way through thick undergrowth, thorns scored bloody scratches on both forearms, until eventually locating the door. Made from a thick-gauge steel, although extensively corroded through neglect and exposure to the elements, razor-sharp scabs of painted rust, mottled and distorted its face. Held shut in its frame by three shoot bolts, each secured with heavy-duty padlocks; fused drawn in their keeps, the bolts had clearly not been drawn in several decades. Something about the door's sheer size and robust construction drove Bruno's interest to another level. What in the world warranted such massive over-engineering?

Bruno returned to the farmhouse, finding Papa in the study, sat in his wheelchair and wrapped in a blanket while reading a book. When he described the overgrown door and asked after its purpose, the old man became edgy, speculatively offering that it could be an old disused storage room. Not put off by this evasiveness, Bruno pressed for more details until his father became irritable, warning that anything stored there should be left well alone. Whatever might be there would either have long since rotted or become unstable and potentially dangerous. Papa's dissuasion had precisely the opposite effect on Bruno, and he took off, realising there to be no point in asking about keys for the padlocks.

Going directly to the old farm workshop, situated alongside a long dried out and overgrown slurry pond, Bruno shouldered the door open. Brushing aside hanging curtains and hammocks of dusty cobwebs to eventually locate an oilcan, club hammer and pair of long-handled bolt cutters. Suitably provisioned, he narrowly avoided a strutting cockerel when racing out the yard and retracing his route to the steel door.

Liberally sousing the bolts and hinges in oil, tapping the bolts along their lengths to encourage the lubricant's penetration, he tackled the padlocks. The shackles of those securing lower and mid-level locks sheared easily under the cutter's jaws but the uppermost stubbornly resisted, being of a different and evidently tougher make. His endeavours were exacerbated by the final padlock being well above head height, remembering passing an old cable drum tangled up in undergrowth. Going to drag it free, rolling his improvised step into place then turning it on one side provided the added reach and purchase needed to overcome the stubborn lock, yielding with a screeching *snap*.

Tapping the bolts from their keeps with the hammer, only heavily corroded hinges now stood between Bruno and whatever Papa preferred remaining hidden. Surprisingly, the door gave way with relative ease, grinding and juddering at first before swinging open to expose a dark space. Fishing a head light from a trouser pocket and slipping its band over his head, he entered without hesitation and was immediately greeted by the odour of long-enclosed abandonment. Turning his head side to side, playing the torch's bright LED beam over surfaces not having seen light of day in more than four decades. Precisely as left on the night Oscar had removed Wagner and his men's bodies, the workshop a clutter of antique machinery, tools and all manner of fascinating junk.

Holding his attention only momentarily, a peculiar-looking contraption of unfathomable design intent sat dejectedly in the far corner. Obviously having taken a beating, whatever the mechanism's intended purpose, things hadn't gone to plan. An open archway in the back wall led to a smaller anteroom where a goods hoist took up one side and opposite, a flight of stairs fell away into pitch blackness.

Steps descending below ground, held an alluring correlation to Oupa's hidden secret. Excitement aroused but cynicism rearing like a shield, fully expecting fantasy to end in disappointment. The stairs in all probability would lead to yet another old storage room, full of worthless trash. Spotting an old-fashioned light switch, he toggled it, unsurprised when nothing happened; power to this part had most probably been isolated within the main building, or disconnected years ago. Following the head lamp's beam, Bruno picked his way down the stairs into a basement lobby, where a pair of doors hung ajar.

A spooky and impenetrably black void lay beyond, evoking elementally primordial fears that were amplified by Papa's warning replaying in his head. In truth, sensible to heed his father's caution, especially when recalling Oupa's eccentricities, deciding to have a quick look but not poke around. Pushing both doors inwards exposed a cavernous space, requiring several passes of the light before fully comprehending what he'd uncovered.

Instilled with a secretive nature from childhood, he would tell nobody else of his find and certainly not confide in Papa. Retaining his role as chairman of the board, the old man still held legal sway over anything relating to the business. Bruno wouldn't put it past him to take drastic measures, if ever ascertaining that his wishes had been disregarded. A radical overreaction could scupper any opportunity to exploit the discovery; he would have to play it cool and bide his time.

Returning topside, Bruno was loath to leave the place open and untended, right then the only option available to him was temporary camouflage. Sweating and cursing while hauling the fallen tree limb from clinging undergrowth, he wedged the leafy end tight up against the door to obscure it from casual view.

A whistle-stop trip into town secured three of the chunkiest padlocks available from a local hardware store, although late afternoon by the time he returned to resecure the place. Snapping the final lock's shackle, he relaxed at having bought himself peace of mind and time to figure out the next move.

In the weeks leading up to Rebecca's arrival from London, Bruno took advantage of every spare waking moment to research, poring over countless internet sites, referencing and cross-referencing. Much of the net's freely available information was clearly contrived bunkum, countless whimsical tales and even scrupulously fabricated, authentic-looking falsehoods. It took time to weed out and distinguish between sensationalism and apparently authentic historical accounts of attempts at reverse-engineering UFO technology. One article in particular stuck out, a column featured in a 1950 edition of *Der Spiegel*, quoting a former Nazi military engineer, Rudolf Schriever who claimed to have worked on developing a flying disc craft in the early '40s.

Seeking out other mentions of similar articles, Bruno learned that the basement's secret wasn't entirely unique; the Germans had been actively studying this kind of technology, even prior to the outbreak of WWII. Beyond that point however, the trail grew cold, yielding no credible information as to what became of this Nazi know-how. Whatever may have remained intact by the war's end had, by all accounts, been divvied up and shared out between America and the Soviet Union; forever vanishing behind an impenetrable veil of secrecy and disinformation. The superpowers' machinations confirmed for Bruno, beyond any shadow of doubt, that the basement's contents were virtually priceless and had to be privately developed.

The day of Rebecca's homecoming turned out bittersweet, when Bruno found his father in the study, succumbed to a heart attack; an irony forever lost, in that Oupa's favourite book lay open in his lap. Naturally, deeply saddened and grieving at his father's passing, another side of Bruno couldn't help but rejoice at the old man's hands finally coming off the wheel. Improvements were long overdue in the core business, and now he could openly begin investigating his find without fear of censure.

Sharing similar interests, philosophies and viewpoints with his daughter, they enjoyed a close alliance and often discussed subjects that were frankly beyond his spouse. A warmly loving, deeply devoted wife and mother, if put sensitively, Zelda lacked intellectual depth and was neither blessed with creative vision nor foresight. Conversely, their daughter had grown into an exceptionally smart and astute woman, endowed with both insight and intelligence. What some may have ascribed to character flaws, Bruno saw as an edge over others; shrewd cunning and the unerring ability to get her own way out of any situation.

A few weeks after burying his father, Bruno took Rebecca into the family business, but since despising nepotism, she wasn't to be accorded any special privileges. Starting in a junior position of the marketing team, like the proverbial duck to water and landing a handsome new supply contract to establish her credentials.

On a hot and sunny Saturday afternoon, some weeks after Rebecca's first coup at VHP, Bruno decided the time had come to confide in his daughter. She'd been lazing on a sun lounger, halfway through a second glass of Sauvignon Blanc when Bruno stepped through the parlour doors onto the pool deck and strolled over. Getting straight to the point, something had come up in the lab's grounds and they needed to go check it out. Since the place they were headed was off the beaten track, Bruno suggested she change into a pair of jeans and long-sleeved top.

Each riding a quad bike, Bruno led the way into the valley where he parked up and dismounted, getting a quizzical look from Rebecca. Saying nothing, he instead motioned for her to follow and set off through overgrown thorny bush, ignoring an ensuing tirade of questions and protestations. Wanting this disclosure to have a similar impact as it had on him, Bruno wrestled the tree branch aside and unlocked the outer door. Before entering, he created context for Rebecca, relating the events leading up to him finding this place. Starting right at the beginning, with Oupa's long ago yarn about a buried secret, then fast-forwarding to spotting the door and breaking in. Groundwork laid, Rebecca looked sceptical, not yet sold on what could be so important as to warrant ruining an afternoon lying by the pool.

Without further elaboration, Bruno started a small generator brought over from the farm earlier, then took his daughter's hand and showed her to the stairs. Earlier that morning, he'd also strung a daisy chain of lights to illuminate their way down into the basement lobby. Here, Bruno paused before pushing the doors inwards and stepping back, allowing Rebecca to enter first. Away from eyes that would see or ears that might hear, father and daughter exuberated, even dancing an impromptu jig.

In Papa's study that evening, they discussed and strategised, coming up with the broad-brushed outline of a plan, snagged by but one obstacle. Precisely the same dilemma as Oupa Andre had experienced five decades earlier, securing the kind of specialised expertise required to move forward. Cutting-edge developmental aerospace researchers, with proven track records, were essential to deliver on something of this magnitude; run-of-the-mill commercial aircraft or rocket builders simply not cutting the mustard. Suitable candidates would also need to possess vision, seeing beyond constraints imposed by current technology's limitations.

Such a venture wouldn't come cheap either, requiring outlay on hi-tech equipment and IT systems needed to achieve the kind of processing capacity envisaged. Access to the basement, logistics, structural repairs and upgrades; all in all, necessitating colossal capital investment, just to get such a scheme up and running. Fortunately, the pharmaceutical business ran at a huge profit margin and could comfortably stump up seed capital, beyond which, Bruno had contacts amongst greedily suggestible people who controlled a far deeper purse.

It was however important for them to demonstrate financial commitment, ahead of tapping into secondary investment streams. Essentially, the Van Heerden's would have to fund and get the facility at least partially operational. To overcome the hurdle of engaging suitable people, a discreetly complex net would have to be cast, far and wide. Specialists in their fields, such researchers would either be employed on high-profile ventures or indentured to top-secret government undertakings. A uniquely incentivised package would be needed to lure the right people away from already prestigious or strategic projects. Money and tangible reward not necessarily being the sole drivers behind personal decision-making; creative inducement, even coercion were sometimes the determining factor.

Before getting into it, Rebecca and Bruno needed to acquire at least a rudimentary grasp of the engineering and scientific disciplines they would be chasing. In a sense, having a research library at their fingertips; piles of mouldering documents stashed away in the basement from both previous enterprises. From living in Luxembourg, both father and daughter were fluent in German, making translation of the documents relatively straightforward.

Weeks spent dredging through reams of mottled paperwork and two swastika-adorned journals provided a fair understanding and moderate insight into the basics. By mutually unanimous agreement, one individual alone could be entrusted with such an elaborate recruitment drive; it had to be Rebecca, the only person with a vested interest and trustworthy enough to maintain confidentiality. Bruno gave her the mandate to make it happen, either through outrageously substantial financial enticement or duplicitous subterfuge.

Years before, Bruno's father had capitalised on an opportunity to diversify, expanding into the manufacture of chemicals and compounds used in the aeronautics and aerospace industries. A fortuitous expansion, since globe-trotting under the auspices of marketing these products provided Rebecca an opening to ingratiate herself into business circles aligned with their target audience. A consummate professional, blessed with the Van Heerden business head, she was also perfectly willing to take advantage of her looks and charms. There would be instances where orthodox negotiation simply didn't actualise an ideal outcome and, if assessing a wavering party susceptible, Rebecca wasn't above going for a "softer kill".

No matter how hard-nosed their business façade, men were hardwired with the basest of instinctual urges and easiest to manipulate. On the other hand, women in positions of power and influence presented Rebecca with an altogether more delicate challenge. Unfettered by ethics or gender-specific preference, occasional intimate entanglements of a less-conventional ilk offered light relief from the infinitely more mundane.

Though extending an element of spice, these trysts never attracted emotional involvement, flings ascribed solely to being a necessary extension of regular dealings. Placing no real value on romance or affection, Rebecca considered these emotions as representing unrealistic fantasies, human weaknesses even. The very notion of allowing another person so close as to connect with one's own thoughts, private desires or yearnings, made her skin crawl.

Rebecca's entrenched phobia towards intimacy and commitment stemmed from a single incident, occurring when she'd been merely six years old. Bruno had been on business in Hong Kong over New Year, leaving her mother to host a dinner, dance bash for family friends and select clients at their Luxembourg penthouse. Mama had been working the room, when a male guest who Rebecca hadn't met before came across and began chatting. About Papa's age and friendly, he seemed nice and quickly gained her trust. When telling him about a new doll's house, he'd asked to see it and they went upstairs together. In the sanctuary of Rebecca's bedroom something terrible had happened, an event that changed her forever. Tormented by shame and embarrassment, never speaking of that horrible occasion with anyone, even her parents, instead withdrawing into a rebellious and calculatingly spiteful shell.

Spending long hours in the office, or travelling on business, Bruno had largely been spared the fallout, everyone else left to take the brunt of Rebecca's outpourings of rage. Around the age of fifteen, she stumbled upon the works of Friedrich Nietzsche; writings that profoundly impacted on her guilt. Finding relief from perpetual self-loathing, by aligning her developing adolescent views on morality with those of the philosopher. An altered mindset henceforth adopted, Rebecca considered herself grown beyond primitive contemporary thinking; establishing a fresh philosophy on life, from which she developed an overriding contempt for the submissive masses.

In this way, albeit built on questionable foundations, Rebecca acquired newly established self-respect. Always one for critical self-analysis, unsurprised, gratified even, when reference to psychology books defined her psyche as narcissistic, with chronic sociopathic tendencies. Disclosure of such nature, likely troubling to most folks, Rebecca conversely took implicit delight in the perceived supremacy this self-diagnosis conveyed.

Whilst talent hunting, Rebecca inevitably networked and rubbed shoulders with corporate or state bigwigs, creatively managing to engineer encounters with those at the coalface. She selectively targeted astrophysicists and next-generation propulsion engineers, robotics and biomechanical researchers. Highly specialised technologists, all-essential doers, with the talkers and self-important egotists simply providing a necessary conduit to fulfil her shopping list.

Identifying prospective candidates turned out being no mean feat, and took time, lots of it, even more so when shortlisting those whose credentials fit the mould. It wasn't only the niche stature of their professions; of utmost import, these individuals must be approachable and amenable to temptation. Once completing a tentative selection list, Rebecca retraced the globe and reconnected with every individual, travelling from the USA to China, the United Kingdom, visiting India, Italy and finally Japan. When meeting her contenders for a second time, she had carefully composed a balance between not divulging too much or saying too little, eventually convincing four to take the bait.

And so it was that Andre van Heerden's great-granddaughter re-established his project, except not in any eulogy to his memory, rather towards perpetuating the family's long-standing tradition of self-enrichment.

CHAPTER 22

"If you place your head in a lion's mouth, then you cannot complain one day if he happens to bite it off." – Agatha Christie

In much the same fashion as at Margie's place, their pursuers had descended on the *Daily Star* with purpose and in force, except this time there had been no question about Craig's next move. Providing ideal sanctuary, common sense dictated going back to the cave; its rudimentary but evidently shielded isolation gave them somewhere to regroup and replan.

Rematerialising at the tunnel mouth, Margie cursed. "Dammit all, that really wasn't the outcome we wanted." Scowling and flopping dejectedly into a chair, to fold her arms. "Maybe Mike can still make something of it though. After all, he's got the video now. Also, he's well connected and respected by all the newspaper's big shots. Even a single column would do, at least your story would be out there," vainly trying to sound hopeful and looking to Craig for affirmation.

Clearly less upbeat, he scowled.

"Mike won't take it any further or run anything, Mags." Pacing like a caged wild animal, frustratedly gesticulating with both arms, he added, "He's right though, we do need solid proof. We've got absolutely nothing to back up any of this and consequently can't substantiate a damn thing."

Going to the press had seemed like a smart ploy towards forcing Govender and his thugs to back off, however there was no sugar-coating their situation.

Plainly put, Margie's press coverage idea, although a good concept, had panned out a non-starter. Mike owed them nothing, and no matter what recording he may have caught of their departure, it wouldn't constitute a credible article. Any number of software applications could simulate that kind of footage, an ever-cynical, tech-savvy public tearing it to pieces. They'd accomplished nothing and were firmly back at square one.

Craig knew a bolder and more direct tactic would be necessary, Sun Tzu's well-known, albeit copiously overused and clichéd quote springing to mind: *"Keep your friends close, and your enemies even closer."* Stood in the tunnel's mouth, a thousand-yard stare drawn on his face, he wrestled with a thought process. An idea that had come to him last night while Margie slept, already certain of its meeting with her scorn. Deciding to discuss it regardless, he pulled the second chair around to face hers, outlining what could only be described as a maverick strategy. A few sentences in, Margie's eyes dropped to the floor, signifying she'd checked out, but Craig pressed on regardless. Eventually, looking up into his eyes, the look of dread plainly etched on her face stopped him dead.

Understanding the logic driving his plan, Margie nevertheless feared the risks involved would far outweigh any prospective gain. Her words came falteringly.

"Okay, Craigy, even if he's not entirely comfortable with…

the human consequences… he's… still following through… doing his job. What makes you think he'd ever consider… helping you? Besides, how would you get to him? You can't just go to the lab's reception and ask to have a private chat, that's never gonna end well."

Taking no heed of her sarcasm, Craig continued.

"Of course not. The lab wouldn't be right anyway. It's got to be a neutral place, somewhere we can be certain of him being alone. That is, if he even swallow's the lure." Without pausing to allow further interjection, going on to explain the rest of his plan.

Downright perilous, probably foolhardy, at this point they didn't have many other options; Govender must be swayed, possibly even brought on side. Lips drawn in a tight line of resignation, Margie reluctantly agreed to go along with Craig's strategy.

He would go alone for the first stage, during the lab's lunch break, knowing Govender's theatre would be unmanned.

Getting up to leave when the hour arrived, Margie caught his hand and pulled herself up from the chair.

"You better darn well take good care of yourself, Craigy. Don't go taking any stupid risks, just stick to the plan."

Self-consciously reaching up and leaning forwards, she softly pecked his cheek. Sparing a brief, reassuring smile, he nodded.

"This is the easy part, Mags. Don't worry, I'll be careful." Adding, "I don't know what would happen if you were in the exact same spot as where I come back to, so probably best if you stay seated in your chair, just in case."

Stepping away, he was gone.

Arriving in the far corner of Govender's theatre, an area mostly obscured by a procession of wheeled screens, the place was deserted. Or so it seemed at first, an indistinct noise startling Craig. Tracking the source to a man strapped on the procedure table, perhaps a few years younger than himself. The unfortunate victim was sweating profusely, his eyes shut tight to repetitively whisper a prayer in his mother tongue. Fighting an overwhelming urge to go straight over, unbuckle the leather straps and free him, Craig instead stood dead still. Foregoing his better nature to instead scan the place, spotting Govender's distinctive mauve laptop open on a worktable near the door. Speaking much of its user, an uninspiring retro screen saver of randomly drifting, coloured bubbles filled the screen.

Not wishing to alert the tethered man to his presence, Craig edged across to the PC. Pulling a folded scrap of paper from one pocket, he placed it on the keyboard and gently closed the screen. The only paper available, Craig had used the chewed stub of a pencil to write on the back of an empty coffee can wrapper: *"North Pier, Durban. Midnight, alone. CF."* Deliberately keeping his note cryptic when scribing, remembering that Govender would occasionally direct his assistant to make entries on the laptop.

Held fast on the procedure table, the captive continued mumbling feverishly, seemingly unaware of his presence. Hesitating to stare across the space separating them, a moral dilemma ate at Craig's conscience, fighting against all too explicit imaginings of the doomed man's potential fate but knowing intervention would be imprudent. They would realise he had been there if freeing the man and taking him away, risking scuppering their strategy. A minute at most had passed and everything was going perfectly, it would be crazy to mess with the plan at this point. Swallowing his principles, Craig departed that place.

Like a spring uncoiling, Margie leapt from her chair.

"Thank God! I was getting worried. Are you okay? How did it go?"

Babbling rapid-fire questions to release pent-up anxiety, then flinging her arms round his neck and whimpered in relief.

Chuckling at her outburst, Craig returned the hug.

"Everything went fine, just like we'd planned." His face changed and took on a haunted look, tone turning sombre. "Horrible though, they've got some poor sod on the table."

Margie's smile flipped to a look of dismay, leaning back and searching his face.

"Oh God, how awful. Did you talk to him?" she asked, partly concerned at the doomed man's fate, although desperately hoping he hadn't.

Eyes squeezed tightly shut, as if by doing so might blot out the man's residually imprinted image, shaking his head. Realising the impact this encounter must have had on him, Margie answered on his behalf.

"No, of course not. You wouldn't take the risk of screwing it all up."

Not wanting to discuss the subject any further, Craig huffed at a choke in his throat and switched topic.

"Well, what's done is done and the die is cast. Now we'll just have to wait, see if Govender reads the note and shows up tonight. If he does, we move onto the next stage. If not, then right now I've got no idea what to do beyond that." Shrugging, he made a face. They stared solemnly at each other for a moment, individually considering the brevity of their situation.

"Well, that's all very cheerful." Margie's expression had hardened, an edge of steel creeping into her voice. "Look, no point in us getting a downer, there's an answer to every problem. Whatever that might be, we'll find it."

Smiling inwardly, Craig knew this seemingly sweet and demure woman to have the heart of a lioness. Something in his face must have given him away because she became self-conscious, deflecting by reaching up to ruffle his hair and cooing.

"We've got around twelve hours to kill before needing to leave, you might as well get some more sleep. Sorry to say it, but you look like death warmed up."

There was no point arguing, mind and body feeling exactly as he must appear.

"Yeah, that's not a bad idea. I am shattered, just too wired to sleep right now. Let's sit awhile and chill out. I'll get a few hours' kip later." Dropping heavily into a camp chair and retying a loose shoelace, he stared wistfully into the distance. "You know what I really fancy right now, Mags?" Continuing without waiting for an answer, "A good meal, a hot shower and an entire day spent sleeping in my own bed."

Margie gave him a look and snorted. "You're torturing yourself, mister. There'll be plenty of time for that when we're done with this whole cursed situation."

After some deliberation, his tone turned pensive. "I truly am sorry for getting you involved and turning your life upside down, Mags, but in a selfish kind of way I'm glad you're here. I wouldn't want to be stuck in the middle of all this without you," immediately regretting how treacly sentimental that must have sounded.

"Now you listen to me, Craigy, you've been there for me during my own tough times, so now it's my turn." Before it could get awkward, she winked at him, adding, "Leave it there. Just don't go getting all cocky."

When she turned away, Craig smiled weakly and they sat in silence, as only two people entirely comfortable in one another's company can. Perhaps an hour passed, when Craig got to his feet. Stretching stiff limbs, he yawned.

"Think I've wound down enough to sleep now, and I've got a feeling this could turn out being a long night." Shuffling past her to reach the tunnel, Craig handed over the Glock. "In case anything happens."

Stretched out on the mattress in their cave's oddly reassuring gloom, his thoughts went to Govender, forming and reforming possible scenarios possibly cropping up that night. Would the man even show up? If so, would he come alone? Craig had chosen the meeting location after careful consideration; the pier should be pretty much abandoned at that time. Long, and surrounded by open water, affording plenty of time to scrutinise anybody approaching. If Govender didn't turn up around the set time, they would have no alternative but to come back to the cave again. Then what?

Tossing and turning on the uncomfortable and smelly mattress, he finally drifted into a restless sleep. There was no way of knowing how long he'd been out, only that it must have been several hours because all daylight had gone from the entrance. Woken by Margie crouched over him, whispering urgently and shaking his shoulder.

"Craig, Craig, get up, they're here." He was instantly wide awake, as if having a bucket of ice-cold water tipped over him.

"Where are they? How many?" also whispering and scrambling to his feet.

"Dunno, couldn't see, just heard them coming through the bush." Finding his wrist in the darkness, she thrust the Glock into an open hand.

Disengaging the safety, he inched the slide back, making as little noise as possible when cocking the pistol. In his imagining, Govender's thugs might already be in the tunnel, almost upon them.

"Whatever happens, stay here," he murmured, squeezing Margie's arm in emphasis, then tiptoed towards the opening.

Holding the Glock ahead of him, in a shooter's stance, hugging the tunnel's craggy inner curvature for cover while creeping forwards. Thankfully, faint backlight from the bore's mouth thus far betraying no intruders. Finally reaching the entrance, dusk had overtaken day and scant vestigial radiance from a long-set sun offered faint definition to the cavern's environs.

Crouching and remaining stock still, listening keenly, the only discernible sound coming from the hammering of his heart. Then, from somewhere in the gloom below, an indistinct noise. Fine hairs on the back of Craig's neck stood on end and he stopped breathing, feeling a warm trickle of sweat slide between his shoulder blades. Adrenaline pumping, senses gone into overdrive, envisaging a squad of night camo'd shock troops creeping across the cave floor. There, another sound, the stealthy shuffling of soft-soled combat boots, interspersed by the faintest snap of a dry twig. It could have been a piece of kindling, dropped by Margie near the stairs, they were closer than he'd thought. Almost certainly equipped with night-vision goggles, they'd already spotted him, in their sights, ready to take the shot. Realisation hit home, the Van Heerden's wanted the Link back at any cost and had given the order to kill on sight.

About to begin backing up, intent on shielding Margie when a familiar odour caught Craig's nostrils, musky, feral and potently foetid. Suddenly, a distinctive grunt gave it all away, a family of warthogs foraging for food. Slowly exhaling released a steel band of tightly wound tension, and he couldn't stifle a snigger.

Lowering the pistol, a sudden touch startled him. Tiptoeing behind, Margie had followed and caught hold of his arm.

"What is it?" Her small voice quaked from fear.

Recovered from his fright, Craig kept his voice low.

"Shh. Warthogs feeding, listen." As if on cue, another grunt was followed by a shrill squeal of protest.

One of the wild pigs had probably uncovered something tasty and another was trying to muscle in on their find. Stretching to see over the edge, Margie brushed up against Craig and he slipped an arm around her shoulder, pulling her close. Shaking, doing her utmost to smother an embarrassed giggle until unable to contain it, she laughed out loud. Alarmed, the hogs stampeded noisily away, back into the forest.

Turning to bury her shame in his T-shirt, she whispered, "Sorry, Craigy. I honestly thought it was those people coming for us."

Craig couldn't help himself.

"Now who's the jumpy one? Never mind. Better safe than sorry." To spare Margie's further blushes, he changed the subject. "It's getting cold, I'll get a fire going."

Squatting to light a candle, he set about stacking the remaining tinder grass, kindling and firewood in sequential order of ignition. Crackling flames soon warmed them and lit the cavern with its flickering, homely glow, seeming to shield against any lurking menace. After eating the second jar of franks, they sat talking, passing the time in idle conversation and casually feigning oblivion at what was yet to come. Shortly before midnight they left the cave, just as the last of their wood sputtered to smoky embers.

At the long breakwater's furthest accessible extremity, they were greeted by a warm and stickily humid sea breeze, fortified with the Indian Ocean's salty, umami fragrance. Roughly halfway along the pier a solitary fisherman trudged landward, two rods and a haversack slung over one shoulder and several pan-sized fish swinging from his free hand. Craig sighed in relief when observing, other than this departing figure, the place looked to be entirely deserted. A brightly lit floating city slid effortlessly past them in the shipping channel separating North Pier from The Bluff headland; a huge container ship entering harbour, its bunker oil-fired engines thrumming and massive thrashing screws churning up a roiling wake.

Opposite, beachfront hotel and gaudy casino lights spilled a multihued splash of colour across a wide expanse of barren sand. During daytime the beach would have been crammed with holidaymakers, bathing or simply soaking up the sun, all the while incessantly plied by soft drink and ice cream vendors. At this late hour, waves crashing on its pale, stretching expanse provided the sole activity. Foaming shore break surf raced up the beach until losing momentum, pausing fractionally before returning to the sea, incessantly repeated, again and again.

Next to them and guarded by a locked gate, a flashing beacon warned of the pier's position. Beyond this, the ocean's dark immensity was sporadically dotted by the lights of inshore fishing boats and further out, those of bigger ships at anchor, awaiting scheduled docking slots.

"So far so good, it's pretty well empty," Craig quipped.

"Including your friend," Margie retorted, unable to keep an edge of anxiety from her voice. The pier's desolation did little to quell a sense of unease, it was far too quiet for her liking.

"It's not quite midnight yet, Mags. Give him a few minutes," Craig shot back, regretting a flash of annoyance. "Sorry, I didn't mean to snap."

In the process of gathering a rejoinder, Margie spotted movement at the pier's shore end.

"Looks like he might be on time after all," pointing towards a lone figure approaching.

Whoever it might be had already drawn level with the departing fisherman, continuing onwards in their direction. Still too far away to make out distinguishing features, nonetheless, carrying a man's gait. Hesitating, appearing as if staring in their direction, he resumed a brisk pace, when a glint of light refracted from spectacles. It was Ruben Govender.

Intending to engage disarmingly with the man, putting him at ease and lowering his guard, Craig would then grab hold and jump them both to the cave. Knowing the side effects of a first jump should keep his mark occupied awhile, Craig intended returning to fetch Margie before Govender managed to collect his bearings. Overall, a sketchy tactic, Govender may be wilier or stronger than his slender frame suggested. If struggling from Craig's grasp at a critical instant anything might happen, worst case, getting to the cave and leaving parts of Govender behind on the pier.

Irrespective, they were sticking to the plan; get the man

alone and interrogate him on their home ground, ideally establishing some kind of reciprocal truce. To have any hope of extricating themselves from this mess, the Van Heerden's operation must be disclosed and made public, the mantis providing concrete evidence that Mike Winter had spoken of. For his part in the bargain, Craig intended offering Govender unreserved cooperation in whatever he was trying to achieve. Willing to do virtually anything that would get them to this point, Craig was ready to use force on Govender, anything at all to save Margie and himself.

By now within earshot, Govender halted and called out.

"Hey there, Mr. Farrant, I got your note. It's good to see you again. I was really worried, thinking something had happened to you."

An inflection in his voice, sounding stilted and rehearsed, except Craig didn't get the chance to process this. Two virtually simultaneous suppressed discharges, *pop*, *pop*, preceded a sharp smack to the neck. Clutching at this sudden, stinging pain, spinning to identify the source and seeing shadowy figures clambering over the pier wall. Distracted by Govender's banter, these assailants had emerged soundlessly from concealment amongst flanking concrete dolos blocks.

"Craig!" Margie screamed.

Whirling again, to see her flailing in the fine mesh of a virtually unbreakable capture net.

They'd been set up and he'd delivered them into a trap, naïvely believing Govender could be enticed. Yanking a tranquilliser dart from his neck and flinging it at one of their attackers, he started towards Margie, but his legs turned to rubber and buckled at the first stride. Dropping heavily to his knees, a buzzing sound filled Craig's head. Vision closing in, everything spiralled, like falling into a psychedelic tunnel. As his face hit the gritty, weathered concrete, the last image was of two darkly clad figures leaping on Margie and pinning her to the ground. His own frenetic whirligig shrieked to fever pitch, slipping into a vortex of oblivion.

CHAPTER 23

"Folly is perennial and yet the human race has survived." – Bertrand Russell

Specialising in artificial intelligence and robotics, Rajendra Mohan Govender had filled a senior post at the Indian Space Research Organisation. Rebecca's second successful recruit, despite being in the latter stages of developing a fully autonomous rover for the country's inaugural moon mission at the time of their initial meeting. Holding doctorates in applied physics, cybernetics and medicine, Govender had filled his spare time with private research on the integration of hi-tech micro and nano mechanics into humans.

A fanatical lifelong disciple of anything science fiction, believing his true calling to be the development of semi-immortal human hybrids for the purpose of extended space travel. Essentially piggybacking on ISRO, simultaneously deriving an income and virtually unrestricted access to the kind of technology required to augment his sideline venture. Although never disclosing these covert activities to his employer, Rebecca had got wind of Govender's moonlighting. Ultimately, it wasn't only the man's professional skill set but also his duplicitous nature that made him a desirable fit.

Born and raised in the clean air of a leafier suburb in Kochi, a bustling city huddled on India's Kerala coast, Rajendra had enjoyed a relatively privileged upbringing. His father's successful tool manufacturing business and mother's partnership in a high-profile law firm had seen the family extremely well off. Both well-educated, his parents had appreciated the financial implications of child-rearing and broke with the cultural norm, limiting the number of offspring they produced. Being one of only three siblings, young Govender and his two sisters had wanted for nothing of a material nature.

Like a fish to water, he'd taken up the game of cricket at school and continued playing into early adulthood, when studying at the Institute of Science in Bangalore. Achieving exceptional final exam results, he'd been tempted into taking a place at MIT in the USA, furthering his studies and gaining three doctorates. Adopting the nickname Ruben during his time in America, as a concession to professors and peers struggling to get their habitually Anglocentric tongues around his given name.

Intrinsically a loner, making no friends to speak of, he'd also steered clear of campus fraternities and parties. Taking advantage of whatever spare time, his extracurricular activities constituted further studies, reading or watching sci-fi movies alone in his dorm. Graduating in the final year of the last millennium and passing over lucrative offers from major corporations on both sides of the Atlantic, he returned home to India. Remaining in America had not once crossed his mind, yearning for home familiarity, traditional cuisines and cultural dialects, even the diversity of smells. Newly acquired credentials under his belt, Ruben Govender secured a hefty research grant from the Institute of Sciences, using the bulk of these funds to set up his private concern.

Realising a steady income to be essential, an offer to join India's own developing space programme had been too good to turn down. Although not enjoying meteoric career progression within ISRO, primarily due to lacking social skills, recognition of technical achievements and work ethic had culminated in his advancement to chief of Robotic Studies. Nevertheless, as in all quasi-government agencies, legislation, regulations, rules and red tape reigned supreme, eliciting an ever-growing sense of frustration and self-limitation.

Thoroughly fed up, after twelve years of bureaucracy, meeting with Rebecca for a second time at a symposium after-party and hearing what she had to offer came as a breath of fresh air. Fairly inebriated by that stage of the evening, he'd been captivated by the woman's charming manner and beguiled when hearing of an embryonic project underway in her country. While references to revolutionary flight systems stimulated interest, the concept of telepathic control had got his undivided attention.

From early life personal interpretations of Vimānas, fantastical flying palaces referenced in Hindu and Sanskrit texts, his imagination drew tantalising parallels with Rebecca's recruitment pitch. Pressing for more information, she'd become evasive, but the tempting morsels disclosed thus far had already set the hook. Even though possessing a superb intellect, Govender was in truth an utterly naïve dupe and incapable of seeing through such skilful manipulation. The evening's event had finally drawn to a close and the temptress bade him goodnight, heading for the powder room. Unwilling to leave their encounter open-ended, he'd loitered outside the ladies' until she emerged, practically begging her to tell him everything. Instead, reeling him in, she invited Govender to visit their facility.

Taking a week's overdue leave at short notice, citing personal circumstances, Govender and Rebecca flew to South Africa a few days later. Landing at King Shaka International the next morning, they were met by her father's driver and taken straight to the laboratory. Due to Rebecca's circumspection, Govender hadn't really known what to expect, just how advanced this tech might be, or even if its inferred applications might indeed be viable. All reservations evaporated when the doors of a newly installed elevator opened at basement level, right there and then, joining the organisation and sealing his fate.

Meeting with Jacqui Lin at some point that day, another recent arrival, with whom he would evidently be working closely. When being taken to meet with his new colleague, she had been sat at a desk, absorbedly tinkering with the fractured remnants of a silver sphere. Taking advantage of this distraction to check her out, immediately struck by the woman's elegant and polished presence. As if tailored, her lab coat fitted snugly over a stylish ensemble of floral silk blouse, knee-length pencil skirt and impossibly high, shiny black wedges. His own red, Ferrari-logoed polo shirt, worn loose over creased grey chinos with three-year-old scuffed trainers poking out below frayed hems, left him feeling at a disadvantage.

Rebecca had caught Lin's attention and made the introduction. Oval-faced and pretty by any cultural standard, the warmth in Jacqui Lin's smile and firmness of handshake hinted at an indefinable moxie, secreted deep within poised oriental calm. Despite their apparent differences, she happened to be friendly and easy-going with an infectious smile, attributes to which he grudgingly warmed from the get-go.

Meeting Rebecca's father afterwards, a burly, stern-looking man and not one for small talk, slicing through any pleasantries to spell out Govender's duties. Given the lead role of exploring the craft's artificial intelligence, he would establish an interface methodology with the talisman's, simultaneously collaborating with Lin to implement control systems pairing. Lin's principal responsibility lay in reverse-engineering the craft's propulsion system and energy source.

At a subsequent gathering, Bruno set performance milestones for their joint portfolios. The short-term goal was production of a fully interactive, functional prototype within twelve months; after three-years, allowing for correcting developmental flaws, to manufacture an upsized scale model, large enough for manned operation. Jointly tasked with growing and managing their own teams proportionately, however, required to support the measure of this endeavour, Rebecca would vet all new recruits.

Hailing from California's Silicon Valley, another new team member started scarcely a week after Govender. An eighteen-year-old 3-D animation prodigy, Gustav Maticek had been hired to decrypt the craft's otherwise unfathomable programming and provide overall tech support. Once deciphering the codes, he was then expected to write compatible algorithms, near as possible mimicking original program functionalities. Acknowledging the enormity and fundamental significance of this aspect, the Van Heerden's had invested heavily in the latest quantum AI computing technology.

Despite having access to the most powerful processing, analytical and diagnostic systems available, the craft's hyper-exotic tech ultimately presented no real mystery to Gus. The holograms, for one; their physical interactivity derived from principles identical to a contemporary capacitive touchscreen. Simplistically, a minute negative charge surrounding the holograms experienced repulsion when in proximity to an equally tiny electrical negative emanating from a human body, thus enabling manipulation of these images.

Beyond basic practical science, Gus's gift made operational grouping, intuitive deciphering and category assignation of holograms and glyphs seem deceptively straightforward. Fascinated from an early age by ancient writing forms and codes, he'd been endowed with an inherent, yet uncannily baffling ability to decode the most obscure of cryptographs. In a manner that most industry specialists could only envy, the languages of computers simply an extension to his own dialect.

To successfully resolve the apparent synergy between craft AI and four talismans, meant identifying an intangible bridge uniting these elements. In amongst this challenging enigma, the same worryingly literal gaping hole persisted, the missing console; self-evident for this unit to be indispensable from the vehicle's overall operation. Analysing icons displayed on the meticulously pieced together console's panel, Gus soon determined its function as relating to the craft's energy source.

A huge blow to the research effort, especially Lin, potentially impacting half of her remit. Gus, however, took a more sanguine view. Since the power system's structural components remained intact and operational, loss of control mechanisms certainly incurred a hindrance, although wasn't necessarily catastrophic. To his way of thinking, the craft's "programming" had to follow a common logic principle, implying that a replacement control system could feasibly be built.

In much the same way as Andre van Heerden, more than sixty years before, Gus became inexorably drawn to the spatial map unit. Unlike the project's earlier patron though, the young tech savant possessed a breadth of abstract technical understanding and quickly mastered this display's manipulation. Discovering that the system had the capacity to navigate off-Earth, out into the wider universe, however electing to keep this aspect to himself. A selfish choice, perhaps, but one he determined ethically justifiable when witnessing the majesty and diversity of life forms inhabiting far-flung exoplanets. Instinctively knowing, if the Van Heerden's were ever to successfully replicate the craft, he shouldn't be the one exposing life's cosmic proliferation to mankind's brutally egocentric desire for conquest and domination.

Outstripping the realms of 3-D lidar cartography or CGI virtual reality, terming the unit a map would be express folly; better described as a real-time universal viewer. Perplexing, even to Gus, that in no way, shape or form could such freakishly comprehensive realism be generated from a conventional database or supercloud uplink. The viewer's capabilities had to be derived from tapping into something infinitely more complex. Derived from his own theosophist beliefs, Gus envisaged this source being more akin to a sentient universal consciousness; the cosmic akashic record, occupying planes elevated beyond mortal existence.

Operating collaboratively, the project team were soon delivering results. Investigating Wagner's wrecked propulsion unit model, Lin 3-D modelled its damaged sphere to ascertain flaws, using the same software to eliminate gyratory turbulence determined as responsible for its failure. Hamstrung by technological limitations of the time, the detail specifications of Wagner's version in fact checked out and would have continued to function, if not for minute manufacturing imperfections.

Simultaneously, employing multispectral analysis of electrical and thermal fluctuations, Govender acquired an understanding of the biomechanical AI's response stimuli. Observing unique reactions from the entity, particularly when in the presence of different team members, concluding the thing recognised people and responded accordingly. An attribute Govender found fascinating and equally unsettling, ascertaining that each person was being subjected to the AI's own critical assessment.

Grouping the cyber-organism's neural activity patterns by regions of stimulus, Govender determined these as similar but infinitely more complex to those of higher order primates and dolphins. On occasion, catching himself detached from reality and staring at the fluorescing blob, as if hypnotised.

Philosophically aligned to the paranormal, he ascribed to the Nazi's theory of communication between crew and craft being telepathic. Late at night when the place was deserted, he would assume the lotus position and meditate for hours, willing the thing to connect with his projected consciousness. Unfortunately, for Govender, a wish that would remain forever unrequited.

Undeterred, rationalising there must be more to attaining connection than merely projecting his own aura, he dug deeper into the science. Convinced that the German scientists had been correct in their beliefs, a wholly evident lack of substantive alternatives providing supporting evidence. Even though still regarded as pseudoscience, the absence of a crew's access hatch in the craft's seamless hull, the most compelling argument against contemporary comprehension. Since, unless employing some form of matter transference, the craft's complement had no way of getting in or out of their vessel. Emboldened by the official sanction of such eccentric conjecture, Stein's team had ventured out on an esoteric limb, daring to propose the concept of teleportation.

Even in modern times, mainstream science discounted these ideas out of hand as outrageously half-baked poppycock, proponents worthy solely of censure and academic exile. Not to Govender's Hindu cultural outlook, imagination further steeped in science fiction, the metaphysical was to be embraced and such theories given credibility. Born into a generation of minds saturated with New Age thinking, an obvious correlation existed, linking telepathy and extradimensional material transmission, with the synergistic potential betwixt man and supersmart machine.

Not needing any justification beyond his own nous, aware of established physicists having already made public their own great strides in instantaneous spatial interaction of subatomic particles. Quantum entanglement, a process still very much in its infancy, was nonetheless a baby step towards the aspirational panacea of instantaneous matter transfer. In simple terms, despite intellectual naysayer's protestations, teleportation.

An accomplishment, likely old hat to a far older and more advanced civilisation, long surpassing such meagre scientific blasphemy with infinitely more complex feats of quantum manipulation. Grasping the underlying principles, Govender could however see that these might manifest beyond the limits of human conception, including his own. For this project to succeed in every respect, it would be essential to determine precisely how the Links were deployed, and their interaction with the AI, before even attempting to replicate this process.

The significance of a Link module accompanying each of the dead aliens had not been lost on Andre van Heerden, nor was it to Govender. Reasoning their colour-shifting peculiarity to hold relevance, he first needed to interpret the implication of this characteristic. Assessing the variety of responses, as influenced by an individual's temperaments, provided the most obvious starting point. Less immediately apparent, the import these personality traits inferred and why not every individual elicited a colour change.

Only three of the ten-strong project team positively affected the Links, and to Govender's disappointment, he fell into the zero-response group. Even so, nothing noteworthy happened when any of that elite trio held an amulet inside the craft; another mystifying fail, so far as Govender was concerned. Unbeknownst in these early stages, expanding his investigation of this aspect would culminate in the project tipping over into a state of premeditated wickedness.

From these preliminary uncontrolled trials, Govender concluded that a colour change didn't necessarily indicate suitable host potential. Not unduly dismayed by initial unsuccessful outcomes, he rationalised that something so fundamental could never be quite as simple. A professional bias towards nanotechnology inevitably influenced his thinking, intuitively knowing that a successful outcome hinged on Link and subject amalgamating, fusing at an elemental level.

Beyond this insight, Govender had no inkling as to how this vital interaction might be instigated. Following scientific principles, by procedurally eliminating causes for failure, he elected to broaden the spectrum; a greater diversity of subjects would inevitably provide a more representative database.

Exiting the restricted zone and leaving his underlings to more mundane tasks, Govender worked his way through the pharmaceutical plant's employees. His search for more compatible participants yielded yet more uninspiring results, until happening upon a young woman in Dispatch. Busy checking off an inbound chemical consignment, she paused, curiously accepting the Link Govender placed into her open palm. The amulet immediately bloomed in an opalescent blue sheen, then after a few seconds, its shape appeared to subtly soften. When the fresh-faced receiving clerk cried out in surprise and dropped it to the floor, Govender realised he'd hit the jackpot. Not only had the Link shown a colour different to any before, more intriguingly another reaction had begun to initiate. A totally unique response, and right away Govender needed to know where that secondary reaction had been headed.

Beside himself with excitement, Govender rushed to Rebecca's office, bursting in without knocking and explaining what had just happened. Not counting on getting rebuked for exposing an amulet to personnel of the wider business, Govender stood his ground, uncharacteristically arguing back. Protocols be damned, he was on to something and needed to carry out multiple trials across a broader test base. To his thinking, sampling the employees had been nothing more than a harmless albeit essential gamble, inconveniencing the employees by no more than a moment's distraction. It had paid off, confirming his assumptions, now needing compliant subjects for the real thing; those where anything untoward happening would be without consequence. Putting aside immediate reservations to hear him out, Rebecca couldn't fault his case, a prospective solution already gelling in her mind.

Recent legislative changes had obligated the Van Heerden's to reactivate thirty per cent of their farm under crops, ten thousand hectares already planted to ripening maize. The timing of Govender's necessity couldn't have been more fortuitous, since government job creation directives also compelled the engagement of unemployed labour in favour of wholesale mechanisation. Consequently, around three hundred indigent men and women were currently working the fields, many coming from remotely far-flung parts of the province. All paid cash-in-hand at the end of every week, by devising a simple ruse, Govender could set himself up in the farm office and test every individual with the Link.

Mostly suggestible rural people, with little or no formal education, they were easily convinced of the Link being a security device; deployed to prevent fraudulent duplicate payment claims. Desperate to keep their meagre jobs, all submitted to this trial by device, none daring to challenge Govender's say-so, for fear of dismissal. By the end of that first payday, four had generated a similar result to the goods receiving clerk and were promptly corralled in an empty, windowless storeroom. Sat in silence, on a single wooden bench, they apprehensively awaited the outcome of their fate. If, during that interval, any had gained the slightest notion as to Govender's intentions, they would surely have fled empty-handed.

Shortly before dusk, the three men and a woman were shepherded from the farm office onto an enclosed pickup truck, then taken to the laboratory. By blind coincidence, the lab's security and detention section happened to be strategically adjacent to Govender's surgical theatre. Locked away in separate cells, over the ensuing days, one at a time, these people would be dehumanised, becoming nothing more than an expendable commodity.

Culturally inculcated, Govender had never knowingly harmed another living creature, even shooing away a bothersome fly or mosquito, rather than killing with a well-placed swat. Years before, wanting to gain background perspective when starting up his sideline research, he'd devoured countless books on atrocities committed in the name of medical or scientific advancement. At first repulsed, ultimately vindicating these acts of barbarism, on the grounds of medical advances derived. An impaired psychological benchmark duly established, his conscience had become inured to such heinous deeds of immorality, consequently experiencing no qualms at using living, breathing human beings like lab rats.

On the morning of the first trial, Govender brimmed with nervous excitement, similar to that experienced when going out to bat for his cricket team. Savouring the moment, however unsure whether this sense of euphoria came from the prospect of what lay ahead, or fentanyl downed with a cup of chai tea. When arriving the laboratory, the middle-aged woman had already been heavily sedated and strapped to the theatre's procedure table. Under close direction, his medical assistants attached electrodes to the woman's torso and head, finally positioning cameras to record the test.

Everything to his satisfaction, Govender placed a Link on the subject's exposed breastbone and stepped away to observe. Immediately colour shifting, for a few tense seconds the Link rose and fell in time with her shallow breathing, then it abruptly liquefied, like wax dropped on a hot plate. Govender stepped forward, concerned about the gleaming bead possibly running and falling to the floor, but instead it adhered and quickly absorbed into the woman's skin. Overjoyed, Govender howled joyously, he'd done it.

Celebrations proving premature and short-lived, when the woman's vitals spiked sharply and went off the chart, monitor's alarms beeping frenziedly. The subject began convulsing violently and an assistant ran towards the table but halted midway, when something truly freaky unfolded. As quickly as going into seizure, so the woman's spasms ceased, slumping to the table, motionless. Then her outline blurred, organic matter diffusing and becoming airborne, as if atomic bonds holding the body's molecular structure together were coming apart.

Everyone in the theatre backed up, sensing something ghastly about to happen, then, sounding like a huge Velcro strip ripping apart, she disintegrated. Instinctively turning to shield his face, Govender peeked but wished he hadn't, witnessing a scene as if taken from the worst kind of horror movie. All surrounding surfaces and nearby assistant had been spattered in a pinky-grey sludge and there, amidst this gelatinous gore, the reconstituted Link. Perched middle of the procedure table, crackling ominously, minute electrical discharges jumping from its periphery.

Shaken by what could only be termed a catastrophic experimental failure, Govender spent days analysing data and video footage. To his exasperation, none of the recordings provided the slightest hint as to where everything had gone so horribly wrong. With nothing of any substance to go on, he resorted to guesswork, imagining subject number one's advancing age may have rendered the woman an unsuitable host. Also, surreptitiously harbouring an innate degree of misogyny, perhaps the Link wasn't intended to sync with females. Forced to discount this fancy however, when recalling one crew's remains exhibiting a wider pelvic girdle than the others.

Fed up with clutching at insubstantial straws, he had nothing to lose by bringing in the next subject, conveniently a male in his mid-twenties. To Govender's disappointment, this man returned a virtually identical outcome, again with the third a few days down the line. Disillusioned at three consecutive failures, he began doubting whether they were even on the right track; after all, despite the alien crew's virtually identical physiology, humans might simply not be compatible.

A week of self-doubt and re-evaluation elapsed. Then, while running on a treadmill in the lab's gym, an idea surfaced, realising it highly unlikely for the crew's systems to contain drugs at the time of merging with their devices. Yet they had pumped a potent cocktail of barbiturates into the test subjects, more so for tranquillity of work environment than as a humane measure. Accepting this to be a somewhat "left field" theory at best, although not entirely unscientific, the benefit of medical insight adjudging this a credible supposition. Just possible that, if detecting these drugs, the Link deemed a candidate's suitability to be compromised, it might then violently reject assimilation.

Coincidentally, this realisation turned out being the self-same insight that led to Craig and Margie's entanglement. Showering after his workout, Govender toyed with the idea of recalling his lab team to prepare their final subject, instead electing to work alone, he ran a series of amended simulations.

Soaring temperatures and the Jag's malfunctioning air con made Govender's drive to work the next morning feel like being broiled in a steam oven. Despite this minor discomfort, nothing could diminish his sense of impending success, knowing he had stumbled on something important. The final abductee, a man in his late thirties, originated from a subsistence farming community in the Drakensberg foothills. Strapped to the table like those before, however without the salve of sedatives, he pleaded to be released and allowed to return home. Entreaties falling on deaf ears, the test began, seeming from the outset to be going down the same disastrous route as the others. Following assimilation, the monitors surged, except instead of convulsing the man's readings gradually stabilised.

Stepping from behind a clear acrylic screen, erected after the first trial, Govender started towards the table then stopped in his tracks. Air surrounding the man suddenly changed, densifying to appear like a rippling liquid, as if from a pebble thrown into a pond. Then, without warning, this atmospheric phenomenon spontaneously collapsed in on itself, and the subject disappeared.

Stupefied, Govender stood motionless, expecting the Link to reappear, only this time it didn't. An exhilarating outcome in one sense, the process having gone exactly as anticipated; conversely, explaining the uncontrolled loss of subject and Link posed a terrifying prospect. Panic set in, needing to take the edge off a soaring sense of trepidation and wanting absolute mental clarity to best deal with this situation, Govender withdrew a blister pack of fentanyl from an inside pocket.

Deciding not to inform Rebecca right away, definitely steering clear of the father, he must first devise a mitigation strategy. Salvation came when the synthetic opioid entered his system; an answer so obvious, realising the craft's map system would reveal the Link's location. Only when once the host's position had been identified would he go to the Van Heerden's, leaving them to organize a suitable recovery plan. Breathing a sigh of relief, he went in search of Gus.

Just as Govender had hoped, a familiar blue dot emerged when Gus widened the map's field of view, seeing it lying roughly a hundred kilometres due west of the lab. Deftly skimming across the landscape until centring on the Link's icon, Gus zoomed, descending in altitude perspective. Dusk had long since settled, and from a height of around two thousand metres the ground appeared rubbed in charcoal, pricked by clusters of light. Continuing to manipulate the viewer, Gus dropped them closer to the target, gleaming pinpricks leaping from the gloom to define light spillout from the windows of huts and houses.

Applying contrast enhancement brightened the scene, revealing a rural landscape strewn with the modest homes of subsistence farmers. Set well apart from other structures, their target comprised a pair of corrugated iron-roofed structures, one larger than its companion. Landscape topographical features showed this irregular pairing to hug the crest of a hillside and served by a single-track dirt road. The Link and test subject were inside the larger building, but to Govender something about this setting felt off; the homestead bigger and better positioned than would be expected of a migrant worker's humble dwelling.

Intrigued, they watched the Link move about inside the house, following a regular pattern as the subject went from room to room. Time had come for the part Govender most dreaded, dropping the bombshell and explaining to the Van Heerden's what had transpired. Surprisingly, they took the news better than anticipated and were at the laboratory within minutes of his phone call. Acknowledging his experimental success, the situation was however critical, both Link and subject beyond the lab and their control. Recovery must be robustly and effectively managed, Rebecca taking charge and electing to oversee the mission personally.

The first order of business lay in retrieving their asset; the most effective means of accomplishing this was to employ guerilla tactics. Any peripheral entanglements, arising from the subject's exposure to third parties, would have to be simultaneously contained or outright eliminated. Specific details and mission logistics would be the sole domain of VHP's head of security, Dariusz Berzins, immediately summoning him to the basement for briefing.

Berzins' pedigree was beyond question, having served in the Latvian army's Special Tasks Unit as a younger man, attaining the rank of major. Retiring after twenty years' service, he'd gone freelance, initially selling his services as a soldier of fortune in the greater Middle East. Badly injured by a Taliban

IED taking out his transport in Afghanistan, he'd moved into the relatively softer field of VIP protection. Around that time Bruno had frequently visited a Saudi sheikh client at his London, Mayfair home and came to know Dariusz. Something about the Latvian's tough inscrutability had resonated with Bruno, and when discovering the wrecked craft there had been no doubt as to who he wanted guarding this treasure.

Skilled in high-level strategic planning, recovering the Link consequently presented no real challenge to Berzins. First requesting an aerial reconnaissance survey of the test subject's location; essential to gain first-hand knowledge of surrounding terrain and assess tactical considerations before dispatching a ground team.

Available on twenty-four-hour standby, the company's chopper pilot was in Rebecca's office within an hour, however expressing reluctance when shown their intended flight path. Intense storms, accompanied by lightning and high winds, had rolled across the province that afternoon and were headed in their direction. Annoyed at the pilot's unwillingness to fly, Rebecca became enraged, demanding that he get the bird airborne. Not wanting to lose a helicopter and lives, Bruno stepped in, taking Rebecca aside and suggesting that she postpone the sortie till morning. Ultimately, a pragmatic intervention, evidenced when the storm hit shortly after, enveloping the region in gale-force winds and torrential rain.

The next day dawned clear and cloudless with the gentlest of southeasters, offering excellent visibility and perfect for flying. Lifting off from the rooftop helipad, Dariusz sat up front with the pilot, turning to follow a west-north-westerly course. They would reach the Drakensberg's foothills in under an hour where, according to the flight chart, their objective lay ahead by a further two minute's flying time. In contact with base via radio, where an operative manned the craft's viewer, directing minor bearing adjustments and counting down closing range.

Streaking up a valley, the Tugela River to port and following a gradually rising ridge line, the remote contact suddenly called out "Contact."

A house and detached garage appeared on the pilot's side, a tall stand of yellowwood trees across the track framing the buildings in backdrop. A kilometre downrange within seconds, by working the Jet Ranger's cyclic stick and collective in unison, the pilot nosed up and banked sharply to starboard, turning one-eighty degrees to overfly the house. Through the footwell window, Dariusz caught sight of an adult male stood outside the dwelling to observe their passage, fleetingly noticing that he clutched a coffee mug.

CHAPTER 24

"Hell is empty, and all the devils are here." – William Shakespeare

A needle prick initiated a flood of muddled thoughts and sensations, gradually restoring Craig's awareness. Still on the pier? The sea air smell and sound of waves crashing on the shore was gone, so they had to be someplace else. Perceiving himself slumped in an uncomfortably hard seat, it could only be the laboratory. Memories were coming back, the ambush, a tranquilliser dart hitting his neck and Margie snared in a capture net. Cautiously moving one hand a fraction, then the other, feeling no restraints, there were people's voices nearby. Keeping his eyes shut tight and feigning ongoing unconsciousness, wanting to eavesdrop, he picked out individual voices. Govender was there, describing the tail end of their capture, Craig could have slapped the man but instead continued listening in.

Another, Rebecca passing a sarcastic comment but there were two more, both distinctively male. That infuriating buzzing in his ears finally cleared, distinguishing the Russian's Slavic-sounding tones, leaving only the last man's voice remaining unfamiliar. He spoke softly and with unmistakeable authority. Risking a sly peek around, Craig immediately became concerned when unable to see any sign of Margie. Of no particular significance or value to these people, they could quite easily have disposed of her on the pier; a crushing blow to the head, then thrown unconscious into the sea and left to drown. Whenever her body washed up, or got pulled from the bay, cause of death would almost certainly be recorded as misadventure. Listening to these people's inane babble no longer of interest, Craig needed to know what had happened to her.

Struggling to his feet, snarling, "What have you done with Margie? Where is she?"

All four turned, momentary surprise on their faces quickly traded for complacency; they had the upper hand and knew it.

"She's fine, so shut up and sit down," Rebecca snapped.

Craig's legs gave way, collapsing back into the stackable plastic chair. Although woozy from the dart's drug, registering a degree of optimism at Margie still being alive.

"I want to see her." He returned Rebecca's glare.

Looking around the room, scanning, desperate to confirm his whereabouts. Immediately recognising the carpet, the same distinctive pattern as seen on the night he'd found Govender's card. Definitely somewhere in the lab. He was in an office, spacious and sumptuously furnished, looking to be the seat of power occupied by a corporate big shot. Glass-fronted, teak bookcases occupied virtually an entire wall, two others covered in richly embossed wallpaper and hung with gilt-framed African wildlife oil paintings.

Standing out amidst these artworks, a framed black-and-white photo of a heavily bearded man, taken in the bushveld, showing him stood holding a rifle next to a reedbuck kill. The head of an enormous warthog hung adjacent with an old bolt-action Mauser mounted below, Craig surmising it to be the same rifle as in the photograph. A dark mahogany desk and high-backed leather chair dominated the window wall frontage, where daylight could be seen through chinks in vertical blinds.

Opposite, a suited operative stood in front of an ornate hardwood entrance door. The Russian, who had been blocking Craig's line of sight to the quietly spoken man separated from the group and took up position at another door, occupying a gap bisecting the bookcases. Now able to see the third man, nonchalantly against the desk and instantly recognisable from his website pic as Bruno van Heerden. He held Craig's gaze, coolly implacable and ostensibly oblivious to his anxiety.

"You'll get to see her when we say you can." Rebecca interrupted the two men's sizing each other up.

About to go on, Bruno stepped forwards, raising a hand.

"Wait, Becca," nodding to the Russian, who opened the door behind him and disappeared through it.

In the flesh, Bruno was unmistakably Rebecca's father, not solely in familial resemblance but in the subtly paternal manner of addressing his daughter. Moving away from the desk to come closer and address Craig, deliberately measuring every word.

"I quite understand wanting to see your lady friend. It's not an unreasonable request, but before allowing that, I need you to understand a few things."

Dressed semi-formal in suit trousers and matching waistcoat over a powder-blue, long-sleeved cotton shirt finished with gold cufflinks, he epitomised elegant power dressing. Tall and broad shouldered, a physically big man of formidably imposing stature, age however beginning to betray him. Posture impaired by a slight stoop, he nevertheless exuded an aura of ruthlessness that most would find intimidating. Just the kind of individual Craig ordinarily avoided, having no time for bullies but right at that moment, he was spitting mad. This wasn't however the time or place for heroics, managing to keep the lid on his temper.

"Go ahead, I'm listening," settling for an undisguised glare.

Paying no heed to Craig's belligerence, Van Heerden continued.

"It's evident you've figured out how to use the Link." He paused briefly, although not soliciting a response. "Seeing as how the Link belongs to me, you will remain here at this facility until Doctor Govender has completed a series of tests. Putting it bluntly, Miss Brooks is our insurance towards your collaboration. If you work with my people, once done with you, she will be allowed to leave."

Despite a neutral facial expression, subtle tonal changes belied the man's bluff; having no intention of ever letting Margie go free. Under present circumstances, with no alternative but to play along, Craig dropped his gaze and simulated contemplation.

"Hmm... Okay, so what guarantee do I get for Margie's release? That is, if I do decide to help you?"

Van Heerden's reply was a fraction too quick.

"I give you my personal word."

The hollow echoed in his reassurance confirmed Craig's suspicion; this character possessed all the integrity of a campaigning politician. Time to probe a little.

"And what about me, when do I get to leave?"

Van Heerden's eyes flicked towards Govender before answering.

"Being completely upfront with you... Look, what we're working on here is completely uncharted territory, experimental and unpredictable, it's almost impossible to forecast outcomes. Unfortunately, that carries a degree of unforeseeable associated risk, so I'm afraid we can't extend the same assurances to you. What I can, however, confirm is that you have value to us and will be treated well."

In this instance, at least being halfway truthful, Craig already knew the possibility of release wouldn't be extended to him. Regardless of Bruno's assurances, Margie didn't stand a chance if Govender's experiments ended badly for him. This was Craig's opportunity to get all cards on the table.

"Okay, we've been here before, but what if I don't cooperate?" Craig eyed up the big man.

To one side, Rebecca visibly stiffened, and her father laughed dryly.

"Come now, Mr. Farrant, surely I don't have to spell that one out for you? You've both been removed from circulation and nobody other than us, and a select group of my people, know of your whereabouts." Making a wry face, he grinned humourlessly. "Whenever your friends, family or work colleagues notice you're missing, where are they going to go looking…?"

Leaving this sentence hanging, he went to the trophy wall and took down the old Mauser, working its cocking bolt to check the breech. Stepping back and raising the rifle's butt into his shoulder, he took aim at the warthog.

"Are you by any chance a hunter, Mr. Farrant?" It was a purely rhetorical question. "Around sixty-five years ago, this animal tore my grandfather to pieces, all because he fluffed the first shot. Oupa taught me the importance of not making mistakes when hunting, a principle which I apply to every sphere of my life. Because of that, I can tell you in all honesty, I've never missed a kill." An implied yet crystal clear threat, his tone changed and became good-natured, as though any souring of their conversation had never occurred. "Let's take you to meet with your friend. She's probably just as anxious to see you."

Turning and heading for the side door without another word, Rebecca followed close on her father's heels. The Russian's number two fell in beside Craig, catching hold of his upper arm to impel him forwards. Passing through what was evidently Bruno's personal assistant's office, vacant at that early hour, they continued into the company boardroom where the Russian waited. Taking up a large proportion of the highly polished green granite floor, a chunky white stinkwood table bore the company's logo, skilfully inlaid in Rhodesian teak. Surrounding this power statement, maroon leather-upholstered chairs were similarly detailed in gold thread. Contemporary modern artwork hung from three gilt Venetian-plastered walls, cleverly illuminated from opposing corners by sun tubes that brought natural daylight to a pair of potted African cycads.

Picking up a credit card-sized remote controller from the table, Bruno touched a button, diverting Craig's attention to the last wall. Made from switchable glass, polarised particles reorientated, revealing a hallway beyond where two more operatives flanked Margie. Sat in a chair, staring disconsolately at the floor, she looked scared and vulnerable. Detecting movement, raising her head to seek out Craig and lock eyes, she smiled briefly. As if sensing Craig's intentions, the minder tightened his grip assertively; it would be pointless getting into a scuffle. Hands cuffed to the fore, Margie got up and came to the glass wall, Craig taking cold comfort when noticing one trailing escort's split lip and the other's black eye. The Van Heerden's security team had come to learn the hard way that Margie could be a wildcat.

"Are you alright?" Raising his voice so she could hear through the glass, Craig wrenched his arm from the guard's grip and took a step closer.

Pressing both hands to the screen, she replied.

"Yeah, I'm okay. Just worried what they'd done with you."

Shaking his head, Craig opened his stance and showed himself to be unharmed.

"I'm sorting something out that works for everyone. It's okay, we're gonna be alright."

Hating lying to Margie, although needing to say something, anything to give her a degree of hope, while hopefully lulling their captors into thinking he'd bought Van Heerden's spiel. Despite Margie nodding, Craig could tell that she knew him to be withholding.

Catching Rebecca sniggering derisively in the glass reflection, he glanced angrily over a shoulder but when turning back, Margie was being led away towards an elevator.

"We'll get out of here, Mags. I promise," he shouted before the polished steel doors closed, turning on Bruno. "Where are you keeping her? It'd better be somewhere decent." Grabbing the man's arm, his fingertips sank into a relaxed bicep and drew satisfaction from his startled expression.

Swiftly interposing himself, the Russian removed Craig's offending hand, simultaneously twisting his arm into a submission hold.

Propelling Craig face first into the glass, the security chief snarled, "Try anything like that again and I will break your arm."

Regaining his composure, Bruno chuckled.

"That's alright, Dariusz. Seeing his friend under these circumstances, it's quite understandable for Mr. Farrant to be emotional." Approaching Craig, still held fast against the glass, he continued, "Just so there's no misunderstandings though, Mr. Farrant, hysterical outbursts and aggression won't be tolerated. Learn to manage yourself better, or you really won't like the consequences. Despite what you may think, we are not savages and your friend is being held in a very comfortable place. To be clear, it's not in this building, if that's what you're wondering. We aren't taking the risk of you getting out and finding her. I must also caution that if you were to make such a reckless attempt, then Marguerite's living conditions would deteriorate significantly. You're a sensible man, Mr. Farrant, and I'm sure you don't need me to paint a picture. It's really very simple, like I've already said, work with us and your friend will be allowed to leave, unharmed. Both of your fates lie entirely in your hands."

Dariusz turned Craig to face an apparently unruffled Bruno who smiled amicably, then continued.

"Who knows, all going well, the two of you may even get to go home together?" Nothing more to add, he turned to his daughter. "Becca, you and I have things to do before our one o'clock, my dear. Over to you, Doctor Govender, keep us posted."

Bobbing his head like an ungainly stork, the mantis cleared his throat.

"Of course, sir. Dariusz, please lead the way." Pushing those ridiculously huge spectacles up the bridge of his nose and signalling for the Russian to go ahead.

Marched through a door in the glass wall and along the same hallway where Margie had been moments before, Craig was guided into the elevator. The Russian, Craig now knowing his name to be Dariusz, pressed B floor selector button and the car dropped smoothly. Absurdly seeming to Craig as if their direction of travel portrayed an analogy to his fate, descending into eternal captivity. Catching himself and internally reprimanding, *Don't be an ass. Get a grip.*

At a discreet *ping* the lift car stopped, its doors slid open and Dariusz pointed for him to exit. Stepping out into the cavernous basement vault, Craig looked up to see an enormous textbook flying saucer filling the space. Amazed but critically assessing the thing to be a full-scale replica; incredibly realistic but obviously a fake, whatever these people were all about had just taken an absurdly bizarre twist. Looking around, half expecting to see a film crew with cameras rolling, except there was nothing of the sort, only a scattering of people in the same white overcoats as Govender. None paid any heed to Craig's bewilderment, all studiously engaged in assorted mysterious tasks.

"I truly am sorry about what happened to you and your

friend last night." Govender hovered at his side.

Having pretty much forgotten about his existence, the man's voice broke Craig's train of thought.

"You've got to understand, Craig, this is my life's work, and I can't let anything compromise what we're so close to accomplishing." His tone had taken on a patronisingly consolatory whine, as if soliciting Craig's empathy or support.

It had the opposite effect, falling like flaming arrows into a vat of boiling gasoline. Craig erupted.

"You can stick your life's work up your arse, Govender."

Before Dariusz or his subordinate could react, Craig launched at his nemesis, grabbing the man's stringy throat tightly with both hands, and together they hit the floor hard. Intervening, the minders were well-schooled in unarmed combat, effortlessly breaking Craig's chokehold and wrestling him away before doing any real harm.

Pinning one arm up his back while forcing Craig's head into the concrete floor, Dariusz knelt on his lower spine, growling, "Easy, now. Easy! Stop it and I'll let you up. Keep on playing rough and I'll put you in a world of pain. Got it?"

Releasing his pent-up rage on Govender had taken the edge off, but Craig knew it wasn't the way to get him and Margie out of this place. Better to hold himself in check, be patient and figure out a way of getting her close, then make a break for freedom. Taking satisfaction from Govender's hacking and coughing discomfort, he nodded, conceding.

"Yeah, okay. Let go, I'm done."

Dariusz's weight came off and Craig rolled over on his back, raising both hands to signify compliance, before slowly getting to his feet.

Taking support from the lift door to nurse his bruised throat, Govender was clearly distraught. His glasses had come off and gone flying during the scuffle, Dariusz's number two retrieving them from under a swivel chair. Straightening up and snatching them, the mantis shot Craig a menacing look before coming over to where he stood.

Folding his arms to disguise trembling hands while maintaining a safe distance, although nothing could mask the tremor in his seething, "Y... you attack me when you and your friend's lives depend on me. Th... that was an incredibly stupid thing to do, Craig. Y... you will regret this."

Govender's voice had reverted to the Malayalam twang of Kochi's urban streets. All academic polish evaporating, his dark eyes sparked with the deadly menace of a cornered cobra.

Unperturbed by his adversary's show of smouldering fury and threatening tone, Craig already knew the odds of their ever leaving this place to be slender. He smirked, not wanting Govender to have the satisfaction of seeing how much that eventuality troubled him.

Holding the man's glare, voice laden with sarcasm, Craig bit back, "If either of us is going down, it won't be me, pal," sneering when Govender looked away first.

Everyone working in the chamber had stopped to spectate the goings-on, seeing this, Govender brushed aside their skirmish.

"Enough of this silliness." Digging deep to resume a degree of professional mannerism, he added, "For goodness' sake, Mr. Farrant, look around you, see with your own eyes, the reason you're here," pointing at the saucer and continuing. "You're privileged to be part of the resurrection of this ancient vehicle. So many less fortunate people would give their eye teeth for such an opportunity." He was waffling, garrulously trying to mask his upset. "I do understand, like anyone seeing this for the first time, you must be wondering how such a craft came to be here."

Craig wasn't pondering anything of the sort, still firmly believing this whole set-up to be a hoax. Unaware of his scepticism, the mantis continued.

"In truth, we don't have all the answers but are certain that it crashed tens of thousands of years ago, lying buried until being discovered in nineteen forty. Where did it come from, you may also be thinking. Well, we can't be certain, but it's obviously likely to be from a different time or dimension, possibly even an extraterrestrial world."

Govender had returned to being overly effusive, but his voice held unfamiliar inflections, affirming he still smarted. Manifestly seeking to paper over these cracks, pressing on unabated in a monologue fashion.

"Perhaps, working together, we may shed light on these mysteries. You're an educated man yourself, Mr Farrant, and have probably now arrived at a correlation between the Link and this vehicle. It's of course the only logical conclusion to explain your recently acquired abilities." Ending his delivery with an arm outflung towards the craft, pausing. Then, turning to face Craig, his mannerism became intent. "I want you to come with me now. We will go inside the craft, just please don't touch anything; there is much we don't yet understand about its workings."

Heading towards a sturdy aluminium staircase, rising from basement floor to a high-level landing, he beckoned for Craig to follow. The mantis' intro ringing in his ears, Craig hesitated; no way could this thing possibly be genuine, rather an elaborate and farcical ruse made up by Govender and the Van Heerden's. But, to what end? Why such an utterly preposterous charade? Nothing about this whole business was making any sense whatsoever, instead getting weirder by the minute. Anyone with the slightest gumption would see straight through such a sham. Whatever their agenda, best to play along for now.

Starting up the stairs after Govender, distortions in the saucer's form framed a very realistic-looking aperture torn in the hull's fabric. Contrasting with its otherwise smoothly contoured lines, this section had been cleverly crafted in support of Govender's supposed crash story. Steadily ascending, getting closer and better able to make out features, everything about this otherwise mundane detail appeared proportionately accurate. Fixatedly focused on the damage, until comprehending that it perfectly replicated the physics of an impact, Craig stopped dead in his tracks. It was the genuine article after all, a crashed flying saucer.

Herein lay the bitterest twist of fate; a treasure of incalculable value falling into the hands of a ruthlessly self-serving mob, exploiting it exclusively for themselves. A nudge from behind snapped Craig out of this consideration.

“Come on, keep moving.” It was Dariusz.

Reaching the landing, Craig followed Govender up the ramp, to a point where he could easily have reached out and touched the craft. Although tarnished, the hull’s surface radiated a lustre unlike anything he’d seen before, his inner geologist speculating at what elements and processes had been utilised to create this alloy. Ducking his head, Govender passed through the opening ahead and disappeared inside the craft, Craig following several paces behind.

In the instant of setting foot on the flight deck, the strangest sense of awareness came rushing at Craig, enveloping him in an unreasoningly warm sense of belonging. Baulking and resisting these ridiculously misplaced feelings; it was the first time he’d ever seen the saucer. Feelings that persisted regardless, as if being welcomed by old friends, seeking to draw him back into their fold. Shaking his head in a vain attempt to physically eject these delusions, but to no avail. Instead, it got a whole lot worse when the befuddled murk of nostalgia became overwhelming, as if becoming another person, returning to his comrades and resuming duties.

Govender’s yelp of surprise distracted Craig’s disassociated state, then observing the source of his excitement. Above three semi-encircling consoles, pencil-thin slices of blue light had coalesced, permeated by crisply defined replicas of symbols rendered on the surface below. A dormant recess ignited in Craig's echo-self, instantly understanding their interpretation and significance, as if undertaking a crash course of the craft's operational systems. Behind these holograms, a hitherto matt grey encircling bulkhead wall abruptly vanished, exposing the basement environs beyond.

Stunned and rooted to the spot, Govender eventually raised an arm to reach for where the vertical bulkhead had been, but his hand met with a solid barrier. The panel still there, except, unlike ultra-high-definition LED screens, it now portrayed crystal-clear virtual reality from outside. Even when viewed acutely, a display without the slightest perspective distortion, as though the bulkhead had become perfectly transparent. Bemused, Govender placed both hands on the see-through surface, and by his reaction, Craig understood this to be a fresh development.

Finding his voice, the mantis distractedly mumbled, "Keep him here. They need to see this." Brushing past and hurrying to the entrance point, pausing only long enough to add, "For God's sake, don't let him touch anything," leaving Craig with Dariusz and his sidekick.

Debateable whether either men had registered this instruction, both so engrossed in their altered surroundings that Craig might have slipped away without being noticed. Recovering, Dariusz grasped his arm.

"You heard, don't try anything." Regardless of the man's aggressive tone, fear welled wholly apparent in his eyes, this thing scared the bejesus out of him.

Realising Craig had picked up on his unease, either fearing losing control of the situation or needing to justify himself, Dariusz's tongue loosened.

"This thing is dangerous. It's already killed a lot of people, right back to when the Germans first came here. Clint will tell you the same," indicating his colleague. "If you do anything stupid, it will be game over for all of us."

Impressing on the seriousness of their situation, Dariusz slipped a hand inside his jacket to where Craig knew a weapon to be holstered.

"Yeah, okay, okay, chill out. I'm cool. I don't want anything going wrong either," Craig raised both hands. Although despite the man's implied threat, his curiosity had been aroused. "What are you talking about? Who were the Germans?"

Not wanting to unsettle the man, Craig maintained a passive demeanour, then Clint joined in.

"Nazis, he's talking about Nazis from World War II. They were sent here to figure out how this thing works and take its engine back to Germany. Hitler wanted to use it, so he could win the war."

Just as rattled as his boss, Clint became animatedly talkative, until a look from Dariusz shut him down.

"Enough. All you need to understand is that messing around in here will get you killed." Regaining his composure, Dariusz knew well enough, anything said out of turn could land them in trouble. "No more questions," glaring first at Craig, then his subordinate.

Conceding with a shrug and pretending at disinterest, Craig looked around, his focus drawn by a square opening in the floor. Evidently an access hatch to someplace below, a ladder protruded above concertina-style safety barriers, guarding against a misplaced step.

Those pseudo-memories returned, something calling to him from down there, the words however muffled and indiscernible. His state of disembodied recall sharpened, the thing's name teasing at the tip of his tongue when Govender and the Van Heerden's burst in. An untimely interruption that frustrated Craig and left him trying to hold onto fading recollections, illusively withdrawing behind a veil. A blurred presence, now skulking in an inaccessible corner of his new-found alter ego's consciousness.

First on deck, Govender had forgotten to duck, catching his head with a satisfying *THUNK* on the low-hanging entrance rim. It had to have hurt but, so enthused by the recent turn of events, he chose to disregard the pain.

"See for yourselves." Babbling excitedly, "It all lit up the minute he came inside and look, look you see." At a loss for further words, he could only point.

Bruno's measured restraint fell away, jaw dropping, then aping Govender's reaction, reaching out to touch an invisible bulkhead. Conversely, Rebecca's only discernible telltale to excitement were flushed cheeks, as easily derived from the exertion of hastening up the stairs.

"Fantastic. Incredible." Bruno acted like a kid in a sweet shop, turning around and around to take it all in, until noticing Craig. "Get him out of here boys, we need to talk."

Making no effort to disguise their relief, neither Dariusz nor Clint spoke while bustling Craig out to the basement floor and into the elevator. Engrossed in a maelstrom of confused thoughts, Craig didn't resist their quickened pace or attempt communicating with the pair. Instead, shutting everything else out, while striving to make sense of the wholesale sensory overload just experienced; most especially, those eerie half-memories and sensations assailing his consciousness.

In a peculiar way, thankful for the lift car opening onto a level where normal surroundings prevailed, recognising the corridor he'd traversed a few nights before. They followed the passageway, until coming upon a door which Clint opened with his ID card. Turning left, after several paces, Craig picked out the theatre and adjacent signed door he'd avoided opening the same night. Opening into a security office, to one side a uniformed operative sat watching two banks of CCTV monitors, while a colleague to one side talked on a two-way radio. Straight ahead the passageway continued, décor here becoming utilitarian and austere; uncarpeted, granolithic floor, walls painted in plain white and modern recessed ceiling lights giving way to single fluorescent tubes.

A few metres apart, steel-faced doors framed either side of the corridor ahead, Craig realising these to be the holding cells.

"Margie, I'm here! Can you hear me?" he shouted, hoping she might respond.

"Shut up! The boss already told you, she's not here," Clint barked, shoving hard at his mid back. "We'd never make it that easy for you."

Opening the nearest cell door, Dariusz turned Craig to face him, leaning in until virtually nose to nose.

"Remember, you are under constant CCTV monitoring. And like Mr. Van said, no funny business or your girlfriend suffers."

Sniggering derisively, Clint steered Craig into the cell and closed the door behind him.

Spotting the spider's web, Craig realised this to be the same cell as during his previous incarceration. Pacing when the door's multi-point lock clicked into place; his idea of getting the mantis on side had been a complete bust, ending in recapture. He would have to come up with a better strategy for getting them out of this place again, the outcome otherwise, only too obvious.

Despite this grim insight, or perhaps because of it, no matter how Craig wracked his brain, nothing remotely workable crystallised. Since being unable to conceptualise any workable escape options, a growing sense of futility blocked out all clarity of thought. Recognising this downwards spiral for what it was, he sat on the cot's edge and glared at the spider bouncing defensively on its web. Shuffling backwards and stuffing the pillow behind him, leaning back against the wall, thoughts returned to that familiar presence occupying the craft's lower deck.

The Controller! Its name came to him in a flash. Then the entity from before, his other self, re-entered Craig's mind;

driving away all angst concerning their predicament, replacing worries with an unquantifiable sense of peace and well-being.

As though his mind were being directed, remembering the mantis saying how each crew's remains had been found with a Link. Sudden enlightenment, the connection made. The crew were connected to the craft at an elemental level and now, likewise assimilated with a Link, so too was he. Those weird half-memories and feelings experienced had to emanate from his Link, a kind of indelibly imprinted residual shadow of the previous user. Data remanence, the only explanation for those shadowy recalls of association and interaction with long-deceased fellow crew members.

Under regular circumstances this would have been a laughably ridiculous notion, except in the here and now making sense of the otherwise inexplicable; even going so far as to explain the craft's responses to Craig. Govender had also spoken of previous experimentations' casualties having perished, apparently this included the unfortunate soul part-rematerialising in Craig's yard. An emergent perception of forces at play began bridging gaps in his understanding, dots mentally joining up and bringing him face to face with an uncomfortable hypothesis. What if the Link coming into his possession hadn't been entirely coincidental?

Govender's inept fumbling's and flawed comprehension of the Link's actuality could quite easily have been manipulated by an infinitely superior artificial intelligence. Nah, his imagination was running away with itself now, getting way too ridiculous. The damned thing landing in his yard was nothing more than a sheer fluke, the worst kind of bad luck.

Another unresolved mystery arose; the logic-defying irony of a civilisation, capable of building a vehicle to skip across perceived light years of space or time, inadvertently ramming it into a distant world. Rolling onto his back and staring at the ceiling, the absurdity of this aspect became all-consuming, when another flashback occurred; this one intensely realistic, as though reliving personal experience.

They had been dispatched on a biological mission, sent to seed the DNA of primitive hominids occupying planet Earth with their own, thereby accelerating this species' evolution. Homo sapiens were selected, since being the closest genetic coding match, and therefore most likely to assure successful integration. Through the universal process of natural selection, the resultant hybridisation would embed and toughen over sequential generations, yielding a smart and compatible primate.

In no way intended as a philanthropic kick-start to mankind's development, the end goal instead a lifeline to their own kind. Synthetic reproduction over successive millennia, tinkering with the helix to augment intellect and stimulate selected societally desirable attributes had backfired. Hardiness and robust physicality, still brimming to a requisite abundance in early man, had long since been sacrificed from their own genetic make-up. Their species had consequently reached a genomic plateau and was beginning to irreversibly atrophy, necessitating a radical intervention. To safeguard the well-being and posterity of future generations, the introduction of fresh and matching DNA into the procreation centres was urgently required.

Implemented by the Administrative Council, this polarising long-term policy agenda had been contentious and divided their society into three camps. Predictably, those staunchly aligned and supportive of the council's move, versus a faction vehemently against, then of course an inevitably ambivalent silent majority. Outspokenly deeming interference with an alien species for selfish ends morally outrageous, the faction successfully established an elected political foothold.

Gaining charter, these firebrands championed stringent adherence to the cyclical cosmic order; self-progression of a dominant species, inexorably leading to its own demise, at a point determined solely by the Great Creator. Likely destined to become the ascendant species of their bountifully diverse world, Homo sapiens should be allowed to evolve at its own pace, either becoming good stewards to their home planet, or perishing consequent to self-induced folly.

Subverting nature's supposedly established limitations, extra-system and intergalactic travel had long since become commonplace to their civilisation. From the perspective of Craig's other self, a former engineering officer, intellectual and technical credit should be duly extended to the human research teams. Over a span of less than eighty years, sporadically tinkering and scavenging from the wrecked craft, they had gained remarkable insight into technology a myriad years beyond their regular development.

Mankind, a relatively primitive being, had already determined the electromechanical concepts of antigravity propulsion and would be capable of building a vehicle capable of extraordinary terrestrial flight capabilities. If left to their own devices, only a matter of time before they gained sufficient further understanding to join the universal stage, slotting right in with a comparatively small clique of similarly warmongering barbarian species.

Currently the humans were hamstrung by basic comprehension deficits, most fundamental of which hadn't even entered their minds. The true magic behind virtually instantaneous travel anywhere in the cosmos, lay in manipulating a universal phenomenon; the concept of which top astrophysicists had only recently begun scratching the surface, some peers still considering its presence entirely hypothetical. The more enlightened had come to recognise this presence as an all-pervading, however virtually undetectable state of matter. In the uninformed absence of more aptly descriptive names, they had termed it "dark matter" and "dark energy". In reality, an extradimensional existence, its sheer mass and force much like an essential glue, holding the universe together.

Accessible only by a craft in antigravitational state, instantly transcending the physical realm to wholly exist in this elevated dimension. A plane unrestricted or limited by the apparent laws of physics, where all imposed fetters of time and distance, inertia and force entirely disconnected. Frail organic beings occupying the vessel, otherwise doomed to be atomised by exposure to dark energy and inertial G-forces, were protected and safely ensconced within the enveloping field.

Bizarrely, connected with his other self, Craig understood everything he was being shown.

All-entraining dark matter gravitons, since existing in a low vibrational state, would violently oppose the craft's highly magnetised antigravity field frequency, instantly seeking to expel this intruder along its integral line of energetic polarity. A concept discovered by advanced civilisations aeons before, they had gone on to become spacefarers. By exploiting dark energy's peculiarities, their craft's targeted destination in space, could simplistically be likened to being connected at one end of an infinitely tautened, imaginary elastic band. The aligned craft would instantaneously be slingshot to a predetermined cosmic destination.

Theirs had been the bioengineering commission's maiden voyage, with more to follow, although unbeknownst to council and crew, the chief officer had been hell-bent on making this a suicide mission. Commander Otan was an undeclared faction member, and while the others busied themselves in preparation for landing, she overrode the Controller's fail-safe protocols, plunging their craft into the planet's surface.

Flinching at the finality of this recollection, left Craig clutching at dissolving filaments of a distant home world and an alternate family he'd never known. Then, all gone in a blink, any access to recall eliminated, like a door slamming shut, instinctively knowing this to be the moment of his other self's death. Intrigued, Craig wasn't ready to let go yet, wanting to observe more of that alternate life, trying futilely to reconnect with the thread. Blocked again, forced to accept the other's right to privacy; nothing in that realm belonged in his reality and gratuitous access would be tantamount to wholesale voyeurism.

CHAPTER 25

"Your worst sin is that you have destroyed and betrayed yourself for nothing." – Fyodor Dostoyevsky

The germ of an idea had sprouted when the door clicked and Dariusz barged in, fragmenting Craig's further scheming. Setting a meal tray down, the Lithuanian spared Craig a glance.

"Your breakfast. Eat."

As he went to leave, Craig blurted, "Wait." Pausing, a look of annoyance crossed the man's face, but Craig continued regardless. "I need to see your bosses, it's extremely important."

Levelling an unmistakable look of warning in his direction, Dariusz responded curtly.

"I will see if they're available, just don't play stupid games with them," he warned, scowling to signify the recklessness of such an inappropriate act, "they won't be happy."

Craig had no intention of fooling with the Van Heerden's, to the contrary, simply wishing to share information since recognising the importance of being considered an invaluable asset. It was crucial that he foster and maintain this belief, although closetly intending to thereby gain time and leeway towards orchestrating an escape plan.

Not having eaten the previous day and feeling famished, he wolfed the food, then sat swigging bottled water. Hours passed, becoming mid-afternoon before Dariusz and Clint returned, accompanied by the Van Heerden's and Govender. This time an oriental woman in her early to mid-thirties joined their group. At first, the newcomer avoided making eye contact, preferring to stand with arms folded, staring impassively at a midway spot on the floor. Unsure quite where and how this one fitted in, Craig didn't get time to speculate before Bruno spoke.

"You wanted to see us, but I thought we'd covered everything earlier. What's this all about now?" clearly agitated, wearing the aura of a man with bigger problems.

Not immune from whatever might be eating at her father, Rebecca slouched to one side, sulkily chewing her lip. Perhaps a father and daughter spat? Something was amiss, but whatever the backstory behind their peevish mood, Craig cared not in the slightest. While waiting for them to show up, he'd put the day's interlude to good use, going over his gambit several times and here was the opening; first the bait, then the hook.

"Sure, but this is unrelated and might be important," he began, engagingly. "Maybe it's nothing, but ever since going inside your flying saucer, I've been getting the strangest sensations. Hard to explain it any other way than to say, like experiencing flashbacks."

As Craig spoke, so the new arrival raised her eyes until meeting his, while Govender took a step forwards, both listening attentively. Father and daughter appeared to welcome the distraction, except unlikely they were deriving the same degree of significance from his words. Craig continued, detailing those bizarre impressions and quasi-memories, although leaving out the revelations occurring in his cell. These would be reserved until another time, for now drip-feeding only sufficient information to portray cooperation and whet their appetites. When he'd finished the newcomer spoke, becoming enlivened and opening her stance, using both hands expressively.

"Thank you for sharing this with us, all most interesting. Tell me, are you experiencing the same sensations at this moment?"

Shaking his head, Craig caught sight of the woman's security badge, bearing a photograph and the name, Jacqui Lin.

"No," sarcastically indicating the cell. "Nothing since I've been back in this cage, only when I was inside the UFO."

A white lie, however, any incentive towards getting time outside of his cell's confines could only be advantageous. Exchanging knowing looks, neither academic managed to conceal their excitement.

"His memories of association are an interesting aside, Ruben, but this could be evidence of psychokinetic projection. It seems the bio-intelligence is connecting with him, of course we'll need to validate through controlled field assessment. I'm thinking EEG and scanner monitoring of directed interactive stimulus anomalies, then utilise files generated to create a model of neural connectivity matrices. If it pans out, we back-feed everything through Quantum, tasking it to crunch the data and spit out control system, command-compatible algorithms."

Lin's mounting enthusiasm infected Govender, stood with one hand eagerly poised in anticipation of getting a turn to speak, silently forming words like a gasping carp.

Stopping to take a breath, Lin's hesitation provided the opportunity.

"Of course, forget the modelling for now though. Don't you see? This is bigger, far bigger."

An exuberantly flailing arm unintentionally caught Dariusz's shoulder a glancing blow. Scowling hostilely, the head of security held his tongue. It was abundantly clear the man didn't have much time for Govender, leaving Craig wondering whether he hadn't perhaps been deliberately slow in reacting when they'd fought earlier.

Govender's clumsiness gave Craig an opening to interject.

"One thing, if I may, Mr. Van Heerden. While we're being held in this place, I'd like to see my friend every day. I don't mean any disrespect, but I only have your say-so that she's okay."

Bruno frowned. "Cut to the chase. Exactly what is your expectation?"

Although not an outright dismissal, the man's expression hardened.

He might only get one shot at this, so Craig went for broke.

"If Margie's somewhere I can see her while assisting Doctor Govender, then I'm not going to be worrying about her and will be better able to focus. For your peace of mind, have a security team present so I wouldn't be able to reach her before they intervened. A simple arrangement really. That way we'd both get what we want. At least think about it, you've got nothing to lose."

A straightforward quid pro quo barter, left entirely up to Bruno whether to haggle or accept Craig's proposal.

Not responding right away, the older man dropped his head and stared at the ground, appearing to be running the odds. A look of incredulity had spread across Rebecca's face, unable to contain herself when her father didn't immediately shoot Craig down.

Furiously directing this wrath on her father, exclaiming loudly, "Daddy, you can't seriously be considering such nonsense. He's playing you for heaven's sake!"

Her challenge lit Bruno's touchpaper, and he wheeled, seeming for a split second as if about to lash out.

"Enough! You heard what Marcus said in our meeting, we need to accelerate. Small things like this might just make the difference."

Craig could only wonder at the reference behind Marcus's assertion, assuming this to be the underlying reason behind the pair's outright tetchiness.

Breathing heavily, Bruno battled to regain his composure.

"It's fine, we could hypothetically manage the kind of arrangement he wants. I'm nobody's idiot, Becca. I know what I'm doing." Turning to Craig, he added, "I'll think it over tonight and let you know in the morning."

Closing the matter to any further discussion, he turned and stormed out. Scowling, Rebecca followed suit, while the rest trailed at a more discreetly measured pace.

When the cell door had shut, Craig allowed himself a self-satisfied chuckle and leapt onto the cot, metal springs screeching in protest. Even if Bruno did agree to his request, how to play out the next milestone remained unclear. The guards certainly weren't to be trifled with; all armed, each carrying the bearing of ex-police, mercenary or military special forces combatants. Making a go for it would certainly be dicey, having to bide his time and remain alert to the right opportunity.

Even if successfully getting to Margie and jumping them both out, their prospects would ultimately be no better than before being captured. For the two of them, the outside world remained a prospectively hostile and unpredictable place. The Van Heerden's had the resources to track them down pretty much anywhere, other than their cave. Assuming they did get out and then split up, Margie remained a bargaining chip and certainly wouldn't be able to resume any semblance of normal life. The only answer, one providing a degree of stability and ending their constant flight, unfortunately, meant self-sacrifice.

Reverting to an earlier solution, Craig would get Margie to a place of safety, then return and surrender himself. The more he explored this scenario, so it gelled as the only option assuring at least one of them survived. The Van Heerden's would get what they wanted and therefore have no foreseeable reason to interfere in her life. A weight rose from Craig's shoulders, albeit clouded by resignation to his own fate; everything about this whole ridiculously sorry mess truly sucked.

Aware of despondency lurking, Craig consciously shifted gear, moving on to the Van Heerden's volatile interaction in his cell. It had been an interesting little sideshow and whatever was going on behind the scenes, the stakes must be high. Whoever Marcus might be, the basis for him advising acceleration of the process, clearly the nub of their joint crankiness. Never one for gambling, Craig would however have taken any odds in favour of the father and daughter's upset being rooted in money troubles. Most times a corporation was compelled to speed up the works, had to do with reducing projected overhead costs and hastening return on invested capital. Circumstantially, it looked as if the Van Heerden's might be in over their heads.

As it happened, Craig would have won the bet. Funding the project since its mid-1900's inception, VHP had been established by Bruno's grandfather as both a legitimate front and cash cow. Predictably, whenever the clandestine sibling organisation progressed in strides, or needed a tech upgrade, the pharmaceuticals business had borne any corresponding fiscal impact. Appreciating the project's potential, Bruno van Heerden had gone all in, and left VHP trading on a knife's edge. Despite being aware of the company's investment limitations, perhaps a rash commercial decision, only time would tell. Safeguarding against bankruptcy, the CEO had however solicited and obtained stakeholder financing from an organisation endowed with virtually limitless pockets.

In the early stages of his European business, Bruno had employed a graduate analyst, a man who would one day become the country's present minister of finance. Prudently maintaining their association, over lunch at his club, Bruno had persuaded Bongani

Thusi to become their champion and key man on the regime's inside. A relatively straightforward coup, financially incentivised, Thusi had convinced his government comrades-at-arms to invest a sizeable chunk of the country's strategic contingency budget into the Van Heerden's venture. Creative accounting, dummy corporations and widely distributed kickbacks meant there would never be an auditable trail leading to VHP's doorstep. For this consideration, Thusi and five more senior ministers became silent shareholders. A deal forged with the Devil, yet a moot point as to whose souls were at greatest risk of damnation.

An elite clique of influential political heavyweights had got their hooks into something truly incomprehensible, nonetheless expecting it to return hefty paydays. The country's political landscape was in turmoil, becoming common knowledge that an election would be driven through the following year. The old guard had repetitively blotted their copybooks, and according to polls taken from an increasingly disgruntled electorate, sweeping changes were in the offing. Suspecting their time in power drawing to a close, the incumbent leadership were becoming ever edgier, outspokenly impatient and eager to cash out.

Darker storm clouds loomed for the Van Heerden's, with savvier political analysts predicting a landslide win in favour of the radically left-wing opposition party. This hot-headed bloc's manifesto contained many tried and tested, repetitively failed socialist ideals, including the nationalisation of private corporations turning over anything above a predetermined threshold. VHP's published trading figures put the business squarely in that danger zone, and the Van Heerden's were fast running out of time.

Unaware of these evolving machinations, Craig had demons of his own to face, deriving meagre solace from having arrived at a plan to remove Margie from the mix. Unlikely to be a simple procedure, needing to patiently bide his time and remain alert to any instant where the guards were either distracted or became complacent. Failing which, and knowing fortune to favour the bold, he would have no alternative but to seize the initiative and create a diversion. Feeling worn out and drowsy, the cot's mattress softer and more comfortable than remembered, he slipped into a deep and dreamless sleep.

Around nine the next morning, Govender and both regular security men fetched Craig from his cell, escorting him to the basement. There was no sign of Margie or the Van Heerden's, the mantis hiving off right away and making for a gathering of lab assistants to rehash the day's running order. Craig hesitated, taking it all in until Dariusz prodded him towards the craft's access stairs. At this point, he resisted though, it was time to play up and shouted.

"Hey, Govender, where's Margie at? Yesterday I told you and your bosses how things are going to work from now on. So why isn't she here?"

Flustered, already having gained a healthy respect for Craig's temper, the mantis fumbled for words until saved by a softly disarming voice that checked Craig's strop. It was Jacqui Lin, approaching from behind.

"Someone will bring her down, shortly," moving to stand in front of him, she smiled genuinely, completely defusing Craig. "Mr. Van Heerden has agreed to your wishes, Craig, so we are happy to wait until she gets here."

Annoyed at being so easily distracted, he scowled, responding brusquely.

"Ah, right. Yeah, okay, we'll wait until Margie's here then."

Craig may have resigned himself to becoming a guinea pig but drew the line at being their patsy.

Unflustered by his abruptness, Lin kept her cool.

"That's fine. Her transport arrived shortly before I got in the elevator, so I'm sure she'll be along soon."

Right on cue, the elevator doors opened, and Margie stepped out into the basement, flanked by both guards from yesterday's hallway reunion. Initially looking up at the craft and predictably taken aback by its presence, she dropped her eyes to seek out Craig from amongst those in the basement. Finding him, she smiled and raised a hand in greeting, but there would be no further opportunity for them to interact. The chaperones whisked her to a simple office chair set against the furthest wall, taking up station either side.

Feeling a sense of relief, Craig was about to call to her, when Dariusz interjected.

"You've got what you wanted, but you need to understand that no contact or talking is allowed. My men have orders to shoot your girlfriend if either of you break those rules or do anything else stupid."

Not for a second did Craig doubt the veracity of Dariusz's threat, besides, it was too soon to hatch his plan. The security detail would be on their toes, alert and prepared for the slightest hint of anything untoward. Also remembering how anxious Dariusz and Clint had been around the craft yesterday, giving any excuse for them to get trigger-happy would be outright stupidity.

"Relax, nobody's trying anything. I just needed to be sure she's alright. Okay, we can get started."

Breaking eye contact with Margie, he made for the stairs; ascending, one, two, three.

Out of nowhere, the Controller's voice rang in his ears, clear and insistent. "Be ready to move fast, they are coming."

Whirling in mid step, Craig fully expected to witness an apparition, seeing only Dariusz two steps behind.

The Lithuanian looked up and frowned. "What now? Come on, keep moving."

Puzzled but complying, Craig was about to take another step, when every hair on his body stood on end and a harsh electric crackle made him duck. All in the basement similarly flinched, then stood fixedly rooted to the spot, their attention drawn to a swiftly evolving mid-air disturbance. On the side opposite to where Margie sat, the basement's atmospheric fabric was distorting, ripples spreading outwards from a steadily brightening core, then "they" appeared.

Emerging from a strobe of blinding flashes came a dozen or so men. All dressed in clothing of a bygone era, some wearing hats, they gathered in a tight huddle, postures and facial expressions conveying naked bewilderment. One in the group, a short, stocky man snapped out of it, becoming indignant and barking out what seemed like a challenge. He spoke in a foreign tongue, and while not understanding the words, to Craig it sounded like German. Incensed at getting no reaction, the angry man came bustling forwards, gesticulating and spewing a renewed tirade of what seemed like questions, wanting to know what the hell they were doing there.

After more than eight decades in an induced state of limbo, Walther Bruck and his team were completely oblivious to time's passing. Their reality existed in 1942, in that split second before being whisked off into an interdimensional state of nothingness. Returning now, their environment inexplicably transformed and occupied by total strangers. By now apoplectic with rage and bouncing on the balls of his feet, Bruck half turned and shouted a command. The little man's tonal shift should have served as a warning but was lost on his modern-day contemporaries.

Bruck smartly sidestepped when several in his group drew handguns, seizing the advantage and taking unimpeded aim at the intruders. Like it was happening in slow motion, Craig watched Dariusz draw his own pistol and winced at the .45's sudden booming report. A hasty and fluffed shot, still finding the SS Sturmmann nearest to Bruck. Clasping at his side, the wounded soldier lurched to join his comrades, by now dived for available cover and unleashing a cacophony of gunfire.

Realising his position to be dangerously exposed, Craig vaulted the handrail and darted for shelter behind the metal staircase. From cover, he spotted Clint caught in the open, taking a hit to the shoulder that spun him over a cowering Govender. Jacqui Lin went to make the same move as Craig, a slight hesitation her undoing, staggering in mid stride as if struck by a baseball bat. Falling face first, a darkly spreading patch of crimson red stained her pristine white coat, where an antique Luger round had severed her spine. A clattering noise overhead wrenched Craig's attention from her lifeless body, catching a glimpse of Dariusz's boots racing for high ground advantage.

From his position of relative safety, looking through a chink between a desk and steel filing cabinet, Craig's heart skipped a beat when seeing Margie's empty chair. Roughly three metres of open ground separated him from the sturdy metal cupboard. If managing to reach the thing unscathed, its bulk and construction would make for sound protection. Better still, he would get an unobstructed sweep of the basement's rear from that spot, hopefully able to determine where Margie had taken refuge. Yelling out her name and getting no response, his only alternative to break shelter and risk being shot.

A movement to his left, briefly catching sight of Govender scuttling on all fours towards the open elevator. Blotting out this distraction, Craig gathered himself to make his move, scrambling over Lin and bolting for the steel archive unit at a crouch. Gunfire had abated, a single whipcrack confirming he'd been spotted.

A wildly inaccurate shot, the 9 mm round went far wide, struck an angular stairs' brace and shattered into a myriad shards of razor-sharp shrapnel. A fraction before diving to safety behind the filing unit, an angrily buzzing sliver of copper jacketing sliced across Craig's cheek. Realising he'd been hit, reaching up to feel his face wet with a warm slickness, withdrawing the hand and seeing all fingers glistening red. Touching again and finding the wound site, it felt completely numb, he managed to discern a ragged gash the length of a thumb. Ignoring the injury, frantically scanning the chamber's rear half, he immediately spotted one of Margie's guards lying lifeless a few paces from her chair, his head framed by a puddle of blood and clearly dead. The firefight had reached this side, and still there was no sign of Margie.

Movement from behind a row of industrial steel storage units projecting from one flank wall suddenly drew Craig's focus, the second minder snatching a peek from cover. Observing one another in the same instant, the operative raised a snub-nosed revolver, then recognised Craig and lowered his weapon. The firefight's tempo had diminished again, both sides taking only sporadic potshots at each other's hiding places, conscious of conserving ammunition. During this lull, Craig again called out Margie's name, hoping she might also have made it behind the units. An immediate reply confirmed she had. Picking a visible point on the wall behind the guard, Craig jumped.

Taken completely by surprise at his sudden disappearance, more so stunned at him rematerialising a few paces away, the guard was slow to react. Needing only this momentary hesitation to grab his gun hand, Craig forcefully rammed the man's head into the steel unit. The unlucky minder crumpled without a sound and Craig turned, seeing Margie crouched on her haunches. Sobbing in relief, she flew into his arms, then pulled away as quickly to look him up down, gasping.

"Oh my God, Craig, you've been shot."

Hands shaking, she pulled a wad of tissues from a sweat top pocket and reached to wipe at blood trickling down his cheek.

Catching her wrist, Craig spoke urgently, "There's no time. We gotta get the hell outta here."

No sooner uttering these words, the voice in his head returned; something had to be done before they could leave. He must give over and surrender all will to the Controller.

Without conscious consideration, he pulled Margie close, and they were taken.

Emerging on what Craig understood to be the craft's lower deck, Margie was wide-eyed in fear.

"What the hell, Craig? Where are we?"

"Inside the spacecraft but don't ask me why. All I know is, I've got to do something here."

An unseen force then assumed control of his faculties.

Like being in a voodoo trance, aware of everything happening around him except unable to direct his own actions, Craig went straight to a bank of holographic forms. A voice came out of his mouth, issuing an unintelligible command that stimulated four contiguous amber columns to rise. Obliquely understanding, accomplishing this task required a specific sequence to be followed, he moved closer. The Controller then placed each hand over the two outermost pillars, and Craig felt a warming sensation flow to his core.

"Stop! Get away from that thing!"

Unnoticed, Dariusz had already descended to the ladder's last rung.

Highly agitated, the man's voice cracked, his pistol aimed squarely at Craig's head however held rock steady. So absorbed in the objective, neither Craig nor Margie had detected him entering through the hatch and descending the ladder.

"Get away from that or you're both dead." Seizing control of the situation, Dariusz dropped from the ladder and bounded nearer. "Do it now, get back!"

Grabbing Margie in a chokehold, pressing the Colt's muzzle to her temple.

"I'm warning you; she gets it first."

The entity released its hold over Craig, allowing him to raise both hands.

"Okay, you win, Dariusz. Now please let her go."

Sneering victoriously, he shoved Margie away and trained the .45 on Craig.

Eyes reflecting a delirious gleam, perhaps battle lust, something about his manner told Craig the man had completely lost it.

"You were stupid coming down here. No one will ever know what happened to you."

Thumbing the semi-auto's hammer back; Craig looked into the barrel's gaping darkness and knew he was about to die.

Like glitter in a shaken snow globe, swirling dust motes suddenly coalesced midway between the men, grouping tightly together. Distracted, Dariusz yelped,

"What is this? What have you done?" Glaring accusatorily at Craig, then inevitably drawn to the gathered particles.

Compressing into a dense cloud and flaring brightly, the swarm advanced. Backing away, Dariusz found himself blocked by the Controller's glass housing.

"What the...? No... no... no, please!"

Poised inches from his face, the fireflies merged to a single glittering point and punched through the man's forehead, instantly pulverising his brain.

Released, the .45 landed with a resonant *CLANK*, fractionally before Dariusz's body hit the deck. Margie shrieked, her face wretched in horror. Pulling her close, Craig turned, shielding from the corpse but she pushed him away.

"Get us out of this thing, Craig."

Only it wasn't entirely Craig. Once more overtaken, ignoring her plea and returning to the unfinished task.

Offering some tactile resistance, the opposing pair of pillars gave way under gentle pressure, descending into their light bed. From the perspective of disembodied spectator, observing his own actions by proxy, Craig understood what this process signified and why it must be done. Where the two outer columns had been, residual amber circles blinked out, leaving dark voids and exposing the glyphs below.

"Craig! Seriously? Let's go!"

Margie's voice was heavily dredged in fear.

Calmly intent, Craig shut out her entreaties.

Frustrated at his indifference, she stamped her foot.

"Be patient, human," Craig's voice a thick mumble, that of another being.

The inner pillars responded alike, winking out, and a shrilling alarm tone sounded when all four exposed symbols flashed red. Releasing Craig, the Controller gradually receded. His essential task complete, it was time for them to leave. Turning to Margie, he shrugged ruefully.

"Sorry, Mags, I can't explain right now, but we're done here and need to get out right away."

Lingering, the entity issued Craig with a final prompt, the image of a tombstone. Puzzled but accepting this cue, he took hold of Margie and in a blink, they were stood at the foot of Andre van Heerden's grave. A picturesque valley lay at their feet, morning sunshine warming their backs, a seeming idyll however blighted by the laboratory clasping greedily at the opposing hillside.

"We're too close, Craigy. They'll see us." Margie made no attempt to disguise her concern.

"Coming here wasn't entirely my idea, Mags. We'll be alright though, just trust me."

Not exactly understanding why they had to be in this precise spot, Craig nevertheless perceived something significant about to unfold.

Reaching an arm around Margie's shoulder, squeezing

reassuringly, when a seismic shock wave and visceral *WHOOMPH* jolted them. Across the valley, unimaginable pressure unleashed within the lab tore a heavy steel door and its frame from the lowest level, flinging it to scythe through brush and trees, finally cartwheeling into the stream. A thick billow of brown smoke poured from the gaping masonry aperture and a yawning crack simultaneously raced up the overlying structure. An adjacent flat area, incorporating the hillside's toe and roughly the size of two tennis courts, subsided then spontaneously dropped away to an audible thud.

Expanded into tributaries, the building's fracture widened, splaying apart, until one half of its riven façade progressively bulged outwards. Weakened, the surrounding structure began tearing itself apart; slabs of masonry falling away and disappearing into the dust-veiled sinkhole. Emanating from within the chasm, a furious hissing arose, triggering more smoke that erupted under pressure, as if from a volcano. A sudden detonation, like from a massive high explosive ordnance, sent a rushing pressure wave radiating outwards and prompted another swathe of neighbouring valley floor and slope to collapse. A smaller concussion followed, flinging a flash of light out of the hole, straight up and gone in a split second, disappearing into the firmament.

Unable to avert their gaze, Craig and Margie watched in wretched fascination as the destruction unfolded. To one side of the growing abyss, a heavily gnarled and extremely old umbrella tree had been undermined, swaying precariously. Suddenly heeling over, essential supporting ground and roots torn away, it desperately clung to life but lost the battle and slid to an ignominious doom.

Seen through seething clouds of smoke and dust, a furnace had ignited in the chasm, burning hotter than a thermite reaction and glowing with infernal intensity. Roaring like a giant acetylene torch, even from several hundred metres away, radiant heat and glare emitted forced both unwitting spectators to shield their eyes. Evaporating concrete, exposing and melting bedrock to lava, this fiery maelstrom continually deepened the void, progressively collapsing more surrounding ground inward. Incrementally devouring the nearby stream's course until inevitably reaching and rupturing Manny Levin's dam wall, releasing a flood. Sweeping into the abyss, this mini tsunami exploded in a thunderous blast of superheated steam.

The workshop section and superimposed double-storey laboratory flank were gone, consumed in the ravenously feeding maw, leaving the building's bulk undermined and clinging precariously to the valley's side slope. Behaving like a gigantic ant lion's trap, the hellish pit increasingly undercut the hillside, all vestigial structure inescapably losing integrity; accompanied by a rumbling roar, it slid into the gulf. Destabilised by this cataclysm, a wide section of the hillside gave way next, sliding fluidly to fill and cover the sinkhole.

As if never existing, the fire pit and every last remnant of the Van Heerden's laboratory had disappeared, entombed under thousands of tons of soil and rock.

Destruction's ferocity at an end, peace returned to the valley. The air become laden with dust and smoke, mingled with a vaporous odour reminiscent of welding fumes to make breathing unpleasant. Wheezing, Margie pulled her sweat top up, using it as a mask but muffling her voice.

"Oh, my goodness, Craig, it's all gone."

Relief plain to see, his eyes however conveyed a sombre acknowledgment of what had just happened.

"Yeah, all gone," Craig could only echo, equally reflecting on the sheer scale of what they'd just witnessed. "Hopefully, this means everything else is over and done with, so we get back to normal."

About to step backwards when Margie grabbed him, just as

a heavy *THUD* shook the ground. Loosened by seismic vibration, Andre van Heerden's massive feldspar headstone had toppled, missing him by a whisker and landing face up. Shaken, Craig read the engraved epitaph and whistled softly.

"Even from the grave, these people don't give up."

The poetic justice of the man's legacy destroyed, and his resting place desecrated, wasn't lost on Craig.

"Yeah, that was close, too darn close. Imagine if, after everything that's happened..." Not finishing this sentence, Margie rolled her eyes. "Anyway, it's a good thing I was here to save your bacon again. Hey, Craigy?"

Sitting side by side on the polished stone memorial, they watched as dust and smoke cleared to reveal the destruction's full extent. Where the lab had once stood, freshly exposed earth and tumbled boulders remained, intertwined with splintered trees and other vegetation. Only one clue to the huge complex ever having existed remained, a small section of the car parking area contained a handful of assorted private vehicles. Of the hundred or so people working in the place there was no sign, seeming that not a single soul had survived.

As if paying respect to the loss of innocents among them, an eerie preternatural stillness descended. For the living, life would however go on; down below, the deathly hush unceremoniously broken by a cackling family of guinea fowl, emerging from an unaffected thicket. The landslide would provide a veritable banquet of unearthed grubs and worms for these ground birds, fanning out, scouring and pecking at the turned soil.

Despite the sun's warmth, an icy chill abruptly enveloped Craig's head, feeling as if frigid water had been poured inside his skull. Panting and shivering uncontrollably, he doubled over when the excruciating cold spread to his abdomen and throughout every extremity of his limbs.

Freaked out, Margie screamed.

"Craaaig, what is it?"

Unable to reply, accompanying paralysis stripping away all motor control, he toppled forwards into the grass. Despite searing pain and disorientation, Craig intuitively felt no fear, the very human urge to panic non-existent.

In a detached fashion, becoming aware of Margie turning him over, registering distress in her voice thickened by fear. Straddling him, she took hold of both shoulders and shook violently.

"Don't you dare die on me, Craig! D'you hear me?" Fuelled by the prospect of losing him after everything they'd been through, her angst transformed into rage, and she slapped him. "Damn you! Get up, Craig!"

As suddenly as the affliction had begun, so warmth and sensation returned to his head, spreading until he was able to speak.

"Hey, I'm okay. But what the heck, Mags." He chuckled faintly, except she wasn't laughing, appearing rather as if she might smack him again. "Whatever that was, it didn't mean any harm, but it sure felt like you did."

A flippancy about his tone sent Margie over the edge, letting loose a torrent of unladylike profanity, then she leant forward until their lips met; not a peck like when they'd been in the cave, kissing him with unreserved passion.

Eventually pulling away, her face only inches from his, she softly murmured, "Okay, so what was that all about then?" Her breath warm and sweet, Craig didn't want this moment of intimacy to end.

"Um, you kissed me." Grinning and expectantly reaching up for more.

Having none of it, Margie sat up straight. "No, you idiot, before that. You, flopping around in the grass like a beached fish." Deadly serious again, frowning, "You scared the crap out of me there, Craig. You'd better tell me what's going on, or you probably will get another slap."

"I honestly cannot explain it, Mags." This wasn't the time for making light of what had happened. Lying back on the grass, head cupped in both hands, he added, "Something to do with the Link, is all I know. It started like brain freeze, then spread all over, through my body, arms and legs. I couldn't move a muscle, but it's pretty much gone now, except for my foot. There's still no feeling there, it's completely numb," he said, pointing.

Rolling off him, Margie helped Craig into a sitting position.

Reaching down and rolling up his right trousers leg revealed a bulging swelling on the lower shin, slightly above the ankle joint. Pulling off both trainer and sock, the exposed skin had become stretched taut to bursting point over a writhing lump. Horrified, Margie went to touch but recoiled as if stung, when a huge gaping pore formed in the mass's centre. Deep inside, something dark moved, forcing its way out and coming to the surface. Like a massive blowfly larva hatching, the pointed end of a familiar shape appeared, expelling itself, until overbalancing and sliding off into the grass.

Following the Link's ejection, the wound closed, skin knitting together without a mark and Craig's ankle relaxed to its regular contour. When the ghastly spectacle ended their eyes met. Speechless, able only to stare at each other. Sensation also returned, along with Craig's comprehension of what had just happened. With the Controller gone and its power source eliminated, the Link could no longer sustain itself, deactivating and coalescing into its base form. Breaking the silence, he explained as much to Margie, before changing the subject.

"You do realise, Mags, that nobody's ever gonna believe a word of this, not even our families. They'll all think we've gone nuts."

She nodded in agreement, smiling until a pensive look crossed her face.

"Yep, probably best keeping this whole episode exclusively between us two. That is, assuming all the Van Heerden's people were wiped out…" Another thought occurred, and she grinned playfully. "Funny thing though, Mike from the *Star* is the only other living person outside of the government who knows anything, and neither are likely to ever breathe a peep. If only Mike knew what a story he'd passed up."

Remembering quite how fixated the man had been about maintaining his reputation, Craig laughed.

"Yeah, after all his pussyfooting and back-pedalling, it would've been the biggest scoop of his career." Scrambling to his feet and extending a hand to pull Margie up. "Time to get moving, I reckon. Only thing is, I'm afraid we're walking everywhere from now on."

Something made him reach down amongst the tufts of grass to retrieve the Link, cold and inert, now little more than an empty husk. Still, to serve as a memento, he pocketed the thing.

"We need to find someone kind enough to give us a ride into the nearest town, wherever that might be. First though, we've got to get those cuffs off you. That'll take a bit of explaining away with the locals." He winked. "You got any ideas, Mags?"

Shaking her head and giving him a look. "Not really, but I'm sure you'll come up with a completely inappropriate story." She replied sweetly.

"Gee, thanks. Leave it up to me to make excuses for you, the one wearing handcuffs. Alrighty then, have it your way, Miss Brooks," returning her look with a grimace of mock distain. "Come on, let's get our bearings and find our way out of here."

Scanning the open veld to see signs of civilisation not far away; what looked like a farmhouse, around a kilometre distant. Scouting about, they came across and followed a well-maintained vehicle track, appearing to run between valley and farm. Chatting as they walked, passing by a flat-topped boulder to one side of the road, Craig noticed a shed snakeskin snagged on a protruding, weathered shard. Nearing the farmhouse, its distinctively Cape Dutch style became apparent, the nearest façade neatly framed by a pair of mature trees.

A little further along the track, signs of activity became discernible; figures bustling around vehicles parked alongside the house, although still too far away to make out what was happening. Something about this hubbub hinted at chaos, the people exhibiting signs of being stirred up, giving Craig an immediate sense of foreboding. Unable to quite put a finger on the reason, this feeling of unease swirled, tugging at recently dormant recesses of his mind.

Catching hold of Margie's hand, he slowed their pace, studying the agitated gathering and watching as everyone disappeared inside the farmhouse. Something intangible had infiltrated his mind, not the Controller or anything specifically identifiable; simply knowing this place to be unsafe and must be avoided at all costs. Catching himself and pouring scorn on the idea, rationalising it to be nothing more than justifiable paranoid delusion. Considering everything they'd been through, hardly surprising that his mind should play tricks. Besides, Govender and the Van Heerden's were certainly gone for good.

His trepidation, nothing more than mental exhaustion and figments of an overstretched imagination, surely?

THE END

Printed in Dunstable, United Kingdom

67766788R10218